fiery
storm

This is a work of fiction. Similarities to real people, places, or events are entirely coincidental.

FIERY STORM

First edition. December 11, 2020.

Written by A.R. Vagnetti.

a.r. vagnetti

ACKNOWLEDGEMENTS

I have several Stormsters to thank for helping me through the research process of Fiery Storm.

My undying gratitude goes to the love of my life, my husband. Thanks, babe, for working to keep your interruptions to a minimum while I created. For knowing when to drag me out of my office, kicking and screaming to soak up some vitamin D, and much needed fresh air. Our trip to Italy all those years ago was so beautiful, it inspired this book's location. Also, for listening to me read my books out loud while we travel. You're my rock.

Gratitude goes to my daughter, Racheal, for always reposting or sharing my marketing efforts.

I would be remiss if I didn't mention my brilliant, amazing, and extremely talented ballroom dance instructor, Lucas Tanner Aldrich. Your instruction was the muse for including ballroom into this story. Thanks for your encouragement, descriptive words, and always making me believe like I could float across the floor even as I stepped on your toes.

And as always, this book wouldn't be possible without my excellent editor, Sam Hendricks. Your comments and uplifting words warm my heart and keep me going.

I'd also like to thank my awesome, devoted beta readers! To my newest beta, Dawn. Your eagerness, keen eye, and quick turnaround times astonished me. My mysterious male beta, Paul. You flew through the Storm Series with lightning-fast speed, but with such a detailed eye. My ever faithful and loyal betas, Mia, and Jodi. You are amazing, and I'm incredibly grateful for your input. I couldn't do this without any of you.

And let's not forget the extremely talented Les at German Creative for creating a fantastic book cover!

Most importantly, I'd like to thank you, my readers. My Stormsters. Without you or your wonderful reviews, my stories would sit on a shelf collecting dust. I hope you enjoy Fiery Storm as much as I enjoyed developing it. Alex's character was a hoot to write. The chemistry between her and Sebastian flowed with ease from my weird brain, through my fingers to the keyboard.

ALSO BY A.R. VAGNETTI
Forgotten Storm
Forbidden Storm
Fiery Storm
Fractured Storm (*Coming 2021*)

CHAPTER 1

Alexandria

"**I**n tango, you must maintain your frame. The movement occurs below the waist and above the neck."

God, why can't I remember? Oh, wait, I know, because my mind is on the billion other things he expects me to work out at the same damn time. Heel leads, knees bent, hold my frame. I can't do all that and pay attention to the cues coming from the six-foot-body-to-die-for dance instructor too. Before long, I'm ogling his six-pack outlined in the t-shirt, and my steps falter.

"Let's try again, shall we?"

Yes, dumbass. Get your head in the game. Nobody forced you into this.

Although today, I'm rethinking this insanity. When Ryen, my mother hen of a roommate, revealed she was taking ballroom dance lessons from a gorgeous Adonis, I thought, *why not?* How complicated could it be? Now my sore abs, throbbing upper back, and aching thighs scream I'm all kinds of stupid for subjecting my body to this abuse.

"In open promenade, keep the front of your thigh flush against the back of mine."

Yup. The primary reason I torment myself for two hours twice a week. Ezekiel Sorath. His solid, flexing muscles pressed against mine is a pleasure/torture I endure without complaint. Well, minimal complaining.

My time with 'sex on a stick' helps me forget the briskly paced chaos of bartending, my jerk of a landlord hounding me for the rent so he can leer at my breasts, and the glorious phenomenon of no recollection of my life before ten months ago.

Flagstaff, Arizona is the longest I've remained in one place since the day I woke to concerned paramedics in a store dressing room in Astoria, Oregon. According to the driver's license, and a black AMEX card in the purse beneath my prone frame, my name is Alexandria Svaldana. I'm a five-foot—clearly a typo as I'm five one and a half—blue-eyed, red-headed Canadian.

The address stumped Google, and the name the DMV says is me... nada, niente, nichts. Oh, and I speak fluent Spanish, Italian, and German. Which means I'm well educated or a world traveler.

Ryen and her techy nerd boyfriend Jose insisted—more like badgered me into believing—that I required professional help to solve the mystery of me. After much browbeating, I caved and bit the bullet.

"Your mind is blocking a significant event, and you need to discover what," she said. "She comes highly recommended by my professor."

"Just because you major in psychology at NAU doesn't mean you know everything," I muttered and dialed the number of the shrink on the business card she thrust under my nose for the hundredth time. Her deadpan stare made me shudder.

"I understand enough to be dangerous." Her cute face, hemmed in by a halo of flaming red curls a shade lighter than mine, morphed into a devious grin, her jade-colored eyes sparkled, and I was beaten.

My first appointment is this evening, and my anxiety is at DEFCON three. What if I'm a fugitive on the run? Did I rob a bank or convenience store? It'd explain the one hundred, hundred-dollar bills stacked in "my" wallet, but not the AMEX card. Who the hell carries around ten thousand in cash?

Paranoid—another oddity about myself I could do without but aligns with the whole bank robber scenario—I've refrained from using the plastic money as much as possible. Between the abundant currency, bartending at night, and working a part-time ER shift at a veterinary clinic, I'm able to handle my share of the expenses with Ry and splurge on dance lessons.

The vet tech gig doesn't pay a whole hell of a lot, but I can't reject this inexplicable draw to animals. They speak to me. Not literally, but I perceive their pain, their fear, and their anxiety. In return, my presence calms them. The talent baffles my boss Dr. Warner.

"How the hell do you calm even the worst patients, Alex?" he asked.

"It's a gift," I replied, my smile strained. How I connect with animals freaks me out a bit.

Over the past month, ballroom dancing has become my escape. I let everything else go and concentrate on following Ezekiel's nonverbal commands, the way his body dominates mine through every pivot and step. The fact the man is freaking gorgeous helps, and hinders, my innate talents. His blond hair looks disheveled, like he's plowed his fingers through the thick strands numerous times or a satisfied woman gripped fistfuls in the throes of a life-shattering orgasm. Either way, it's hot.

Those deep-set hazel eyes scrutinize every nuance of my body during class, and it's disconcerting. I prefer to pretend it's because he appreciates the dips and curves of my well-toned frame, but it's more likely the slave driver is eyeing my limbs for proper placement.

"With tango, your feet make love to the floor," he asserts as he propels me backward across the dance studio. "They slide sensually, like a lover's caress, then hard and aggressive, full of passion."

His words elicit a visual of us writhing on the gleaming hardwood surface in the throes of ecstasy, and I throw a mental fist bump for executing the next open break without tripping over my feet.

I love the tango's intensity and passion. The waltz's fluidity and grace. The provocative, down-and-dirty-acts of the salsa. When I set aside the sexual attraction to my teacher, I have an instinctive, effortlessness to my movements.

Or my scrummy coach is blowing smoke up my ass because I'm paying him.

Either way, watch out Fred and Ginger.

Today Ezekiel's heavenly body distracts me as I carry out my next turn, and I realize too late I'm peering at the outline of his sculpted pecs showcased in his tight t-shirt instead of following his wrist like he directed a zillion times.

The toe of my right foot hits my left heel, and with my balance off, I go careening towards the floor with a very unladylike, "Fuck."

Before my cheek slams into the gleaming hardwood, brawny arms grab my waistline, suspending me mid-faceplant. Ezekiel tugs me against his torso and my cheeks heat with chagrin, and a smidgen of lust. Just a smidgen.

"You okay?" he asks in a sensual, wet-my-panties voice, getting me even more flustered.

"Yeah, of course. Thanks for saving me." I chuckle, going for humor. "My life flashed before my eyes." An extremely short flashback.

Ah. There it is: the stimulate-my-nipples smile I stumble over my own feet to witness every week. Oh boy. Tonight, B.O.B. (battery operated boyfriend) will have double duty.

Ezekiel's gaze falls to my lips, and I clutch his shoulders in response. My nails digging into his skin urge him to close the distance and ravish me.

Okay. Note to self, no more trashy novels. Ravish? Really?

A muscle pulses in his jaw. My lids lower in anticipation. For once, we're the sole couple in the studio, and with no obstacles in his path, he can finally make his move. He's kept me at arm's length for four weeks now, and I'm about to combust. The teacher/student taboo is a real downer.

Strong fingers tighten on my waist and my breath hitches, already feeling his lips on mine when the exquisite warmth of his arms falls away. I huff in frustration as he saunters over to the sound equipment in the corner with powerful, agile movements. What's his deal? He's never alluded to a little woman waiting in the wings. Is he gay?

"You performed well today, Alex," he says as he powers off the computer. There's a new roughness to his voice. Ah ha! Mr. Playing Hard to Get is not as unaffected as he appears. "I'm astonished at how you've advanced in such a short time."

"Well," I laugh, sashaying over to one of the small tables bordering the dance floor to retrieve my water bottle. "I have this amazing, patient instructor who makes learning fun. And lucky for me, he has quick reflexes to boot."

Once Ezekiel has the computer and sound equipment taken care of, he strolls over, his intense regard accelerating my heart rate. Damn, he's beautiful. Strap a sword on him and white wings, and he'd be a splendid portrayal of an angel ready to battle evil.

"Need to quit the trash novels, Alex," I murmur under my breath.

He throws me a quizzical glance before retrieving his phone off the table and pulling up the calendar. "Same times next week?"

"Yup," I respond between loud gulps of water.

"At the rate you're learning, you'll be competition ready in a couple of weeks."

The notion of competing sends adrenaline zinging through my system. Another matter I've learned about myself: I'm an adrenaline junkie with a ruthless competitive streak. I just hope I'll still be around in two weeks. The impulse to continue my search escalated several days ago.

"That sounds awesome. Can I wear a sparkly, skimpy outfit for the salsa? Oh, or a flowing gauzy dress for the waltz?"

His laugh does bizarre things to my abdomen. "A ballroom competition wouldn't be complete without them?" He holds out his hand, ready to escort me to my car as always.

"Hey, um... if you're interested, a few of us from work are getting together for karaoke tomorrow night at The Zoo. Nothing serious or intense. Although I attempted to spin it into a real singing contest on the first occasion, and my friends about lynched me." I can't stop babbling, but I'm dying to spend time with him outside the instructor/student situation. "So, no taking up the mic if you don't wish, but there's a live band after and dancing. We could put your lessons into actual life practice."

Please say yes. Please say yes.

"While I encourage all my students to take part in those types of scenarios, I do not socialize with them." *Well, shit.* "However, since I am pressing you hard toward the competition arena, it might be beneficial to further your comfort level in front of an audience."

Yeah, what a crock of crap. Mr. Yummy wants me as much as I want him.

Chapter 2

Alexandria

Why the hell did I let Ry talk me into meeting a shrink? This is for crazy people, right? On an emotional level, I'm about as stable as a mobile home during a tornado, but I don't long to harm myself or anyone else. Except for my landlord. I'd enjoy eviscerating him.

Annnnd, that's why I'm here, lounging in this god-awful chair, struggling to appear as the most put-together chick on the planet.

"Tell me a little about yourself, Alexandria," the classy woman with black hair cut into a perfect bob, the straight edges resting on her collarbone, asks from her *cozy*-looking chair across from me. What did she say her name was? Dr. Horawitz... Horbowski?

Shit. "Doc" it is.

"Well, that's the million-dollar question, isn't it, Doc?" I attempt to cross my legs, but my butt's sunk so deep into the cushion, I wind up looking like I'm seizuring. "Before six months ago, my world is a total blank."

I played with the notion of fucking with her, making up an elaborate story about how I'm a secret agent for the CIA on a mission to thwart terrorists and only here to keep my cover. But then I thought, screw that, I'm paying this gorgeous woman to help me recall my life. I need to get serious.

Another fact I've learned regarding myself: I'm rarely serious.

"What's the last thing you remember?" she asks and jots something on a yellow legal pad resting on her wool-covered thighs.

"Waking up half-naked in a woman's dressing room." I give up on trying to appear cool in the stupid chair and perch on the edge of the seat.

"Is there a probability the purse they found with you was not yours?" Her red-tipped finger pushes up the purple-framed glasses sliding down her slim nose. She should go back to her optometrist and have those things adjusted because the slide, push, slide, push thing is driving me crazy.

"Anything's possible, Doc, but since the picture on the license is my image, I'm guessing it's mine."

"Strange. When you called for your appointment, I scanned every database available, and nothing surfaced. It's like you never existed."

"Not making me feel any better here."

"I apologize. I just find it incomprehensible the system didn't produce a single strand of evidence the name on the driver's license possessed a life. Ninety percent of the population today has surfed the web, emailed, had a social media account or applied for a loan. Something."

I feel bad for the tall, stunningly beautiful shrink with eyes the hue of the midday sky. She's perplexed by my lack of existence.

That makes two of us, sista.

Doc waves a delicate hand in the air. "Let's move past that,"—hey, I wasn't the one stuck on it—"and concentrate on what we know. Then we can talk about ways to help trigger your memory. Okay?"

"Sounds great. Fire away." My aching spine pushes back with a vengeance, and I inspect the couch with longing. Although, isn't lying down on a sofa in the shrink's office cliché?

"So, your first recollection is waking in the dressing room. What happened after that?"

"When I refused to go to the hospital, the hunky paramedic asked for my number." I shrug with a smile.

"Why not seek medical attention?"

"One, I felt great, except for the blanks in my brain, and two, what if I was a fugitive from the law? They report cases like mine to the police."

"Why would you think you are an outlaw?"

Outlaw? Old school but okay, and a damn good question. "I don't know. Maybe I saw it on tv or as a criminal possessed firsthand knowledge of how the system worked?" This is becoming interesting. Let's throw her a curveball. "I could be an undercover detective."

"Do you want my help, Alex?" A dark eyebrow arches.

By her tone, she's not buying it. "Not a cop or fugitive, huh?" When she continues to regard me with her lips pursed, I drop the bullshit and go with honesty. "Okay, here's the deal." I climb my way out of the stupid chair and stroll over to the windows to gaze out at the snow-covered sidewalks. Christmas is right around the corner, and I think every house in Flagstaff has an inflatable Santa in their yard.

"My life started six months ago in that dressing room, and since then, a strange compulsion to run consumes my dreams. It's a driving force hammering away at my brain, insisting I keep searching for someone." I spin, cross my arms at my chest, and pin my shrink with a desperate regard. "With no idea who I am, where I come from, or how to resolve this obsession and get my memories back, I'm an emotional wreck. I can't solve this on my own."

"That is the first honest thing you have said since you strolled in here. You took the initial step by seeking professional guidance, my dear. Next, we must understand the cause of the amnesia. An individual can suffer minor, temporary amnesia from a car accident or other common head injury. It rarely lasts long or causes significant problems. More serious neurological amnesia results from brain damage or severe injury, which arise from tumors, diseases like Alzheimer's, oxygen deprivation to the brain, stroke, or brain inflammation. Amnesia also develops from alcoholism or a reaction to certain drugs."

Hmmm. I do consume large quantities of tequila on the weekends. But it's a safe bet I did so before the memory loss. I'm not the professional here, but I don't think weekend overindulging counts as alcoholism.

"If we proceed, I will insist on a battery of tests with a physician to rule out neurological amnesia or any underlying medical condition, although I do not believe those are your diagnosis." Doc picks up a purple mug next to her with a tea bag string dangling from the edge and takes a rather loud sip.

"What kind of tea is that?" I ask. "I've never seen a red-colored tea before."

"Rooibos tea, native to South Africa," she answers before enjoying another slurp. "I am addicted to the sweet, woodsy, earthy flavor." She lowers the cup. "Dissociative amnesia, also called psychogenic amnesia, is rare but usually follows an emotional trauma. We do not connect it to any neurological or physical injury. It is limited to memory surrounding a traumatic event or period of life. In your case, it may have wiped everything prior to the trauma."

"If it's dissociative, how do we resolve it and get my memories back?"

"There are a collection of methods available. EMDR is one. Eye Movement Desensitization and Reprocessing. This method can help integrate the two hemispheres of the brain to help recall events." The loud slurps between sentences grates on my nerves. "Hypnosis is another approach if the subject is susceptible. Through relaxation and a process called age regression, it is possible to retrieve lost remembrances."

Well, hypnosis sounds more charming than the whole eye movement one.

"This all seems invasive, time-consuming, costly, and overwhelming." I sigh and pinch the bridge of my nose to alleviate the emerging pulse of a headache.

"The good news, Alexandria, is there is hope of recovering your lost memories."

Yeah, but the enormous question remains: *do I want to remember?*

Chapter 3

Alexandria

"**A**lex!" Ryen shouts in my ear, her jade gaze having trouble focusing on mine. My 'always level-headed' BFF is tripping the line between tipsy and drunk. "Sss your turn," she slurs loudly, and I'm forced to lean away to preserve my eardrum. "Geyur cute asssss up there."

When she points toward the restrooms, I giggle and nudge her hand at the karaoke stage, where a dainty Japanese woman is attempting to sing Peaceful Easy Feeling by the Eagles.

I exhale with contentment. The Museum Club, affectionately referred to by the locals as "The Zoo", has been an icon in Flagstaff since the early 1900s. Situated right on Historic Route 66, the upside-down wishbone tree over the front entrance draws you inside. In contrast, the western décor, complete with wagon wheels over the bar and petrified tree trunks hugging the dance floor—one actually smack-dab in the middle—is a dichotomy to the rising college presence monopolizing the place.

The owners are amazing and working here is a blast. The Zoo welcomes locals, students, and visitors to share in dime beer nights, happy hour, country music, karaoke Tuesdays (my personal favorite), live bands, and even open mic nights.

After the last five shots of good ole Don Julio, I've plunged headfirst into tipsy land, so I'm easy prey to Ry's not-so-subtle peer pressure. Not that I need coaxing. At all. I'm like Rhianna, or Ariana

Grande—or hell, Demi Lovato! I'm fucking incredible. Sure, it could be the tequila talking, but either way I'm gonna own that stage!

I need to eliminate today from my mind and drown the insistent urgings to find the mysterious individual I've sought for the last six months or my head will explode. The Doc insisted we schedule a complete physical exam with a colleague of hers tomorrow, and a follow-up appointment with her to start hypnosis Friday evening.

"Danger Will Robinson, danger," keeps shrieking through my brain repeatedly, like something truly horrible will emerge while I'm in a trancelike state. What the sweet sugar cakes it could be is the big, fat, hairy question and the reason I'm saturating my brain cells into oblivion.

After several minutes of staring into space, the perfect song pops into my alcohol-sodden brain just as Ezekiel walks through the door. Holy shit. He's so damn hot. My heart rate accelerates as those incredible hazel orbs search the bar. For me. The blond Adonis blends in perfectly with the young crowd in faded blue jeans with a black Henley hugging his perfect torso. I think he mentioned once he was twenty-nine. Still, he could easily pass for a college student with all those beautifully sculpted muscles, tight ass, and adorably disheveled locks.

I hop up and wave to draw his attention, and the room tilts slightly. Whoa. I better slow down, or I'll make an ass of myself on stage instead of killing it.

Just as Ezekiel turns my direction, the hairs on my nape tremble, and a bolt of awareness shoots through my body. I freeze. A soul in this bar is igniting me like a match to dry timber, and it's not my dance instructor.

I pivot in a circle to scour the room. There. A broad shadow lurks in the corner. But when I stare straight at it, it's nothing but blackness. I shift my head somewhat to keep the presence in my periphery.

Whoever is hiding in the dark is significant, well over six feet, but that's all I can make out.

Some deep-seated yearning takes hold, and I pant with excitement. A sensation brushes my hair, like a sensual caress sifting through the curls, but when I whirl around, no one's there. Okay. This is freaking me out—time to investigate the darkness.

Before I take one step, Ezekiel blocks my route. I gaze into his handsome face with a glower. For several weeks, this scrumptious dancer has consumed my thoughts and libido, and breaking down his defenses has been my top priority. Right now, all my inebriated brain can fixate on is investigating the shadow. Somehow, it calls to me.

I tilt sideways and peer past Ezekiel's nicely muscled bicep into the blackened corner. A spark of blue lights up the space, and I gasp. *WTF!* My skin tingles, and my nipples stiffen.

"Alex? Are you alright?" Mr. Yummy asks. "Maybe you should sit. You are quite pale."

"Did you see that?" I ask, never taking my scrutiny away from the wraith across the bar.

"See what?" Ezekiel turns to examine the place.

"That flash of blue in the corner. It was so pretty."

His gaze swivels back, and he scrutinizes me more closely. "There is nothing there," he says abruptly, gripping my shoulders and hindering my view once more. "How much have you drank?"

I hear the censure in his tone, and my hackles rise. "Oh, I'm just getting started, *Dad*. Have a seat and enjoy the show."

Wow. Way to get in his pants, Alex.

Dismissing him, and the something or other in the corner shifting my hormones into overdrive, I head to the stage with a determined stride, my chin raised. I'm gonna ensure Ezekiel falls in love with me tonight, and sex with him will be epic.

Somewhere in the back of my mind, I recognize it's the tequila talking, but I don't care. Besides, I'll have a better view of the mysterious corner from the stage. It baffles me why I'm captivated with a mere shadow. I should chalk it up to the booze and resume my original mission, seducing Mr. Twinkle Toes.

"What's your song choice, love?" Becky asks, holding out the mic. She must have drawn the short straw this evening because the young, stupidly beautiful blond usually handles the bar.

Becky and I met over my obsession with unique coffee mugs at Black Hound Gallerie in the Old Town Shops by my apartment. We reached for the same mug etched with the words "Zen as fuck" and hit it off immediately.

My grin is evil. Or I hope it is, but since my face is slightly numb, not too sure I nailed it. "Touch it by Ariana Grande."

The big blue eyes widen. "Bold option. Some guy in the audience you're trying to fuck, Alex?"

"Isn't there always?"

Chapter 4

Sebastian

My insides ignite with rage when the mortal male blocks my scrutiny of the little redhead. After months of hardly any sleep, even less nourishment, and traipsing across this damn continent, my female is finally within my grasp.

No. Not my female. Alexandria is my assignment. A burden I will walk away from the second her mind is whole, hand her off to her family, and fulfill my vow to my queen.

I devour her luscious body as she mounts the steps to the stage. I forgot how tiny she was, toned and curvy, but hardly over five feet. I prefer my subs tall and willowy, so the fact her compact little frame stirs my cock both surprises and irritates me.

How did she discover this small college town in Northern Arizona? Alexandria is a long way from home. The Valkyrie Regency territories in the U.S. encompass Louisiana, Alabama, and Kentucky with their headquarters in Ontario, Canada.

Arizona, controlled once by the Vampire Nation, is now a demon realm, and while the city is beautiful, hemmed in by dense woodlands and situated at the base of a massive dormant volcano, it reminds me of our stronghold in Nunavut, Canada. My home.

I am impatient to get back and resume my obligations as head of the queen's Guardians.

When Icarus, our High Priest Oracle, crowned Nicole, my brother passed the reins of Commander to me to become her Consort. An adviser to our young Halfling queen in vampire law, strategy, and etiquette. And even though Logan is a warrior through and through, a legend in immortal society, the responsibility ensures he remains at her side. Since the scare of her death at the great battle, he keeps his mate within reach at all times.

With well over a hundred Guardians under my immediate authority, the responsibilities of Commander are time-consuming. Every night I assign soldiers to safeguard our territories based on intel I scour from various sources. I am especially interested in threats of unrest, chatter overheard by the Council of Unity members, and posts on the dark web—where curious humans talk about "strange phenomenon" like alien encounters... and mystical vampire sightings.

One primary law all immortal species adhere to is keeping our identities secret from humans. Mortals are a complex and fragile race content in the knowledge they are at the top of the food chain—the higher evolutionary ladder. And while immortals are superior in every sense, humans possess vast numbers and advanced weaponry. A war with the mortal world would be an extinction event.

The Guardian's role, along with other elite fighting forces in the immortal realm, employ our enhanced abilities to hunt for rogues out of control, young ones enjoying a little too much fun in public, or malicious individuals with prejudice against humans.

Sad to say, but werewolves and vampires are the most likely offenders; the pull of the moon and our insatiable lust for blood is a perpetual battle many lose.

Even though I have taken to the technological advances like a valkyrie to lightning, I miss the periods before technology, when concealing our identities to mortals was simpler.

I examine the bar, noting every smartphone clutched protectively, a linked life-force to their fragile minds. Many bend over their devices texting, taking pictures of their decorative drinks for Instagram or Snapchat, or posing for selfies with friends. I shake my head at the tremendous extent of intimate information this generation naively grants the world.

My gaze turns to the redhead on stage. How is she dealing with her capabilities? According to Viessa, the new Oracle in training, Alex does not understand who or what she is. In fact, she believes she is human.

Well, I am about to blow shit to high heaven.

My task was to locate her. Done. Now, contact the demon king who interfered with her mind in the first place by telepathically placing an overpowering compulsion to kill Nicole and have him attempt to reclaim her lost memories.

If that fails, our High Priest Oracle, Icarus, dropped the bomb: the only option left is me, her fated one. I am expected to perform the mating bond by having sex with her while exchanging blood, effectively linking us for all eternity. Once the link is accomplished, I am to thrall her and restore her missing life.

Fuck.

Simply thinking about it messes with my mind. The valkyrie is my one true mate. I do not need or want a meddlesome female able to perceive my emotions and pinpoint my location. I am content with my BDSM lifestyle—enjoying a new submissive every week. No commitment. No emotion. No mess.

Now the gods have bound me with this female. Based on what I have witnessed so far, a goddamn emotional, partying, sarcastic spitfire. Even if I wished to integrate her into my life—which I do not—there is nothing passive regarding this woman, and I demand control. Always.

She seizes the mic with determination, the compelling blue gaze seeking my position once more, and I discover I am captivated by her beauty despite my reservations. What she lacks in stature, she more than makes up for in charisma. Her inviting smile is riveting, and my lips curve in response.

The strength to keep my body camouflaged to these mortals is as effortless as breathing. Humans whisper of our existence, but few believe. Those that do consider us alluring, seductive, attracted to us in a manner their feeble minds can't define. But we are much more. Our appetites run rich and varied. Thirst consumes us. Hunger cramps our innards. Vampires are carnivorous creatures of the night, lusting for flesh, salivating for blood.

The sassy valkyrie senses my presence. Not just because of her immortal abilities, but because I am hers. My vampire stirs with yearning at the notion, but I squash him deep, weave the shadows tighter, and settle back for the show.

Alexandria's voice surrounds me in a sensual haze. The drumbeat pounds through my veins, and I cannot take my gaze from the carnal beauty. She is in tight jeans I crave to peel from her hips and thighs, a black V-neck sweater—allowing a hint of enticing cleavage—and she possesses the voice of a naughty angel. I envision her petite form in one of my playrooms, her skin coming alive under my touch, her moans of ecstasy filling my ears.

I recall the first time I laid eyes on the redheaded valkyrie. It was the night my brother Logan revealed the prophecy to his mate, Nicole. The mating bond sang through my veins with exigency, stunning me speechless. It filled me with a demand to protect and shelter the distraught little beauty with tears shimmering below irises the color of a blue morpho butterfly.

Thank fuck, I wizened up and did not fall at her feet like a simpering fool, pleading for any morsel of affection. That is what a mate does to a male. I have seen it countless times, even in my own brother.

My gaze narrows on the minuscule diva performing, and I am hypnotized by the swaying of her hips to the erotic beat, her hand running suggestively up her waist, sweeping the side of her breast, before threading her fingers through the luxurious hair the hue of sugar maple leaves in the fall. A sudden eagerness for it to be my hand plows through me.

While still clutching the mic, Alex sashays down the steps, her tone as sultry as her strut, her destination clear. Me. The little minx is too damn erotic for her own good, but I cannot help being captivated by her performance.

She teases and flirts with the men around the bar as she makes her way toward me. Jealousy rears its head, and a growl hovers below the surface. Does she wish to play with fire? I can oblige.

Bit by bit, I allow the darkness surrounding me to disperse, never taking my scrutiny from the hellion sauntering my direction. She hesitates for a split second, the blue topazes devouring my frame before she continues her path to destruction.

I slip from the corner, and she halts, not even bothering to sing anymore. Her heart rate spikes, along with her breathing as I slide my gaze from her delicate boots to the flaming mane cascading over her shoulders.

"You like what you see, Red?" The nickname falls smoothly from my lips as I step closer, inhaling her bouquet of vanilla, lilac, and tequila—her scrumptious neck arches to keep those dazed blues locked with mine. A pink tongue darts out to moisten her lower lip. I follow it with hunger.

"Who are you?" she whispers, shuffling closer before setting the mic on the bar top next to us.

'*Yours*,' hovers on the tip of my tongue, and I frown in irritation.

"Do you know me?" The petite female asks before boldly placing her palm on the center of my chest. I nearly leap out of my skin at the current arcing through my sternum.

"Would you like me to?" What the fuck is wrong with me? Why am I playing this game with her? I should retreat from this situation before my other brain takes over, and I do something we will both regret.

"Hell yes."

"You wish to get out of here?" *A fucking lousy plan, Bastian.*

"Am I safe with you?" she has the foresight to inquire.

"No."

"Then, yes," she grins, and I am lost.

Chapter 5

Alexandria

The icy December wind slaps my face as we exit The Zoo, dulling my buzz somewhat. Deep down where I refuse to explore, a nagging fear prods my mind. Leaving the security of the crowd with this six-four dark-haired god, with piercing blue eyes and the cutest cleft in his chin that makes me crave to run my tongue along it, is probably not one of my better decisions. In the last few months, anyhow.

"Do you have a name?" I think to ask as he escorts me around the building with a palm between my shoulder blades.

Is it me, or does something happen when we touch? It's more than lust, although I have that in spades too. Who could fault me? This man fills out his black sweater to perfection. I can see his bulging biceps and bite-worthy pecs underneath, and my eyes follow the fabric down to where it disappears into black cargo pants. A long leather jacket hangs over his arm; the dark ensemble adds to his appeal.

"Sebastian Moretti."

Something zings inside my brain. Sebastian Moretti. Wow. I let the name slide over my tongue, savoring its texture. Italian. Hot.

I stumble in the snow, and he tightens his hold, drawing me to his side. Damn. Hot is right. The warmth radiating from him makes me want to snuggle closer. Without clothes.

"Do you have a vehicle here, little red?"

I positively adore his nickname for me, and it's entirely accurate. With a foot and a half in height variation, he towers over me. Instead of being intimidated by it, it ramps up my lustful fantasies of straddling his trim hips and riding him like a bucking stallion.

"Yes, but I don't think you want to take mine."

"Why?" he asks with a curious lift of an eyebrow while examining the dim, snow-covered lot.

"You won't fit." I point to my beat-up car, smirking as those sapphires widen in dismay. The image of him squished inside my compact Fiat almost has me doubling over with laughter.

"Is that even roadworthy?"

Okay, nobody insults my rust bucket and lives to tell about it. Yes, I admit the years have not been kind. His once beautiful paint job has faded to a cringe-worthy turquoise, the bottom's nearly rusted out, and the poor dear has coughing fits on the highway, but his insides are in mint condition. The little gem is all mine, and eighty percent of the time, he gets me where I need to go.

"Hey, don't diss my ride, you'll hurt his feelings." It's all I can do to keep a straight face when Sebastian turns an incredulous expression my direction, surveying me like I've lost my mind. Technically, I have. Well, most of it anyway.

He blinks several times before guiding us away from my little deathtrap. I think I've flummoxed the sexy beast. Tonight is lookin' up.

An alarm chirps, and I stop dead in my tracks, gaping at the wet dream showcased in the faint glow from the parking lights. This Superman lookalike drives a 1986 cherry red and white Ford Bronco, Eddie Bower Edition, with big, sexy-ass knobby tires and shiny rims.

"Holy shit, Batman! You own this sweet ride?"

He grins down at me, enjoying my exuberance. "One of the best automobiles ever invented."

"Where have you been all my life?" I whisper to the Bronco while caressing her side fender. "This baby sports a 5.8-liter, high output V-8 with 210 horsepower and can do 0-60mph in 10.5 seconds flat. Back in its day, it was the beast."

"You know cars?"

I glance over my shoulder at his stunned disbelief. "I recognize great machines. This gem was by far the best full-size SUV of its time. I mean, just look at her. She's damn sexy."

He chuckles, and my insides readjust. "Hop in, and I will take you home."

When he reaches around to open the door, I'm struck with a case of the 'what ifs.' What if he's a serial killer? What if he's a rapist? Although, I can't imagine him doing anything to my body that would cause me to object. Scream his name in ecstasy, on the other hand, damn skippy.

He observes me with a predatory awareness making the hairs on my arms stand on end, and I hesitate in the open door. Inside the bar, when I'd asked if I was safe with him, he'd answered no. No hesitation whatsoever. What does that mean? As much as I'm *dying* for a ride in this baby, I'm not too keen on dying for a ride.

This is wrong and dangerous, and honestly, downright asinine. Still, I've never reacted to anything, since waking up on the floor of the store dressing room, the way I respond to Sebastian. Smart or foolish, I hop up onto the gray and red seat and pray I didn't make the biggest mistake of my life.

When the engine roars awake, I nearly squirt, forgetting in an instant all my reservations, or my friends partying in the bar; even my mission to get into Ezekiel's pants.

Ezekiel who?

The deep sapphires twinkle in the gloomy light. "My car turns you on. I do not know whether to be offended, jealous, or kiss you."

I'm definitely on board with the kissing.

"This is not a car, Sebastian. This is a chick magnet, which I'm sure you are well aware of."

"I like the sound of my name on your lips, little red. And I do not require a vehicle to get... chicks."

Yeah, I bet not.

When the locks engage, I nearly jump out of my skin as he maneuvers out onto Route 66.

"My name's Alex, in case you were wondering." I peer out the window. It's mid-December, and very few cars brave the icy roads at this late hour on a Tuesday.

When he stops at a red light, he shifts in his seat to face me. A swarm of emotions flits through my system as he regards me with those beautiful but savage eyes. With one glance, he manages to make me feel like the sole focus of his thoughts and words.

"Why did you get in the car, Alex?" A cute line forms between his dark brows. "Are you sure you have no idea who I am?"

Well, shit. Don't freaking throw my fears back in my face. "I'm a good judge of character, and my gut tells me you won't hurt me." Man, could I lay the bullshit on any thicker? "I expect you are as curious as I am."

"About what?"

"This peculiar connection between us." If I have to spell it out, maybe he's not experiencing it as intensely as I am.

"What is it you feel, Red?"

How does he make me go from wanting an escape one minute to wanting to wiggle across the center console and straddle him? "I'm not sure, but every instinct I possess tells me you have the answers I seek."

"What are the questions?" he purrs low, leaning close, one arm draped over the steering wheel, the other resting casually on top of the red leather divider.

This guy and his eyes are unlike anything I've ever encountered before, that I remember—icy blue like the sky, glittering and bright. I ease closer, my heart rate spiking, and a pleasant hum settles in my abdomen.

Now probably wouldn't be an ideal moment to inquire if he knows who I am or where I belong. We barely learned each other's names. I prefer this man between my thighs, not running for the hills to get away from the crazy woman.

I twist in my seat and answer his question. "If you're as good in bed as you look," I whisper and boldly close the distance between us to seal my lips over his.

Chapter 6

Sebastian

Long ago, I sealed the door to my heart. Too much hurt and disappointment. Too many tears and broken promises. I allow no one close. Especially a female, and one who is obviously as promiscuous as the night is dark.

Is this how she reacts to any handsome face? Jumps into a vehicle with a random stranger and hopes they want the same thing she does and not to slit her throat or worse.

The thought of someone hurting this little fireball constricts my chest, even as I struggle to not respond to her skilled mouth. Her tongue darts out, running along my lower lip, enticing me to open.

She does not understand who she is messing with—the strength of my control, the dark depths of my passions. As much as I want this small minx, my vampire craving to make her ours, I pull away without touching her.

I have a mission. Now that I have found her, first things first. Contact the demon king, Jagorach Darath, and get his ass here to break this mental block. If he fails, I must mate her. But I refuse to do so until she knows all the facts. I will not deceive her into mating.

"Alex…"

"Oh, God." Her face blooms, matching the color of her hair. "I'm sorry. I totally misread the situation, didn't I?" A horn blare behind us causes her to jump and drop into her seat. "If you want to take me back to the bar, I'll drive myself home." She turns away to stare out the window.

Without a word, I face forward and ease through the intersection, shifting slightly to reduce the pressure of the zipper constricting my hardness. "I am happy to take you home." In reality, I need to know where she lives. "Give me directions."

"Now, I'm thinking that's not such a good idea," she mumbles, the disappointment in her tone apparent.

"Little late for that, Red."

"Just so you know, I'm a black belt in Taekwondo."

I snort at her sudden influx of bravery. God, she is cute. "You have nothing to fear from me, little one. Please allow me to take you home."

"Says every serial rapist in the world."

"I need not force women into sex."

"I bet not," she mutters under her breath before offering directions.

After only a couple of miles down the main drag, and two turns later, we arrive at an apartment structure called Village at Aspen Place. It is located within the Historic District and appears to be a great location and a well-maintained facility.

She directs me to the attached parking garage, and I slide into an open guest spot, turn off the engine, and face the biggest challenge of my life. If things go south with the demon, I need Alex to trust me, to be a part of her life. If I leave things as they are, her thinking I do not crave every inch of her skin against mine, we will have no need to see each other again. I cannot allow that.

"Let me be clear. Please do not mistake my reservations. I want you, Red. From the second, I laid eyes on you, I needed to fuck you," I murmur, reaching over and plucking her off the seat and across my lap.

When her hip contacts my throbbing hardness, I growl low, and her pretty eyes widen before dropping to my lips.

"Yes."

The word is nothing more than a desperate whisper, but it sets me ablaze. Alex slants her mouth over mine once more—hungry and demanding. Her tongue flicks the seam, and this time, I open up and deepen the kiss, taking control.

My hands spear into the luxurious mane with a rough growl, tilting her head to devour, delving deep, exploring every inch of her mouth with my tongue. Her low moans set me on fire, egging me on, nibbling at her plump lips before diving back inside to duel with her tongue. She tastes so damn good. Too good. I fight the insistent urging from my inner vampire to take over.

Small, but strong fingers grip my shoulders as her hips start a delicious rocking along my length, and I grasp her waist, hard enough to bruise, to keep her immobile. It is like I am some newbie vamp, ready to shoot my load at the mere sight of this pretty female. It has taken me centuries to cultivate and control my inner beast, and with one touch of her soft, supple lips, it all flies out the window.

"Christ, I want you," I groan before trailing my lips across her cheek, nibbling, and kissing my way to the erratic pulse calling to me. I glide my hand up her flat stomach, encasing a generous breast in my palm.

What the fuck is happening to me? I cannot control my raging lust for this woman. I crave to touch and taste every mouthwatering inch of her body, to sink so deep into her I will never let go.

But you will let her go. Do not break her heart too, Bastian.

The thought sobers my inner vampire as the past slams into my brain with the force of an explosion. I do not want this—a mate. Never have, never will. Alexandria is a means to an end. The completion of my vow to my queen.

As abruptly as I grabbed her, I toss her back into her seat, needing some distance before I lose complete control and fuck her senseless in my car like a crazed teenager.

She blinks at me several times to recover before surprising me with a hard slap across my cheek.

What the fuck.

"Your whole, on-again, off-again thing might get some girls hot, but I'm not one of them."

I watch in fascination as the blue of her irises flickers silver with her anger. How has she kept those hidden from the mortals around her?

"Alex..."

"We're done here."

When she reaches for the door handle, I gently halt her progress by grabbing her hand. "I am sorry," I grate between clenched teeth, working on getting my breathing under control. Apologies do not come easy for me, but I need her trust.

Those three little words freeze her in place, and I am relieved when she releases the handle. Her scrutiny sets my nerves on edge, but I unflinchingly hold her gaze.

"Why do I get the feeling those words don't come out of your mouth too often?"

"That would be an accurate statement."

"You talk weird. Like you're from another time." Her fingers caress mine, and I realize I am still holding her hand.

The darkness of the parking garage is broken by the soft illumination of the low lights placed throughout. It is intimate, sensual, and my jaw clenches with the knowledge of how much I like it.

"I mean, I'm not complaining," she continues. "I just haven't figured you out yet, or our instant connection." She leans against the door, facing me straight on, and I could drown in the blueness of her gaze.

"It was rather expedient. The reason for my hesitancy." I gently tug on her hand, easing her closer. "As much as I want you beneath me, moaning my name, I would like to get to know you first."

"You want to take things slow?" A dark-red eyebrow arches.

"Yes."

"Well, this is a first. The guy is turning down sex to know me better?"

The thought of her with other men sets up an ache in my gums, longing to rip out their throats. "They were fools."

Her smile lightens the darkness in my chest. "Where have you been, Sebastian?"

For a second, I am thrown by her question, imagining a scenario where she knows who and what I am, my sinister proclivities, and wants to be with me anyway.

"Waiting for you, Alexandria."

She frowns at the use of her full name just as her door flings open, and she is hauled out with a scream.

Chapter 7

Alexandria

Strong arms yank me from the warm cocoon of Sebastian's vehicle. I spin in their embrace and stop cold at my dance instructor's angry face.

"What the hell, Ezekiel?" I shove against his chest, knocking him back a step. That's when a black blur whooshes by me. My hair flies in a frenzy across my face. When I finally manage to flip it out of my eyes, Ezekiel is pinned to the concrete floor with an enraged Sebastian on his chest, fingers squeezing his throat.

"Who the fuck are you?" The enraged, sexy as hell man growls low, and I swallow at the dangerous visual he presents. Holy shitballs. If I were smarter, I'd be petrified to be alone with this guy.

"Sebastian." Not wanting to get caught between these two if a fight breaks out, I ease closer. Although, an Ezekiel and Sebastian sandwich would be my idea of heaven. "This is my dance instructor. Please let him go."

The sapphire eyes blink up at me several times. "Dance instructor?"

"Yes, asshole. Now get the fuck off me." Ezekiel's demand is a mere squeak around the vice on his throat.

Bastian—cause why not—rises to his feet with such grace, I'd swear he was the dancer. E puts on quite the show of wheezing and coughing up a lung. I bend down and offer him my hand. "You okay?'

Once on his feet, he ignores me and faces off with his replacement for the evening. "What the hell is your problem?"

"Why are you in Alex's parking garage?"

"Yeah, good question. Why are you here, Ezekiel?" I ask, my gaze bouncing between these two impressive men.

Bastian is several inches taller than E and broader in the shoulders. They both possess drool-worthy physiques and model perfect appearances, but it's Sebastian I'm drawn to with a fierceness that scares me. No objection would have left my lips if he decided to have his wicked way with me in his Bronco, in the middle of my parking garage.

"I saw you leave with him, and I wanted to make sure you got home safely."

He turns those hazel irises entirely on me and... nothing. I step closer, waiting for the butterflies to appear in my gut. Still nothing. I gently place my hand on his bicep, and low growl permeates our little trio.

Oh, there they are, undulating in flapping waves in sync with Bastian's inhuman growls. Not wanting to enrage the blue-eyed beast further, I remove my hand and take a stride back.

I don't get it. Just yesterday, I thought E was the end-all-be-all and couldn't wait for him to be *the one*. Now? While I still think he's hot and his dance moves sexy, I'm in tune with Superman's doppelganger. I would gladly turn away from E to be with Bastian.

What the fuck is wrong with me? All of a sudden, I can't wait to have a man in my pants. Have I always been this way? Maybe I was a high-class call girl for the mafia. It would explain the money, and my need to be on the run, but not this nagging compulsion to find someone.

Maybe Sebastian's the one I've been seeking. It would explain this instant connection with him. One thing is for sure: I need to find out.

Decision made, I step in front of Bastian and face E. "While I appreciate your concern, Ezekiel—although stalking a girl is probably not the best way to go about it— I'm fine. I left with Sebastian of my own free will."

"Are you sure about that?" he asks, never taking his piercing gaze from the man at my back.

I step next to Bastian and lace his fingers with mine. He frowns down at our entwined hands like he's never held hands with a girl before, and then those delicious sapphires with the longest black lashes lift to mine. Their directness lances through me with the speed of a bullet, causing my heart rate to skip and my lips to part remembering his searing kiss. The control he exerted over me was spectacular, and I'm itching to explore more.

"Go inside, Red. Your *friend* and I have things to discuss."

"Excuse me?" *What the fuck?* "Are you dismissing the little woman so the men can talk? Really?" I drop his hand like a hot potato. Okay, it seems I like a man in control sexually, but don't fuckin' dictate when, where, how or what any other time.

"No, I...."

"Smooth, jackass," E says with a sneer.

"This is my place. I'll come and go whenever I want. It's the two of you who are leaving." When nobody moves, I place my hands on my hips and give them both the evil eye. "Right the fuck now. Can I make that any plainer?"

Sebastian's jaw clenches tight as he glares at me, then E.

"Is there a problem here, Alex?" Ry's boyfriend, Jose, questions with a frown as he strides in our direction. "Is Ryen with you?"

"Jose, you were supposed to meet us an hour ago." Great, now I'm facing off with three men. This night keeps getting better and better.

"I know, sorry. I got held up at work." His frown deepens as he takes in the large amount of testosterone bouncing between the he-men.

"You planning a ménage à trois, Alex?"

I snort. "I wish."

That gets me another glare from Bastian. "This idiot will never lay his hands on you."

Whoa, Nelly! He did not just... "Listen here, Bas," another ominous glare. "I don't know you from Adam. Who I date, party with, or decide to sleep with isn't any of your damn business." I turn to E. "Or yours, for that matter."

"Alex, please calm down," E dares to say.

"Calm down? Never tell a woman to calm down, because guess what, you won't get the reaction you're hoping for. Now, you two can kill each other for all I care. I'm going home." I turn on Jose, beyond pissed at this point, and he wisely backs up a step. "You. Get to The Zoo. Your girlfriend is drunk. Bring her home." With that, I pivot in a beautiful spin and stalk through the darkened garage to the apartments.

What the hell happened back there? One minute I'm all hot and heavy with Mr. Dreamy, and the next I'm yelling at them and escaping to my apartment. Alone.

Every instinct I possess demands I twirl around and run into Sebastian's arms. No. I refuse to let a man control me. If that's his thing, then good riddance, I say. But, the thought of never seeing him again produces a tremendous icky feeling in my chest.

Is Bastian who I've been waiting for all these months? Why else would I have such an inappropriate reaction to him? I mean, I sensed the man in the bar before I even saw him. How does that happen?

It goes along with all the other freaky things concerning me. Like the fact, I hardly need to eat and never feel hungry, but I don't lose weight. Or the fact I'm drawn to lightening like a gnat to fruit, which I hate—pesky little buggers.

Just the other day, I cut myself chopping veggies for Ry and nearly took my damn finger off. I made a quick getaway to the bathroom before she noticed. By the time I rinsed it, applied antiseptic ointment, and searched the medicine cabinet for a bandage, it healed. I couldn't believe my eyes. And after an hour, only a thin white line remained.

There is something different about me, and it scares me shitless.

Chapter 8

Sebastian

"How the fuck do you deal with a stubborn mate, Logan?"

After watching Alex's delightful ass walk away last night, the dancer and I parted ways, but not before I made it perfectly clear who Alex belonged to, and if he valued his life, he would keep the dance lessons purely platonic.

Not that she will be taking lessons from him again. I will not allow another man's arms around my mate. When I see her tonight, she will come to understand that. Period.

I glance at my brother's smirk and must curb the urge to plow my fist into his face. Logan and I are equally matched. It would be a long, painful incident, and right now, I need his advice more.

Logan's mated to my queen. The most powerful vampire on the planet is a kickass, take no prisoners, zero- filter-between-her-mouth-and-brain halfling who has the voice of a sex goddess. I have come to adore her quirkiness, the way she names inanimate objects, and the rarely seen vulnerability. But then again, I am not mated to her.

Alex lives up to her thick mane of red hair. She is stubborn, hot-tempered, and worst of all, promiscuous. It grates my nerves to think she might have slept with the human from last night or the other one named Jose.

"The valkyrie giving you trouble, brother?" Logan grins, leaning against the conference table in the castle's war room. The frigid

Canadian climate penetrates the stone walls, and I ease closer to the fireplace.

"She is a fucking menace."

"Hey!" Nicki admonishes as she saunters in and heads straight for the heat of the flickering flames. "Don't be badmouthing my best friend. And you guys need to get with the twenty-first century and start contracting your words. It's more efficient. Just saying."

I cannot help but snort at the words on her hoodie. *I have a black belt in sarcasm, a degree in Smartass, and I'm just a few credits short of being a bitch.* It could not be more perfect.

"When you have spoken one way for centuries, my love, it is hard to break the habit of *proper* English," Logan smirks.

"Proper according to whom?" she taunts back with a wicked grin.

"Your master and mate."

"Mate? Yes. Master? You fucking wish."

I have never seen my brother this happy and relaxed, bantering back and forth with his pregnant female. He is giddy with excitement about this baby. We all are. The child will be the first natural born vampire with the ability to walk in the sun and eat human food, procreating a long line of daywalker vampires.

The queen held serious reservations at first about being a parent. I think she is still worried concerning her ability to be a good mother. Who could blame her with her upbringing? Her father, the former king, sexually abused her while her mother looked the other way.

Logan strolls up behind Nicki and wraps his arms around her slightly swollen belly, nuzzling her neck. "Alex is giving my brother fits."

She glances up at me, the gray eyes dancing with humor. "Well, I'd be disappointed in her if she didn't, but don't tell me the renowned ladies' man, Sebastian Moretti is having trouble getting one little female to swoon at his feet."

"Laugh it up all you want, but if King Darath fails to restore her memories, I will have no choice but to mate her, and I refuse to commit her to a lifetime bond through deception or force."

Nicki's grin vanishes. "Force is not an option, Bastian. I know I said 'by any means necessary', but I hope you know it excludes rape."

My irises heat, and my fangs descend. The blue glow diminishes the warm orange light of the fire.

"Alexandria Svaldana is not only a princess to the Valkyrie Regency but my mate. I would sooner die than cause her harm." I take a step closer, and Logan's arms tighten protectively around his mate. "Not to mention, I would never abuse a female in such a way. How can you even say such a vile thing to me?"

"I know, Sebastian. I just needed to hear you say it." She shrugs at my display of aggression and extends her hands toward the flames. "What's your game plan?"

"I have no fucking clue." I run an agitated hand through my hair. "I deal with subs who follow my every command; I do not comprehend how to deal with a redheaded, sarcastic hellion with an overactive libido."

Nicole barks out a laugh. "Overactive libido? This coming from the male who has a different submissive every week."

"Submissive and obedient is how I like them. When I issue a command, I expect it to be followed without hesitation." Why is she pressing me on this?

"Don't piss off the pregnant woman, Bastian. I'm running out of places to hide the bodies."

"Brother, approach this like you do everything else. Formulate a plan based on the parameters laid out before you. In this case, Alexandria. Learn her wants and desires. What her hobbies are, what movies she likes, or her favorite flower or food, and then use those to your advantage."

"Listen to you, Casanova," Nicole scoffs.

"Okay. Yes. Thank you, brother. The first sound advice."

"Hey, my advice usually goes down like a fat kid on a see-saw, so listen closely. Alex is in love with the idea of love. She falls hard and fast. Be as honest and upfront about your commitment issues as possible without freaking her out enough she disappears again."

"I understood half of that."

My queen steps forward, lays her palm on my chest, and my lungs compress at the energy flowing into me. "Don't close yourself off, commander. You're gifted one mate throughout eternity. Don't throw it away because you're too stubborn to try."

I have no idea what the trauma in your life was, Nicole whispers in my mind, her powerful empathic abilities picking up on the turmoil within. *But I'm going to offer you the same advice Jimmy, the great werewolf king, once told me: to get over the past, first, you must accept the past is over. No matter how many times you revisit it, analyze it, or regret it, it's over. It can't hurt you anymore.*

Oh, but it can. "Yes, my lady. Profound advice."

"See, I can..." Nicole suddenly doubles over, clutching her protruding stomach, a deep groan of pain escaping her lips.

"Baby?" Logan and I reach for her at the same time when Icarus, the High Priest Oracle, rushes into the room. The blue tattoos all over his face and body pulse with energy, and I grit my teeth against the powerful magic radiating from him.

"Icarus," Nicole wales. "The baby."

"Yes, my lady. I am here."

"What the fuck is happening, priest?" Logan bellows before lifting her in his arms and sitting in the overstuffed chair by the fire.

"I am sorry, my lady. I assumed I would pay the price for bringing you back from death."

"Oh, no! I would gladly pay the price, Icarus. Anything but this." Tears run unchecked down Nicole's face. I think this is the first time I have ever witnessed her cry, and it breaks my heart.

"What fucking price?" Logan demands, glaring daggers at the Oracle while rocking his weeping mate in his arms.

"Bringing your mate from the depths of hell carried a heavy price, my lord. I assumed the price would be my life, but it seems the gods are demanding your unborn child."

"No fucking way," Logan bellows. The priest's face is awash in Logan's tormented green glow.

Holy hell.

I glance at my brother, and his anguish nearly brings me to my knees. How could the gods demand an unborn child? This baby is supposed to be the prophesied daywalker.

"Can you not plead with them on our behalf, Icarus?" Logan demands.

"You have two options, my lord. Your unborn child or both of them."

"That is utter bullshit!" Nicole yells, her body tight with agony.

"If you do not consent, the miscarriage will take them both."

"What kind of choice is that?" I demand.

"The only one we are offered, commander."

My mind flashes to Lucretia's trial and her sisters' manic ravings. She kept repeating, 'Not this child, not this child.' Did the mentally troubled vampire, now Oracle in training, foresee this?

Logan cradles his mate's face, peering deep into the shimmering gray depths. "I lost you once, and it nearly broke me. I will not lose you again."

"No. There has to be another way." Tears stream down her flushed face, her eyes pleading with my brother to find a different answer.

I plow my fingers through my hair, pacing in agitation. What can I do to solve this?

"Since the gods are angry with you, Icarus, maybe your daughter could plead their case. I know she is only in training, but..."

"You do not negotiate or bargain with the gods, my lord. We—I defied them, and in doing so, I assumed the price would be my life." The priest's weird blue eyes glaze over in anger. "It appears I was wrong."

Nicole's scream pierces the tension.

"Choose, my lord, before it is too late."

"Nicole," Logan whispers as a tear rolls slowly down his cheek, and I want to roar with anger. "I always choose Nicole."

Nicki weeps harder, burying her face in her mate's neck, and holding on to him for dear life as her belly visibly rolls.

Holy Christ! This cannot be happening.

Icarus kneels at their feet and gently lays his pulsing hands on top of Nicki's shifting stomach. I join him, grabbing my brother's bicep, trying to offer as much comfort as possible.

"You will get through this, brother. You both will."

"As long as I have her in my arms, I can get through anything."

Logan's words dig deep within my soul, wrapping around my blackened heart. To him, his mate is his greatest strength—the purpose of his life and sole reason to exist. She is his sun, moon, and stars, the light in his darkness. I see it in his gaze. Without Nicole, Logan would wither and die.

And that scares me more than the loss of this child because I see my future in those troubled eyes.

Chapter 9

Alexandria

"How are you feeling after last week, Alex?" Doc asks from her customary spot, savoring her tea.

I didn't even bother with the ridiculous chair; I flew straight for the couch, which I'm now laying on like a freaking cliché.

"Fan-fucking-tastic, Doc."

What a pile of bullshite.

"We agreed on complete honesty during our sessions."

"Yeah. Okay. I'm miserable and pissed at myself. I still can't believe I walked away from—not one—but two gorgeous men last week. Both tall, scrumptious morsels of man meat wanted me, but a girl's gotta draw the line. Right?"

"And what was the line?"

"I will not be dictated to like a child who needs to obey."

"Perfectly understandable, but from what you told me, Bas apologized."

I snicker. No way was I going to expose their actual names, so I went with the little nicknames I invented. "Yes, that's true, but I get the impression the role of dictator sits comfortably on his shoulders. Not to mention, the clashing emotions he creates tear my insides to shreds. Like I'm not certain whether to strip him naked or pack up and disappear."

Or slip a silver dagger through his heart. A dreadful sensation pounds in my brain when I judge him as if he's standing in the way of something I need. What, I have no idea, but this compulsion to kill him or fuck him frightens me.

"And what about the other gentleman, E?" Doc asks around her mug while balancing a laptop on the arm of the chair and typing with one hand.

Since big fat snowflakes descend in rapid succession outside the darkened window, the designer skinny jeans tucked into low-heeled boots, and the thick red sweater seems a more appropriate choice than the outfit I shuffled into this afternoon.

Although, some part of my brain was working before coffee because I remembered to layer warm cuddle duds under my periwinkle blue scrub top and pants. I start my ER shift at the vet hospital after this head shrinking session.

"According to him, he merely followed me to make certain I was safe. But it still seems a bit stalkery to me," I answer.

"Has either contacted you since that night?"

And there's the jab through the heart. "No, but I have a dance lesson tomorrow with E." It smarts how much I yearned for Sebastian to appear in my parking garage over the past week. He was such a dynamic and compelling personality, and I crave to be back in his arms. Hopefully, not to murder him.

"Good. Keep me posted on how it goes. In the meantime, I received your test results from the physicians this morning. By the way, thank you for squeezing those into your work schedules." At my nod, she continues. "We can safely rule out neurological amnesia or any underlying medical condition."

"Okay. So, what happens now?"

"It is my professional assessment that hypnosis is the best course of action if you're susceptible."

Why does the concept of the doc probing around in my mind cause heart palpitations?

"I've placed you on the schedule for next week. We will begin with the Stanford Hypnotic Susceptibility Scale or SHSS."

"That sounds ominous." I sit up and gather my unruly mass of hair into a high ponytail in preparation for my vet assistant gig.

"It isn't. They developed this to measure susceptibility to hypnosis. The higher the score, the more responsive one is to it. I will perform a standard hypnotic induction, and then you are given suggestions pertaining to a list."

"Please don't make me suck my thumb or cry on command."

"Ha ha, very funny." The doc is finally coming out of her shell. "No. It is more like posture sway, eye closure, left-hand lowering, etcetera, etcetera. The form comprises twelve items with progressive difficulty and generally takes fifty minutes to perform. It's rudimentary and mainly consists of motor and cognitive tasks."

"What makes a person susceptible?" This is fucking scary and fascinating.

"Individuals of extremely high hypnotizability are termed fantasizers. They exhibit a cluster of traits. Fantasizing much of the time, describing their imagery was as vivid as actual perceptions and experiencing physical responses to those imageries."

Oh shit. It sounds like me.

"Also, bearing an earlier than average age for first childhood memory, and finally having grown up with parents who encouraged imaginative play. About 60% fit into the fantasizer group while 40% we term dissociaters. These are individuals who experience daydreaming mostly as "spacing out" and not remembering what transpired for periods of time. We can count that out.

"Second, dissociaters possessed parents who were harshly punitive and/or encountered other juvenile traumas. Again, we have no way of knowing whether such a scenario is true for you." Blue eyes pin me to the couch.

Oh crap. I never considered the probability I might have suffered a traumatic upbringing. That would totally suck.

"Fantasizers experience hypnosis as being much like other imaginative activities while dissociaters reported it was unlike anything they'd ever experienced. Individuals with posttraumatic stress disorder, which I surmise is your issue, have the highest hypnotizability."

"You believe I suffer from PTSD?" *What the fuck?*

"I suspect, but we will delve into it more next week." She stands gracefully and sets her laptop on the cushioned coffee table, her tea mug gripped firmly in her hand. "Our time has ended for tonight."

"Oh, okay. You threw a lot at me today, Doc." I frown as I slip into my shoes.

"Try not to fret, Alexandria. Google it if it will make you feel better, but I've done these numerous times with remarkable success," she declares as she approaches her desk. I peek at her nameplate again. Dr. Sarah La Borski. See, I knew it was a Ski-something-or-other.

I can't help but marvel at the way she moves, like a model strolling down the runway. If I were to guess, I'd say she was in her late twenties, but with all the degrees on her wall, it's more likely she's in her thirties.

"Oh, and steer clear of Bas until we get your past resolved. Keep your dance lessons with E strictly professional. The last thing you need is the added complexity of a romantic involvement right now."

Shitballs.

"Yeah, makes sense. Keep my pants on until I find out who I am."

"Precisely. See you next week, same time."

"You know, I could make our appointments during the day if you needed."

"No, evening hours work better for me. My daytime appointments are booked solid."

"Well, I appreciate you squeezing me in, Doc."

"Alex, you are my priority."

Aww. Isn't that sweet? I'm someone's priority.

"THANK YOU FOR ALL YOUR help tonight, Alex," Dr. Gorgeous murmurs while removing his lab coat. All the women vets wear scrubs, including the owner, Doc Julie, but the muscle-bound god wears jeans, a button-down dress shirt rolled up to expose brawny forearms, with a white medical coat.

Usually, I'm what they hail a floater—a vet assistant who bounces between all the ER docs, helping where needed. The first time a technician called me that, my hackles rose, and my head spun in her direction like the girl in the Exorcist movie. Then I settled down.

When Doc Julie hired the amazingly, swoon-worthy, Dr. Steve Warner last week, I wonder if she did it to provide all the women some eye candy to gaze at during the long hectic nights. It pissed the other techs off when she assigned me to his rotation exclusively. He's an excellent vet, easy-going, and meticulous with both patient and client and is quite comfortable being the only male in the clinic. In fact, I suspect he basks in it.

But why are all the individuals around me freaking supermodels? It's like someone planted them in my world to make me feel crummy. I'm not ugly by any means, but geez, these people should star in Days of Our Lives.

"It was a crazy one tonight," I respond, throwing my suture scissors, white tape, thermometer, sticky notes, and various pens in my locker. "That Rottie nearly ripped your arm off."

"Yes." The frown provides him a stormy, brooding expression that gives women heart palpitations. But the good doctor has never peered at me as anything other than his assistant. Which is a damn shame because the 6'3", body to die for, dark-haired, dark-eyed beef-cake is enough to drive any woman to swoon and beg to be his.

"Do you require a lift home, Alex? I noticed your clunker wasn't in the parking lot."

"Hey, why does everyone diss my ride?" He shoots me a deadpan stare, not bothering to answer. "Whatever. Ry dropped me off." I mutter and twirl the combination lock before grabbing my down jacket off the hook on the wall. "Since it finally stopped snowing, and I live half a mile, I figured I'd catch a little fresh, brisk night air and walk home."

"It's one in the morning. Do you consider that a wise idea?"

"I think it's a brilliant idea, and this is Flagstaff, Dr. Warner, not Los Angeles. I'll be fine."

"If you're certain? I have several more charts to type up before I leave. See you on Thursday?"

"Yes, but remember Christmas is next week, so I'm off until the day after."

"How did you manage that?"

"Doc Julie loves me," I grin and head for the exit.

The second the icy temps slap me in the face, my eyes water, making me rethink this lunacy. No. I need this chance to think. Walking always helps clear the clutter and cobwebs.

Instead of taking the long way down Butler Ave, I skirt around a semi loading facility, jump the brick wall onto Sawmill RD, and head to the frozen parking lot of Whole Foods. This path cuts out several blocks, and when it's December in Northern Arizona, the quicker you get inside, the better.

I'm halfway across the property when a powerful force slams into my side. The impact sends me careening head over ass through the air until my spine crashes into the unforgiving steel of a vehicle. Figures, the only car in the lot is a 1967 Ford Fairlane. No crumpling fiberglass to cushion the jolt.

Holy fuck! What the hell happened?

Pain lances down my vertebrae as I struggle to push myself up, but my left arm refuses to cooperate, and darkness encroaches on my vision. I shake my head, blinking several times when a blurry white form takes shape on my right.

Shit, Alex. Get the fuck up!

On instinct, I reach for the small dagger hidden in the inside pocket of my jacket even as I battle through the ripples of pain to gain my feet.

The colossal threat approaches. My vision clears, and it takes a full ten seconds for my brain to assimilate what I'm seeing. I gape at the magnificent, bare-chested being towering over me, a ten-foot, blinding white wingspan unfurled behind him.

Shit. Did I die? Is this angel here to faery me off into the afterlife?

"Alexandria Svaldana?" The voice is deep, rich, with a rough Scottish brogue, and I stupidly nod. "Kin' Grayflame desires yer company. Come willingly, lass, or Ah will tak' ye by force."

Okay, I adore the accent, but it doesn't sound very angel-ly. And who the hell is this Grayflame character? Not God. Maybe this white-haired, silver-eyed creature is an evil angel, here to toss me to a warmer climate and the *other* guy. Shouldn't his wings be black, though?

I flip the dagger, keeping the blade along the inside of my forearm and pray my fractured arm hurries and heals.

"Well, handsome, you can tell your king to go fuck himself. I'm not traveling anywhere with you."

With astounding agility and a high-pitched shriek, I leap into the sky, higher than an average human could—I'll contemplate this new ability later—and meet the beautiful being mid-air as a lightning bolt streaks across the star-filled sky.

Another fact: lightning emerges when I become emotional.

Before the jackass can wrap those massive arms around me, I slash my knife through his left bicep and down his rib cage. A big meaty fist sails by my head, missing me by mere inches as I whirl away, spiraling down to the parking lot.

I land with a soft thud, slushy snow soaking through my stupid tennis shoes, and drop into a crouch. My arm screams bloody murder.

The angel charges, and this time I sink to my knees, plunging my dagger into his thigh with a twist and pull. His bellow fills the night, but before I can give his other limb the same treatment, he seizes a fist full of my hair, yanking me to my feet.

I yelp as fire spreads over my scalp, and jab forward with the dagger, aiming for his gut when he tosses me across the parking lot.

Shitballs. This is gonna hurt.

Metal buckles. A loud pop in my shoulder brings tears to my eyes as my limp body crumples to the icy snow. *That's twice the fucker slammed me into this beautiful car*, I reflect stupidly through a haze of pain.

Everything hurts. My back sings in agony, my shoulder pulses in rage, bone on bone grinds in my forearm, and warm blood streams down my face.

This is it. I'm going to die in a Whole Foods parking lot, 500 feet from my apartment.

Why didn't I let Dr. McDreamy take me home?

Chapter 10

Sebastian

Where the hell is the little minx? I peer at my watch for the hundredth time. It is after one in the damn morning, and I have worn a track in the concrete outside the apartment's main lobby. Her rust bucket of an automobile is in the parking garage, but I did not scent Alexandria anywhere in the building.

Earlier I hacked into the apartment's computers, but her name was not on any of the rental agreements. I have no notion which residence is hers.

She should be here by now. The trek from the clinic is only ten minutes, if she crawls. I should have waited outside her work and escorted her home. I am going nuts imagining another male picked her up for a date. The visual of their limbs entwined as he savors and touches what is mine spreads fury through my veins.

The previous week was a total cluster fuck. Logan and Nicole sequestered themselves in their suite, grieving the loss of the baby. Vampire business settled on mine and Icarus' shoulders. At every meeting, we concocted reasons for the couple's absence.

The minute I discovered Alexandria's whereabouts, I incorporated one of my most trusted Guardians into her life. It soothes my mind somewhat knowing Christoph watches over her while I am consumed with tedious meeting after meeting, but dammit, I miss the little spitfire. Her vivid blue eyes haunt my dreams, and her vanilla scent stirs me in ways I do not wish to ponder.

A high-pitched scream rips through the night, accompanied by a blinding streak of lightning. Only one phenomenon produces such an ear-piercing shriek followed by those eerie dazzling bolts—a valkyrie.

My fucking valkyrie.

I draw on the surrounding shadows before ascending into the frigid sky toward the sounds of a skirmish.

When I catch a splash of red, rage fills my vision, honing my senses, and I sink into a crouch at the fringe of the frozen lot. My mate engages in battle with a winged fae twice her size, but her speed and agility, the quick, efficient strikes with the blade has pride warming my chest. Each slash and stab are meant to hit vital areas for maximum effect.

Thank goodness the store is closed, and no humans mill around at this hour. The dark fae took an enormous risk exposing his true self out in the open. An offense punishable by death.

Tonight, I deem myself judge and executioner.

When the feathered immortal grabs the little redhead by the hair, tossing her across the parking lot, I pitch all discretion to the wind and trace in front of the winged creature, halting his advance toward Alex, who is making a valiant effort to stand. Her left arm hangs at an odd angle. The spice of her spilled blood fills my senses, and my fury darkens.

My heated gaze lights up the fae's startled expression, and before he can recover, I drive my fangs into his neck with a feral growl, ripping the artery from muscle. Ruby gore spews like a geyser in every direction. Gods. Magical power infuses fae blood, but it tastes like rusted metal, and I yearn for my swords.

A meaty fist slams into my cheek, and I laugh at his pathetic attempts to halt his death. "You dared touch what belongs to me."

Silver eyes widen while his fingers attempt to stem the tributary of crimson flowing from the gaping wound. "Th' valkyrie is yer mate?"

"Yes, young fae," I snarl. "You just sealed your doom." I charge, latch onto the other side of his neck, going deep, while fisting his silver locks and snapping his skull down hard to his shoulder, tugging at the same time. Desperate fingers shove against my shoulders, wings flap in a relentless beat, seeking to break loose of my grip.

Within moments, my fangs tear through his flesh until the fae's head rips free, and his body collapses to the frozen ground.

During the famous battle with King Dimitri last year, the dark fae battled the shifters and valkyrie, steering clear of the Guardians. They are no match for our speed and strength, especially if armed with swords.

"Oh, my God."

The tortured whisper dims the violence consuming my thoughts, and I pivot to face my mate, the fae's head still clutched in my fist.

Huddled against the side of the car, clinging to her left arm, mouth hanging open, Alex appears diminutive and frail. A misconception. Red is a fierce little warrior. As I observe her tremble, something in my chest catches, as if pierced with the wicked dagger dangling from her lax fingers.

What the hell?

"Alexandria..."

"What the fuck are you?" She grates out between clenched teeth as if she is barely holding on to her sanity.

I release the head into the snow. "I appreciate you are scared and confused but do not fear me." I maintain a soft tone and ease closer, raising my palms as proof I mean her no harm. Until I notice the dark red staining every inch of them.

I groan inwardly as I take in the rest of my condition. Jeans, sweater, and leather coat are all drenched in blood. Jesus, it is probably all over my face as well. I would not be surprised if she hightailed away from me as fast as possible. "I am not your enemy, Alex."

"You—you took his—that thing's head off with... fangs." She wavers, drawing a deep, shaky breath. "So, I'll ask you again, Sebastian, what the fuck are you?"

I slide a few feet closer, and she presses harder against the car. The trembling in her limbs intensifies. I halt a foot away. "I am here to protect you. The creature meant you harm, and I will not allow it."

Before I realize she has advanced, the tip of her silver dagger rests between two ribs, directly above my heart.

Chapter 11

Alexandria

He holds my glare, not even blinking. The seconds tick by with every heartbeat until he confounds me by spreading his palm over mine.

"Let me be clear, Alexandria," he declares, his tone deepening on my name, and I tremble. "I never give up control, but I am now, for you."

He strides into the tip of my dagger, pressing it deep. "You have authority." His hand slips away from mine clutching the hilt, leaving behind a sticky smear of blood across my knuckles. "You have two options," he continues. "Trust me as I am trusting you, or plunge your blade through my heart. Decide now."

Even though Bastian scares the ever-living-shit out of me with his otherworldly gruesomeness going on, he still appeals to a deep part of me. An element craving him even after everything I witnessed. And unlike the winged monster, I sense this creature possesses no inclination to harm me.

I lower the blade and step back, leaning against the dented fender of the car once more. "I can't hurt you, Sebastian."

He draws a sharp breath. "Not true. You are the most dangerous woman I have ever faced."

What does that mean? "Are you a vampire?" I ask with nervous excitement as he continues to regard me with a perplexed countenance.

"Yes."

Shit.

"And the thing with the wings?"

"A dark fae."

"Why did he want to take me to someone named King Grayflame?"

Sebastian's eyes narrow. "Is that what he claimed?"

"Yes. He informed me a King Grayflame desired my company, demanded I come voluntarily, or he'd abduct me by force."

"If he had prevailed, you would be lost to me now." His frown deepens, and the beautiful sapphires pulse with a peculiar light.

"Where would he have taken me?"

"Scotland, most likely." Sebastian steps closer, and the warmth from his body lessens the trembling in my bones, but he reeks of blood. "We must get off the street, Alex, before someone spots us and signals the authorities."

He's right. We look like we just stepped out of a horror movie. "My roommate is staying the night with her boyfriend, so I have the apartment to myself. We could clean up and wash our clothes."

A smile lifts the corner of his blood-tinged lips, and my stomach flips. What is wrong with me? The dude's freaking covered in disgusting gore and a goddamn vampire! What the hell happened to my world?

"We can share the shower," he suggests, and tugs at a red curl stuck to my cheek.

I gulp at the imagined visual of water sluicing down his muscular body. His powerful arms hauling me to him and taking me against the tiled wall while steam billows around us. Heat infuses my tummy. Did the temperature rise?

"How bad are your injuries?" He asks, running the tips of his fingers along my broken forearm. I suck in a gasp at the pain the gentle touch produces. "I can help heal them."

Why do I get the impression I won't like what he's going to suggest? "How?"

"My blood will restore you in an instant."

"You want me to drink your blood?" Eww... and kinda hot.

"Strangely, yes." The glower he's sporting shouts otherwise.

"Wait. I'm bleeding. Doesn't that bother you?" Is he going to go berserk, sink those sexy fangs into my neck, and suck me dry?

"Alexandria," he smiles. "I am 500 years old, I have lived and traveled around the world, speak multiple languages, fought in numerous battles, and while the delicious bouquet of your blood calls to me, similar to a craving for chocolate for a mortal, I mastered the bloodlust long ago."

Holy shitballs! Five hundred? "So, you were born in the 1500s? No wonder you don't contract your words. I can't imagine the things you've experienced."

Bastian's every word entrances me. The fact he's a vampire should terrify me, especially covered in bloody gore, but he fascinates me. This creature is knowledgeable, well-traveled, and a ruthless fighter. The man carries himself with graceful confidence. We are so different, yet; I feel a profound connection to him I can't explain.

I shove off the car to get closer to the vampire until my gaze veers to the mutilated monster staining the snow red, and my lust cools.

"What about his body? We can't leave it here." Yup. Those words just fell out of my mouth. My shrink would have a field day with this, if I were dumb enough to inform her, a man with white feathers tried to kidnap me until a 500-year-old vampire tore his head off with his teeth.

Padded cell here I come.

Bastian frowns before dragging a cell phone from his front jean pocket. He rubs his palms down his pants several times to erase enough blood his pads contact the screen. I watch with raised eyebrows as his fingers flutter over the keys with such velocity it's hard to follow.

Shit. That's handy.

"An associate of mine will take care of it. Now drink some of my blood to mend your wounds."

"Um, thanks, but no. I'll heal in a few hours."

His jaw clenches, and I bite my lip to check a smile. Aww, Mr. Dictator's pissed I disobeyed him. Hilarious.

"Are you a drug lord or mafia king?" I inquire as we dash across the street into my parking garage. He laughs, and my chest tightens at the deep masculine melody. I'm guessing this creature doesn't indulge in laughter regularly. Beneath the cool blue eyes lies a great torment.

"Would it sound better than vampire?"

"Actually, yes." At least it would be more plausible.

One minute, I'm minding my own business, struggling to get through life with no past, and then, BAM! I've become embroiled in the fantasy world of vampires and guys with wings.

My brain hiccups. "Hold on a damn second." I halt at the elevator doors and pivot to face off with the vampire. "I find it strangely odd you've suddenly appeared at the same time some winged creature wants to capture me and take me to his king." Shit, sounds weird saying it out loud, but I step closer and stretch my neck to scowl at him. "Sebastian, do you know who I am?"

He considers me, the pretty cerulean irises roaming my face. "Yes."

Holy fuck!

"What am I?"

"You, my kind-hearted hellion, are a valkyrie."

"What is that?" I attempt to block the keypad with my throbbing arm as I punch in my access code to open the elevator. He chuckles behind me. "What?" I ask innocently over my shoulder.

"Even covered in dirty snow and injured, you are delightful."

"Yeah, well, coming from the man soaked in an angels' blood, that's just creepy."

"He was not an angel," he murmurs in my ear as I hit the button for the 5th floor and a shiver runs down my spine.

"Angel, fairy, whatever. All I know is it wasn't freaking human. And apparently, neither am I." In truth, I've suspected something was off with me the minute I came to in the dressing room.

"Wait! How old am I?"

His grin heats my insides further, calling for his hard flesh on my own. "You are a baby. A mere century."

Geez. I'm a hundred years old? Damn.

Entombed in the metal box with a murderous villain saturated in crimson, I welcome the few precious moments to evaluate the last hour. When I opened my eyes this morning, never in a million years would I have guessed my evening would catapult into such a wild ride?

On the sunny side, I discovered what I am, and it explains so much. Not that I even remotely understand what the hell a valkyrie is, my friend Google will educate me later, but at least I've met a... being—I would say man, but is a vampire a man?—who knows me.

Sebastian and I have an odd connection, and my instinct whispers I can depend on him, but my mind is screeching to move slow. Trust is earned, and even though he saved my life tonight, I know less than zero about him or vampires, besides what I've picked up from books and movies over the last six months.

The doors glide open, and thankfully the corridor is empty, but I insist we take off our shoes. Don't want to track blood across the carpet. Nothing says, 'there goes the murderer' like a trail of bloody footprints.

As we silently walk to my apartment, a warning pricks at the back of my mind. Letting this individual into my home is probably *no buena*. Not good.

But as usual, I discount the voice and unlock the door. "I'll use my roommate's shower, you can have mine," I say as I traipse through the kitchen, but when I turn around, the handsome devil covered in gore, black biker boots dangling from his fingers, has paused at the entrance. What the hell? The second someone sees him, they will call the police, thinking he's massacred everyone in the apartment.

"What are you doing?"

"Invite me in, Alexandria."

"Oh. This is a vampire thing, eh? You can't cross the threshold until you're invited?"

"Exactly."

"Hmm. Let me ask you this; can you teleport like in the movies?"

He cocks his head to the side. "Yes."

"Great. Then I suggest you teleport to wherever your home is and shower there because I'm not stupid enough to invite you inside." And with that, I stomp over and slam the door in his stunned face.

Redhead one, vampire zero.

Chapter 12

Alexandria

After a grueling ten-hour day shift at the clinic, I race home, in my car this time, needing a little one-on-one with my computer to delve further into what I am.

A scalding hot shower and several doses of Ibuprofen later, I lean toward the steamed mirror. The gash in my forehead healed, and while my forearm is still uncomfortable, it's mending nicely.

I'll never forget the expression on Ryen's face when she strolled out of her bedroom the morning after what I've dubbed "The Ferry Debacle". She took one look at my bruised body and nearly called the police. After an elaborate story about how a Great Dane knocked me across an exam room, and an even more scintillating tale of Dr. Warner checking me out, she relented and headed to class.

At my dance lesson last night, E pushed me hard, and it was all I could do not to cry uncle since my back and shoulder still throbbed from the beating it received the previous evening. What developed after astonished me.

As expected, he escorted me to my car, but instead of walking away with a wave, he gathered me in his arms and kissed me. At first, I was frozen in shock, but the persistent skill of those sensuous lips encouraged a response. Tingles raced along my spine, and my heart sped up, but I soon recognized it wasn't the all-consuming, can't get my clothes off fast enough, fiery lust I experienced with Sebastian. My vampire.

I'm not sure when my mind started referring to Bas as mine, but the reminder urged me to step away from Ezekiel. I smiled gently, opened my car door, and mumbled something about seeing him next week.

The hurt on his face still haunts me.

I pluck the laptop off my bed and beeline it to the kitchen, pour a generous glass of wine, and settle into the comfy high back stool at the island. It's time for a little research.

Before opening the computer, I reflect on the positive things in my finite life and peer around the apartment.

I'd never be able to afford such extravagance on my own. Our floorplan is the largest unit in the place with approximately 1300 sq. Ft. of space and an excellent split bedroom design. Ry and I each enjoy a master suite with a spacious open living room and modern kitchen between us. We even have a washer and dryer, and a large balcony overlooking the pool for entertaining.

I glare at the front door and imagine Sebastian on the other side. He holds all the answers to my former world, and I shut the door in his face. Not to mention, he saved my ass. If the vampire hasn't washed his hands of me, he could explain to me why I have this over-powering compulsion to find someone—no idea who, but the sensation pushes at me like a life quest.

It also scares me because I believe I aim to hurt this person, or they mean me harm. In either situation, my gut is advising me to steer clear of uncovering the answer no matter what.

In the meantime, I'm gonna discover what a valkyrie is, and find out what abilities I possess, besides the ones I already experienced.

Two hours later, my lids grate like sandpaper with every blink, a major jackhammer has taken residence inside my skull, and I'm more confused than I was before. Google gave me way more information than I can process; most of it is utter malarkey. I don't have wings;

they exaggerated the pointy ears, and I certainly don't parade around with gold armor on my head and skimpy clothes.

The one part I found fascinating was the mention of lightning as an energy source. It would explain my scarcity of appetite and my preoccupation with storms.

It's time to face facts. I require the devilish vampire if I wish to discover my past. I must have family out there, and he might be able to help interpret this incessant need for someone.

Just as I resolve to let it go, veg in front of the TV with some mindless show or movie, a heavy knock has me almost jumping out of my fleece jammies.

"Alex, it is me."

Oh, God. The sexy vampire came back. It's like I summoned him.

With as much stealth as possible, I ease off the barstool, tiptoe over to the entrance in my fuzzy socks, place my palm on the wooden surface, and lean up to peek out the peephole.

"I hear your heartbeat, Red. Open the door."

Shit. The warped image shows thick, dark hair lying in perfect waves on his head, and a clean-shaven jaw. Wait. Are those leather pants? This I gotta see.

I swing the door wide, and the vision of the man takes my breath away. And yup, he's wearing leather pants that hug his hips and powerful thighs, a snug black Henley with the top two buttons undone, and a long, dark leather duster.

Holy crap, he looks like every vampire fantasy I've ever imagined.

"If you're trying to keep the fact you're a vampire secret, then you might want to rethink this outfit."

"Says the female in unicorn pajamas and pointy ears."

"Touché."

"Invite me in." When I hesitate, his manner shifts. "Now, Alex."

Oh God, his voice is sin. The perfect tenor mixed with a dark sensuality reminds me of sex. "You sound kinda angry. I'm not certain I...." The sapphires spark. "Come in, Sebastian."

In a blink, he's across the threshold, kicks the door shut, grips my shoulders before spinning me around and smacking me sharply on the ass.

Pain ripples through the flesh of my cheek, and I twist, my hand going to my smarting butt. "What the hell?"

He stares me down, no give on his grim face. "You placed yourself at risk by keeping me out. Remember the dark fae? Do you assume he's the only one? You will feel my palm every time you stupidly put yourself in jeopardy."

My jaw drops. "You've got to be kidding me."

"No. You need discipline, and I am the vampire to provide it."

"Now, wait just a goddamn...."

His fingers sink in my hair, and his mouth devours mine, cutting off my angry retort. Every thought in my brain scatters into oblivion. Lust pools hot and tight as I clutch his waist and hold on for dear life.

The technique of his lips astounds me, wets my panties, and stiffens my nipples. I am warm and sheltered. Being in his arms, devoured beyond anything I've experienced, so far, is perfect in ways that make my lost memory, and the fact he just spanked me, second to this. To him.

"Alexandria," he breathes across my mouth.

I squeeze my eyes, suppressing a shiver at the ring of my name in his deep rasp. It's as if with one word he caressed my breasts.

"I need to fuck you," he murmurs against my lips. "Need to sink my fangs into your throat and drown myself in your essence while hearing you scream my name."

I press my body against his and a growl vibrates his chest. "Yes." The word is nothing more than a frantic whisper before I lean up on my tiptoes and slant my mouth over his, hungry and demanding. My tongue flicks across the seam of his lips, and Sebastian deepens the kiss, seizing control, and I'm lost.

He backs me against the wall, lifting me against his chest. My legs automatically encircle his hips, drawing his hardness against my core as his mouth suckles at my neck.

God, why do I crave those fangs embedded in my flesh? I even tilt my head, granting him better access, and clutch his broad shoulders in readiness.

"Bite me, Bastian." At my order, his withdrawal is immediate. I peer into the face of the devil. The blue irises glow with indignation and passion. The huge incisors I wanted deep, now terrify. What did I say to piss him off so quickly? "Sebastian?"

"You need to learn something about me, Alexandria. I am a Dominant. I demand control in all situations and complete submission from my... sexual partner."

My breathing quickens. "What do you mean? Like... BDSM stuff?"

He cocks his head with a raised eyebrow. "Does the notion turn you on?"

I bite my lip, and his gaze zeros in on the movement. "I'm not sure. I have no idea whether I'd enjoy that. No memory, remember?"

"Shall we find out?" He gently lowers my feet to the floor and my eyes widen. "Do not panic, Alex. Your initiation will be gradual."

What the hell does that mean? Initiation into what? Shit, maybe I should've conducted research on BDSM instead of valkyries.

"Which chamber is yours?"

Oh, fuck me. We're starting?

"The one on the right." I manage to rasp out. I'm turned on and scared shitless. "Bas..."

"Speak now if you wish to stop. Once I have you in that room, there is no going back."

His words are demanding, but his touch is gentle as he brushes his knuckles down my cheek.

A part of me wants what he's offering more than I crave my stolen memories, but there's also the side petrified I'll either like it—and what type of woman does that make me—or loathe it, and lose any chance with this extraordinary being.

"I'm scared, Sebastian," I admit with a whisper.

"Of me? Or yourself?" he asks.

Wow. How does he understand me so well already? Oh, wait. Because he does know me. From before.

"Can't we just make out in the living room?"

"Make out?"

"You know, kiss and touch and stuff." Gawd. My face feels hot.

"If I did not know you better, I would claim you were a virgin with such talk." He smirks.

"That's because I am." The grin disappears. Shock widens his eyes.

Redhead two, vampire zero.

Chapter 13

Alexandria

" *Buon Dio*!" Good, God! The vampire staggers back a step, stunned disbelief etched all over his face. "*Fanculo! Tu menti.*" Fuck! You lie.

"I wish I were. Trust me; I was as flabbergasted as you when the doctor informed me." It's stupid, but I can't help being upset by his utter incredulity. I twist away from the panic on his face and move into the living room. Well, I suppose the whole make out option is off the table. Did he have to look so appalled by my lack of sexual experience?

"Why did you solicit a physician, Alexandria?" He inquires from the spot he's glued to in the kitchen.

"I see a shrink for my memory loss, and she requested a battery of tests. In order to rule out various physical or psychological traumas, they did a rape test and bingo, not raped."

"Your memory loss has nothing to do with physical or mental injury or any human issue whatsoever." With his hands in his pockets, like he can't trust himself not to touch me, he strolls over to the couch where I plopped.

"You know how I lost my memories?" That perks me up a bit.

"Yes." He perches on the coffee table facing me, his forearms resting on his thighs. "For months, I have searched for you to resolve your mental block. We have two options to restore your mind. But I must caution you, either comes with a price."

I draw a deep breath. Do I entrust this creature with my innermost secrets? He holds the key to everything. What if it's him I mean to harm?

I want to laugh out loud. As if I could injure a vampire.

"I fear what we will reveal. I've experienced visions and dreams of hunting someone. I think I'm supposed to punish them."

"Oh, Alex. Those were commands imprinted in your brain by your best friend's enemy."

"My best friend?" I knew there were people out there who cared about me.

"Yes. Her name is Nicole Giordano, and she is my queen."

"My BFF is a vampire and queen?" Sweet. I got connections.

"A halfling. Half-vampire, half-human. Five years ago, your mother, the valkyrie queen, assigned you to her protection detail. It was your responsibility to insinuate yourself into her life and watch over her during the day."

"What was I guarding her against?" How fucking cool. I was a bodyguard.

"Her father, King Dimitri. It is a lengthy story, but the upshot is, Nicole is the prophesied bringer of peace to the immortal world that has been at war for centuries. She conquered the king by killing herself and..."

"Wait! She's dead?"

"No. Icarus, our High Priest Oracle, brought her back."

"From the dead?" What can't immortals do?

"Yes," he grins, and something pricks my spirit.

"So, how did I lose my memories and go into hiding?"

"The demon king, Jagorach Darath, manipulated your mind by implanting a command to kill Nicole. He underestimated the depths of your emotions for your friend. You resisted his mental commands, which is virtually impossible for someone so youthful, and then disappeared."

"Holy crap. There are demons? And if my mother is a queen, then I'm a... a princess, right?"

"I realize this is overwhelming, but once your memories are reinstated, it will all make sense. I promise."

"If you say so." I pluck at the frayed edge of my sleeve. "In my life, are we friends?"

All of a sudden, the arrogant, confident vampire vanishes, and his lids lower. "You, uh... we..."

"Oh, for Pete's sake, spit it out." His hesitation spikes my heart rate.

"It's not a secret you hate vampires, Alex."

"But... isn't Nicole, my supposed BFF, half-vampire?" He merely nods, scrutinizing me carefully—a muscle pulses in his jaw.

"Our races have been at war for an extensive period of time." Sebastian reaches for my fidgeting fingers, clasping them between his. "I am everything you loathe, Red. We have no common ground."

"Then why would you help me?" He stiffens. "Did this, Nicole, your ruler, order you to?" If that's the sole reason he's here with me, it will shatter my heart.

When did I become so attached to his creature? I've only been in his presence on a couple of occasions, but I can't avoid thinking about him, wanting him with a single-minded desperation bordering on obsessive.

"Yes. That is the entire reason I am here."

Well, shit on a stick. That sucks balls.

"I see," I whisper and work to present a brave face even though his admission produced a fissure to surge through the gullible, overeager organ pumping blood from my brain.

The vampire sighs heavily. "I am no good for you, Alex. You are innocent, sweet, loving. You care for people deeply; you are fiercely loyal and stubborn as hell, with a fiery attitude I somehow find captivating. I am dark, hard, damaged, and I would consume the light inside you. When your memories return, you will understand that."

"What if I don't want them to return? Would you still walk away from me?" God, why am I sticking my heart out there? He admitted he'll stomp on it without a thought.

He hesitates. "My duty is to protect you from any outside threats. You need to secure your heart."

I might be overly tired right now, and my insides misfiring, but even with half my life missing, I recognize when a dude is warning a girl, he will crush her if offered a chance. "What do you want from me, Sebastian?"

He rakes his fingers through his hair and considers me, his cobalt gaze glittering with fire. "I crave to bury my face between your legs and make you scream my name."

Heat lances through me so swift, I gasp.

"I want you spun around, beneath me, knees spread, face in the mattress with my dick so deep inside you, I will never be free. I crave to smack your delectable ass until you come."

Shit. His words alone could take me there.

"But in reality, you would sooner run a silver dagger through my blackened heart than allow me anywhere near you."

That can't be true. I underwent an instant passion for Bastian the second I sensed him in the bar. If I despised him enough to want him dead, wouldn't I feel it? The demand for my old life pales compared to my appetite for this vampire: dominance and all.

"I must depart soon." I'm startled when he shifts over to sit next to me instead of standing to leave. His ocean scent wafts through my senses, the warmth from his body tightens my aching nipples. "Come with me. I cannot protect you during the day."

"Why do you care? Oh, wait, if I died, then you failed your queen, right?" Sarcasm drips from every syllable.

He grimaces. "I lied, Alex. You are more than an assignment, but it does not negate the fact I am no good for you. I am treading new territory here. It is not my intention to hurt you."

I'm not certain if he's conscious of it or not, but his fingers absently trace a unicorn on my thigh. Perhaps this vampire is not so cold. Maybe he needs to be warmed up, and I have just the nature to do it.

"What if I suggested, hypothetically, that for one night, I wished to forget our pasts, and surrender ourselves to each other? I—I may be a virgin, but I'm far from innocent. The things you require excite me, and I want to experience it with you." I watch as his breathing accelerates with each word, his jaw clenching.

"And if I said I wanted to tie you up, have you submit to my will, spank or flog you?" He grasps my wrists in a crushing grip, and I swallow at the appearance of his true nature. "This is your choice, Red. Yes or no. It alters nothing. But I can never commit to you."

My chest tightens with the enormity of this moment. At the mix of nerves, lust, and tenderness Bastian stirs in me. And even though his sexual proclivities frighten me, my need for his touch overrides my fear. Or common sense. Samesies.

"Yes," I sigh.

He examines me for several seconds, his blue gaze penetrating, as if he's seeking to peer into my soul.

A few strained minutes later, he rises and holds out his hand. "Have you ever been to Italy?"

Chapter 14

Sebastian

The little valkyrie fooled everyone, including my lie-detecting queen, into believing she was profligate. It never dawned on me her persona was anything but real. Now I realize every excuse she proposed to be away, was a subterfuge to deal with her obligations for the Valkyrie Regency.

Alex guarded Nicole during the day, which means she took every opportunity throughout the night, while a Guardian stood watch, to navigate her responsibilities as a Protector—the valkyries elite fighting force—and as a princess, her duties to her people and queen. Her only reprieve was when Kurtis or Liam was on guard. Talk about an exhausting assignment.

The joy filling my chest at her revelation appalled me. So innocent. So pure. No male claimed what belongs to me. The knowledge sent panic and elation coursing through my nerves, while my mind roared with what I could teach her. I yearned to strum the exquisite body like a fine-tuned guitar. Her moans and cries of ecstasy music to my greedy ears.

Then reality punched me in the gut. How could I defile something as precious and rare as my mate, with my darkness? And I am quite aware the minute she remembers; the warrior will seek to slay me for touching her.

She threw me for a loop when she proposed we forget both our worlds exist and become lost in each other for one night. The situation went from zero to fucked up in less than a second. This hot-headed adorable little redhead will be my demise. With her words, she stripped my hard-earned control to shreds. I wanted to disregard all my carefully laid out methods, the ones to never trust another woman again, to always maintain my lovers at a distance. On their knees. Submissive.

But surprisingly enough, those are not our biggest hurdles. If I fuck her without her memories fully intact, even though she is begging me to, it would be no different than if I violated her. The true Alexandria Svaldana would never consent to sex with a vampire, and I damn well know it.

I may be dark and demented in my sexual inclinations, in my philosophy and expectations toward females sexually, but it goes against everything I am to manipulate a woman into bed, no matter how extraordinary my appetite for her.

I have lived 500 years, battled horrendous creatures, performed abhorrent tasks in the name of my king. Nothing scares me anymore. But my petite mate terrifies me. Long ago I sealed the door to my heart. Too much misery and disappointment. Too many tears and broken vows. No one will hurt me anew.

"You have ten minutes to change and pack a bag, Red." I realize my manner is brusque, but I must maintain a distance between us. As much as I crave this trip to be about exploring every inch of her skin and testing her tolerance, I need to drill it into my skull, and jam it down my beast's throat, it is purely for her safety I am absconding with her to my home country. Safety. Nothing more.

"It's not my fault if your relationships have consisted of only submissive women who jump when you snap, but trust me when I say, it's inconceivable for any woman to get ready in less than twenty minutes."

My growl has her rushing for the bedroom, and I can't help but chuckle. If any sub dared question my command, punishment would be forthwith. Alex tests me, and I struggle to keep a grin at bay.

Yeah, I am fucked.

THIRTY MINUTES LATER, we appear in my darkened bedroom at my villa in Northern Italy, outside Florence. It is well past dawn here, but my staff keeps the shutters sealed tight during the day in preparation for my arrival.

"I can't see a damn thing. Are we in Italy?"

"Yes. We can turn on a light, but the shutters remain closed."

"Oh, sure. Vampire. Sunlight bad." She stifles a yawn.

I grunt. "Correct." I drop her bulging suitcase next to the bed. "Did you require so much stuff for one night?"

"It's Italy, baby," she announces like her statement justifies everything.

"Right, what was I thinking?" I flip on the bedside lamp and observe her eyes expand as she takes in the chamber.

"Holy shitballs! Your room is the size of my apartment. And the ceiling, wow. It's waves of brick separated by beams. A real stone fireplace in the bedroom? That's super-indulgent."

I shrug out of my heavy, weapons filled duster, drape it over a wingback chair by the crackling fire, and smile at her exuberance as she explores.

"The brick archways are magnificent. Is the bathroom through here... Oh my fucking God! This is... I can't even express how decadent everything is." The lovely blue irises flicker silver in her glee, and I want to keep the bright smile on her face. Always.

But we are not gifted forever. We promised each other one night, and I must somehow dissuade her of that concept. Tonight, when we wake, I will wish nothing more than to explore every exquisite inch of her body. Hear her moans and screams of ecstasy, realizing they will be my sole companions throughout the centuries. Her beautifully expressive face will haunt my dreams.

Maybe I can relish those things without taking her innocence. It would require an iron fist clamped tight on my beast. To touch her, taste her, but never sink deep into her, might be more than even I could handle. I would have to fight, not merely her passion, but mine and my inner vampire's demand to claim its mate.

I rub at the pang in the center of my chest. Red will take off the second her memories return. No matter how fucked up I am, fate brought us together, and despite the misgivings and obstacles, my vampire desires to make her ours. Mind. Body. Soul.

What a fool I am to imagine such an arrangement feasible. Alex is an innocent, in many respects, and a future ruler who abhors the sight of me. And I? I am depraved. A sadist who gets off on inflicting sexual pain on others to appease the demons of his past. We could not be more opposite.

When she stifles another yawn, I stride over and gently lift her chin. "We both require sleep. Tonight, we can explore Florence or San Gimignano if you like." Her tired smile stirs my cock, despite the slumber pulling at me in the current time zone.

"That sounds perfect." The grin fades. "Bastian I..."

"Worry not, little one," I interrupt, sensing her anxiety as my own. I lean down and brush my lips across her sweet, succulent mouth, groaning at the contact. "We will take things slow." A lot slower than either of us would prefer. "No expectations for this evening."

"I don't want you holding back. I need everything in the next twenty-four hours because if you're correct about me hating you; then these moments together are all I'll have to hold on to."

Fuck. Her words pound at my defenses. "Make no mistake, Alexandria, after tonight, you will never forget who owns you." At her raised eyebrow, I spin her toward the entrance to the lavatory and smack her ass. "Now, go do whatever it is you need to do to get ready for bed."

"Yes, sir," she salutes saucily, snatches her bag, and beelines it through the archway.

While Alex rummages in the bathroom, I slide two blades between the mattress on my side, and undress down to my boxer briefs, establishing various weapons throughout the area.

My villa is under an assumed name. No reason to suspect the fae knows of its existence, but as my queen is enamored of repeating; It is better to have it and not need it than need it and not have it.

When I hear the shower turn on, I clench my fists to keep from striding in there and joining her. Instead, I snag my phone and call Nicole.

"About fucking time! What is happening, Bastian?" I do not object to her harsh tone. I understand her apprehension regarding Alex.

"She is fine, but King Grayflame ordered a dark fae Custodian to kidnap her."

"That stupid son of a bitch dares to start a war with the Valkyries to call me out? I can't wait to rip his pointed ears from his head and shove them up his ass."

"The soldier is dead, but I am not sure if he obtained time to report Alex's whereabouts before I arrived on scene. I traced her to my villa for safekeeping."

A weighty silence permeates the line. "Have you told her?"

"Only bits and pieces. The sleep is tugging at me, and she is exhausted. We are secure here for now. As soon as she has recovered, I will contact King Darath to undertake the memory restore."

"For both your sakes, I hope it works."

"Agreed. I do not desire to be strapped with a mate any more than she wishes to be bound to a vampire for all eternity."

"Good luck, Bastian. Keep me posted."

"Yes, my lady. How are you doing?"

"Oh, you know me. Tough as nails and all that shit."

Translation? My sister-in-law is suffering. Never having experienced children myself, I toil to fathom the anguish she must experience at the loss of her unborn child. But if I recognize one fact regarding my queen, she will pour out her torment in a song, thrust the pain into a corner, and fixate on the dilemmas at hand.

"Guard her, Sebastian," she orders softly.

"With my life, my lady."

"In the meantime, Logan and I will work a little recon in Scotland, see if we can determine what they know or if they are mobilizing against us."

"Please be vigilant."

"Will do. Get this shit show completed, Bastian. I require my commander and my friend."

"What's a mate?" The tired little redhead asks from the archway as I end the call and set the phone on the wireless charging pad on the nightstand.

Damp curls caress bare shoulders; her body is enveloped in a black towel. The silver eyes take a languid stroll over my near-naked frame. I kept my boxer briefs on in the hope the thin barrier would somehow keep me under control when lying next to this enticing creature.

"Please tell me you will wear pajamas to bed."

In response, she drops the towel, and I nearly fall to my knees at the perfection of my mate's nude visage.

"Fuck me," I breathe and grasp the bedpost in a desperate attempt to retain my sanity.

"I believe that's my line." Her saucy grin sets me on fire.

Chapter 15

Alexandria

"**A**lexandria," he warns gruffly. "You do not understand what you are unleashing by your brazen behavior."

He's right, but I can't deny my body's reaction to him any longer. Based on my responses to him and Ezekiel, I would have wagered my Fiat I've done the deed. I certainly talk like I've experienced multiple partners/ orgasms.

This vampire sets off fantasies in my head I never realized I wanted. Apparently, I crave a man to be in command in the bedroom, or at least the current me does, because he's threatened it's the only way this will work.

I gulp at the flawlessness stalking toward me. I didn't know ab definition like that existed without airbrushing, and his pecs are thick pads of sleek muscle my fingers itch to explore. I eyeball the intricate black tattoo swirling over his chest and sculpted shoulder, down the bulging bicep.

My gaze stalls on the gigantic bulge in his boxer briefs. Good grief, I think I need to reevaluate this seduction because no way in God's green earth that scary thing is gonna fit inside me.

Should've thought things through before you dropped the towel, dumbass.

His hands clutch my arms. The sapphires brighten. I stare in fascination as the deadly, sharp fangs descend, and choke down a gasp as a surge of heat rushes through my veins at the visual of those piercing my skin.

How will I ever get Sebastian out of my head when his effect on me is instant, visceral, and absolute?

"Red." The low growl clenches my insides. "Listen to me closely. I would love nothing better than to fuck you senseless, but the dark circles under your eyes, not to mention the damn sleep tugging at my brain to shut down, say otherwise." He stoops and picks up my discarded towel, wrapping it gently around my shoulders. The slight tremor in his hand soothes the sting of his rejection somewhat.

"Do you want to bite me as well?" What the heck am I doing jabbing the beast?

He nods, shifting closer, his gaze latched on my neck. I hate him this close. It makes my body go stupid. Really stupid. Hell, my brain drops in IQ simply being in the same room. Like towel on the floor dumb.

"You tremble," he whispers, rubbing his palms up and down the soft cloth covering my arms. As if the shivers are from the coolness of the room.

"You scare me."

His body stills, the blue orbs lift to mine, and I gape at the intensity of his stare. "I vow never to harm you, physically, Alexandria."

Ah. There it is again. The subtle reminder he will injure me emotionally.

"Did you bring something to sleep in?" he asks again, and I'm both relieved and disappointed he won't drink from me.

"Yes. The unicorn pajamas you admire so much." I grin up at him attempting to calm his intense glower.

"Go put those on, now. You like this severely tests my iron control."

Geez, he's bossy, it makes me want to jerk the towel off again for spite. But, I'm sensible enough to accept I'm in over my head with this... vampire.

Before I can spin and retreat into the bathroom, he grips my shoulders tighter. "Remember the plan," he whispers against my lips, making it difficult to breathe. "We sleep until nightfall, and then you are all mine. Every square inch of your skin will feel my lips, tongue, and fingers. No escaping me now, little red."

"I never wanted an escape." The emotional depths of his cerulean irises fascinate me.

"Oh, but you soon will. Right now, your baby blues beg me to make you mine, but when your memories return, they will swarm with contempt and vengeance."

How could my subconscious loathe this being with such viciousness, but my conscious mind desires him with a tenacity that takes my breath away?

In any event, I overheard his discussion on the phone. He despises the notion of a—what did he call it? A mate?—as much as I apparently detest him.

"I devised the plan, remember?" I reply, wrapping the towel tighter. "I get you don't wish to be shackled to me any more than I to you. Or so you keep telling me."

"Alex..."

"Please, Bastian, let me change. I'm drained, and my brain is not firing on all cylinders right now. You want me. I want you. The rest just sounds like blah blah blah."

He snorts. "Your mind fascinates me."

"You and me both." I scoff before pivoting and beelining it to the bathroom.

Once my comfy jammies cover my frame, I pause and peer at my reflection. It's the same image I've studied for the last several months. Nothing has altered. My hair, while slightly damp from my shower, is still a wild mane of crimson, and my irises are still bright blue. I lean forward and prod the skin under my eyes. Yup, and he was correct about the dark circles.

The bottom line is when I look in the mirror, I can't imagine changing so drastically when my memories return that I'll despise him. I'll still be me. Right?

When my phone buzzes on the counter, I snatch it up and groan at the caller ID.

"Hey, Doc."

"Good morning, Alexandria. I wanted to remind you of your hypnotherapy session on Monday evening."

"Yeah, about that. I'm not positive I'll require hypnosis anymore."

"Oh?" The subtle shift in her tone has me cringing. "How so?"

"Trust me when I say, my memories will return by then." Even though Sebastian didn't indicate as much, I'm pretty sure revealing his kind, or mine, to humans is probably forbidden.

"Have you started to..."

The door crashes open with such velocity; the handle impales into the drywall behind it. "Who the fuck is on the phone?" The enraged vampire demands.

What in the holy hell? "My shrink if you must know," I whisper with my palm over the phone.

When he jerks it from me, I yelp in surprise. "Hey!"

"Who is this?" He practically growls at the doc on the other end.

What the ever-loving shit is his problem? Maybe he is correct; I will hate him.

I can't determine what the poor doctor is saying, but when the Italian's skin pales, and his eyes start glittering, sweat breaks out on my forehead.

"Stay the fuck away from her, Rowena."

Rowena? Her name is Sarah. "Bastian, I think you're confused. She..."

His fangs lower, and he hauls me against his rib cage in a possessive gesture. Oh shit. I peek up at the stone-cold regard drilling a hole in my skull.

"*Stai lontano da lei o implorerai la morte.*" He whispers before hanging up and dumping the phone back into my bag.

Stay away from her, or you will beg for death?

What the fuck is happening?

"How do you know my shrink, and why are you threatening her?"

"She is not your psychiatrist."

Coolly, as if nothing transpired, he steers me out of the bathroom and over to the enormous bed.

"No?" I question with skepticism while climbing between the sheets. "Then, who is she?"

Bastian tucks the blankets tight to my body before strolling around the bed and sliding in on his side. His side. Like this is a normal routine for us.

"Sebastian? Who is she?"

"My mother."

Chapter 16

Alexandria

Warmth blankets me from all angles. A massive hardness lays cushioned between my butt cheeks. I'm cocooned, protected, and no nightmares plagued my dreams. I never want to leave this haven.

When Bastian and I climbed into bed, to my internal clock, it was past midnight, and I'd been awake for roughly twenty hours. I wanted to investigate Sebastian's claims concerning my shrink being his mom, but my mind refused to cooperate. Besides, Sebastian was out as soon as his head struck the pillow, but not before he made certain to place as much distance between us as possible.

Was it because I was too much of a temptation, or because he wasn't used to sleeping like the dead with anyone?

Well, I concluded the chasm simply wouldn't do. I slithered across the mattress, raised his distractingly bulging bicep over my head, and positioned my cheek on his shoulder, my leg over his hips, and my arm draped along his fit waist. The heat from his body soothed me. He was like a personal heating blanket.

It alarmed me for a few minutes when the thumps of his heart slowed to virtually non-existent, and his breathing was barely discernible. I knew next to nothing about vampires. Was he even aware I was in bed with him? No wonder these creatures keep their existence secret, they are defenseless when they sleep.

My mind, of course, moved straight to the gutter, and I wondered if I licked or bit his nipple if he would stir. Unable to help myself, I drew soft circles across his chest with my fingertips, sketched the tattoo as far as I could reach before smoothing them down the bumps and ridges of his abdomen.

A quiet rumble vibrated my cheek, but he never stirred. It was like his mind was aware I was taking advantage of him while he snoozed, but the slumber paralyzed his body from objecting.

A naughty, delicious vision of sampling his hardness flashed through my brain, and before I could stop myself, I was sliding the sheets past his hips. The black briefs hugged the massive erection in soft microfiber, and I licked my lips in greedy anticipation as I scraped a fingernail down solid granite.

When it twitched, I jerked my hand back with a squeak, peeked up at Sebastian, expecting to meet blue sapphires glaring down at me. Nope, still out cold. That's when my moral compass was like, *"Pervert. Stop taking advantage of the sleeping, sexy vampire."*

"Buzzkill," I sighed before pulling the sheets up and settling my cheek down on his chest. I zonked out within minutes.

A glance at the glowing lights of the bedside clock shows its 8:00 pm. We slept a solid twelve hours. Wow. I don't think I've relaxed this deeply since my life re-started in that changing room.

My mind slithers to our discussion last night, or I suppose early this morning here in Italy. Sebastian never acknowledged my question. What is a mate? Is it a term vampires use for lovers or girlfriends?

He'd claimed he exhibited no wish to be *strapped* with one, which, if the jargon is correct, leads back to the BS he spewed earlier of no commitment.

I offered the proposal of a one-night stand, but now I'm not sure if my heart will allow me to walk away from this vibrant being, no matter how desperately I crave my first initiation into sex to be with him.

But here's the mammoth elephant in the room. Do I? Would my real self-surrender to this vampire and grant him the wonderful gift of my virginity? According to him, that's an emphatic, NO.

And what the hell is wrong with me I waited one hundred freaking years to have sex? I mean hashtag, WTF!

"You are thinking too loud." The sexy male rumbles above my head, his arm tightening around my midriff.

"I can't help it. You've hurled a ton of crap at me." His heavy sigh brushes warmth through my curls.

"Alexandria, we can spend the next twenty-four hours talking, and working with the demon king to restore your memories, or do as you proposed." His hips nudge mine, causing his erection to slide along my ass. "Fucking forget everything and become lost in each other."

I groan, pressing against his firmness. He nuzzles my nape while he continues to undulate against my backside. "Sebastian," I whimper.

Warm fingers gently sweep the heavy curls from my neck and shoulders. "I require a favor before I devour your luscious body."

"Anything." I shiver when scalding lips graze my neck, his tongue running along the surface, and I strive to control my ragged breathing. It would suck if I passed out from asphyxiation before we even began.

"It has been quite some time since I fed," he murmurs before suckling the skin above my vein. Dampness floods my core. "It would be prudent if I did so before we begin. It will strengthen my command over my inner vampire."

A slight scraping has me quivering in anticipation. "Will it hurt?" I think to ask, not actually caring.

"Quite the opposite. It is extremely pleasurable and can bring you to orgasm."

Well, shit. Why would I say no?

Before I answer out loud, the solid hand clamped around my waist, slips into the waistband of my pajamas, delving into my slick folds, while the other slides under my shoulders, his palm coming up to rest on my forehead.

"Christ, Red. You are wet for me already." The inhuman growl accelerates my overworked heart. "Say, yes."

His words are all authority, but I'm finding it challenging to focus on what specifically I'm saying yes to, but who the hell cares as long as he doesn't stop the circle-y thing with his fingertips.

"Yes," I sigh, driving my swollen nub harder against the skilled fingers.

The palm on my forehead eases my head to the side. I don't even register the slight sting because in the next instant, an orgasm blasts through me with such force, I'd swear my body burst into a million fragments around the room.

"Bastian." I keen low, opening my legs further to provide him better access.

With the next glorious pull on my vein, he inserts a finger into my soaked core, and an intense build-up to another life-shattering orgasm sparks anew. I grind against his hand, demanding more, and he growls, vibrating my neck, down my chest, and tightening my nipples into hard achy points.

When he introduces a second finger, I whimper. Christ. The fullness is too much. How will I ever accommodate his girth?

When the pads softly strike the sweet spot, all fear flies to the wind. Between the continuous tug on my vein, the deep feral growls, the glorious pressure of his fingers thrusting inside me, and his heavy cock rubbing against my ass, it's nirvana.

I reach behind me and dig my nails into his muscular thigh, urging him on, imploring him to shoot me over the brink once more. Bastian answers with a possessive growl and clamps down hard on my neck, and the delicious pain erupts fireworks through my abdomen, the heat building and spiraling up through my chest. My eyes roll back in ecstasy.

"Oh, God!" The world tilts dramatically before imploding with a fiery storm so profound my entire body trembles in its wake.

Fuck me! That was... incredible. Mind-altering. Cosmic shattering.

I wince slightly when his fangs withdraw. Fangs! Holy shit. His teeth were in my flesh, gulping my blood, and I fucking exploded from it. Well, also because of his skilled ministrations between my thighs. This guy is changing me into a vampire junkie. No orgasm, in the history of orgasms, was ever this epic.

A warm tongue slides over the puncture wounds, and the skin tightens as it heals. I groan, my core convulsing around the fingers still buried inside.

"Thank you, Alexandria," he murmurs between kisses along my shoulder. "You honor me with your gift."

Well, isn't that sweet? Underneath, Bastian's not as hard or cold as he wants everybody to believe.

"Sebastian?"

"Hmmm?" he purrs.

I suck in a gasp as he slowly withdraws from my core, skimming the responsive, slick flesh.

"I'm not sure you'll fit."

He chuckles before flipping me around to face him. My eyes widen in fascination when his mouth closes over the long digits just buried inside me. Dark lashes lower, shutting out the blue glow as he suckles his fingers drenched in my juices, growling with pleasure.

Fucking, eh. That is the hottest thing I've ever witnessed.

"Your taste is addictive. Sweet and delicious. I cannot wait to devour every last drop with my mouth. But do not fret, Alexandria. The prudent course, in light of your missing past, is for me *not* to take your virginity."

"Mmm-hmm," I mumble, still lost in the afterglow of multiple orgasms and his hypnotic comments.

Wait. What?

"I thought we agreed on one night together. Was I wrong to assume it meant sex?"

When the vampire's phone vibrates on the nightstand, he snatches it up with a sharp, angry growl.

"This better be fucking important," he snarls, and I feel sorry for whoever is on the other end, while still reeling from his announcement.

His body stiffens. The irises, generous with passionate promises moments ago, brighten into ice-cold orbs. "I will be there in ten minutes."

When his gaze settles on mine, regret fills the depths.

"What's going on?"

"It appears your mother has waged war with the Vampire Nation."

Chapter 17

Sebastian

"Goddamnit, Arra. We just discovered Alex's whereabouts, and you wage fucking war?" Queen Giordano's gray eyes blaze with fury at the head of the conference table, and I share her rage.

After a brief quarrel, that still has my teeth-gnashing in anger, I left Alex behind to explore the Villa, on the condition she did not step foot outside the grounds until I returned or there would be severe repercussions.

I almost changed my mind and threw her over my shoulder at the defiant lift of her chin, but with her compulsion to kill Nicki, no way in Hades I could bring her to the castle, and it was still too dangerous for her to go back to her apartment.

Eventually, she consented. I am utterly out of my depth with this little spitfire. When I give an order, I expect an obedient 'Yes, Sir' with eyes lowered. Not a middle finger flipped in my face with the threat of my balls shoved down my throat.

Why do I enjoy her defiance so much?

"You find this humorous, Commander?" Arra demands in an angry rumble from the monitor on the wall.

"No. Quite the opposite." I erase the smile and focus on this pivotal meeting. I see where Alex gets her irrational behavior. Even though Queen Svaldana is a blond, dark-eyed beauty, her graceful demeanor cannot disguise the wild valkyrie bubbling below the surface. "Your actions are a detriment to your daughter, Arra."

"You were supposed to bring her to me the minute you discovered her, vampire. Where is she?" In the large window behind the dainty queen, bright bolts of light streak across the vivid blue sky. A testimonial to her seething emotions.

The jump from one time zone to the other is interfering with my internal clock. Exhaustion wears on me even though I just slept twelve hours, and while Nicole isn't a slave to the damn sleep, my brother's bloodshot eyes reveal he is resisting the effects of the ascending sun.

"I made no such agreement, my lady. My pledge to find Alexandria and recover her memories was never to you."

"If you've mated her, bloodsucker, there is nowhere for you to hide."

"You dare threaten my commander?" Nicki shoves the table, sending it sailing across the office. Logan traces out of its path barely in time.

Ever since losing their child, a mere week ago, Nicole's temper has become volatile. Nothing seems to mollify her, not even Logan. This display of aggression from Alex's mother has thrown fuel on the fire.

I glance at my sibling, but his face remains passive. The sole clue to his inner unrest is the clenching of his jaw. I suspect my brother is at a loss on how best to handle her tumultuous emotions. He is grieving, but like always, the fierce warrior thrust his own needs aside to aid his mate's.

"You don't want to be my enemy, Arra," Nicki growls, her irises lighting up the room, her body rigid with fury. She is attired in skinny jeans, boots, and a simple blue sweater. No smart-ass quotes don her clothes. The ever-present smirk is absent from her mouth.

My heart bleeds for them, and I'm as clueless as Logan on how to help her heal.

"Tell me where Alexandria is, and we can lay this behind us." I softly snort as Arra backpedals in the face of Nicole's wrath.

Need to diffuse this situation before it escalates out of control. I stride forward to confront my mate's mother. "Your daughter is safe. Unharmed. Untouched." The black eyes tighten, striving to determine if I speak the truth. It is a partial lie.

Even now, her potent blood courses through my system, the sweet perfume of her vanilla and musk scent linger on my fingers, filling my nostrils. I marvel at the effect the exquisite, little valkyrie has on me. Every second I am away from her presence seems like hours. My skin itches with the desire to have her beneath me, sunk deep in her tight flesh, commanding her body, bringing it to pinnacles of euphoria she has never imagined.

A visual of her wrists bound above her head, her legs spread, her slick folds begging for the rhythmic tapping of a crop, sears my brain. I covet her submission, her trust. But in all honesty, I would welcome her any way I could right now. We are on borrowed time.

Christ, Sebastian. Focus, or you could face a war with your mate's people.

I clear my throat. "Our sole objective here is to restore Alex's memories. You cannot do that without our assistance."

"King Darath is a close friend to my mate Cipher. Bring her home, and with his aid, we will attempt to reconstruct her mind."

Cipher Ruse, Kurtis' father, and the former shifter king is Arra's fated one, and she is his. Until recently, the law forbade their love. For over a century, they managed to keep their relationship concealed. The deadly shifter would do anything for his mate, and his beast would destroy anyone who dares upset his female.

The Vampire Nation has the highest population among all the immortal clans, and with Lucretia mated to King Ruse, our accord with the Shifter Territory solidified.

"And if it doesn't work?" Nicki says in a deceptively calm tone. "Will you allow your stubborn hatred for my kind to cloud what's best for Alexandria? If so, you deserve my wrath. A child should *always* come first." Her icy glare slides to Logan.

For the first time, my brother backs down from the frigid regard. His lids close, and he lowers his chin to his chest in defeat. What the fuck? She blames him for choosing her. What was he supposed to do? Let them both perish?

'Brother.' I whisper in his mind, and his head lifts. The anguish in the green depths terrifies me, and even knowing Nicole can hear our private exchange, I continue. *'She's grieving. Give her time. Your mate conquered hell to come back to you. Together, you will get past this as well.'*

'I choose her. Always. She is my soul. The death of our baby crushes my heart, but she will not fucking let me in, Bastian, no matter what I say or do.'

I feel Logan's heartache and despair as my own. *'It has only been a week, brother. Give it time.'*

Nicole shoots me a glare. *'Really? You're selling him the "Time heals all wounds bullshit?"'*

While Nicki hears all internal dialogue around her and can speak to anyone telepathically, only blood relations or mated couples are able to communicate with each other. Which means I cannot respond. I offer a slight shrug in lieu of an answer.

Nicole turns to Queen Arra. "We stick to the plan. I'll not allow your prejudice to hurt my friend. If you don't agree, tough shit. You should direct your wrath on the dark fae. Syn Grayflame attempted to abduct Alex, presumably to use as leverage to draw me out, and if it weren't for Sebastian, your daughter would be in Scotland right now at Syn's mercy and beyond your reach." Nicki leans back and crosses her arms, smirking at Arra's outraged expression. "So, I would think twice before threatening war with the Vampire Nation. With me at the helm, you *will* lose." Nicki's smile is savage.

Son of a bitch. Where is her fucking diplomacy?

"Arra." I step next to my furious, hurting queen and stare straight at the beautiful valkyrie. "I would never mate your daughter against her will. If King Darath fails, Alex will understand all the facts involved and decide for herself."

"If she answers no? You'll bring her home?" She asks suspiciously.

"Yes. This I vow."

"You have one week to deliver my offspring, vampire, or the Protectors will come knocking," the valkyrie growls before her image dissolves.

"Bitch," Nicole mutters.

I round on my queen. "I realize you are grieving, and I cannot comprehend the anguish you must be suffering, but are you willing to start another war with the Valkyrie Regency? We are already at war with the Dark Fae Kingdom."

Her regard swivels my direction, the deep auburn waves settling around her shoulders. "You're not my consort, Bastian. I'm not soliciting your council. Do not question my authority."

Wow. Nicole has always been a hard ass, but over the past year, she learned to curb her anger with fun-loving sarcasm. It is like she has reverted to the furious, bitter, and scared young woman before her transition.

"Yes, my lady." No matter how her words infuriate me, I must remember; she is not merely my sister-in-law. She is my queen and should be treated with the respect she has earned.

Nicole's sigh is heavy, her tone softens. "Does Alex recall anything? She still wish to kill me?"

"She remembers nothing. But she possesses a compulsion to search for someone, someone she worries she intends to hurt."

"Which means the risk is too great to bring her here."

"Yes, my lady." I glance at the male I have looked up to my entire existence. He has not moved from his spot by the exit, his iridescent eyes watching Nicki's every action. "We have another complication." Emeralds lift to mine.

"Well, my world wouldn't be complete without multiple fucking problems," Nicki sneers with hands on her hips. "Let's hear it."

My brother moves closer, sensing my inner angst, and I shift my full gaze on him. "My mother is back, and she has wheedled her way into Alex's life."

"How so?" Logan asks with a worried frown.

"She is Alexandria's shrink."

"And why is this a bad thing?" Nicki inquires with a confused lift of her eyebrow.

"The vampire is much like your father, Nicole. An evil, manipulative, bitch who hides behind a charming, kind-hearted smile and polished demeanor."

"Wow. How do you really feel about her?"

"She has an agenda. Guaranteed." I scowl. Worry and anger wage war in my gut.

"You think Rowena is using Alexandria?" Logan asks softly.

"Yes. And knowing her the way I do, the petite valkyrie is just a puppet in her crusade to get to me. I will execute the female before I allow her to come near me or my mate."

Chapter 18

Alexandria

This blows. I've showered, shaved, including my girly bits, and slathered on my favorite lotion in preparation for getting my freak on with Bastian. Three hours later, the jerk is still a no show. Tonight is our only night, and he's wasting it doing God knows what.

I've explored every nook and cranny of this elegant villa. The ground floor includes a spacious kitchen done in warm earth tones with surprisingly modern appliances, a casual dining room with a beautiful hand-carved table, and a fireplace. Across from the kitchen is a formal dining area with seating for twenty. It surprised me to discover a gorgeous guest bathroom off the tiled entryway, and a drool-worthy media room. I see myself spending hours watching reruns of Game of Thrones.

My eyes rolled when I discovered the freaking billiard space, cause a house wouldn't be complete without one. By the looks of the sunken living space, with its ooh poopy doo furniture, which doesn't look comfortable at all, it's not used often.

The second floor boasts nine bedrooms with sensational views of the surrounding Tuscan landscape. I adore everything about this impressive structure, but the undulating brick ceiling with dark beams throughout is what sets it apart.

In the summer, outdoors is the place to be. It is divided into four types of gardens. An extensive grassy section immediately in front of the villa, a covered terrace, and BBQ area, you know, because vampires eat. Who does he entertain here that requires normal food?

Has he ever brought a submissive here? The thought sparked the green-eyed monster, and I viciously kicked a stone into the inviting pool gazing over the breathtaking view, gnashing my teeth at the notion of my beautiful vampire skinny dipping with other women.

I wandered down the slight hill to a shady garden-like setting with trees the staff informed me later, were hundreds of years old and plopped down on a wooden bench. The sense I'm in over my head pressed on my shoulders again. The 'what the fuck am I doing' sensation sent me into a panic attack. I allowed the lightning to soothe and fuel.

No matter how much I crave the powerful being, nagging dread pecks at my subconscious. I can't define it or rationalize why it's there, so I keep pushing the impression deep and work to ignore it. I could chalk it up to virginal fear or my insecurities regarding his sexual preferences.

Yup. That's what it is, end of story.

From wherever I am around this immense property, you can see vineyards extending in all directions, and I'm dying to experience the view in the daylight. But the higher the full moon rises in the sky, the pissier I become. Maybe deep down, he doesn't want to be with me. "Shackled to a mate" is how he expressed it.

Well, fuck him. I'm in freaking Italy, baby, and these boots were made for walking.

I amble down the long drive, inspecting the locked iron gates at the end with a smirk. Like these could keep me confined. Bastian commanded me not to leave the compound, but he's not my damn father, and I'm an adult woman, no scratch that, a valkyrie who can handle herself just fine.

Besides, nothing will stop me from strolling along the ancient Via Francigena, the road the pilgrims followed from Canterbury to

Rome in Medieval times. I mean, come on, how cool is that? Plus, it's only a fifteen-minute hike to ancient San Gimignano. Which, according to Wikipedia, is identified as The Town of Fine Towers and is renowned for its gothic architecture. The city sits on the edge of a hill encircled by three walls.

I'm about to vault over the intricate iron, when a tall, burly black man steps from the shadows. Dressed similar to Bastian's 'come fuck me' leather outfit, I'm guessing he's a vampire. The dark as night irises give me the heebie-jeebies.

"Might I be of assistance, my lady?" He asks in a rich, cultured Italian accent.

I snort. My lady. Oh wait, that's right, I'm a freaking princess. Ha!

"Only if you can open the gate."

"I'm sorry, but you're not permitted beyond the entrance." The deep grate of his speech causes goosebumps to advance over my flesh.

"Am I a prisoner?"

No fucking way will they hold me against my will. I shuffle my feet, solaced by the weight of the dagger in my boot.

"No, my lady. It is for your protection."

"Riiiight."

"Shall I accompany you back to the villa?"

"Listen up, Mr. Tall, Dark, Slightly Scary Vamp, this is my first time in Italy, and I am going to explore San Gimignano. Now, you either step off and let me pass or tag along. Then you can inform Mr. Control Freak you monitored my every move. Either way works, you decide."

Geez, when did I grow a brass pair?

"My lady," he rumbles, stepping into my personal bubble. "You either stroll up this drive to the residence, or I will trace you and tie you to the master's bed."

Master? What the fuck? Did I step into the stone ages when we teleported here? By his expression, I'm guessing he's not messing around. Well, neither am I, buddy.

"Fine. I'll walk." I smile serenely.

When his shoulders relax, it takes everything to keep the evil grin off my face and the word 'Sucker' from escaping my lips. Men. So predictable.

As we start up the drive, I pause, creating a pretense of tying the laces on my boot while slipping the blade into my jean pocket. I don't wish to kill him, just incapacitate him. Can you knock a vampire unconscious? It's not like I can trip him up and make a break for it, the bastard will trace to me in a nanosecond, and before I could blink, he'd have me hogtied to the *master's* bed.

Jesus. If he ever asks me to call him that, I'll deck him.

I rise to my feet and grace the dark beauty with my best come-hither smile. "You're a handsome one. What's your name?"

"Quillon." He bows dramatically. "At your service."

"Nice to meet you, Quill." His grin is dazzling white with enormous fangs. He's adorable. I hate to get him in trouble, but I'm escaping this luxurious prison. Me and my AMEX card have some serious Italian shopping to accomplish.

Several steps later, I'm still racking my brain on how to bust free from the sweet, sexy, somewhat scary Quill when my phone in my back pocket rings. I stride from my bodyguard in the direction of the gates with a raised finger to answer the call.

"Hey, Doc. Or should I call you Rowena? Are you even a licensed psychiatrist?"

"I'm sorry, Alex. I never meant to deceive you, but you were my only link to my son." The desperate ring in her voice gives me pause. "And yes, I possess many degrees. When you've survived as long as I have, and your appearance never alters, you have many opportunities to expound on an education."

Wow. How cool is that? A perpetual college student. But, if Sebastian is half a millennium, how old is Rowena?

"Care to tell me the drama between you two? He clearly wants nothing to do with you." I roam a couple more steps toward the exit, kicking a pebble, my head lowered. *Don't mind me, vampire. Little miss innocent here.* "In fact, I'd take it so far as to state he hates your guts."

The doc's heavy sigh draws my attention. "It's a lengthy story loaded with misunderstanding and regret. I would love to meet with you, get everything out in the open, therefore we may continue our sessions. I still believe I can help you, Alex."

"If this were a typical situation, with ordinary human beings, I would agree. But we are way beyond normal hypnosis resolving my blocked memories. Apparently, I require a *demon* for that." I cross myself uttering the term demon.

"So, my son hasn't mated you yet?" The relief in her tone irritates me.

"If you're older than Bastian, why is it you contract your words, and he doesn't?"

"I've spent decades at various universities and in the workforce among humans. My only child chose a different path, one with little to no interface with mortals. Have you mated Sebastian?" She asks again.

"I'm not even certain what that means, but I'm guessing no."

"Excellent. Believe it or not, that's a healthy thing, Alex. For you." Did she just threaten me? "Let's meet. I will explain everything. Where are you?"

"Italy."

Quill steps in my path, a worried frown marring his expression. "Who is on the other line?"

At the same time, Rowena asks, "Are you inside the villa?"

Glaring at my prison guard, I drop the cell to my chin. "None of your business." Then bring it back to my lips to answer my shrink. "No, by the gates." Not sure why my exact position would make a difference.

Several things develop at once. Quill snatches the phone from my grasp, crushing it in his enormous fist. I raise my hand to bitch slap him when Rowena suddenly appears behind the angry vampire, and before I can call out a warning, she's snapped his neck, and his powerful body lands hard on the dirt at my feet.

"Now," states the beautiful, crazy killer in designer jeans. "Let's go shopping."

Chapter 19

Sebastian

"What the fuck do you mean she is gone?" I glare with murderous intent down at my guard pinned to the concrete floor in the kitchen, my boot pressing viciously against his windpipe. "You had one duty, Quillon. Keep her here." How could my little mate overpower my best guard?

After the showdown with Arra, Logan crashed, powerless to fight the sleep a minute longer. Nicole demanded an update on the happenings in the Nation during her grieving sabbatical, and considering the vast holdings, it took over an hour to get things finalized.

Just as I started to take off, Viessa appeared in the office, alarming us both. Her frantic gaze zeroed on mine as she clutched Liam's gold necklace around her neck.

"Your highness." I edged closer, not wishing to spook her further. "How may we serve you?"

"Much suffering in you. Can't help that." Viessa twirled and slapped her palms on the desk in front of Nicole. The queen jumped, eyeing the Oracle warily.

"Heal the rift. The first was destined to perish."

"Oookaaay," Nicole muttered, rising to her feet, but before she could respond further, the vampire marched straight toward me, clutched my sweater in both fists.

The amber gaze, identical in color to her twin, Lucretia's, pulsed brighter. I wanted to reach out and grasp her shoulders to calm her, but it is forbidden to touch an Oracle, even one in training.

"What disturbs you, Viessa?"

"It is better this way. For you. The valkyrie will grieve. Make her forget, Commander."

What the hell was she talking about? "Why will she grieve? What will happen?"

"Her light is divergent and brilliant. The princess must live, no matter the cost." She shakes me, and I am astounded by her strength. "Answer you understand, vampire," she growled with sudden authority and shoved me against the wall.

"I will protect her with my life, Oracle. This I vow."

My promise seemed to soothe her enough that a small smile graced her lips before she released me and spun away, her long dark hair fanning out around her. The fire lit her from behind, causing the toga-like robe to become translucent, highlighting the elegant womanly curves beneath.

"Many battles and heartache behind and ahead. Need my king. Icarus is angry with me. Be well."

The second she vanished, Nicole and I stared at each other for several long moments before she finally shattered the silence.

"Fuck all. She freaks me out."

I nodded my agreement. "She will be a great Oracle one day if she can obtain control of her mind."

"Yeah. Let's hope she gets it together soon. For all our sakes."

"Apologies, Master," the big brute beneath my boot wheezes, refocusing my thoughts to the present. I ease off somewhat to receive his report. "She planned to leap the gates when I intercepted her. I was escorting her back up the drive when she received a phone call from a woman. The valkyrie informed the female where she was before I could stop her, and the next thing I knew, I'm waking in the dirt with a severe neck ache."

Fear coats my gut. "Did Alex reveal her name?" Only one female vampire, with such speed and strength, knows of this location.

"Yes, Master. Rowena."

Son of a bitch!

My mother could trace her anywhere. Would she harm Alex, even knowing such a measure would trigger the beast to avenge its mate?

My mind darts to the vile things she inflicted upon me. Terror coats my innards at the prospect of my innocent valkyrie in her clutches. If the bitch lays one finger on Alexandria, I will hack her fucking heart from her chest.

But overshadowing the fear, a wave of deep-seated anger develops. Alex disobeyed my orders and sought to leave. Her disobedience cannot go unpunished, no matter how pure she claims to be.

"The only thing keeping me from ripping your skull from your body is my mate's blood running through my system." If Alexandria is within a fifty-mile radius, I will locate her. But where would Rowena take her? San Gimignano? Florence? Pisa? She might not even be in Italy for fuck's sake.

I rake my fingers through my hair in agitation. Dammit. I should never have left her side.

I remove my boot from Quillon's collar, grasp the lapels of his leather jacket, and haul him to his feet. "Gather five of my best guards and meet me at the well in Piazza Della Cisterna. We will start there. I will tear Italy apart to find my mate."

Viessa's comments haunt my thoughts. Moments ago, I vowed to keep Alex safe, and I've already lost her.

"Yes, Master." Quillon dutifully lowers his head.

"Do not fail me anew, or you will greet the mid-day sun."

EVEN AT THIS LATE HOUR, many of the shops and restaurants are open and crowded with patrons. Above the well in the center of the Piazza little white lights fan out across the square in a tent-like fashion for the coming holiday. The towers blaze with fire against the night sky.

I would have loved to escort Alex around this fascinating town. Shower her with gifts from the stores and enjoy watching her sample all the incredible food. Instead, I'm inspecting the beauty from the shadows as she dines with evil incarnate.

Seeing Rowena after all this time ties my gut in knots. This female is the cause of all my pain, shame, and rage. She is also a powerful vampire, and I must tread carefully.

I note the position of my guards at every exit to the square and hope this encounter does not require open combat. To be on the safe side, I shoot a quick text to my brother, giving him my exact coordinates.

Within moments, Logan appears next to me, a worried line between his brows, his hair slightly mussed from his rest. I am comforted to discover he showed up dressed for battle, minus the swords, of course. The Polizia would besiege the Piazza in seconds if seven warriors stepped out of the shadows with broadswords strapped to their backs. Then again, in Italy, you never know.

Logan takes in the square, noting my men in a heartbeat before his widened gaze settles on Alex and Rowena seated at an outdoor café.

"What is the plan, Sebastian?" My brother is shrewd enough to use telepathy, knowing the bitch would overhear our conversation.

"Not sure yet. She went with a public venue, so I take it to mean she does not wish open conflict."

"You believe Ro plans to harm Alex?"

"Only if she gets in her way."

"Mayhap I should confront your mother, find out what she demands. It is probably not a safe plan to have the two of you in proximity among mortals."

Logan and I are half-brothers. His mom was our father's one true mate, and according to him, she was a loving, generous female who doted on her husband and son.

Not long after Logan's transition, a herd of centaurs trampled her to death a week after the Vampire Nation slaughtered their army in battle. Devastated by her loss, father nearly joined her in the afterlife.

Somehow Rowena manipulated her way into his life and persuaded him a companion would kindle his will to live once more. Even though the female was not his one true mate, Voila, nine months later, I popped out—a miracle baby. The gods despised me to allot me such a mother.

"No. I will handle Rowena. I required your presence as a further deterrent against a public tantrum. From her, or me." I offer with a strained smile.

"I have your six."

We gradually move forward, and I signal my team to maintain their positions. Two six- and half-foot males dressed in leather draw more than sufficient attention.

With each passing step, my heart rate increases. My hardened gaze never deviates from my deceptively beautiful mother. Even though my inner vampire demands I snatch Alex from her chair and teleport her to safety, I do not.

When Rowena's blue eyes lift to mine over Alex's red locks, I nearly stumble as white-hot rage fills my vision. It is all I can manage to hold the fierce glow from my gaze and my fangs from descending. This bitch destroyed me, and if she weren't my flesh and blood, I would have ripped her head from her body with my bare hands long ago and damned the repercussions.

The radiant smile lifting her lips is in complete contrast to the illuminated evil brightening her irises.

"My son," Rowena breathes, and I want to gag.

Alex's head whips around, but I ignore her. The little minx will have my complete attention in no time.

"Bastian…"

"For once in your life, Alexandria, shut up." When she opens her mouth to protest, I slant her a livid glare, allowing a slight gleam of blue to fill my gaze. She wisely snaps her lips together before shifting to gape at Logan.

The only thing my brother and I share in looks is our stature, dark hair, and Italian complexion, otherwise we look nothing alike. Logan keeps his locks on the longer side, brushing his shoulders. His irises are a brilliant iridescent green, and he always sports a sinister-looking goatee. He resembles our father in many ways.

I was unfortunate enough to inherit my mother's sky-blue eyes with the ridiculous cleft in the chin. While hers is barely an indent, mine is more pronounced and the source of considerable ridicule as a youngster.

I flip an iron chair around and straddle it, propping my forearms on the low back. Logan eases into the seat opposite me. "What is it you want, Rowena?" I ask, not bothering to conceal the contempt in my voice. Alex fidgets nervously in her chair.

"You didn't need to bring your big brother for backup, son. I mean you no harm. On the contrary, I've missed you."

When her ice-cold palm lands lightly on my forearm, I jerk as if scalded. "You touch me again, and I do not care where we are, I will rip open your throat and dance in your blood."

"Brother, calm yourself." Logan turns a livid stare on my mother. "Rowena, I recommend you keep your vile hands to yourself, or this will be over in a heartbeat."

The bane of my existence visibly swallows at Logan's display of hostility. My sibling and I are fairly matched in skill and speed, but my brother's ruthlessness on the battlefield is legendary. And since she is not his flesh and blood, the infamous warrior would have no qualms in slaughtering her.

Alex clears her throat. "It's apparent this is a family matter. Why don't the three of you hash this out, and I'll catch up with you later?" She whispers and attempts to rise.

In a millisecond, my palm slams down on her shoulder, holding her in place. "You so much as twitch, and I will tan your hide in front of all these witnesses."

Cerulean eyes narrow, but she remains seated. "No need to get pissy," she growls fearlessly.

"Son, I wish to make amends."

"Amends?" I bark out a cruel laugh, and several human heads swivel our direction. "By abducting my mate?"

"I did not kidnap her, Sebastian. She came voluntarily. Isn't that correct, Alex?"

Alexandria's uncertain gaze bounces between the three of us, and I can hear her mind spinning. "Your mom didn't abscond with me, Bastian. I wanted to go shopping and explore a little."

"You could not await my return?" I grind out between clenched teeth.

"Well, the night was wasting, and I didn't know if you were coming back," she retorts.

Her defiance produces a twitch in the corner of my eye. "I will deal with you later."

"Please, Sebastian. Don't be furious with Alex. It was my fault."

"Of that, I have no doubt, Rowena." I scowl at the vampire who birthed me. "What the fuck do you really want?"

"As I mentioned, to make amends." She leans back in her chair, crossing her legs. "I returned to atone and solicit your forgiveness."

She cannot be fucking serious. Nothing she could say or do now would redeem her sins. "Is that it?" My gaze narrows.

"No," she replies coolly.

I knew it. "Spit it out, Rowena. I do not have all damn night."

"I..." she swallows and sweeps a speckle of lint from her jeans. "I would appreciate the opportunity to get to know you again, to be a part of your life."

I throw my head back and roar with laughter. It is manic to my ears. Logan tenses, bracing to back me up no matter what goes down. My inner vampire thrashes for command, and I squeeze my lids shut to hold in the blaze in my irises, but I cannot contain the elongating of my fangs.

I am on the verge of vaulting over this table and eviscerating the woman who gave me life and then brutally defiled it when a small, warm hand closes over my fist. A sudden stillness invades my spirit, and I shake my head at the immediate impact of Alex's touch.

I lift my lids and peer into the troubled scrutiny of my mate, and the need to comfort her eats away at the violence. I gape at this petite valkyrie in bewilderment.

She smiles in tender support before turning to Rowena. The blue irises flicker silver. "Doc. It's obvious there's bad blood between the two of you, and honestly, I don't know either one of you very well, but your presence upsets Sebastian, so either you leave, or we will." I ogle this remarkable creature when she leans across the table, her posture menacing. "Don't ever fucking use me as a pawn again. You're fired."

Rowena's brow lifts, and my lips twitch in delight. Christ. Not merely did her touch soothe me, but her actions warmed my chest. The fierce little princess is defending me.

"Well," Logan chuckles. "I believe you have your answer, Ro." He stands and captures my mother's chair, indicating she rise. A courteous gesture for the occupants of the café, but the keen emerald regard fills with savage intent.

"Very well." Rowena gains her feet with fluidity and grace. "But this isn't over, my son. I will do whatever it takes to be a part of your life again." With that, she spins on her heel and melts into the milling crowd.

Relief floods through me, and my muscles relax for the first time in hours. A day of reckoning is coming between her and I. One long overdue. Because Rowena's objective is not absolution. In her sick, twisted mind, the only thing she did wrong was love her only child. No. Mommy dearest wishes to punish me for forsaking her.

She wants retribution.

Chapter 20

Alexandria

When we materialize in the cozy dining room of the villa, a roaring fire crackles in the fireplace, but I immediately take a stride back from the livid vampire. I'm not positive what shit was flying between him and his mother, but holy hell, it was extreme. And his brother? For the love of God, he was a gorgeous, powerful dude. The whole erotic pirate vibe he was sporting was downright provocative.

The eerie silence between us becomes suffocating, and I can't help the sigh of regret. Tonight, our one and only night, is FUBARed. Fucked up beyond all recognition. So much for allowing this spicy beast to initiate me into the pleasures of sex.

Back to plan A. Ezekiel. I know he will be a gentle, patient lover, and that's what I need. Not this overbearing, angry, non-human glaring daggers at me. Something in the vicinity of my heart tweaks at the prospect of never being close to Bastian again, but I ignore it and turn away to go pack.

"Stop."

The sharp command has my inside fluttering, and the breath in my lungs freezes. I falter in the archway, refusing to confront the anger pulsing into my spine.

"I asked one thing of you, Alexandria."

I bite my lip at the low, threatening tone. "You didn't ask. You ordered."

"Yes. And you disobeyed. Look at me."

I prefer to run from the room and barricade myself in the bathroom. Not that a puny lock would block him from barging in if he desired. But a small part of me is animated by Bastian's strength, the authority in his tone. And if I dared to probe deeper, I'd recognize my foolishness tonight was to seek this backlash. I lust after the darkness in him. How sick is that?

I pivot slowly, and my heart leaps at the beauty of the vampire, but the cool indifference in his expression gets my juices flowing and clenches my body tight.

"When it comes to your safety, I demand obedience." He strolls toward me, and I swallow. It's all I can manage not to retreat in the face of his dominance. "You placed yourself in grave danger tonight, little red. How can I do my duty in shielding you when you defy me?"

"I'm capable of taking care of myself." I hoist my chin. Who the fuck does he think he is? I'm not some errant child in need of a scolding.

But, if Rowena's objective were to injure me, and with no understanding of the scope of her abilities or mine, would I have stood a chance against her?

His gaze hardens. "In a blink, your heart could have been in her hand." He moves closer. "I will slay anyone who threatens you with zero remorse, even my own mother."

No matter how savage the words, they are real. He is real. No longer the wolf disguised in sheep's clothing, his brutality is part of his appeal. This part frightens and excites me, but according to him, he's off-limits—six feet four inches of supernatural bad news. And I don't fucking care.

"There's a darkness in you, Bastian." My words seem to startle him for a moment.

"Yes," he replies quietly. "Are you afraid?"

"Yes. But what scares me even more, is the darkness inside me begging for yours."

His eyes widen, and he sucks in a deep breath. "Red. I cannot offer you..."

"I know," I interrupt, swallowing away the fear and thirst for more. "No commitment. Got it. But I desire everything else."

He contemplates me for several minutes, doubt clouding his expression, before his demeanor reverts to the fierce Dom, and my belly quivers.

I frown in confusion when he turns and discards the armchair at the head of the table. What the hell is he doing? I expected him to gather me in his arms and trace us to his bedroom.

"You fancy a glimpse of my blackened soul?" He waits for my nod. "Remove your clothes."

Wait. What?

"The longer you defy me, the harsher the punishment."

Punishment? Shitballs, this is happening. "You said my first time would be gentle."

"And so, it shall. This is just the beginning."

At his pointed look, I unbutton my blouse with slow movements. I'm not trying to be seductive; I merely require the precious moments to garner my courage. I can't lie; I'm a little petrified. While I trust Bastian would never hurt me, the scary unknown is ramping up my heart rate, and to this adrenaline junkie it's like he's injected pure heroin laced with ecstasy into my veins.

The cobalt irises spark, observing my movements with bold hunger until I stand before him completely nude. My fingers tremble as I tuck a thick curl behind my ear and wait.

Patience is not one of my virtues, so when he slowly circles me, not touching or saying anything, I gnaw my lip to keep from blurting out zillions of questions. Is this part of the game? Is he going to undress? Why isn't he fucking touching me? I. Need. His. Touch.

"Walk to the head of the table," he breathes in my ear and shivers ripple down my spine.

Amazingly, I don't collapse in a heap on the stone floor as I amble to the oak table. The heat of the fire warms my side, and for the first time, the thought crosses my mind there might be servants in the house.

"Lay your chest on the surface, hands stretched out above you."

A swift peek over my shoulder shows Bastian hasn't moved. Broad, muscular shoulders still encased in his black leather lean against the archway. The brilliant sapphires collide with mine. Waiting.

Okay, Alex. You asked for this. Stop being a pussy and fall in line.

When the cool wood connects with my aching nipples, I nearly groan at the torment. They beg for Bastian's hands, the full lips and warm tongue. An image of his fangs piercing the delicate flesh has me rubbing them against the grain as I slide my palms above my head.

"Good girl."

I bite the inside of my cheek to keep from smiling. God, I'm pathetic to respond so eagerly to his praise. Am I truly a submissive, or do I just love the role play?

I nearly jump out of my skin when warm fingers dance along my spine, over my exposed backside, and quivering hamstrings. I didn't even hear his approach.

"Never be frightened to explore your fantasies and desires, Alexandria. Embrace them. Make them yours. They are a part of who you are."

"Do your recommendations extend to someone else after tonight?"

Before I can lament myself for the dumbass question, a resounding slap bounces off the brick ceiling, and a biting sting spreads across my right butt cheek. Instinct demands I jerk upright, but somehow, I don't. Instead, I dig my nails in the wood above my head and remain completely still.

"Do not speak of that again. Understood?" The tone is harsh and guttural, and my core clenches.

"I'm sorry." I murmur and settle my forehead on the table. It was a bitchy thing to mention at this intimate moment.

In response, his broad palm glides over the area he just smacked, and a heavenly warmth spreads through my flesh, straight to the bundle of nerves craving his touch. I moan low and rub my pelvis against the curled edge to alleviate the throb.

"Hold still." His stern command wets my opening, but I do as he instructs. "Do you understand why I am spanking you?"

Holy shit! Why is the word spanking fucking hot?

"Yes." *Please don't make me state why out loud.*

"Tell me."

Damnit.

His powerful hands resume their exploration of my posterior, and I forget the question.

A little lower, sir.

Whoa. Sir? This is not me. I don't bow down to any man. But when his palm strikes the same spot as before, and the addictive heat expands, my reservations spiral into the dancing flames and lust pools hot and rapid through my body.

"Because I disobeyed your command." Who is this breathy, submissive woman? Certainly, not me?

"Christ, Red." Soft lips kiss along my shoulder blade. "You astound me."

Yeah. I'm fucking amazing myself right now.

"I will give you a safe word." A warm tongue licks the feverish skin on my ass, and I moan deep, craving him lower. "If at any point, the situation becomes too much, I want you to utter the word..."

he pauses as if pondering. "Unicorn," he whispers against my lower back, and I feel the grin on his lips.

I snicker. "Unicorn?"

"What can I say, I adored your pajamas."

Oh, the many layers to this man. They run deep and wide.

When his warmth leaves my side, my smile vanishes, replaced by nervous anticipation.

"You ready to begin?"

Umm. No! My anxiety shrieks, but the carnal passion slamming through every nerve in my body ignores her.

"Yes."

Chapter 21

Alexandria

"Since this is your first time, that we know of, it will be challenging for you to remain still, therefore I want you to cross your wrists at your lower back."

Every sound in the deep sexy timber causes an answering throb between my legs, and I immediately obey. A warm hand firmly clasps my wrists, and I bite my cheek to keep a moan buried at the delicious stricture.

"Remember your safe word, Red."

And before I can even smirk at the reminder, his wide palm lands on my ass with a ringing slap. I jerk, but his firm grip keeps my hips in place. Bastian gently caresses the sting, but I don't get a chance to revel in the sweet burn expanding before he strikes the other side.

Holy fuck. Why does every slap shoot raptured bliss straight to my brain? My clit pulses in cadence with each smack, my nipples tighten into hard, painful points, and I grit my teeth to keep from rubbing against the table. As the fever in my backside spreads with each impact, my lids lower in ecstasy, and I turn my head, resting my cheek on the warm wood as an orgasm smolders below the surface.

"Bastian," I whimper softly.

"Do not come unless I grant you permission."

His barked command has me clenching my insides to stave off the impending explosion as his fiery palm continues to work my flesh. This... these sensations he's evoking are fucking incredible. I take pleasure in this way too much not to have indulged before my memory loss.

Maybe I'm a masochist. And even though the word sounds scandalous, if the reward you receive for being one is this, then I'll gladly shout it from the rooftop.

I'm so caught up in the mind-blowing tingle and burn spreading through every nerve in my body, it's several moments before I realize the blows have ceased, and Bastian is gently running his palm across my tender cheeks.

"You did well, Alexandria." I nearly bolt upright when his fingers glide along the seam in my ass before delving into the evidence of my desire coating my folds. He tightens his hold on my wrists, stepping between my legs.

"Stay put, or this ends," he commands, nudging my feet wider before his lips begin a gradual, sumptuous exploration of my heated ass, down each leg and up again. My muscles twitch in response to his caress, yearning more. Like those soft, full lips and tongue exploring the pulsing need splayed out before him. What the fuck is he waiting for?

"Please, Sebastian." I don't care if I'm begging. I'll plead, sob, and offer him anything to ease my torment.

Soft, cool leather brushes my calves as he kneels between my thighs, his tight grip never leaving my wrists. The second his heated breath cascades over my soaked pussy, I nearly combust.

Yes, yes, yes. Closer. Taste me, vampire.

A warm tongue circles my opening, and I keen low. It dips inside, then drops down to lap at my clit before departing.

"Dammit, Bastian," I growl against the wood, and his answering chuckle has my head lifting in irritation. Enough of this game already. I need to come like yesterday.

I attempt to rise, but my lower back and hips stay fastened to the table by one dominant hand.

"Do you wish me to stop, Alex?"

"Fuck, no." I grate out.

"This is your last warning. Rise again, and I cease."

How can he sound so calm and in control? A forest fire rages under my skin, obscuring all rational thought, but I lower my chest down to the oak, and I'm rewarded with his wicked mouth clamping onto my sensitive flesh, devouring me, consuming me. He growls and sets in; one hand crushes my wrists, the other plunging into my core and setting up an exquisite, addictive thrust.

This is bliss and torture at the same time. I'm on the cusp of fracturing into a thousand tiny fragments. It's all I can do to hold my hips still, so I grind my forehead into the hardwood to check my pending eruption.

"Come, Red," he commands roughly. Savage flames burst from my body, shattering my sanity, and spiraling me over the precipice into pure fucking nirvana.

"Oh, God!" I cry as he doubles his efforts, extending my orgasm beyond anything I've ever experienced. My core convulses around his thrusting fingers once more when a sharp sting penetrates my clit. "Oh. Yes."

His low hungry growl vibrates along my slick folds, and I spread my legs further to allow him better access. I crave this man between my thighs 24/7. How will I walk away from this? From him?

As soon as my shudders diminish, Sebastian releases his grip on my wrists, and I drop them to my side with a groan before slowly dragging them up, stretching the stiff muscles. Bastian rains tender kisses over the sensitive flesh on my backside, along my spine, before brushing my hair to the side and nibbling on my neck.

Twice, the vampire has brought me to orgasm without worry of himself. An image of his girth sliding over my lips and down my throat has my insides humming anew, but I'm finding it challenging to move. My muscles have entered a state of relaxed lethargy.

Gentle hands lift my languid form from the dinner table, cradling me in mighty arms. Deep darkness envelops us, and in the next breath, we're standing in the center of his room. Wow. Teleporting is damn convenient.

Bastian lowers my feet to the floor, and I clutch his jacket to keep from collapsing in a heap at his feet. Jesus, my legs are like jelly.

"Take a minute."

It's then I realize the man is still fully dressed, leather duster and all. Shit. This exquisite specimen carried my body to such extraordinary heights of euphoria while fully clothed. How fucking erotic is that?

But now, I crave to explore every hard inch of his body, run my tongue over the dips and valleys of his impressive abs, navigate the sexy tattoo with my fingers. I close the narrow gap between us and rub my stomach against the enormous erection straining against his leather pants. His grip on my shoulders tightens painfully.

Not as in control as he prefers me to believe.

I lock my knees and arch my neck to gaze into the soft blue glow. I don't care how languid my muscles are; nothing will stop me from watching his iron restraint crumble to dust under my hands. The occasion for caution has passed. I covet what remains below the surface—the beast sparking those baby blues to life.

Before dawn intrudes, Sebastian Moretti's discipline will snap. I'll make certain of it.

Chapter 22

Sebastian

I never imagined in a million years; Alexandria Svaldana, the assumed promiscuous hell-raiser, quick-witted smart mouth with a shopping addiction would get off on being spanked, or I would be the one spanking her.

When she started moaning and writhing, I couldn't sway the descent of my fangs, or the blaze from behind my eyes. For the first time, in all my centuries, the beast craved domination. During a session with a submissive, I keep him locked down. His baser instincts have no place in such a performance.

But with Alex, she challenged me at each turn, and it took every morsel of my hard-earned restraint not to rip my leathers open, bury my throbbing cock deep inside her tight sheath, and sink my fangs into her neck. The result? The completion of my side of the bond, tying the little valkyrie to me for eternity.

Gazing down at her now, I read the determination in her silver gaze. She wishes to take over, watch me surrender my steely discipline. The beautiful spitfire does not understand the inferno she would unleash. I never give up control, especially during sex. No woman will ever wield such power over me.

"Go lie on the bed." Her eyes widen at my harsh tone. I soften it by gently running my knuckles down her cheek before tucking a damp curl behind her ear. She hesitates. "Before we proceed, let me be explicit. You will never have control during sex. Do as I command without hesitation, and I will reward us both great pleasures." I stride away and shrug out of my heavy duster laden with weapons before draping it over a chair by the crackling fireplace, allowing her a moment to decide.

"I may not remember many details about myself, and as much as I got off on what transpired in the dining room, I'm pretty sure submissive does *not* describe me."

The beautiful minx has the spunk to oppose me completely nude. The orange glow from the fire licks over the heavenly body, showcasing surprisingly full breasts for someone so slight, with rosy, puckered areolas—a trim waist flaring slightly into curvy hips and toned thighs. The glistening folds beg for my attention once more.

I drag my gaze to hers. My cock hardens to the point of pain at the rebellious, determined gleam in her eyes. She wishes to battle for domination. With anyone else, I would shut her down with a harsh word and walk away. For some goddamn reason, her opposition heightens the lust coursing through my nerves straight to my other brain, throbbing in my pants.

"You think not?" I whip my black t-shirt over my head and stalk toward her. I am pleased to see her eyes expand as they devour every inch of my exposed skin. "Then why did you enjoy the spanking, my fiery hellion?" I stop mere inches from her, and her warm breath fans over my rib cage. I bite back the groan begging for release at the blaze of lust in her gaze.

"I..." She reaches out to touch my stomach, but I seize her wrist, holding it immobile from her target.

"Answer me. You got off on being restrained, spanked. Your heart rate spikes with every order I utter. Why?"

"Because..." she huffs out a sharp breath. "Because you're sexy as fuck, and for some goddamn reason, I want to please you."

I inhale sharply at the shouted confession, letting her go when she jerks her wrist free. Pleasure spirals straight to my groin, but it is the excitement growing inside my heart that snags my attention, and I frown. Her words mean more than they should.

She pivots toward the bathroom, but I latch onto her elbow and twirl her into my chest. No way in hell is she running away from me.

My lips claim hers in a searing kiss nearly buckling my knees. My small, precious bundle grasps my waist in a painful grip and opens for me, her tongue dueling with mine, her whimpers and moans music to my ears.

I grasp the delectable ass I enjoyed warming with my palm earlier and hoist her up until strong legs wrap around my midriff. A rumble of pleasure rips through my throat when she clutches fistfuls of my hair, wiggling to get closer. The slick heat of her core rubs against my belt buckle, and the hardened nipples scrape my rib cage with each pant of breath.

Fuck. I never wish to never leave the warmth of this female's embrace. I could devote the next five hundred years enjoying the vibrations of her moans, relishing her sweet essence each night, and it would never be enough.

I strive to keep my fangs dormant as I explore every inch of her mouth and drift toward the bed. I slip a finger between her cheeks and rub the pad against her puckered hole. She stiffens, leaning away to study my face.

"What are you doing?"

Fuck, she is adorable. "Do you trust me?"

So many wondrous things to teach this female, and as much as I wish to take it slow, we have but one night. Tomorrow, my mate will reject me. The remembrances of these precious hours will be an excruciating pleasure to occupy the endless nights ahead.

I vowed not to deflower her while her memories stay buried, but I am a selfish prick, demanding the fantasies of her writhing under me, my name on her lips as I pound into her untouched flesh to assuage the agony of her absence later.

When her hatred returns, our time together will either fan the flames or perhaps soften them enough we could work through her prejudice against my kind. Either way, I am not prepared to let her go just yet. The incessant demand to claim what is mine cannot be denied any longer.

"Yes." No hesitation in her response and the gift humbles me; even as a part of my brain shouts, I am not worthy.

"You are petite, Alex. I must prepare you to receive my girth, or your initial time will be quite painful."

"Okay, but what's that got to do with your finger on my ass?"

I chuckle and kiss her neck. "You will see," I say before tossing her into the air to land with a soft "oomph" in the center of the bed.

"Stay put," I order with a pointed finger.

Instead of arguing, she settles against the pillows like she is the Queen of Sheba. When I unbuckle the belt she eagerly ground against, a teasing smile lifts her lips and she drapes her arms over the cushions, her spine against the headboard.

"Are you going to strip for me, Sebastian?"

"Why, yes, my lady," I retort, toeing off my boots.

I could disrobe in a blink, but her full, eager grin warms my black soul, so I take my time.

"We need some sexy music," she giggles, her gaze glued to my hypnotic moves.

"Alexa, play Two Feet."

"Look at the 500-year-old vampire rockin' the twenty-first century."

When the heavy, sensual beat of Love is a Bitch fills the chamber, I grin devilishly, allow my fangs to descend, and the fever in my irises to expand. With slow, intentional movements, I stalk my prey lounging wide-eyed in the center of the mattress surrounded by plush pillows.

"Divine Mother of God," she pants, climbing to her knees, her nipples hard little points begging for my tongue.

I slide the leather and boxer briefs to the floor and toss them aside, pausing at the end of the bed. I note her ragged gasps, the hands clenching and unclenching, itching for a chance to explore. The lovely silver eyes widen when they take in my erection, licking her lips, and the traitor jerks in response, a victim to her unspoken demand.

"You are beautiful, Bastian. The way you move..."

"Imagine those moves while I am deep inside your sweet pussy, driving hard and fast."

"Yes, please. I'm ready."

I bite back a grin and kneel on the bed in front of her. Her bright gaze wanders down my chest, admiring the Moretti tattoo spiraling over my pec, shoulder, and bicep, before traveling on to my abdomen, and ending at the cock straining toward her.

"I want to taste you," she whispers before raising those appealing, enchanted eyes to mine. "Please, Sebastian."

How could I refuse this fascinating creature anything? Plus, her pleading thrills me. I tuck a silky curl behind those exotic ears begging for the caress of my tongue or the sting of my bite. After a little investigation into valkyries, I discovered the tips of their pointed ears are an erogenous zone, and I can't wait to reveal if that's true.

In answer to her inquiry, I assume her previous position on the bed, draping my arms across the expanse of pillows. A deep, shadowy part of my subconscious balks at giving her even this minuscule amount of authority, and I clutch the cushions, my jaw clamping down hard.

When a sub pleasures me, it is always on her knees, wrists bound behind her as I grip fistfuls of hair and fuck her mouth. So, to lay here submissively on my back, letting her take control, causes my skin to crawl with images of my past. The burn of silver on my wrists and ankles. The bite of sharp nails piercing my flesh, as my traitorous body responded to every lick and glide of her vile mouth.

I shift forward to reverse our positions when Alex's words freeze me in place.

"You have all the control, Bastian. Guide me where you demand. Show me what pleases you."

Fuck.

I sense the desire coursing through her, but also need, not merely for my commands, but her reluctant urge to satisfy me. The spitfire's willingness to submit to my will blasts the horrendous images from my mind and I settle against the cushions once more.

Alex can protest all she wants about not being submissive, and it might be true in her day-to-day life, but here, whether in the bedroom, playroom, or dining room, she craves domination.

It suddenly dawns on me, we may come from divergent backgrounds and of different species, but Alexandria Svaldana was created for me.

Too bad, my blackened soul will devour any spark of hope.

Chapter 23

Alexandria

My eagerness to be with this vampire outweighs the dent to my pride at following his orders. I'm not the shrink here, but I'd bet good money something from his past shaped this demand for complete control. Based on their interaction at the café, I'd wager his mother is the culprit.

I shove everything aside and scan the magnificent specimen before me. I've given the lounging god the green light to guide my every action, and my insides have gone all squirrely in the desperate hope he allows me a chance to sample and explore.

"Straddle my thighs, Red."

Crap. I can't help it. The low sexy command in his tone heightens the wobbly things in my gut, my nipples harden, and my empty core clenches for fulfillment. Namely, the enormous Johnson laying strong and proud against his abdomen.

Holy Christ. No way he's going to fit.

Reservations bounce through my brain, but I do as he directs, and straddle his thighs.

"Speak your desire." The vivid sapphires watch me with a fierce predatory, yet elusive scrutiny. Sebastian scares me, but he's like an obsession I couldn't walk away from even if someone stuck a gun to my head.

Somehow, staring into his keen regard, I recognize his past seeking to encroach, to slither between us, and if I color outside the lines, even a little, it's game over.

"I want to taste you," I whisper, never removing my gaze from his.

"Take me in your hand."

I immediately comply, and gasp at the silky-smooth texture stretched over rigid iron. Oh wow. My initial impulse is to lean down and lick the droplet beading at the tip, but I can't make a move unless granted permission. Instead, I slip my fingers around the impressive girth.

"With a firm grasp, glide your fist up and down with slow movements."

Fuck, me. This is hot. And the best part? I don't even have to determine what to do next. Bastian's commands instruct me every step of the way.

"Hmmm. Just like that. So good, Red."

I bite my lip and beam, thoroughly enjoying myself. Bastian's hips move in opposition to my hand, and I peer up at him. Those sexy irises glow with an inner light as they study me. His lips part, and I'm pleased to note the orgasm-inducing fangs hang low.

I run my tongue over my parched lips and increase my pace, hoping he won't halt my initiative.

"Kneel between my legs," he pants, spreading his limbs to grant me room. The insides of my thighs are slick with my desire, and my clit throbs for attention, but I ignore it and concentrate on my vampire.

"Lick me from base to head."

About fucking time.

The second my tongue slides along his length, I groan low at the extraordinary texture and sweetness, and I think nothing could be better than this. Until the drop of moisture at the tip flares across my taste buds, and I understand how fucking wrong I was.

His essence is pure ambrosia. Salty and sweet at the same time. "Jesus, your flavor is incredible," I whisper in awe, gradually working my tongue along his length again.

"Take my balls in your other hand and roll them gently. Yes, like that," he groans. "Now, continue the slow glide with your fist, but I want you to suckle the head with your mouth."

Shit. He doesn't need to tell me twice. I soften my lips, stretch them over the enormous head, and moan low as his addictive ocean scent fills my nostrils.

"Good girl. Perfect."

When his fingers fist in my mane, I nearly combust at the sting on my scalp. Sebastian begins thrusting deeper, and I greedily devour him.

"You like that, Red? Sucking my cock?"

I moan my response. Holy shit. The dirty talk spikes my heart rate. Every word flares through my core. And the rougher he fists my hair, the harsher his thrusts, the more I crave.

"I love fucking your hot little mouth. Is your wet pussy begging for me?"

I growl low, fixed to explode, and he hasn't touched me.

"Draw my balls between your lips. Yes. Perfect."

I continue pumping his shaft while sampling the delicacy below. The fact he's utterly devoid of hair down here makes me want to sprawl out on my stomach and feast on him for hours. Maybe even explore farther down.

What in holy hell has gotten into me? I crave to lick, bite, and suck every glorious inch of him, no matter how taboo or naughty. But is it? Vampires don't eat, and the blood they consume redistributes throughout their bodies as fuel. So, I could....

One second, I'm kneeling between his spread thighs, devouring him, the next I'm on my back, and Sebastian is over me straddling my shoulders, his bulbous head pressing against my lips once more.

I blink several times at the abrupt change before peering up his stomach and torso to gape into the near-feral gaze of the vampire. The ferocious beast is evident in his harsh breaths, glowing irises, and enormous fangs.

"Open up. I am going to fuck your mouth until I come down your throat."

Holy shitballs. Sebastian is scary and beautiful and sexy all at the same time.

I part my lips, and he slips inside, all the while pinning me with a sharp scrutiny. He grasps the bedpost with one hand and plants the other by my head.

The minute the shallow thrusts begin, I grip his thighs and hold on for dear life, scissoring my legs to alleviate the ache his dominance creates with each drive forward. My eyes water, but I relax my throat even further, yearning to observe him come apart.

It doesn't take long. When the big body stiffens, I reach around his hips, and clutch the base, while cradling the tight sac.

"Fuck! Alex!" He bellows before hot liquid gushes down my throat, and I eagerly swallow every last drop of his salty goodness.

Goddamn. That was extreme, carnal, sexual, and I crave to do it again, but he's already easing from my mouth and dropping to settle between my thighs.

The second my slick core contacts his still hardened length, my eyes nearly roll back in my skull, and I can't help grinding against his solid thickness.

Surprisingly, he doesn't stop me. Instead, he leans up slightly and palms a breast. His hand trembles as he peers at me with a focus I find a bit disconcerting. As I glory in the exquisite friction between my legs, the pleasure-pain of his fingers rolling and pinching my aching nipples; the unnaturally blue eyes gleam with some inner fire imprisoning me.

"What do you want from me, Sebastian?" I pant, grinding faster and harder, my nails digging into his muscular ass.

"Everything," he groans. I swallow at the primal aggression in his expression. "I want the beautiful light inside you. I crave to glutton myself on your rich blood while I fuck you senseless until you never forget who owns you. I covet to possess you, bend you to my will until you'll do anything I demand."

His words still my hips and my heart. Someone claiming that much of me, knowing every little nuance, is a threat. He could expose me, use me, and then hurt me in ways I have yet to imagine.

"You ask too much."

"I am not asking, Red. This is who I am."

Sebastian's offering me an escape, a now or never ultimatum. Either I submit totally and take a chance, or he will end things with him cradled between my thighs. When I hesitate, his eyes dim, and his expression shuts down. He is stone. Immovable. Emotionless. Stone.

Bastian's words disturb me down to my foundation. How can I permit this vampire authority over me? Yes, I get off on his dominance and so far, the foreplay has been downright spectacular. I imagine sex will be just as mind-blowing, and an experience I'll never forget, but he's asking, no, demanding, a part of my soul.

When he tenses to move away, I tighten my legs around his waist, not ready to let this creature go. My lungs cease inflating as I stare into the steely blue eyes of the one man who holds the power to destroy my heart.

Oh, God. I need Bastian like I need air, and it terrifies me. But I think deep down; it frightens him as well. He experiences this undeniable connection between us and is working to scare me away. Too bad. I'm composed of stronger shit than that.

"Tonight, Sebastian, I am yours, in any way you desire."

"Who are you?" He mumbles, his gaze drifting over my face before his lips lock onto mine with a frenzied urgency.

I relish his hunger, his passion, his claim to me. I realize now he wants, even needs, to own me. This revelation should scare me, but his clean ocean scent is damn familiar, both soothing and arousing, I let my worries go and submit.

The glide of his silky hardness against my slick folds has me gasping for breath, and when he lowers his lips to my neck, suckling my skin, I throw my head back and grip his waist harder, urging him to a swifter rhythm.

My skins on fire and the blood in my veins is pulsing so strong I sense each beat. My nails sink into his spine, and he growls, the sound deep and sensual. My muscles respond by pulling tight, an eruption on the verge.

"Fuck," I wail, my eyes unable to remain open at the exquisite, erotic sensations this man draws from me. Each thrust hits my clitoris, causing the little bundle of nerves to tingle, and tighten.

Bastian leans away somewhat, gently inserts two fingers, and my core convulses—shattering like glass. No checking it even if he ordered.

"That's it, baby," he pants in my ear. "Come for me."

When a third digit nudges lower, demanding entrance, I let go of my reservations and relax, allowing his finger, coated with my juices, to slip inside.

I nearly pull away at the extreme stretching, in my core and below, but somehow, the pleasure-pain of his gentle thrusts, the splendid weight of his body between my thighs, and his rigid cock tapping my clit catapults me over the edge once more with a startled scream.

Once the tremors ease and my breath evens out, I force my eyes open. "Now, Bastian. Please. I need you."

He hesitates, and I see the doubt enter his gaze. "Are you certain? Once your innocence is gone, there is no going back. You cannot even recall who you are, Red."

I reach up and frame his face. "It doesn't matter. I'd want you in this life or the next."

A deep exhale, and his expression softens before he gradually withdraws his fingers and positions the enormous cock at my entrance. I lift onto my elbows to watch the show, but he grasps my chin, pushing my head back onto the mattress, his stare direct.

Those talented fingers, which just pleasured me so thoroughly, bury into my hair before his hips drive forward enough my walls welcome the rounded head.

"You are fucking tight," he grounds out, his eyes squeezed shut.

He thrusts a little deeper, and his erection spreads the inner walls wide, the nerve endings sparking like fireworks. I tense at the discomfort.

"Relax, Red," he murmurs before his lips claim mine in a searing kiss.

Desire liquefies my tendons, and a moan, filled with longing rumbles between us. I attempt to undulate my hips, to take him deeper, but the firm grip on my waist holds me immobile.

"Do not move." The warning in his tone is enough to suspend me in place and wet my opening around the bulbous head.

Another shallow thrust and he inches further, hitting the thin barrier. We both freeze. Our gazes lock for a split second, his filled with wonder and regret before he drives his hips forward.

The burst of pain leaves me gasping and clinging to his shoulders. Holy shit. He's ripping me in two. Wait. I can't do this. It's too much.

"The suffering is over, little one." His anxiety at hurting me settles me somewhat, as do the kisses he rains over my face. The pain slowly ebbs as the vampire begins a gradual, steady glide back and forth. I revel in the completeness as he stretches me. So large. So perfect.

"Jesus. What are you doing to me?" His bewildered tone has me peering up into the grandeur of his gaze.

Sharp, deadly fangs descend past his lips, and I lift my hips to match him thrust for thrust. Something deep in my brain screams for them entombed in my neck once more. I swing my head to the side, exposing my vein to the beast thrusting between my legs with wild abandon.

When soft licks graze my collarbone, I keen low. A spiraling fire escalates inside my core. Muscles never touched convulse around his driving thickness.

"Please, Bastian." I have no inkling what I'm begging for, his bite, or his permission to come, but I am coherent enough to recognize that, at this moment, Sebastian is setting a standard I will judge every man by in my life. None will ever measure up to my scarred and broken vampire.

"Come my sweet, fiery valkyrie, shatter around my cock."

His words splinter my meager resistance, and my muscles clamp down as my world bursts into a thousand bundles of light, each overflowing with ecstasy.

"Bastian!" I shout, my spine arching as intense pleasure skyrockets through every nerve ending. He thrusts harder, driving my hips into the mattress, and all I can do is hold on to this magnificent male as he sends me careening over the precipice once more.

"Fuck." His body tenses before he plunges deep, and hot liquid spears through my core, warming me from the inside.

Holy shit. I lost my virginity to a vampire.

Chapter 24

Sebastian

"When can you be here, Darath?" I growl into the phone, pacing under the covered patio outside. A cool night breeze, with a hint of vanilla, swirls around my bare chest, and I grit my teeth against the urge to trace to my bed where the petite redhead slumbers.

I am still in awe of the gift she bestowed, and my heart skips a beat, knowing I am the sole male who has ever been inside her delicious tightness. I huff a breath, marveling at her responses once more.

She recognized just what to say to halt my attempt to end things. Willingly granted me all control at the precise moment I felt trapped in a corner.

And the way her skin came alive under my touch, her throaty moans, and her sweet pleading for more, drove me insane. Everything about Alexandria Svaldana intrigues and captivates me.

Through every gasp, every stroke, I cautioned myself. She was not my submissive. This was her first time. Even though Alex possesses a genuine inclination toward it, she is ignorant in the ways of BDSM. For some odd reason, a part of me longs to keep her oblivious. Not that I wouldn't kill to enjoy her scrumptious body in one of my playrooms. The picture of her blindfolded, tied, and gagged has my cock tenting my sweatpants.

I refuse to undertake anything remotely that intense until she reclaims her memories and can decide for herself. It would only make matters worse when her past slams to the forefront. The last thing I want is for her to look at me with hurt and betrayal—anger I can handle.

Who am I kidding? I already violated my oath by taking her virginity before Darath fully restored her mind. Not just once, either. I plunged into her from behind. While on all fours in front of the fire with my hand clamped around her throat. Her body braced against the wall of the shower, her strong legs gripping my waist.

If she did not despise me before, the second she remembers, the fiery little warrior will aspire to drive a silver dagger through my heart. And I wouldn't blame her.

In all my centuries, I have never craved for the difficulties of a relationship, a true mate. That was my brother's thing, not mine. Sex, for me, was always about complete control—dominance over the female's responses and my own. It gratifies me to bring pleasure to females through pain. In a contained environment. No raging hormones. No lovey, do anything for you type of nonsense—no lifetime promises.

Alex is the type of female who will demand commitment. Love. The eternal bond. The prospect sends panic searing through my veins and my erection deflating. I do not possess the capacity to love or trust. Those emotions died long ago.

My world is all discipline, from my obligations as commander, to my sexual propensities. Nothing will change that. Not even my one true mate.

Dawn approaches, and it is time for Alexandria to remember who she is and where she belongs because it is not by my side. She stated she was okay with the whole one-night stand, no commitment deal, but since I have consumed her blood, I perceive her desire for more.

"I am not your 'Beck and Call' demon, Mr. Moretti. The Realm will not run itself," the red-eyed bastard informs me before carrying on a muffled conversation in the background.

"Just give me a timeframe, Darath. We are in this quandary because of you, so I would appreciate it if you could expedite the resolution to our little problem." The demon king needs to get his ass here ASAP. The sooner Alex starts hating me, the better.

"Most males would postpone the inevitable showdown and relish the little vixen. I would," he all but purrs and my hackles rise. The seven-foot, crimson-eyed spawn of the devil beds anyone who tickles his fancy. Male or female. After two millennia on this earth, I suppose you would do anything to keep the boredom at bay. "You realize when her memories return, she will most likely kill you?"

I freeze mid-step. Darath has been inside Alexandria's mind. He knows better than anybody the extent of her angst with my kind and the reason for it. "You learned why she hates vampires?"

"Yes," he jeers. "But not vampires as a whole. Her hostility is solely for you, my friend."

What the hell?

"How could she possibly hate me so profoundly? She does not even know me."

"You will find out." He speaks to someone, and I clench my fist to hold my temper in check.

Why would Alex loathe me specifically? The first time I cast eyes on her was the night at Nicole's cottage several months ago when the mating bond blindsided me like a baseball bat to the temple.

Looking back on that night, I remember tears spilled down her pale cheeks, upset by something Nicole said to her before I arrived. But the second those glittering blue eyes settled on mine; they hardened with malice.

Why? My interaction with the Valkyrie Regency over the centuries was nominal. Skirmishes here and there. One major battle nearly three hundred years ago, which had nothing to do with Alex, she was not even born.

An image of Queen Arra during the battle flashes through my vision. The little valkyrie fought fearlessly, with quick, stealthy movements inherent to her kind, but we never crossed swords.

"It is almost dawn there. We will tackle the memory recovery your time tonight. Say 10:00 pm. Since I have never been to your villa, meet me at the entrance to *Torre del Diavolo*."

I scoff. "You wish to meet at The Tower of the Devil? How appropriate."

"Who do you think the legend is about, Commander?" He laughs before ending the call.

I shake my head, recalling how ancient the eerily handsome demon is. According to the myth, the devil himself built the grand tower: its proprietor at the time went on a lengthy journey, and when he returned, it astonished him to discover his tower to be much taller; and was convinced it was the work of the devil. Maybe it was.

I exhale and dial Nicole.

"Please tell me Alex's memories have returned, and she is safe at home."

No, 'hey, how is it going? Heard you encountered your mom. Are you alright?' Nope. Not from my queen. But her abrupt nature is precisely what I need.

"Afraid not. Darath is otherwise engaged until tonight."

"Son of a bitch. Arra is breathing down my neck, and I'm 'bout ready to bite her."

"I apologize, my lady. But I gleaned some disturbing news from the demon."

"Those are comments you don't want to hear. Wait, let me put you on speaker so I don't have to repeat it to Mr. Broody."

Well, it seems they have not worked out their issues yet.

"Brother," Logan's deep rumble over the line instantly comforts me. "Are you alright?"

Even though Logan is a century older than me, and was out of the dwelling and a king's Guardian by the time I was born, he has always been the closest thing to a friend I have ever experienced. We fought wars together, fucked women together, and traveled around the world. I could not imagine my existence without my brother by my side. There is not much we do not know about one another.

"No. King Darath informed me Alex's contempt for vampires centers on me."

"What?" Nicole chimes. "Why?"

"No clue. I was hoping you might enlighten me, brother."

When Logan doesn't immediately answer, my muscles tighten, and my calm evaporates.

"Oh, yeah. He knows something," Nicki murmurs. No doubt sensing some emotion from her mate.

"Sebastian, if it is what I suspect, when her memories return, I recommend you trace home and let Darath take her to her mother."

"What the fuck did I do to her?" This is asinine. These last two days are the most contact I have experienced with the valkyrie. Ever.

"You killed her father."

Chapter 25

Alexandria

The sound of my bare feet slapping the cobble street bounces off the dark, abandoned buildings. Each breath sends fire lancing through my ribs, but I push harder. I need to reach him before it's too late. Cool wind flares every cut and bruise to life, and my blood-soaked jeans slow my pace. The tattered remains of my shirt flap with each pump of my arms, and I grip the hilt of my sword tighter.

Bolts of lightning streak across the star-filled sky. My lightning. Proof of the turmoil boiling inside. Fear. Rage. Desperation. I stumble when a rock slices open my heel, but I push aside the pain and dig deep for added strength.

Skidding around a corner, I stop dead at the carnage before me. "Oh God," I mumble in horror, my hand clamped over my mouth to keep down the vomit threatening. Severed limbs scatter the filthy alley. They appear to dance in the strobing flashes from the sky.

"Please be alive. Please be alive," I chant, making my way through the bloodbath. Dark congealed blood oozes between my toes with each step. I gag against the putrid odor of copper, trash, and decay.

A moan in the far corner snags my attention, and I sprint over severed heads, both valkyrie, berserker, and vampire.

There. Under the butchered torso of a nightwalker, my father's hazel, pain-filled gaze pierces my heart.

"Daddy!" I toss the muscled corpse off my dad and drop to my knees, clutching his outstretched hand. Tears stream down my cheeks as I view his wounds. They crushed his sternum. Things I can't think about hang from the gaping wound in his stomach.

It takes me a second to comprehend my father is mumbling. "Don't talk, Daddy. Save your energy." For what I'm not sure. My mother is miles away. No backup is coming.

He grips my shoulder with surprising strength, pulling me closer. I position my ear above his quivering lips and try to make sense of his frantic whispering.

"Avenge... me... daughter." The sound is a wet gurgle, but I hear it loud and clear.

"Who, Daddy? Who did this?"

"F... vam.... Vampire. Fallen... Moretti... kill..."

"Daddy!" I shake him, frantic for him to stay with me. "No!"

"Alex."

Horror and despair crush my spirit as the beautiful eyes glaze over in death. "Please don't die, Daddy. Come back."

"Alexandria." The sharp, rough voice calling my name from the darkened corner penetrates the anguish clouding my brain. I glance up and stare wide-eyed as Sebastian Moretti emerges from the blackness, his hand outstretched, beckoning me. "Come to me."

Rage lights my skin on fire. The silver glow from my irises dissipates the eerie shadows. On wobbly legs, I rise and stumble over mutilated bodies to advance on the vampire.

"You killed my father." I don't even recognize the tormented, guttural voice as my grip tightens on the sword still clutched in my fist.

"No," he whispers, regret softening his gaze. "Trust me, Alex."

"Liar!" I scream and lunge for the beautiful creature of the night. He doesn't block or evade, and it's the acceptance in his stare that frightens me more than my blade plunging into his heart.

His body crumbles at my feet, and I wait for the elation at avenging my father to course through me. But as I stare into the vacant sapphire gaze of my enemy, devastation slams through my mind, buckling my knees.

"What have I done?" Despair crushes my chest. I murdered my mate. The vibrant beast who lights my nerves on fire, who not only claims my soul, but soothes my spirit.

"No. No. No." With trembling hands, I lift Sebastian's head into my lap, curling my body around his. Thick, crimson curls shroud us as I rain kisses saturated with tears over his forehead, closing the lids before pressing my lips to his one last time. "I'm sorry, Bastian. I'm so sorry."

"Alexandria!"

I jerk upright, and I stare in horror at the image of my father standing above me, hurt, anger, and betrayal etched in his face. His finger points at me in accusation, but it's the intestines spilling from his gut that's my undoing. I throw my head back, offering my warrior scream to the night.

"Alex!"

I ignore the low, urgent command, screaming my angst and heartbreak to the gods at my failure. Rough hands grasp my shoulders, shaking me.

"Red. Wake up."

Bastian's worried expression comes into focus as the nightmare dissipates. He's bare-chested and perched next to me on the edge of the bed. His bed. At the villa.

Oh, thank God! It was only a nightmare. But even as the last visage of the alley massacre fades to the background, I can't help but sense this was a foreboding of things to come. Or at the very least, a warning.

Gentle fingers brush my sweat-slicked curls from my cheeks. "It was a dream, Red." His reassurances bring fresh tears to my eyes.

Just a dream? I killed him, thinking he murdered my father. I dart out from under the covers, not caring I'm butt-ass naked, and crawl into his lap, gripping his broad shoulders. I bury my nose in his neck and let go. Tears stream fast and furious down my cheeks and over his chest, darkening the Moretti tattoo.

Sebastian hesitates for a moment like he's not sure what to do with the bawling, naked woman clinging to him with desperation. The second his tender embrace envelops me, the tense knot between my shoulders loosens.

Warmth seeps into my bones, and a sense of sheltered peace invades my system. He feels right in ways my lost memory and the lingering terror of my nightmare dull in comparison. But he holds me a little too tight as if he's certain something will rip me from him. After the dream, I fear the same.

"Hush, baby. You are safe. Nothing can hurt you here," Sebastian murmurs into my hair, stroking my bare back and rocking me side to side.

"It felt real," I hiccup, my sobs lessening as the horrible visions fade, replaced by warmth and arousal at Bastian's soothing caresses.

You'd think after being fucked six ways to Sunday for hours on end; the lust would've cooled somewhat. Nope. I grip him tighter, diving my fingers into the short, thick strands at his neck, and press my lips against his jugular, enjoying the feel of each pulse beneath my mouth.

My tongue darts along the heated flesh, and the powerful arms tighten. "Make me forget, Bastian," I whisper in his ear. "Take control. Let me lose myself in your world, your every command. If tying me up and whipping or flogging me pleases you, then I submit once more before reality rips our little piece of heaven apart."

"Christ, Red. I crave that more than you can imagine." The grip on my biceps is painful as he sets me away from him on the bed. The loss of his heat has a shiver chasing up my spine. "You do not even understand who you are. Last night was a mistake, and I assume sole responsibility. I took advantage of you. I will not do so again. Especially not in such a way." He pushes off the mattress and strides to the fireplace. His knuckles whiten as he grips the mantle, staring into the flames.

Saliva pools in my mouth at his powerful body outlined in the flickering glow. The sweatpants hang low on his hips, showcasing the sculpted abs arrowing down with the perfect muscled V disappearing below the waistband.

"The demon king, Darath, will arrive tonight, and attempt to restore your memories. Until then, I think it would be best if I slept in the other room." He turns, pinning me with a hardened blue stare. "By tonight, you will hate me with every fiber of your being, and lament your stolen purity..."

Sebastian goes on as if each word isn't blasting apart what is left of my heart. He's eager to walk away. I see it in the tense muscles and tight jaw. Relieved would be a more appropriate analogy. And even though his words devastate me, I refuse to let it show how much.

"You're right," I interrupt, gathering the sheet around my nakedness. "You should leave. Thank you for saving me from myself. Go sleep like the dead somewhere else."

His jaw clenches, irritated at my command. Well, fuck him. He's correct about me subjugating myself to his dark desires, to him. It was a horrible idea. He opens his mouth as if to say something, but clamps it shut. With a tight nod, he disappears.

My lips tremble with suppressed emotion, and I squeeze my eyelids shut, clutching the sheet to maintain my composure, to stop myself from racing after him. I am not that pathetic.

Last night wasn't a mistake. It was incredible. But I understand sex between a Dom and his subs isn't like anything we did. Yes, it was rough and raw, intense, and erotic, but there was emotion involved. Passion soared between us, igniting in every glance, every touch.

I did a little research while he assumed I was sleeping, and the things I discovered intrigued, heated my face, and appalled me.

Might as well throw in scared the bejesus out of me. But, for Sebastian, I'd willingly dip my toes in the sadist/masochist arena.

Several—okay a plethora—of hard limits exist for me, but I assumed we could work it out. Come to a compromise to satisfy us both. I realize now; those fantasies were just that, fantasies. With the return of my memories, any chance we obtained together is about as likely as pigs flying out my ass and singing dixie.

After several minutes of meditative breathing, I leap from the bed and head for the shower. The vampire may have to sleep during the day, but I do not. I need to get out of this house and away from his alluring scent.

It's time this girl did some much-needed soul searching. Italian spa here I come.

Chapter 26

Alexandria

It was a piece of cake to escape the Villa during the day. No one leaped out from behind a tree to stop me. Although when I asked the housekeeper Helga for a map of the city, she reluctantly handed it over with a warning about girls wandering around alone, and how the master wouldn't like it.

The Master. I cringe every time someone says that. It's so freaking medieval. But then again, Sebastian was born in the 1500s. Maybe it reminds him of his past. Keeps him grounded.

Yeah, and chocolate-covered almonds will rain down from the sky any second. No, it's a controlling, dominant attitude. Mr. Moretti gets off on the peasants bowing to his commands and hailing him master.

Well, he can count me out. That word will never escape my lips. No way. No how. Does he expect his submissive of the week to call him Master too, or is it simply, Sir?

A vision of him with another woman sends pain lancing through my chest, and rage clouds my vision. 'The shithead is mine!' my mind shrieks.

No, he's not.

The vampire made it quite clear he abhors commitment, and I refuse to be another sub he casts away when he grows bored. I have more self-respect than that. More pride. Although, I could easily imagine carrying on a sexual Dom/sub relationship with the erotic brute. But no way will a man ever dictate to me what I can and cannot do outside the bedroom. And I require some control during sex from time to time. I'd love to have the vampire submit to me, follow my directions.

A picture of Sebastian kneeling between my bare thighs, his hands tied behind his back as he laps at my core has me pressing my legs together. Holy shit, that's hot. But I realize now, Bas will never permit me such a level of control over him. Commitment takes trust, and much more. Like him letting go of the demons in his past.

Why are my thoughts progressing down this track, anyway? The vampire and I have no future after tonight.

Something in my heart cracks. In a few hours, it'll be over, and a part of me would readily give up my former existence to be with him. Yeah, the stupid, giddy in love part.

Even with all the turmoil swirling through my brain, I've quite enjoyed my outing today. The map Helga gave me listed the history along the path the pilgrims traveled. The Francigena road sent a thrill straight through my bones as I imagined trekking alongside them centuries ago, the same sun warming their shoulders, the aroma of earth and grapes filling their nostrils.

San Gimignano is a beautiful town. Rowena and I meandered through a few stores, and I relished the ambiance of the place at night, but during the daytime, many more shops propped their doors open in invitation. Along the main street of Porta San Giovanni, bars, souvenir shops, and restaurants line both sides.

I would define San Gimignano as a medieval Manhattan because of all the massive towers dominating the skyline. When the town was in its heyday, over seventy-two towers, built by the wealthy families as a symbol of their magnificence and power, spanned the horizon. Now only thirteen remain.

A little lethargic from vigorous sex, lack of sleep, hours of shopping, an excellent massage, and mani-pedi, I decide to relax at the

Locanda di Sant'Agostino restaurant for sustenance and alcohol before starting the hike back to the Villa. A shopkeeper insisted this was the place to dine, and he couldn't have been more correct.

The atmosphere is serene and tranquil, and even though a cool breeze rustles through the plaza, I opt to sit outside and savor the view of the historic well and the Sant'Agostino church. My skinny jeans, low-heeled boots, and thick sweater were a wise choice.

The waitress wanders over and hands me the menu with a polite smile. My mouth waters and my stomach grumbles with hunger. When was the last time I ate?

"Tu devi essere affamato," the tall, slim brunette with sparkling green eyes exclaims with a laugh.

"Yes," I grin. "I'm starving."

I order the big bruschetta at her recommendation, a healthy pour of a super Tuscan red, and even place a to-go dessert order of Crème brûlée. After tonight, I doubt I will ever come back to this town—the reminders of what could have been too painful to relive.

An hour later, the beautiful oranges and reds of the sunset keep me entranced, and I'm captivated by the old-world flavor of this place as lights flicker to life around the center in the waning light. With a full belly, and the pleasant buzz from the wine dulling my thoughts, it's a miracle my languid muscles don't melt down the chair to pool on the ground.

It would probably be a safe idea to head out before it grows too dark, and Sebastian wakes to find me gone. I'm sure Helga will inform him where I went, but I don't wish to encounter an enraged vampire on my last night in Italy.

"Alexandria Svaldana?"

The fine hairs on the nape of my neck rise at the rich voice. The rasp grates along my nerves, but I swing my head to gape at the beauty of the behemoth circling my table. This man has half a foot on

Sebastian. Gorgeous dark brown hair tumbles in waves to his broad chest, but it's the ruby irises that captivate my awareness.

Are those contacts?

"Does your mate know you are out here alone?" The giant asks, and I glance around at the other patrons, noticing all eyes fastened on the sexy goliath dressed in a black three-piece Armani suit.

You can put this man in a suit, but he'll never be tamed. He's got this otherworldly vibe going on, and those eyes draw you in, like a fat kid to a candy factory.

"Who are you?" I ask with a frown when he occupies the opposite seat.

"Your mate summoned me to recover your wayward memories."

Ah. So, this is King Darath, the demon, and the reason I have no past. "You mean the ones you stole from me," I accuse, staring him down.

He chuckles, easing back in the iron chair. "Your fiery reputation precedes you valkyrie. I assure you; it was for a good cause at the time." He signals for the waitress and orders a bottle of their finest Super Tuscan.

What the hell? No remorse or guilt of any kind from this creature for stealing my life? "The cause better have been saving the world because that's the only excuse good enough to justify what you did to me."

"Actually, it was to avenge the death of my mate and daughter."

His quiet response stuns me, reminding me of my nightmare. Avenging a loved one is something I understand.

"Okay, two excuses then." I amend softly, and he tips his head, studying me like a bug under a microscope.

"Do you recall my original command?" The irises brighten, making mine water.

Buried deep, a muffled voice shrieks to glance away, but my eyes seem attached to the scarlet depths.

"What the fuck do you think you are doing, Darath?"

Sebastian's angry rumble from behind me breaks whatever spell the devil was attempting to cast, and I jump from my seat, back-peddling into the square away from these two potent beings.

"Easy, Commander," the demon coos before swallowing a gulp of the deep ruby wine the waitress practically dropped in his lap before beelining it inside. "I was just testing the waters, seeking to establish what barriers she has constructed."

"Out in the fucking open?"

I can't help but admire the furious vampire dressed in leather once more. The long, black duster appears heavy. I'd bet his various weapons weigh down every pocket.

"Do not blame me for your lack of discipline over your mate, Moretti. I was walking innocently through the area when I spotted her sitting all alone."

Oh, I could smack the evil grin off his smug face as Bastian's ice-cold stare swivels to mine. The demon king said exactly the right thing to shift the vampire's wrath in my direction.

"Sit down." The quiet demand lifts my chin.

"I'd rather not."

"I was not asking, Red. Sit and finish your wine, unless you would enjoy the sting of my palm on your backside once more."

Heat infuses my face as the seven-foot fucker chuckles.

"Who in the holy hell do you think you are?" I grate out between clenched teeth—my resentment and humiliation overriding common sense. The less, in your face, out in the open option, would have been to clamp my mouth shut and sit down. But I will not tolerate him demeaning me in public.

"Would you like to find out?"

Okay, running from a vampire isn't feasible, but he might be less prone to create a scene in front of all these wide-eyed tourists watching the show.

"You dare lay a hand on me, and I'll shriek bloody murder. And we both know my scream is powerful enough to signal the authorities and shatter every window in this square."

Yeah, put that in your pipe and smoke it, douchebag.

"No need for theatrics, young valkyrie," the demon says with a cheeky grin before ascending to his imposing height. He swigs the remainder of the wine, throws a couple hundred on the table, before capturing the bottle. "As much as I would enjoy watching this showdown, or indeed taking part, I have several matters to attend before our little rendezvous later tonight." Unaffected by the angst flowing between Bastian and me, he saunters away.

Livid sapphires never veer from mine. But it's more than anger sparking the air. Sexual tension builds like a ticking time bomb waiting to detonate.

I start to mouth off again, the crowd around us bolstering my courage when something odd happens. A loud hissing fills my ears, red curls swirl across my face in slow motion, and every muscle from the neck down locks tight in some sort of stasis.

I scan the square, and it appears as if time stood still. The people milling the area are frozen mid-stride, mid-conversation. Everything, the birds flitting to and fro, the steam rising off plates heaped with pasta, has ceased.

I peer at Sebastian several feet in front of me, hoping it's him who froze time somehow, but his muscular frame is as stationary as mine. Irises blaze with violence and... uncertainty.

And that's when I hear it, the soft whooshing of wind through wings directly behind me. Sebastian's eyes widen in fear, and if my lower body weren't arrested in some limbo, I'd have pissed my pants because what in holy hell would produce such a reaction in the powerful vampire?

'*Alexandria*,' Bastian's rich baritone penetrates my mind, and I inhale against the breach. '*Whatever transpires, I will find you. Do not resist. Blink if you understand.*'

I flutter my lashes several times when what I prefer to do is peek over my shoulder and see what's behind me. Better to confront the unknown head-on, then imagine the worst.

The vice constricting my muscles vanishes with an abruptness that causes me to stumble, nearly falling to my knees. A cursory glimpse around confirms I'm the only individual able to move. A rough, frantic rumble vibrates from Sebastian's throat, the widened sapphires pinned over my shoulder.

"Alexandria Svaldana, turn and face your doom."

While the voice is melodious, the words send panic through my brain. With one final peek at Bastian's crazed stare, I slowly pivot.

Sweet Mary, Mother.

Three beings of extraordinary beauty wrapped in long, dark robes interwoven with silver stand a mere fifty feet away. From their backs, incredible black wings extend twelve feet in either direction. The dark obsidian feathers fuse with the night sky. Shiny silver swords hang from their hips and gleam with exquisite light.

"We are the Watchers, the wardens of the immortal world. Our mission is to preserve the balance of power and nature. Your mating is an abomination and will not be tolerated." They speak as one, but their mouths never move.

The heavy rumble behind me intensifies, and I clench my fists to keep from running to Bastian. He can't help me now. I'm on my own.

"Um, we're not mated," I argue and snort when I realize I'm negotiating with angels.

"We know all. You will never be permitted to procreate, Alexandria Svaldana. Your mere existence should not be. Come with us now or forfeit the vampire's life."

Hell no! They touch him, and I swear I'll go all Sarah Connor on their asses.

"Not great choices there, guys."

What the fuck does he mean I can't procreate? Who the hell gets to decide that?

"We do." They boom.

Oh shit. They can read my mind?

The middle one with long golden hair and penetrating black eyes steps forward. "You have chosen."

"No! Wait. I... I didn't choose." I declare in alarm, inching away.

"You chose his life over your own. Make your peace with God, child. Your hour is at hand."

Chapter 27

Alexandria

Oh, shit. This is it. My destiny is to perish at the hands of angels. Wait. Does that mean I'm going to heaven?

"Halt, brothers," suggests a fourth voice from behind me, and I whirl to confront the new threat.

What the fuck? I gape in bewilderment as Ezekiel Sorath, my dance instructor, navigates through the frozen bodies to face off with the terrifying winged angels of death.

"What the hell are you doing here, Ezekiel? Stay back," I whisper frantically, trying to grasp at his sweater to drag him away.

"Alexandria was my task, Kalaziel, not yours."

His task? Fucking, eh. He lied to me. All this time, he was some dark angel assigned to monitor me? Oh, he is so getting an earful when this is over. How did I lose complete control over my existence?

"You failed to protect her from the vampire. She is no longer untouched."

Heat spreads over my cheeks when E shoots me an ominous stare. How the hell do they know that? And why should my sex life be of any interest to these celestial beings?

I narrow my eyes at his bitter glare. Ezekiel never hinted he wanted more, no matter how many times I sought to encourage advancement from him.

"Regrettable, but they remain unmated." E steps between me and the trio calling for my death. "Allow me to reveal the past. With such knowledge, the inclination to mate with the vampire Moretti will terminate."

"It is forbidden to restore what was absorbed by the demon," the big blond, Kalaziel answers coolly. Apparently, he's the spokesperson for the three. "Your sentiments for the valkyrie cloud your judgment, brother."

Does E have feelings for me? News to this girl.

I peek over my shoulder at Bastian, but his attention is laser-focused on Ezekiel. *'Ease behind me, Alex. Help is coming.'*

It's so bizarre the way he speaks into my mind. I wonder if I can respond. *'Won't they notice?'* When he doesn't even blink, I want to growl in frustration. Must be a vampire only thing.

Never taking my focus from the winged creatures arguing with E, I shuffle backward several steps, then halt, expecting them to draw their swords and skewer me like a shish kabob. When no eyes swivel my direction, I ease backward even further until I'm level with Bas.

'Good girl.'

Questions by the dozen spiral through my brain, but since I don't wish to attract attention, I keep my lips sealed and wait. The deflowerer of my virginity is delusional if he thinks I'll take off like some coward. If Sebastian plans to engage, then by God, I will fight by his side. No way he gets all the fun.

The second the deadly trio's gaze pivots to mine, several events develop at once. Bas growls in my brain to run at the same moment Ezekiel unfurls massive black wings, blocking my view of the Watchers. Within seconds our group is hemmed in by dozens of powerful creatures dressed identically to Sebastian with huge broadswords clutched in their fists or strapped to their backs.

I recognize Bastian's brother, Logan, front and center, but the woman next to him draws my awareness. She is stunning. Thick, dark auburn hair tumbles in loose waves to her shoulders, and hardened gun-metal irises glow with malevolent intent.

She's decked out in leather pants hugging shapely hips, with deadly looking guns strapped to each thigh, and a smaller sword hilt juts up over one shoulder. But it's the words etched on the long-sleeved red shirt that almost has me laughing out loud.

'*I'm allergic to stupidity. I break out in sarcasm.*'

I would so wear that.

"For your own safety, step away from the valkyrie," the woman announces with an evil grin and a wink in my direction.

The husky tone misfires something in my brain. I recognize this chick. She's the source of all my misery these past few months. It was never Sebastian I was searching for; it was her.

A tremendous compulsion to end her life invades my head, and I stoop, slipping my fingers inside my boot to retrieve a concealed dagger. Killing her would solve all my problems.

'*Alex, don't!*' Bastian yells telepathically, and the steely gray eyes of my target swivel my direction.

A well-placed throw straight into her heart should do the trick. The woman regards the blade in my raised hand with sorrow.

'*I am not your enemy, Alex,*' she whispers sadly inside my mind before her expression hardens. '*I'm here to save your ass. Stand the fuck down.*'

I hesitate a split second before sending the weapon soaring through the air.

"NO!" Right before the pointed tip penetrates her sternum, Logan's enormous frame steps in its path. It impales him in the gut with a soft oomph.

Oh shit! I stabbed Sebastian's brother.

The woman peers around the bulging bicep decorated with a dark tattoo identical to Bastian's, contemplating the hilt of the dagger protruding from his abdomen. She squints at him with a raised eyebrow. "I had that you know."

"Of that, I have no doubt, my love," he replies before jerking the knife from his flesh and tossing it aside. I watch in fascination as the wound seals in seconds.

Shit. I thought I healed fast.

The blond angel strides forward, addressing who I now realize is Sebastian's queen. "The Watchers have no conflict with the Vampire Nation, young ruler."

"Yeah, you kinda do." She steps next to Logan. "The Valkyrie Regency is under our protection, and since Alex is the future queen, we strongly object to you killing our ally."

"You have no sovereignty, Halfling. Only God determines our movements, and he ordered us to halt the mating between Alexandria and Sebastian by any measure."

"So, you're God's Angels?" she asks curiously as I slip my fingers into Bastian's coat pocket, searching for a weapon.

"We were once, but now we are fallen, tasked as wardens of the immortal race. We preserve the harmony of power and nature, safeguard humans to earn favor with God." He states it like it's no big deal—a simple errand that needs running.

"Oh, I see. You're like Lucifer. What did *you* do to get the boot out of heaven?"

I detect Bastian's stare boring into the top of my skull. '*Stop, Alex. Nicole is your best friend. You love her. This urge to kill is from the demon king's mind control.*'

Yada, yada yada. He's speaking, but it makes no sense. The only element predominant in my brain is ending the vampire queen.

"We chose the wrong side," the angel responds.

"You're determined to repeat your mistakes then because you're choosing the incorrect side now. I will not allow you to harm her."

"Vampires are no match for the power of the fallen, no matter your number."

What an arrogant dick.

"Oh. I'm sorry. Did I neglect to mention we brought friends?"

Movement in all directions has me pivoting in a circle. Several packs of wolves, lions, panthers, and tigers emerge from the shadows, navigating their way through the throngs of motionless tourists, and I forget the dagger in my palm.

What the...

'*Alex, stay close to me*,' Bastian urges.

"Why?" I hiss back. "You can't even move."

'*Then get to my brother, he will protect you.*'

"And who will cover your frozen ass?"

'*Goddamnit, Red, for once, do as I say.*'

The mental growl shakes me to my core. I twist away from the feral glow and watch in fascination as a magnificent, deadly version of an Alaskan Malamute saunters over to a tall, beautiful woman attired in leather with two large swords strapped to her back. A long black braid cascades over one shoulder, and the most stunning amber eyes peer down with devotion at the beast, her hand falling to settle on its neck.

And if that visual wasn't ridiculous enough, an enormous white wolf with striking blue irises takes a position on her other side, nudging her waist with its muzzle.

I've somehow died and been transported to Narnia. If the animals start talking, I'm so out of here.

"So, you see, Mr. Fallen Angel, if you proceed, the Watchers will upset the balance, and not in the immortal world's favor."

I gotta hand it to the vampire queen, even though every instinct I possess is screeching at me to kill her, she's handling the angels like a pro. But can the three beings—correction, four beings if I include my lying bastard of a dance instructor glaring daggers at me—really take out all these immortals?

"If God's will is to eliminate your resistance, you would not be standing here negotiating for your friend's life, youngling."

"Far be it for me to go against the big guy upstairs, although I do have a bone to pick with him on another matter." Her tone drops to a dangerous growl.

"You speak of the loss of your child."

Oh, man. Her kid died? Sucky. This vampire queen, Nicole, seems like someone I would totally hang out and drink with, so why am I bent on murdering her? Oh right, the demon. Why isn't he here, anyhow? Every other immortal in the world appears to be.

The queen's eyes harden, and her lip curls into a sneer. "Care to explain?"

"Your Oracle crossed the line when he brought you through the gates of purgatory."

"Whose decision was it to destroy my child? Yours or God's?"

The angel peers down his snout at the queen, a condescending grin lifting one corner of his mouth. Okay. I've suffered enough of this. I flip the dagger, raise my arm, and take aim on the big blond asshole. If I'm destined to die anyway, why not take a few down with me?

'*Alex, no!*'

Before the blade leaves my fingertips, the red-headed angel on the right raises his palm, and I'm suddenly flying backward, crashing spine first into the stone building of the restaurant. Agony shoots through my lumbar as I collapse on top of an iron table and chairs, snapping my forearm, *again*, before bouncing to the ground with a bone-jarring thud.

Holy fuck!

A mighty, ground-shaking roar penetrates the veil of pain hovering over my vision. In his expanding rage, Sebastian breaks the influence over his frame. Huge, menacing fangs drip with saliva as rumbling snarls emanate from his chest. The radiant blue glare lights up the whole square.

"I will fucking eviscerate you, Gadriel!" Bastian bellows before reaching into his duster and whipping out two small swords with a metal ring of sound. Blackness seeps along the edges. I shake my head to clear it, fearing for Bastian's life. Logan struggles to hold onto the queen.

Must get up, help him. I can't let the vampire die because of me. I gain my feet, swaying unsteadily, my vision a pinpoint of light.

"Bastian." My croaked plea snags the vampire's attention.

Everything tilts, and the ground races toward my face. Right before my cheek slams into the unforgiving pavers, strong brawny arms engulf my torso.

"Bas?"

"Yes, I am here."

"Don't you fucking die for me," I mumble before the sweet bliss of oblivion takes control.

Chapter 28

Sebastian

"You did the correct thing in backing down, brother," Logan reiterates as I pace outside the castle's medical room. The Oracle snatched the unconscious valkyrie from my arms the second we arrived and refused us entry. "It is forbidden to engage a Watcher. One swipe of their sword obliterates your soul. Our force tonight was merely for show."

As soon as I had turned my back on the Watchers to catch Alex, Icarus appeared. The puissant individuals stared each other down for several minutes before the angels, including the bastard Ezekiel, nodded, unfurled their wings, and fluttered off into the starlit sky.

It appears our blue tattooed Oracle has some clout with the Watchers.

I will never forget the impotence rushing through my immobile frame when Alexandria flung the dagger at Nicole. It would seem the mind control is still anchored in place. When I warned Nicki, I was taking Alex to the castle, she nodded, fixed to trace home with us despite the abiding threat. I scowled, even though my brain acknowledged her omnipotent abilities, I was torn between my duty to protect my queen and caring for the precious bundle in my arms.

My brother seized the choice from me when he stepped in front of his mate, threw her over his shoulder, and traced away.

"How are you keeping Nicole from teleporting here and kicking your ass?" I smirk, requiring a diversion. "Your female is the most powerful vampire in the world."

"Chained her to the bed at her old cottage." He shrugs, a devious smile lifting his lips.

"With what?"

"I arranged for Icarus to construct mystical shackles. You remember, the ones he claimed he designed for Dimitri but never produced. I cannot strong-arm my female anymore. I required them to protect her from her own stubborn ass."

"Jesus, Logan." I cannot help but admire my big brother, but I would not wish to be anywhere near these two when he eventually frees her.

"It was the sole means to keep her away from Alex for now. I will exhaust her sexually while shackled and hope it slows her down." His grin says it all.

"That is your plan?"

"You have a better solution?"

I open my mouth but shut it again at a loss. "When Nicole gets something in her head, nothing can sway her," I finally offer.

"Exactly." Logan chuckles, and it is the first occasion since losing the baby, the veil of grief lifts, and the dark humor seeps to the surface. "She vowed to serve up several of my body parts to the wolves." The grin broadens, and the emeralds sparkle.

"Well, good luck with that," I mutter and pivot on my heel, determined to get to my mate. Before I reach the door, Darath materializes in front of me.

"What are you doing here?"

"The Oracle summoned me." Carmine irises turn to Logan. "So did your woman, but I assumed it judicious to ignore her demands to trace to her bedchamber in someplace called Newport."

"You are not as dumb as you look, Jagorach," my sibling responds with a rough growl.

"I have my moments, Moretti."

The door behind him swings wide, and Icarus motions us all inside.

About damn time.

After everyone files in, I halt in the doorway; a vice cinched around my heart. Alex sits perched on the edge of the stainless-steel medical table, petite feet swinging above the floor. A black sling cradles her arm, and a purple bruise mars her pale cheek. She appears diminutive and fragile. Those vivacious Azul eyes seek mine, and the vice tightens.

"I see you're still alive," she says nonchalantly even as I observe the tension leaving her shoulders at my arrival.

"Yes, princess. Alive and well. How are you feeling?" I inquire from the doorway.

My inner vampire shouts to go to her, take the fiery hellion in my arms, rain kisses over her face before plunging my fangs into her neck to ensure everyone understands she belongs to me.

She eyes me curiously. "I've been better." At the small admission, I grip the rock to keep from tracing to her side. Every gaze in the room bores into me, but my concentration never falters from my mate.

"My lord, come in and close the door," Icarus demands. "We are about to begin."

Christ. No. I need more time.

"Allow Alex and me a minute, please." I shove away from the entrance, and everyone shuffles past. The soft click of the door is a portentous echo in the empty room. Now we are all alone, I am not certain what to say.

"I won't bite, Bas. You can come closer."

I perceive the smile in her tone, and it only ratchets up my anxiety. What in Christ is wrong with me? I am acting like a prepubescent immortal.

With a sharp inhale, I stride over to the table, clutch the edge on either side of her thighs, and lean down until my lips hover over hers. "Red, no matter what you might think of me in a few minutes, I wish for you to understand something." The gentle whisper of her panting breath against my chin makes my gums ache, and my cock hardens. "Whatever your perceptions about me, I will always be there for you, waiting, watching, keeping to the shadows. The second you need me; Nothing will stop me from protecting what is mine."

"Am I yours, Sebastian?" The irises flicker silver.

"For all eternity," I mumble, my gaze locked on her lush lips.

"If only that were true." When she eases back, I mark the sorrow in her expression. Feel it as my own.

She is right. I offered her nothing but a night of passion. I convinced myself it was because when her memories returned, so would the hate, but it was more than that. This is on me. I am the ruined one, incapable of providing a female love or commitment, only pleasure and pain.

"Alex, I am not worthy of you. It is beyond my capacity to offer you what you solicit, what you deserve. You will forever be my one true mate. The valkyrie I would sacrifice anything to keep... safe."

"You're wrong, Bastian. You *are* deserving of my love." She gently cups my cheek, but it's the tears glistening in the blue depths that is my undoing. "I just wish you could see what I see."

"Alex, in a few minutes, King Darath will attempt to restore your memories and clear away the mental command to kill Nicole. If he is successful, love will be the farthest thought from your mind regarding me." I tuck an unruly curl behind her ear. "No matter how extreme your hatred rages, do not shut me out. Let us make sense of it and discover a resolution."

The prospect of her turning away from me sends panic searing through my brain, even though some long-buried noble part understands it is the best course for Alex. I tap the fear down and step back.

"I must inform you of the alternative option if Darath fails."

"Okay." The little redhead eyes me warily.

"I can recover your memories." Her eyebrows lift. "It requires a mating."

"What is a mating, exactly?"

"Vampires are gifted one true mate in their entire existence. If he or she dies, the vampire is so lost, they soon lose the desire to live. Few overcome the despair. Valkyries, on the other hand, are intrinsically designed to acquire additional mates if need be throughout their lives." I take another stride back, putting some much-needed space between us. "You are my one true mate, Alexandria, and I am your fated one."

"Is that why I experienced an instant connection to you?"

"Yes. And I to you."

"So, it's a biological phenomenon? A physical link?" She frowns up at me, and I open my mouth to answer yes, precisely right, but it would be a half-truth, for I have grown to care for her, beyond the mating call. The notion shakes me to my foundation, penetrating years of barricades around my heart.

But what can I offer a princess? I am a soldier with dark needs and an even darker soul. I refuse to contaminate such perfect purity any further than I already have. For the first time since laying eyes on this splendid creature, I lie.

"Yes. Nothing more." At her wince, I crave to shove the words back down as if I never uttered them. But what is done is done and for the best. "If we were to complete the mating bond, which requires an exchange of blood during sex, we would be psychologically and physically tied to each other until death. But with such a connection,

I gain the ability to enthrall you and help rebuild your lost memories."

"What do you mean by psychologically and physically linked?"

"We will perceive each other's emotions, communicate telepathically from across the globe, and I can trace to your location, even if I have never been there."

"And that's forever or until one of us dies?"

"Correct." I drive my fingers through my hair in agitation. "Because of the enormity of the commitment, it needs to be your decision. I refuse to force you into a mating to reclaim your memories."

"Will I be able to sense if you are with someone else... or vice versa?" Alex stares at the stone floor, fidgeting with her sling.

"Yes." It is precisely what could drive me insane.

"Then let's hope the demon can fix me because I don't think I could endure that hell."

I swallow at the intensity of anger bubbling behind her irises and step close once more. "Alex. Let me set your mind at ease. I never have, nor will I ever, have an emotional partnership with another. My sexual interactions are pure control. You will perceive nothing from me. Emotion has no place in my BDSM world."

"Oh. I see."

"Do you?" I grasp her shoulders, mindful to keep away from her injury. "You are the epitome of emotion. You feel everything on a visceral level. Every spike in your heart rate, every elevation of desire, lust, love, and hate, I will experience as my own and discern the second you take another lover or fall in love."

"And will that bother you?" she questions softly, settling her good hand on the center of my chest, scalding the skin through my shirt.

"It will fucking eviscerate me." I plunge my fingers through the thick, silky mane of curls to clasp her neck, before devouring her sweet lips. All the fear, anxiety, and resentment at our situation flows into the kiss. I have wanted nothing in my life the way I crave this female.

Her soft moan escalates my feverish desire, and I step between her spread thighs. Every whisper of breath skitters along my nerves, lighting them on fire. Her little moans of excitement shoot straight to my cock. The metal zipper digs into my hardened length, and the pain shoots my heart rate into overdrive.

I need the sweet essence of her blood, the intoxicating taste of her sex on my lips, and her screams of ecstasy filling my ears as I pound deep into her tightness.

Jesus. A part of me hopes the mind-meld with Darath does not work, and Alex chooses to mate with me. And indeed, it would permit me one more chance to fuck her senseless, but the aftermath would result in the same outcome.

The sick, twisted side of my darkness contemplated finishing the mating bond and then claiming I could not return her memories, leaving her ignorant of her hate, and longing to be with me. But even I am not so cold.

I ease back. Our panting breaths mingle as I rest my forehead on hers. "I will miss you, little red. More than I dreamed possible."

"Bastian," she pleads, gripping a fistful of my sweater. "I don't want to lose you."

Her frantic plea constricts my lungs, and I clasp her face in both palms. "Our fate is inevitable, Alexandria. One day, you will become a great queen, and fall in love with a valiant berserker to rule by your side. But hear me and remember; I will always be here whenever you need me. This I vow."

To witness her anguish, with a glimmer of moisture on pale cheeks, tears at my blackened soul.

Chapter 29

Alexandria

"Concentrate on my voice, Alexandria. Block everything out," the gorgeous demon king with the peculiar red eyes insists for the second time.

I can't help it. My sole focus is on the sexy vampire brooding in the corner. Deep down, I don't want to remember. I want him to whisk me away from these strange people, chiefly the bizarre little Oracle dressed like Caesar, his body painted in blue symbols. Something about him sets my nerves on edge.

Bastian's comments earlier cut me to the core. What an empty existence the warrior lives. To never experience the joy and pain of an emotional connection with someone would be a living nightmare for me. And while I perceive his love for his brother and queen, and I suspect he cares for me beyond the bond, I picture him with one of his subs, his expression cold and detached while he whips, flogs, or fucks her. No doubt his administrations would bring her immense pleasure, as he allows himself to quietly orgasm, but a part of me breaks for the damaged man behind the stony mask.

"Dammit," Darath growls, and I jerk in response. "Sebastian, you need to leave the room. You are too much of a distraction."

Bastian's jaw clenches, but he nods and heads for the door. Panic surges through me. "Bastian," I plead, and I'm not sure for what. "Please." He hesitates in the doorway. The sapphire depths clouded with regret.

"I will be right outside. Open your mind, Alex. Let Darath aid you."

"I don't wish to," I confess quietly, and his gaze softens.

In two strides, he's by my side, and the demon takes a step backward. I can't help the tears threatening to spill over. I don't want to remember if it means I'll despise him. Without his touch, the sound of his firm voice commanding my body to his bidding, I will wither and die.

"Red, you have a family and friends who miss and care about you. A glorious life beyond this." Rough knuckles graze down my cheek.

It means nothing without you! I silently shriek, but nod my head like a good girl, knowing this is not what either of us wants.

Ignoring everyone else in the room, I grab Bastian's nape and bring his mouth to mine. I delve my tongue between his lips, confessing all my turbulent emotions in one kiss. I hope he recognizes how much he affects me, and no matter what I recall, I will always want him.

He responds, his tongue dueling with mine for a brief second before he abruptly breaks away. "You ready?" he asks roughly.

No! My valkyrie shrieks, but I surrender my grip and nod. "Yes."

Without a word, Sebastian pivots and strolls out the door. The wooden barrier between us crushes my heart, but I shift to the giant demon with a harsh sigh.

"Clear your mind. Allow me in." When the ruby irises glow bright, I let go of my fear and doubt and concentrate on his directives. "Visualize a barren room. Black walls, black floor. A vacant dark space with one exit. Nod when you are there."

The stygian void suffocates, soundless as death, but I order myself to envision the door. Agony infuses my bloodstream as every instinct shrieks that the single nondescript doorway is about to transform my world. I swallow the panic down and nod.

"Good. Now proceed to the door and open it. I will be waiting."

I falter. It's not just him on the other side; it's my life, everything I've forgotten. My family, my obligations, my friends. But to gain it all back, I must cast away the creature I covet the most. Sebastian. My inner warrior rebels, roaring, nothing is worth the loss.

"Open the door, Alex." The demon insists.

Even though my muscles strain to run in the opposite direction, I stare in dismay as my hand grasps the doorknob. A quick twist and the barrier opens inch by reluctant inch.

White light sears my eyeballs, and I squint against the glare. An enormous dark figure fills the entrance, and I step into the towering shadow to block the harsh illumination. Strong hands clasp my biceps in a painful grip, lifting me until my gaze is level with the spine-chilling crimson glow.

"Remember." The giant mutters before planting his lips against mine in a scorching kiss.

Fire lances through me, igniting a blazing inferno inside my brain. Image after image bombard my cranium, even as desire floods my core. Unaware of my injury, I reach up and clutch the broad, bulky shoulders with both hands before wrapping my legs around his waist. The deeper the kiss, the quicker the images flash behind my lids, and the sharper my lust rages.

My fingertips delve into the heavy mane of dark tresses as powerful arms lock me to his chest. Our tongues duel for control, and I grind my aching core against the solid planes of his abdomen. What is happening? I'm supposed to be remembering not getting down and dirty with the demon king.

When long fingers graze the hardened point of a nipple, I groan with pleasure, even as my past slams into my brain like a category five hurricane. The infinite love of my mother and father. My older brother, Tedri's relentless teasing and overbearing protectiveness. Teaching my little sister, Skadra, how to hold a bow. Nicole's cautious but cherished friendship. The joy of singing backup, and bartending at the LeLoo Blues Bar. The tremendous battle with Nicki's psycho of a dad, Dimitri. Her death and resurrection.

Every burst of my life stimulates the rapid lust flaring through me, but in the dim corner of the room, a soft cerulean glow diminishes my craving. This demon isn't my mate. And as yummy as he is, it's not him I truly desire.

I'm about to draw back, when Jagorach locks a giant hand behind my skull and intensifies the kiss with a mental order. "Remember, it all."

With an abrupt mental shove, I'm transported into the alley from my dream. Blood and death surround me. My father's hazel eyes plead with me to avenge him. As the life drains from his gaze, his clenched fist opens. I snatch the gold ring from his palm, glaring in disbelief at the Moretti emblem embossed on the surface. Rage billows.

Sebastian must be the vampire my father indicated with his last gasp. He killed him. Butchered him in cold blood and left him to die in that alley. My mother confirms the ring's owner when she arrives on the scene moments later. Her ear-splitting shriek at losing her husband discharged through the lightning-filled night sky. I pledged not to rest until Sebastian Moretti paid with his life.

With a sudden jerk, I leap from the demon's exotic embrace and sever the mind meld, only to realize I'm still perched on the edge of the metal table, and King Darath hasn't even touched me.

Icarus and Logan watch me intently, and I can't help but note the enormous erection straining the zipper of the king's trousers. Within seconds the fuzziness in my brain dissipates, supplanted by an uncontrollable fury. I tear the sling over my head, ignoring the sharp pain in my forearm, spring from the table, and stomp for the exit to murder the bastard with my bare hands if necessary. Before I make it two strides, a large muscular arm snatches me up by the waist.

"I cannot allow you to hurt my brother, Alex," Logan says, keeping my spine clamped to his chest.

The fucker took advantage of my memory loss and seduced me. I enjoyed sex with my father's killer, offered him the precious gift of my innocence. But that's not what infuriates me the most. It's the part of me raging against my own feelings for the murderer. Even now, with all my memories intact, I crave to be mistaken. I want to neglect my vow and seek my mate's embrace.

How fucked up is that?

Over the years, I carefully plotted my revenge, and when the protection detail for Nicole presented itself, I jumped at the chance to get close to Sebastian. The night he appeared at Nicole's; shock stunned me immobile. He was my fucking fated one. My inner valkyrie waged war against my desire to slit his throat.

And during the great battle, I grappled with my duty to protect Nicki and the compulsion to sneak up behind the Guardian and plunge my silver dagger through his heart.

The stupid bond links me to him, but Bastian betrayed me by twisting my feelings against me, forcing me to want him, care for him. Jesus, I fell in love with the bloodsucking bastard who slaughtered my father.

"Sebastian!" I struggle against the vampire's hold. "I will fucking kill you!"

Chapter 30

Sebastian

Why does losing her hurt so damn much? The screamed threat through the door was like a silver arrow through my rapidly beating heart.

According to Logan, the Valkyrie Regency imagines I killed Alex's father. But I knew Gadr. He was a good man, devoted to his family and people. He boasted a bit of a temper, but what berserker did not. They are notorious for their short fuses.

One fact is for certain; I need to cull this out, find out what Alex remembers, and work to convince her I did not slay her father.

But would it not be better for her to loathe me? It would expunge the constant yearning to be with me and could eclipse the mate connection altogether. The prospect shoots pain through my chest, even as the guilt at stealing her innocence when she did not know who she was, eats at my innards.

The realization she slept with her parent's murderer has to be tearing her up inside. My inner vampire rages against causing her anguish of any kind. I must determine who slew Gadr, for both our sakes.

'Brother, retrieve Nicole,' Logan mentally orders. *'The shackles will release with either your thumbprint or mine. Alexandria needs her. And I highly recommend you hightail it out of here. Go work over a sub and get your mind off this.'*

'We need to find out why the valkyries believe I killed Gadr.' Does he honestly imagine I could tuck my tail between my legs and hide-out in one of my clubs?

'And we will, but the priority is to calm Alex down enough we can talk to her. Right now, all she wants is to kill you."

Her valkyrie scream pierces my ears. My lids close. *'Do not hurt her, brother.'*

'I vow it. Now go get my female. Oh, and be careful. She is bound to be livid.'

"MY QUEEN, PLEASE SET me down, and I will release you." My jaw clenches, suspended against the ceiling by Nicki's telekinesis. Livid does not begin to express her state of mind.

"The fucking coward couldn't come and get me himself?" She hisses from the center of the bed, her back against the headboard. The chains rattle as she jerks forward.

"He is with Alex, my lady. She needs you."

The gunmetal glow dims somewhat. "She remembers?"

"Yes, but she..." I sigh with frustration. "Put me down, and I will explain everything."

Her eyes narrow, but she slowly lowers me to the carpet. The second her kinetic hold releases, I traipse around the bed and press my thumb to the shackles.

She hops off the mattress, yanking her boots off the floor. Apparently, Logan sought to make her as comfortable as possible before he left.

"Your brother is in serious shit, but first, inform me what's going on with Alex."

"He did this to protect you and Alexandria." At the glower, I raise my palms in surrender and immediately explain the situation while she slips on her boots and grabs her jacket from the chair.

Before we clasp hands and trace to the castle, I place my finger under her chin and lift her gaze to mine. "My lady, everything Logan has done since the moment he cast eyes on you was to protect and keep you safe. You are his life. Without you, my brother would cease to exist."

"As would I," she says with an exhale. "I didn't realize the death of our unborn child would affect me so strongly. You know me and emotions. Don't worry. We will get through this." She reaches up and pats my cheek. "You going soft in your old age, Sebastian?"

"Just a little wiser, my lady."

The second we materialize outside the medical room, blue fire locks on my eyes.

I am outraged to discover her chained to the wall. "What the fuck, Logan." I round on my sibling, knocking him into the stone, my forearm against his chest.

"Easy, brother." Logan clamps my shoulder. "It was the only means to control her without injuring her."

"You sure have a thing for chaining up women today," Nicole mutters.

"Yes." Fire sparks in my brother's green depths. "Too bad, I could not relish you bound to the bed."

"Sucks to be you," she retorts before freeing Alex's chains with the flick of her wrist, and I step away from my brother to confront my furious mate.

But instead of flying at me in a frenzy, she launches herself at Nicole, draping her arms around her shoulders and squeezing her tight.

"Whoa," Nicki exclaims softly before awkwardly hugging her friend, but I am pleased to observe the relieved smile on my queen.

"I'm sorry, Nicki. I hated not being here for you, but I had to stay away." She leans back, gazing up at her best friend. "You understand that, right?"

"I do now." Nicole steps to the side and pats Alex on the shoulder, her discomfort at the valkyrie's display of affection apparent. "But don't you ever fucking take on something like that alone again, or I will kick your ass. Feel me?"

Alex's glowing smile catches my breath. I would give anything for her to look at me in such a manner. "Yes, my lady." The petite princess twirls her arm in the air before bending at the waist in a dramatic bow.

"Ha-ha, very funny."

"We have much to catch up on, but first," fierce blue latches onto mine. "I need to kill your commander."

The hatred radiating from my little mate sends ice slithering through my veins, and my eyes narrow in anger—enough of this bullshit.

"You think you can take me, Red?" I advance a menacing step in her direction, but instead of backing down, she charges forward, and before I blink, her small fist connects with my jaw, whipping my head to the side. Shit. She delivers a hard punch for someone so tiny, and maybe I deserved it for bedding her before we revived her memories.

When she raises her fist to go at me again, I stoop low, catch her around her thighs and haul her over my shoulder. With one arm, I pin her legs down, eliminating her ability to kick anything vital and raise my other to smack her hard on her jean-clad butt.

"Enough!" I bark. She stills immediately, but I sense the fury coursing through her.

"Mayhap we should give them some privacy," my brother wisely suggests.

"Oh, come on. This is a popcorn moment," Nicole whines.

"Nicki." Alexandria raises up to scowl at her friend. "Don't you fucking leave me with him."

"Alex." The queen strides over to the prone valkyrie hanging off my shoulder. "You're a skilled fighter. You got this."

"Wait!" My mate makes a grab for Nicki as she and Logan disappear. "Dammit."

"Hold still." At my command, she tries to punch my kidney, but instead her fist strikes the hilt of a sword concealed under my coat.

"Ow! Son of a bitch."

I smack her twice more, vigorous enough for my palm to sting. "We need to talk, but not here."

When she realizes I intend to trace, she instinctively goes limp, clutching my duster as I teleport us to my suite on the third floor.

Instead of dropping her right away, I stride over to the massive fireplace flooding the room with warmth. The bitter cold of the Canadian winter seeps through the stone walls, and with no central heating, the servants keep the hearths lit round the clock.

"Are you going to behave if I let you down, or do I need to take you over my knee?" The hope of spanking her heart-shaped butt has my cock stiffening.

"You strike me again, and I will stab you through the heart." Her tone is stock full of menace, but the quickened pulse and the fragrant scent of her arousal say otherwise.

"We have to talk, but not until you have settled down. If a spanking accomplishes that, then so be it."

"Fine," she grates out between clenched teeth. "I'm fucking calm."

I cannot contain the grin. She is damn adorable. "That does not sound convincing." Perhaps I should not feed the fire, but the sadist in me cannot help it. I smack her bottom again. "Are you temperate enough to carry on a rational conversation?"

"Yes," she all but growls.

I slap her rump again. "Yes, what?" Why am I pushing her this hard?

"No fucking way!" Without the ability to hit anything vital due to all my weapons, I am startled when her palm connects with my ass, several times. With my layers, it barely registers, but the impact through my brain is like a canon explosion from my past. Red clouds my vision.

In one swift movement, I am seated in the chair, my mate lying prone over my femur. When she attempts to push up, I slam my palm down on the middle of her back and pin her legs with mine.

"Let me go, Sebastian." Her furious command ignites the simmering lust.

I reach around her waist and unbutton her jeans before shoving them down her hips. She struggles in earnest, and I temper my strength, so I do not injure her.

"You fucking bastard. If you do this, I will hate you forever."

Something in her tone stops me. What the fuck am I doing disciplining a female against her will? This is not who I am.

"Alex," I murmur low, fondling her posterior, and she stills. "I merely wish to talk."

"Oh, really? Is this how you *talk* to everyone?"

At her sarcasm, I raise my palm and smack her bare bottom. Fuck, that felt fantastic. My muscles tense, expecting her to fight me harder. Her hands grip the bear rug beneath us, but she remains perfectly still. Opening my senses, I bask in her rapid heartbeat, the trembling breaths, and the inviting perfume of her arousal. Alex is resisting her desire, struggling to hold on to her temper with gritted teeth.

With slow movements, I brush my fingers over my handprint on her flesh, fondling the perfect roundness. The impulse to rain down more slaps to her bottom is overwhelming. I have never fought for control this fiercely before, and for the first time, I am at a loss on how to proceed without surrendering my hard-earned restraint.

"Are you ready to talk?" I ask, the coarse rasp of need in my tone surprising.

She hesitates—another whack.

"Red, answer me."

Silence. A loud slap fills the room and contentment courses through my veins at the husky moan escaping my female's lips.

"Fuck, I love how you respond to me," I proclaim before shifting my fingers down to her sex. Sweet Jesus, her delicate folds are slick with her desire. I graze her swollen nub, and she cries out with pleasure.

"Are you ready to talk, my delectable valkyrie?" As much as I crave to slip her to her hands and knees and fuck her from behind, it would simply escalate the problem.

"Yes, Sir." At her breathy sigh, my lids close in ecstasy as I battle to keep from devouring every inch of her.

Chapter 31

Alexandria

How dare he deliver me so close to orgasm when I should detest him. And why am I not more humiliated by this power play?

My cheeks heat when he gently pulls my jeans up before lifting me from his lap to settle in the armchair opposite him. Instead of zipping them closed, in one deft move, I reach into my boot for my dagger and launch myself across the space to straddle his hips, the tip of the blade pressed against his chest.

The vampire sighs. "You wish to kill me, Red?"

"You brutally murdered my father." Why am I hesitating? I can finally avenge Daddy, but staring deep into the sapphire depths of my mate, a tormented darkness bubbles behind the cool exterior.

"No. I did not. Your father was a good man. I possessed no reason to assassinate him."

"His last words were of you, Sebastian." The dark eyebrows lift in surprise, and I clutch my rage and grief to my breast like a lifeline.

"You were there when he died?"

I press the knife deeper. Bastian doesn't even flinch. "Oh, yes. I arrived too late. You murdered, no, you butchered all those valkyries, berserkers, and vampires, making certain to leave no witnesses. But I guess you failed to make sure my father was dead." I clench my teeth against the evoked anguish, but a tear escapes, and I clutch the hilt of my blade tighter.

My demand for revenge is warring with the mate bond and my inner warrior. I'm torn in two. If I skewer Sebastian, Nicki will turn against me, and probably drag me before the council to be tried for murder if she doesn't annihilate me herself.

The beautiful vampire has the audacity to reach up and gently wipe the tear away. "I am so sorry you endure such anguish and violence, little one, but I vow to you I did not kill Gadr."

"Stop lying!" I shout and drive the tip deeper between his ribs.

At his sharp inhale, another tear rolls down my cheek, and my spirit splits in two at the pain I'm compelled to inflict. This is not at all how I envisioned this. In my fantasies, I only hesitate for a second to let the vampire understand why I was ending him before plunging the silver dagger through his rapidly beating heart.

Again, he rubs the moisture away, then grips my head between both palms. With one squeeze, he could crush my skull between his mighty hands like a ripe melon, but his touch is gentle. His intense stare ignites a deep trembling in my soul. "Do not do this, Red. The burden of killing your mate, no matter how much you despise me, will haunt you forever."

What the fuck? He's worried about what the aftereffects of terminating his life will do to me? Why can't he be pissed? I don't know how to handle the tenderness and regret in his gaze, the gentleness of his touch.

"Before he passed, my father begged me to find the vampire as he clutched your ring." No way he can dispute the evidence. His hands are tainted with the blood of the fallen in that alley.

Sebastian stills, his focus sharpens. "What ring?"

"The gold ring with the Moretti emblem." Try to deny that, bloodsucker.

Bastian's eyes widen. "Are you certain?" He asks, his arms falling to the chair.

"Stop acting surprised. You were there. My father implicated you. The evidence clutched in his fist."

"The ring was not mine, Alexandria."

I bark out a hysterical laugh saturated with disbelief. "Since it held the Moretti emblem, that only leaves your brother. Are you accusing Logan of disemboweling my father?" Shit. I didn't even consider that.

"No. It was our father's."

"Nice try. Your father has been dead for centuries."

"Yes. He lost the ring. We assumed in battle."

Wait. What?

"What are you saying, Bastian?" For the first time since I learned my fated male was responsible for the death of my father, a small glint of hope ignites in my gut. Could my mother and I have been wrong all these years?

"I did not kill Gadr, but whoever possessed my father's ring, planted it to make it appear as if I did."

"Why? It makes no sense."

"Agreed. Unless it was to ensure your hatred and keep us apart."

Hmm. Back in the square, those angels were ready to eviscerate me to prevent Bastian and me from being together. Some bullshit nonsense about me being an abomination, and our union was forbidden. Maybe, just maybe, some truth exists in Bastian's statement.

I cannot destroy an innocent guy. Not even a shadow of uncertainty can linger. If I murdered Sebastian, my mate, only to discover he had nothing to do with my dad's death, my soul would shrivel and die. I would end my existence by my own hand, or willfully surrender it in battle.

Relief floods through me. Through no choice of my own, fate gifted this commander to me, but I've also fallen in love with the sexy beast, and I can no longer imagine my life without him. He stole my heart when I didn't even know who I was, and with my memories intact, those feelings haven't changed.

Am I pissed he bedded me before my past returned? Yes. Would I take it back if I could? Hell, to the no. Bastian's mouth, hands, and cock directed my body like a master conductor of a symphony, and whether we end up a couple or not, I wouldn't trade it for all the lightning in the sky.

I waited a century to relinquish my virtue. Never in a million years did I imagine it would be to a vampire, but after our time together, I wouldn't have it any other way.

"Do you think it was the Watchers? They seemed hell-bent on keeping us from mating."

"I am not sure, but I promise you this, I will not rest until I find out who is behind this. They will pay for the lives taken that night." The determined glitter in his gaze leaves little doubt in his pledge.

With the blade still embedded between his ribs, I lean forward until my lips are an inch from his. "I don't trust you, vampire. We do this together, or I end it right here and now, and figure it out on my own."

The rough, threatening growl has my stomach quivering with nerves, but I hold his lethal stare. "You run your silver through my heart; it is because I allowed it. Do you understand me?"

Basically, he's informing me the sole reason I'm not prone on the ground or sailing across the chamber is because he's choosing not to resist me. Isn't that a humbling thought?

"Vow to me, mate. We'll pursue this together, and I will withdraw my blade." No way in hell, I'm backing down like a frightened puppy. I'm Sebastian's. I'd seen it in his shell-shocked expression the night at Nicki's cottage, and he confirmed it in the medical room. His inner vampire would never allow him to injure me, just as my valkyrie warrior is fighting me tooth and nail right now. I have to keep believing that.

"Mate?" The blue glow sparks to life, and my insides quiver in response.

In a quick motion, I withdraw the blade from his ribs and force it against his jugular. "It means nothing between you and me, but with one sip of your blood, Bastian, I will experience the truth."

Valkyries have the ability to see an individual's history by consuming their blood. It's not something we often utilize because having your own thoughts clouding your brain is more than enough, but to have the highlights of another person's life bombarding you is too much.

For some, it develops into an addiction, eventually taking over their reality, and they have difficulty discerning between their memories and the ones they pilfered. Check another box in a long list of reasons a mating with this vampire scares me. It requires an exchange of blood during sex. Although, the mental chaos at drinking him would be worth it to learn what trauma damaged this male so profoundly.

"I will *never* allow my past to poison you," he growls before gripping my skull and slamming those hard, full lips against mine.

As his skilled mouth manipulates with an expertise taking my breath away, lust slams through me like a locomotive, and the dagger lies forgotten against his neck. The delicious sting on my butt as he grips it kindles the fiery storm brewing in my veins, and I groan, grasping a fist full of the dark tresses at his nape, reliving the scalding heat of his palm on my backside. His every stroke, hard or soft, leaves me craving more.

I'm an addict, and Sebastian is my drug of choice.

Bastian grabs the dagger and flings it across the room, the tip sparking the stone wall before clattering to the floor.

"Never threaten me with a blade again, Alex, or you will not like the consequences."

Oh, but maybe I would.

Chapter 32

Alexandria

"**B**ut Christmas is in three days, and none of us have even put up a tree," I whine to my reunited BFF before flopping on the couch in the living room of Nicki's —now my— cottage. "That's like sacrilegious or something."

Nicki smiles. "God, I've missed you."

"Wow. Did you just admit to an affection? Who are you and what did you do with my best friend," I tease, but her smile fades, and a heavy sadness shadows her gray eyes. I pat the cushion next to me. "Sit. Tell me everything."

After Sebastian's alluring threat, I concluded the most reliable course of action was to hightail it out of his bedroom. I observed the effects of the sleep tugging at him, no matter how hard he resisted. And the last thing I needed was to have his vulnerability tug at my tattered heartstrings.

I can't believe I surrendered my virginity to Sebastian Roman Moretti. My father's killer. No, *alleged* killer. I promised to give him the opportunity to disprove the evidence, and if he can't...well, I'll leap that proverbial bridge when and if I get to it.

I spent hours prowling the monstrous castle, searching for my best friend, hoping she wasn't sleeping like the other hundred or so vampires living here. I've missed my relationship with Nicki, our talks over wine or coffee, and I needed her again.

The only individuals milling about were the servants, hauling in firewood, stoking the numerous fireplaces throughout, cleaning, and polishing everything.

I eventually located her in the enormous gym beating the shit out of a boxing bag and persuaded her to get cleaned up and trace us home.

The two of us spent four amazing years in this cottage. What better place to catch up than here?

Nicki moves to the piano under the bay windows instead of the couch, and I focus my attention on her. The midday sun shimmers through the trees outside, illuminating the gleaming baby grand and the halfling vampire like a soft spotlight on a stage.

My roommate has always been remote, a little standoffish, and uses sarcasm to deflect emotions she can't grapple with, and even though her start in life was a bitch, there's a newfound sorrow emanating from her.

"Please talk to me," I whisper, watching her slide onto the piano bench. The second her fingers lightly tap the keys, her lids close, and she inhales deeply. A heartbreaking melody fills the room.

"When Icarus brought me back from hell, he did so at a price." She continues a gentle strumming across the ivory. "He assumed the cost would be his life. But instead, the sick, twisted fates demanded my unborn child. A girl."

Oh shit. That's right. I'm still experiencing difficulty synchronizing the incidents between my old and new life.

I leave the couch and slide next to her on the bench. She'll object to a hug, so I bump her shoulder with mine. "I'm sorry, Nicki. Sorry I wasn't here for you."

"It's okay. You made the correct move. Spared us both the turmoil of me kicking your ass."

I snort, knowing her remark isn't just a gentle ribbing. Nicole could mop the floor with me and then some, but it would have wrecked her.

"How are you and Logan coping?" Even with the crap going on after the arrival of my memories, I still noticed the strain between her and the warrior.

"Honestly, he doesn't know what to do with me. I've shut down. At first, I was furious, but I soon understood his decision was the only option, even though it hurt like hell." I'm stunned when a solitary tear courses down Nicki's cheek. I have never witnessed her cry. "I'm coming apart, Alex. I've said and done things to him which can't be undone. And I am petrified my failure to deal with this will destroy us."

Cautiously, I lay my palm between her shoulder blades. If Nicole is sharing her insecurities and emotions, then she is in a world of pain, and it shatters my heart. "Logan doesn't merely love you, Nic, you are his everything. He would willingly die for you without hesitation. And no matter how long it takes for you both to surmount this, he'll be waiting with open arms."

"I hope you're right." She shoots me a shimmering glance. "So, tell me what's been going on in your life. How many times have you fallen in love since you left?"

"Oh, you know me, a hundred times, at least." Old habits die hard as I veer away from the truth.

"Ouch." Nicki winces, and I suddenly remember how lies affect her.

"Sorry. Guess I don't need to maintain the charade anymore."

"Why did you?"

"Well, I couldn't reveal I was performing duties for the Valkyrie Regency, now could I? So, I invented the promiscuous persona as a front." I shrug and hope she doesn't drill deeper.

"Okay. I'll let it pass." Her intent gaze has me swallowing. "Tell me about your hostility for my brother-in-law."

Dammit. How much do I reveal? The demand for space has me wandering over to the potbelly stove to toss another log inside, buying me some time to consider. Do I spill my guts to Nicki? I could certainly use her opinion, but I don't want to burden her with my shit.

"I require a distraction. Spit it out."

"Bastian makes me feel things I never thought possible, but," with a sigh, I plop down on the couch and draw my feet under me. "His remote, controlled demeanor scares me more than his anger. He stated he abhors commitment and cannot offer me love. I don't know if I can submit to him without those things."

We might not have a chance to find out if the Watchers have anything to say about it.

"Alex, it's the surrender he needs. Your complete capitulation to every touch, word, and stroke. For Sebastian, it's your submission that will break the control and allow his sub-conscience to commit, to love. It's the bond between you he requires. And whether he acknowledges it or not, he craves to trust you, to believe he is more than a lover, he is your other half, the keeper of your soul. His past demands no less. Let go. Give him your trust, your submission. And in turn, you'll become his everything, and together you can conquer his demons."

Wow. When did my friend gain such profound insight? Or is she speaking from experience?

Tingles race up my arms, and hope warms my chest. Could it be that simple? Well, surrendering is by no means easy, but it *is* doable. Until I recall all the other shit standing in our way.

"Sebastian and I have some gigantic hurdles to overcome before we can even contemplate any kind of relationship. The problem is, for years, the Valkyrie Regency believed a Moretti killed my father, Gadr."

I confess everything to my best friend while she proceeds to play a haunting melody that only adds to the tragic, gruesome retelling. Every once in a while, she glances up or nods, so I know she's listening and not lost in the melody her fingers perform.

"Sebastian claims the ring was his fathers, thought lost in battle."

"What does your gut tell you?" she asks, glancing up from the keys.

I shrug, tucking a curl behind my ear. "My gut shrieks that he's responsible somehow, but my foolish heart prefers to think he didn't do it."

"If Bastian says he didn't, I believe him." She peers at me intently. "He'll stop at nothing until he discovers the truth."

"We both will." My chin lifts with determination.

"Fair enough."

"You up for some coffee?" Time to change the topic.

"Is that a real question?" She counters with a smirk.

"Right, what was I thinking? Why don't I put a pot on, and then we can drag the Christmas tree out of the garage, play some annoying Christmas music, and decorate?"

"That sounds like a horrifying plan. I'm in. But do you mind if I sing first? There's a song burning in my gut, and I have to get it out."

"Of course not. Do you prefer me to leave the room?"

"No. Start the coffee and ignore me." She smiles, but it doesn't touch the sorrow in her gaze.

"What's the song?"

"Aptly, Undone by Bonnie Raitt."

I'd never heard of it, but when she plays the soulful intro, I mentally prepare myself for the heartbreak about to emerge as I set about preparing our brew. This will be cathartic for Nicki. A beginning to the healing process. She's always been connected with the songs she sings, requiring them to force out her suppressed emotions.

Somehow knowing Logan needs to hear and see this moment when he rises, I snatch my phone and start videoing as the coffee perks. Halfway through, tears stream down my face, and I'm clutching my phone in my fist to hold it steady.

The lyrics are about shattered romance, and the first verse is quintessential Nicole.

There's a sword at the tip of my tongue. It shows no mercy on the latest one.

The melody is soulful, her voice throaty and laden with regret. How can she not keep from blubbering like an idiot singing this?

Or I'm possibly projecting my own struggles with Sebastian. I readily accused him of, not just murdering my father, but butchering a dozen or more immortals. I never investigated whether my vengeance was justified. I couldn't get past the misery of failing my dad or the self-betrayal I went through when I discovered the killer was none other than the vampire I've secretly lusted after for years, and my fated one.

How screwed up is that? I realized it was a Moretti who murdered my father, and while rage consumed me, it didn't break the connection I felt with Sebastian. I longed to despise him. Fantasized about plunging a silver dagger through his heart. But those weren't the only fantasies I enjoyed of him.

Even with my memories obliterated, everything about Sebastian drew me in, like a cockroach to shit. He dominated my every waking thought and my dreams at night. I craved to drown in the cobalt ocean of his gaze and surrender to his demands.

Everyone knows Bastian's sexual predilections. The fact he owns several BDSM clubs says it all, but he never sought to hide it or seemed ashamed of it. It's weird, but I find his confidence and assertive presence sexy as hell. I'm intrigued by his lifestyle. Just recalling the scene at the villa gets my juices flowing.

What would it be like to have him tie me up, maybe blindfolded and at his mercy? What delicious, wondrous things would the vampire do to me? I relished the sharp sting of his palm on my backside, but what about a crop or flogger? Would I be able to handle losing all control? And as much as the remote Dom turns me on, he also frightens me.

It doesn't matter, anyway. Once Sebastian and I figure out who murdered my father and I have my vengeance, he and I will have no further reason to be together. The Watchers will never permit our union, and Bastian has made it abundantly clear he's unable to provide me commitment or love. Two qualities I demand in a partner.

If I were to take Nicki's advice and just go with it, who's to say the damaged vampire could overcome his past, or even want to try. I will be completely shattered when he walks away.

I rub at the throb in my chest, refocusing on my best friend who needs me. The last note reverberates through the room, but I continue to video as Nicki hangs her head and grips the edge of the bench in a vulnerable moment. The second her shoulders shake with heart-wrenching sobs, I quickly send the clip to Logan before racing over and wrapping my arms around her trembling body.

"You'll get through this. You are a warrior queen who can kick the shit out of anyone. You will annihilate grief's ass too. I promise. But Nicki," I draw away and force her to look at me. "Stop shutting him out. You need him as much as he needs you. You're not the only one grieving."

"I know," she sniffs.

"He lost you once, and it nearly destroyed him, now he's lost, not merely his child, but the warmth and love of his mate."

"Fuck. When you put it like that, I am a total bitch."

"No," I chuckle. "You're a woman who's suffering and doesn't realize what to do with the emotions raging inside you. You never have."

"I have to get my mind off this shit. Let's drink this pot of heaven, put up the damn tree, and then go to the LeLoo and rock it out with Liam until the guys wake up. He's hurting too."

"What? Why is the werewolf upset?"

"I'll explain while we trim the tree, but I prefer to drive to the bar. Teleporting is uber convenient, but I miss my truck, Riddick."

"By the way, I arranged to have his front bumper fixed before I disappeared." Nicki's black Ford Raptor, a.k.a Riddick, took a beating when dickwad Nathan Connor decided to run us off the road. Nic's quick reflexes saved our asses from a violent shootout.

"I knew there was a reason I liked you. Your weird obsession with vehicles."

"It's not weird. It's pure unadulterated lust."

Chapter 33

Alexandria

The thump of the bass vibrates my chest. The excitement of the crowd, jammed with only immortals since Liam shut the bar down for this reunion, fuels my adrenaline. Even though I'm merely a backup singer, I totally understand Nicki's addiction to being on stage. And coming back to the LeLoo, where it all began, makes me nostalgic for a time when matters seemed so black and white. At least on my end. Nicole's life was all kinds of crazy.

I can't believe Kurtis mated Lucretia. Who would've thunk it? A shifter prince turned king and a vampire warrior. Or the mind-blowing fact Lu has a twin who's an Oracle in training.

Whaaaat?

A ton of shit went down while I was running around the states resisting the urge to murder my best friend and later completely losing my identity.

And Liam, holy shitballs, the wolf buffed up. Gone is the sweet, fun-loving ladies' man. He's replaced by a harder, more serious version, with a strange despondency in the chocolate eyes. I can't help but appreciate the muscled physique in worn jeans and t-shirt, or how hot he looks with a Stetson covering the unruly dark hair and a guitar strapped to his chest.

In the past, when we would tend bar together, I'd hear him singing under his breath as he served drinks to the salivating ladies, so I recognized he boasted a fine, seductive tone. But seeing him on stage, his raspy voice and blues inflections filling the speakers with an entire band backing him up, is like hearing a sexy cross between country singers Chris Stapleton and Brantley Gilbert. It sends pleasant shivers up my spine, and I could tune in for hours.

Even though Nicki and Liam perform in different genres, I can tell she enjoys collaborating with him and vice versa.

I glance at my watch again. The sun set an hour ago and still no Sebastian. Logan appeared, along with two dozen Guardians not on rotation; the second the fiery ball dipped below the horizon. The sexy brute with the iridescent irises offered a brief nod in my direction. I'm assuming an acknowledgment he received my video before his fierce regard shifted to his mate behind the piano.

Not long after, Kurtis and Lucretia arrived with my mother and Cipher in tow. I was delighted to see her, but the queen's smothering presence overwhelmed me until the former shifter king finally snagged her attention. They sought to control their love for each other, but I was aware of their bond. And sadly, I suspect my father was as well.

My old man always advised me, "We don't choose our fated ones, daughter. We make the best of what the gods hand us."

Whether it's the gods or fate or whatever, they certainly have a sick, perverse sense of humor sometimes.

The front door opens again, and I tense, desperate for the magnetic presence of my mate, but also apprehensive. Instead, I'm astonished when Dr. Warner saunters in, and when he and Logan clasp wrists in greeting, my mouth falls open, and I don't even pretend to sing.

I fire a glance at Nicki behind the grand piano, and the smirk on her face says it all. Dr. Warner is a fucking Guardian, established at the clinic to watch over me. By her or Sebastian?

I shake my head. A vampire veterinarian. Who knew?

When the sexy vamp smirks up at me on stage, I itch my nose with my middle finger, letting him observe precisely how much I appreciate his duplicity before I resume harmonizing with Nicki and Liam.

Was Doc Julie in on this little farce? I know she's not a vamp; she works general practice hours. Maybe the hunky vet did some weird thrall thing on her to finagle his way into a position.

With a shrug, I let it go and direct my wrath on Ezekiel. Mr. Twinkle Toes was assigned to get close to me, to thwart a mating by any tactics necessary. Translation; my death. I can't believe I considered doing the sneaky snowplow with the backstabbing fucker. There must be a special place in purgatory for people who boink an angel.

When the last notes of the music fade, Liam announces the band is taking a short break. I step from behind the mic as the werewolf places his guitar on the stand and encloses me in a warm bear hug. Or...wolf hug. Summer rain and leather surround me as I squeeze his waist.

"Missed you, pipsqueak." His low rumble vibrates my cheek, and I raise my chin to gaze at the handsome cowboy.

"You've buffed up, wolf boy," I say with a grin. "Still working to impress the ladies?"

He chuckles. "You're all the woman I can handle, Valkyrie."

"Hey, Alex?" Nicki calls from behind me, motioning me over.

"Let's catch up later, eh."

"You got it," he answers before hopping off the platform to greet Kurtis and Lu.

"What's up?" I ask.

"I have a song in mind, but I need you. Do you know 'Tell Me You Love Me' by Demi Lovato?"

"Shit, who doesn't? I adore it. If you're singing this to Mr. Green Eyes then I think the lyrics are lit."

"Yeah, I thought so too." She twists and sets up two standing mics at the front of the stage.

"Oh. I'm in front with you?" At her nod, I grin. "Sweet."

A quick glimpse over my shoulder and I notice Logan in the VIP section below, lounging in the center of a couch, his gaze fastened on Nicki. Liam, Kurtis, Lu, my mom, and Cipher have joined him in the makeshift living room set up.

Perfect. But where's Sebastian?

Nicki and I assume our places at the mics, and I'm suddenly nervous. For her and me. I want the delivery of the message to be the focal point.

"Before the band takes their break, I would like to perform a special song. This is for you, Logan." At his name, he sits a little straighter, his body tense.

The musicians begin the intro, and I wipe my damp palms down my jeans. The first few sentences are an apology and Logan's eyebrow lifts.

"Oh no, here we go again, fighting over what I said. I'm sorry, yeah, I'm sorry."

I chime in on the chorus, harmonizing. But it's the last few lyrics that sharpen Logan's gaze.

"Through the ups and downs, Baby, I'ma stick around. I promise we will be alright, alright. Everything I need, is standing right in front of me. I know that we will be alright, alright, yeah."

The message is a promise. No matter what life throws at them, she will always wish to hear he loves her, and she is nothing without him, even if she doesn't express it correctly.

Before the final note fades, Logan is on his feet, the emeralds shining in the low lights, and meets his woman halfway as she leaps from the stage, straight into his waiting embrace.

"I love you, baby," he growls in her ear while holding her tight against him, her legs wrapped around his waist. "Nothing in this world or beyond can change how I feel, not even you."

"I'm sorry. Forgive me." Nicole's whispered plea stuns me.

"Always." He grabs a fistful of her hair, forcing her head back and plundering her mouth with his own.

Their kind of love is what I seek. An all-consuming passion and desire that eclipses all the shit life hurls at you. What must it feel like to understand you always have the rock-solid faith and love of someone forever?

Sebastian and I are mates. Our biological link will invariably steer us to one another if we're ever in need. But I seek more. Demand more. Love. Trust. Commitment. I deserve no less.

Once we resolve this issue regarding my father, could I persuade the vampire to trust me, to let go of the monsters in his past, and take the leap? A tiny glint of hope burns in my gut. I've witnessed the tenderness in his gaze, experienced the gentle side of his lovemaking. Bas's emotions petrify him, so he chooses to confine them in a shadowy corner of his mind to ward off the possible pain or misery he believes attaches to such feelings.

But what if I could...

The front doors open and the object of my thoughts saunters in, dressed in a dark turtleneck and jeans. My heart stops, and at first, I don't notice the striking woman on his arm. But when they pause in the entrance, a growing dread drops in my stomach like a cannonball as the slim blond bows her head, eyes on the floor. He bends to mutter something in her ear, and that's when I catch the black choker around her throat.

Son of a bitch! He brought a submissive to the bar.

An acute pain invades my system, penetrating my spirit like shrapnel from a dirty bomb, and for several moments, I stare dumbfounded at this intentional move to hurt me. The entire reason he led a sub here was to make it glaringly obvious what he expects—a fucking collared, subservient female.

Fuck me.

Logan strides up to his brother, his expression livid. Sebastian ignores him, his cold, indifferent regard aimed at me as he plants his palm on the female's shoulder, and she automatically drops to her knees.

Everything inside me shuts down. I can't pretend this doesn't bother me. Bother me? Fucking eh, it destroys me. He might as well have sliced open my rib cage with a sword, reached in, and crushed my heart in his fist.

A part of me recognizes the message he's trying to convey, and the sub was a visual aid to establish his point. Well, I read it loud and clear. I will never tolerate a male collaring me in public like some fucking sex slave from the stone ages. If that's what he requires, then we'll never have a future.

I need... to get out of here.

I pivot, turning away from the hellish scene, but my muddled brain has no idea where the exit is, even though I've passed through it a million times.

"Alex," Nicki's fingers grip my elbow. "He's being a fucking dick. Why don't you step outside and get some fresh air? Let Logan deal with him."

She points me in the right path, and I don't even realize I moved until the metal door slams shut behind me. I gulp in lungfuls of crisp December air, force the tears away, refusing to weep over the bastard. He sauntered in with the sub to prove a point. Well, he fucking proved it. He's an asshole.

"Good evening, Alex."

Oh, just perfect. The other jackass on my shit list, Ezekiel. "You dare to show your face in a place overrun by immortals after what you did? Those are some big brass balls you're toting around, E."

"I was merely doing my duty. Surely you understand that?" He steps closer, and I can't help but marvel at the beauty of the male in his bad-boy attire, complete with a biker jacket, even if he's a fallen angel.

"If that were true, I'd be dead."

"Yes. My affections for you complicate matters."

Something he declared in the plaza bounces into my recovering brain. "You know who killed my father, don't you?" When he doesn't respond, I walk closer, letting go of the shit show behind me. "Cat got your tongue?"

"I am incapable of lying, so I find it best not to answer."

I snort. "You lied to me for months."

"No, Alex, I did not. I simply withheld the truth."

"Same, same." Hazel eyes regard me expectantly. "How about we play a little yes or no game, and you respond with a nod or shake your head? Does that fit into your no lying scenario?"

"Sounds logical." His smirk says it's utter bullshit but he is willing to play along.

"Oh, goodie. I'm overjoyed you approve." By his blank expression, the sarcasm is totally wasted on him. "Did Sebastian Moretti murder my father?"

He shakes his head.

Holy shit! I was quite prepared for him to answer, yes. "Okay. Did Logan Moretti kill him?"

Another shake.

Well, crap. Now what? The only other Moretti I know is Rowena, a.k.a Dr. LaBorski, my shrink. Former shrink.

Wait. A light bulb bursts in my brain. "Did Rowena kill Gadr?"

A sharp affirmative.

Oh. My. God.

"Why?" I whisper in bewilderment. Silence. Shit. Think Alex. A yes or no question. "Did she plant the Moretti ring?"

Nod.

"Was she acting alone?"

Shake.

Fuck. Who was working with her, and why?

Bench those questions for now. "Can you inform me why the Watchers want me dead?"

"They fear a mating with the vampire will upset the balance of power and nature."

"Yeah, Yeah. They indicated as much, but why? Kurtis and Lu mated."

"Yes, and the former Guardian is watched closely, but Lucretia's shifter side has never re-surfaced after her turning."

"Hold on. I'm confused. How is there situation any different from Bastian and me? He's a vampire, and I'm a valkyrie."

"That is all I can report. I came here to warn you." He cups my cheek and steps close—warm tingles cascade along my nape at the contact. "Steer clear of the vampire if you value your existence. I couldn't bear it if anything happened to you."

"Ezekiel, what do..." The gentle caress of his lips shocks me. I daydreamed about this moment during our weeks of training, but the knowledge of his lineage, his mission, contaminates the experience. Not to mention the stupid vampire's image appears behind my closed lids, but so does the visual of the female on her knees.

The back-door crashes open, and I jump away like a guilty teenager caught making out in the bathroom on prom night. A broad figure blocks the light from the bar, but there's no mistaking to whom the brilliant blue glow belongs.

"Remove your hands from my mate, Fallen, or I will break every bone."

Oh no, he didn't. He strolled in tonight with a submissive on his arm, and he's demanding no other guy can touch me?

I whirl and face off with the livid vampire, the manifest of my rage streaking across the moonlit sky. "Go back to your sub, bloodsucker. I'm certain she's waiting in anticipation of your whip."

"That honor is now bestowed on you, Red." Never lifting his gaze from mine, the dangerous predator eases down the steps.

"Never in a million goddamn years." I spin to E, observing the exchange with interest. "Get me out of here."

"With pleasure."

I gasp when his enormous black wings unfurl with a shrug before he yanks me to his chest and takes flight. My stomach drops at the velocity of our ascent, but it's the enraged roar from below that has me risking life and limb to peer over Ezekiel's bicep while clutching his shoulders in a death grip.

My mouth drops open, and legitimate fear spikes my adrenaline. The radiance of my mate's feral expression is gaining fast.

Holy shitballs! Sebastian can fly.

Chapter 34

Sebastian

M_ine!_ The beast rages for control, the wind rushing by at near-supersonic speeds waters my eyes. The goddamn Watcher dared to handle my mate, kiss her, and then abscond with her.

At her fucking behest, I remind myself.

Somewhere in the sane fraction of my intellect, I comprehend I have no call for acting so possessive. The reason I brought a sub tonight was to display to Alex my authentic character. I expected her to turn away in revulsion, but the hurt and betrayal on her face branded my soul.

Nothing can steal away what I already identify down deep in my gut; Alexandria threatens every lifestyle choice I have established over the last couple of centuries. In a brief time, she transformed my life and my shriveled heart forever. Part of me hates her for it.

When the Watcher nose dives for a nearby rooftop in downtown Newport, I adjust my course to pursue. Rage clouds my vision, but an underlying apprehension in facing off with the fallen angel spirals through my gut. I cannot keep Alex safe if I am dead.

My boots land without a sound as Ezekiel positions my mate behind his enormous wings. "You would be wise not to engage me, vampire."

"Probably," I concede. "But you have something that belongs to me."

The little redhead ducks under the Watcher's feathers to challenge me, delicate fists perched on her hips. "I am not a piece of property, asshat. I belong to no one."

"Asshat?" What the fuck?

"Yes." She steps forward. The angel reaches for her, but she flings him off, which soothes my seething vampire somewhat. "You made it abundantly clear, Sebastian, a single night with no commitment. Which you reinforced by flaunting your sub in front of me tonight." I flinch at the reminder of my arrogant stupidity, remembering Logan's harsh criticisms. "Who I date, kiss or fuck is no concern of yours any longer."

She's right, but I cannot leave her alone, and the prospect of anybody else touching her satiny skin, sampling her sweet essence, ignites a blazing need to lock her away in my bedroom forever.

"Unless you've changed your mind." She takes a tentative stride forward, and I recognize the kindling of hope in the blue irises. "If so, declare it now or leave. I can't deal with your on again, off again bullshit." Another small step, and she's halfway between the angel and myself. "But understand; if you walk away, we are finished."

The fierce tenacity in her gaze terrifies me, and I swallow as panic fires in my gut. I want her. No. I need her, but can I let go of centuries of mistrust and rage and allow this valkyrie to scale the defensive walls I erected around my heart?

"Alex," Ezekiel interrupts the stare-off with my mate. "The Watchers will never permit a union between you and the vampire."

She twirls in his direction. "Why E? The council reversed the law regarding different species mating. Why are they so resolute against ours?"

Yes. I would love an answer to that question myself. I ease several strides forward until I am a mere foot from Alex's back. "Why are the fallen fixated on Alexandria?"

The angel shoots me a ferocious glare before dropping his gaze to my mate. The devotion and admiration shining in his eyes shames me. This is what Red deserves. A male worthy of her affection, capable of returning it tenfold.

I can defend her, keep her protected, and provide us both tremendous pleasure. But to love her in the manner she deserves?

The valkyrie has a big heart, a caring spirit craving a nice, stable, sensible lover. The only thing my blackened soul can offer is pain and submission. It would kill me to watch the fire in her eyes diminished by my dominance and control.

"You know I cannot answer your inquiry," the angel responds with regret shining in the hazel depths. "Please recognize, my objective is to keep you alive and safe. If you choose the vampire, I cannot defend you from my brothers."

"She does not require your protection, fallen. The princess has several armies ready to fight for her with their lives."

Alex pivots, but I maintain my glower on the immortal behind her. "Why would they need to, Sebastian?" Reluctantly, I lower my regard to the hope in her gaze. "Are *you* choosing me?"

"I..." Fuck. I am wedged between a rock and a hard place. If I answer yes, her survival is in peril from the Watchers, and I risk losing her to not only them but to the darkness inside me. If I reply no, I damn us both to a life of torment, but she would be safe. "Ezekiel is correct. Us being together puts a bullseye on your back."

Ice smothers the hopeful spark, and a part of me dies with it. She shifts to the fallen, moving in his direction.

"Wait."

She pauses, her spine stiff. The barrier around my heart cracks, realizing I am about to break her. If I were a selfish male, uncaring of her safety, I would sweep her up in my arms and fuck the consequences. But my inner vampire will always protect what is ours. I must crush any glimmer of hope we will ever be together.

"Alex." Azul fire peers at me over her shoulder. I harden my resolve and force a bored weariness in my tone. "The reality is, you cannot provide me what I truly need any more than I can grant you what you seek." I lift my lip in a sneer. "Love. Commitment. A mating. It is best if we go our separate ways."

Fuck. Agony spears though my chest and I grit my teeth against the torment.

My mate lowers her lids and turns away, but not before I read the devastation in her eyes, the tremble of her chin, and my vampire rages, desperate to shove the words hovering in the space between us back down my throat. I reach for her, to drag her against me and express how sorry I am, that I do not mean it. But my arm falls to my side, and my lips remain sealed.

Instead of stepping into the angel's embrace, Alexandria veers toward an exit on our right.

"Alex? Where are you going?" The angel inquires.

"Anywhere away from the two of you." She grips the doorknob, hesitating. Her shoulders stiffen as she delivers the message to dismantle the shields centuries in the making. "I love you, Sebastian." Pain lances through me, and I squeeze my lids shut against the invasion. "But right now, I hate you. Never come near me again."

Without a backward glance, Alex jerks open the door and escapes into the bowels of the building under my feet. I glare at the metal contraption, silently praying she returns, but knowing what just transpired was for the best. As much as her confession of love spreads warmth through my soul, I cannot return the sentiment. I am incapable of such an emotion.

"Advise your brothers there will be no mating between princess Svaldana and I. They need not pursue her any further." At all costs, I will ensure my mate's security, even if I must do it from a distance.

I now understand the misery my brother suffered forced away from Nicole for years for her own safety, only capable of invading her dreams. How did he stand it? My beast is deranged with the need to pursue our mate. Will I be strong enough to merely observe from the shadows? See, hear, and scent the beautiful valkyrie, but never caress, taste, or sheath my hardness in her tight core?

You will do what needs to be done, Sebastian. You are the commander of the queens' Guardians. You must protect your mate at all costs, even from yourself.

Then why does it hurt so fucking much?

Chapter 35

Alexandria

Nervous butterflies dance in my gut as I await with E on the sidelines for the announcer to call our names.

Instead of running home to my mother, who would have droned on about how I made the appropriate decision regarding the fiasco on the roof two months ago, I returned to my old/new life in Flagstaff. I instructed her I required time to heal my shattered heart before I resumed my commitments to the Valkyrie Regency.

For the first week, I stayed holed up in my bedroom, refusing to eat, drink, or see anyone, even though my roommate Ryen threatened to break down the door on several occasions.

The weather channel marveled at the weird lightning storms with no rain or clouds. They eventually chalked it up to a dry lightning phenomenon, but a deluge of meteorologists converged on Flagstaff to film the strange bolts dancing across the sky day and night. Little did they realize it occurred from one tiny female whose heart was broken by her man.

After the third day entombed in my room, Ryen slipped juice packets and protein bars under the door in an effort to keep me alive. They laid untouched on the carpet. The lightning fueled me. Too bad it couldn't strike the pain into oblivion as well.

Ballroom dancing preserved my sanity. It's curious. I should be pissed at Ezekiel for being part of the plot to kill me, but instead, I sought his calming nature. His apparent devotion to me is a balm to my bruised and battered psyche, my heart. Because of the many absences, I lost my job at The Zoo and eventually abandoned the veterinary gig too.

Since I'm cognizant of who I am, a valkyrie princess, I no longer need to be frugal. My finances are such I never have to work another day in my life, but I'm not the type of immortal to lay around eating Bon Bons and watching soap operas, so ballroom and E have become my entire world.

Nicki and Logan visited many times over the last couple of months, but neither of us mentioned Sebastian. By the twitch in her eye, I sensed Nicole would love to whack me upside the head, and her restraint was a testament to her growing maturity. Although she advised me to 'suck it up buttercup and return to the land of the living.'

They're both here tonight, along with Kurtis, Lu, Liam, and surprisingly Christoph Nox, a.k.a. Dr. Warner—still having trouble with that one—ready to cheer me on during this competition. The impressively beautiful beings draw every eye, and I must agree; they do stand out in their formal attire. Everyone in this area is dressed to the nines, but the immortals are just... more. Their bodies are perfection, their looks are movie-star quality, and mortals are helplessly attracted to the supernatural aura they exude.

The announcer calls our name, and I fidget with the number pinned to my chest one last time before taking E's outstretched hand.

"You ready?" He whispers in my ear.

"Oh yeah. Let's go kick ballroom's ass." His smile is beautiful, but it no longer makes my heart stutter. Only one male on this planet with the power to escalate my pulse, suspend the breath in my lungs. Sebastian Moretti.

After my week in hibernation, I beelined it to my fake psychiatrist's office to confront the bitch, but as expected, it was vacant, like she never existed. I'm debating whether to inform my friends and mom on what E revealed about my father's death. I could use their aid in locating the vampire shrink, but I don't wish to start an all-out war and get Bastian's mother killed until I have proof.

At E's tug on my hand, I let go of my tumultuous musings, straighten my spine, and sashay onto the dance floor like I own it. The vociferous cheering and whistling from my friends inch my smile wider as E twirls me front and center. The other dancers attempt to ignore us and concentrate on their own movements, but the immortal thing set fear alight in their eyes.

Watch out, bitches. I'm about to own that trophy.

Our first dance is my favorite and most challenging; the Tango. Good. If I nail this one, the others are in the bag. We take our opening positions, a dozen couples frozen in place, awaiting the music. An expectant hush settles over the audience and excitement burns in my belly.

I set my frame, settling my lower body against Ezekiel's when *his* presence cascades over me like a heated blanket, and it takes every ounce of discipline I possess not to inspect the crowd for the striking blue gaze.

He came. Nicki mentioned she left the invite on the dining table, but I didn't know if he would show up or not.

Instead of it troubling me, a peace invades my mind and body, and I'm thrilled he will witness me dancing. Even yet, with our future bleak as the winter skyline in Alaska, for some stupid reason, I crave him to be proud of me. His remarks two months ago split me in two, but I realize now he said those awful things because the noble bastard assumed he was acting in my best interest to protect me. And maybe he was. It kept the Watchers off my back. But being this close to him after all this time, I perceive his suffering as my own.

Whether he chooses to admit it or even realizes it, the idiot loves me. He simply doesn't know how to handle the emotion. His past prevents him from opening up, becoming vulnerable. So, he's taking the only action he understands; protect.

One day, I hope and pray he conquers his demons, and somehow, I get rid of the Watchers scrutiny so we can be together. I recognize this is a huge fault of mine; I'm a hopeless romantic. I covet the happy ever after. Is it too much to ask, to spend the rest of my existence with the male I love? My goddamn fated one?

As soon as the vigorous, seductive music of the Tango thrums over the speakers, I let go of all the idiocy, all the what-ifs, and follow the subtle commands of Ezekiel's frame against mine. The long slit in the black skirt allows for ease of movement. The sequined bra shows off my slender waistline and toned arms as I pivot and twist, bend and lunge to my partner's directions. The rhythm is dramatic, and Ezekiel takes full advantage of my expertise and the floor.

When the melody ends, and E spins me out to perform our bow, I scan the crowd under my lashes. The second I sight him in his black tux, my heart nearly bursts from my chest. My God, he is the perfect package, beautiful, provocative, and dangerous, with a fierce stare that gets my juices flowing.

And then he smiles. It's subtle, a brief lift at one corner of those kissable lips, and I want to weep. His expression says it all. Everything I craved and more. But when the grin fades, I notice the sorrow in the blue irises. They overflow with regret, and my heart breaks anew.

He isn't here to declare his love for me. He's here to demonstrate support for his queen's best friend.

I glance away, and E twirls me one more time before we head backstage to change for the next round.

"You were flawless!" The angel declares before wrapping his muscled arms around my shoulders. I plant my palms on his solid, naked abdomen under the short, black jacket and lean backward. He picks up the hint and steps back with a pout. "You okay?"

"Yeah. I should get changed. You know how long it takes for per-fection," I tease and veer towards the dressing rooms.

The second I turn the corner, away from E's watchful scrutiny, my limbs give out, and I grab the wall for support. Why do I let my hopes consume me when I see him? Like the stoic, stubborn ass will suddenly alter or abandon centuries of doubt and mistrust for me.

"Alex."

Goosebumps spring along my skin at the dark, sensual voice be-hind me, and my breath catches. Oh shit. Time to force an Oscar-winning performance and convince the vampire I am quite content without him in my life.

Inhaling a sharp breath, I slowly turn and confront the hand-some creature who seized my body, heart, and soul. I'm startled by his haggard appearance. Dark circles shadow his eyes, the Italian skin alabaster in its paleness. My gorgeous mate is suffering. And by the looks of him, starving. Good. I'm glad it's not just me.

"I'm surprised you showed up, Mr. Moretti."

An eyebrow lifts. "Mr. Moretti?"

I shrug. "I guess it's best we keep things formal."

A muscle pulses in his jaw. "You were amazing out there. You have more talent than all of them combined."

I'm baffled by the praise. When he steps closer, I stiffen, my la-tent desire sparking to life. The heady spice of a refreshing ocean breeze fills my senses, and I want to bathe in his fragrance. I expel an unsteady sigh and tackle my rising lust with sarcasm.

"I know." I attempt to laugh, but it comes off as a throaty moan.

"Alexandria, we need to talk."

Dread filters like thick honey through my veins as muscles tight-en over bone. '*You've survived worse. You can survive the words he's about to spew from those lush lips you're craving to nibble and lick.*'

Nope. No, I can't. I'm a coward. "I have to get changed for the next dance, Sebastian." A scantily clad dancer goes scampering by us down the hallway to the dressing rooms.

He frowns. "Tonight, after the competition then," he insists before barreling into my space and clasping those big palms on either side of my head.

"Oh... okay," I stammer, curling my hands into fists to keep from reaching for him and cursing the repercussions.

He leans in, and my breath stalls in anticipation. "I stayed away," he growls against my mouth in ruthless passion. "Cannot be near you without wanting you. Cannot want more..."

His words cut off as his lips descend. He dives deep, his tongue hard, dueling with mine, enticing me to suck it. When I pursue the urgent instinct, the light pull draws a guttural moan from his throat. Shivers course down my spine, and I clutch the lapels in desperation, never wanting this to end.

Somehow, I discover the fortitude to break free, backing away along the wall, the hard surface keeping me vertical. The vampire watches me. His breath is as harsh as my own, the sapphire gaze tracking.

"Tonight, Red. We settle this." And with that, he turns and stalks down the corridor before disappearing around the corner.

Holy shit! What just happened?

Chapter 36

Alexandria

"**Y**ou fucking rocked it out there!" Nicole declares before wrapping me up in an unexpected hug. I grip the trophy tighter and slip my free arm around her waist, savoring the rare affection from my BFF.

"I did," I grin when she steps back, making room for Logan's warm embrace.

"I have observed many dance competitions over the years with Sebastian, and you, little one, are far superior in skill to my brother."

My lids expand so wide enough I fear my eyeballs will pop out of their sockets and go bouncing across the makeshift wooden floor. "Bastian dances?"

"Oh, yes. His mother was a champion ballroom dancer centuries ago, and he was her partner until his transition. After that, he never danced again," Logan says with a frown.

"I didn't realize ballroom went back so far."

"Indeed. The Viennese waltz originated in the Provence area in France in the mid-1500s."

Wow. A new wrinkle in my brain, and with it, my imagination ignites with all kinds of possibilities. It would be the ultimate fantasy to dance the tango with the sexy vampire. The tall, dashing male controlling my body with a turn of a wrist, his solid frame pressed to mine. Crickey, I'm flushed merely thinking about it.

"Where is your brother?" I ask, noting he isn't among my group of friends. Did he stick around and watch the rest of the competition after our kiss, or did he take off for parts unknown? Like one of his fucking clubs? Disappointment settles in my gut.

"He hightailed it out of here a second ago," Kurtis responds before enveloping me in a bear hug. Geez, he's like Goliath to my David. "He said to meet him just inside the rear entrance in ten minutes."

He stayed. Tingles spread along my skin. The prospect of being alone with him sends my fervid thoughts into overdrive. God. I detest how much my soul cries out for him.

When Lucretia bends to embrace me, I'm in sheer awe of her. She is the offspring of an Oracle, and her twin is an Oracle in training. Not to mention, she was the first and only—so far—female Guardian. I can't imagine the dedication and discipline that level of training required.

"That salsa was the sexiest thing I've ever witnessed," she declares with a grin before stepping back into Kurtis' grasp. They make such a beautiful couple. Her height fits perfectly with the 6'8 powerful physique of King Ruse.

"Thanks," I smile, before winking up at the sexy shifter. "And congrats on the promotion dude. Should I bow or something?"

Kurtis barks out a laugh, but I'm startled when Lu leans down again and whispers in my ear. "Only if you wish your ass smacked." I gape at the shit-eating grin on the stoic warrior's face.

"Hey, pipsqueak. My turn to extend congratulations," Liam says before stealing his arms around my waist and hoisting me up for a crushing hug.

I choke out a laugh. "You're gonna squeeze the life out of me, you big oaf." I kiss his cheek before he lowers me to the floor. "No lady on your arm, handsome?"

The smile vanishes, supplanted by a dark melancholy. "Nah. Between running the Werewolf Provinces, managing the LeLoo, and maintaining my ranch, I'm too damn busy." A teasing glint enters the somber gaze. "Besides, you've ruined me for other women, pipsqueak. I only have eyes for you."

"Yeah, and I'm the queen of England," I snort.

After hugging my mom and Cipher, I hand them my trophy for safekeeping before turning from the group. "Meet up with you all at the LeLoo later tonight," I say over my shoulder as I rush to the changing rooms.

Excitement bubbles in my gut as I quickly don a pair of black, fleece-lined leggings, a heavy wool turtleneck, and white snow boots. When I showed up at the hotel earlier this evening, big fat snowflakes were tumbling from the sky, and this girl's toes do not get cold.

I finger comb my curls into some pretense of order before glancing in the mirror to inspect my makeup. Still perfect. Thank you, MAC.

Practically jogging to the exit, I pause at the door and inhale several deep breaths to steady my erratic heartbeat. Jesus, you'd think I was meeting a celebrity or something the way I'm acting.

With a shake of my head at my silliness, I shove open the door and step into the frigid night. Kurtis mentioned waiting inside, but I need air.

The once gloomy and dirty alley became a snowy, white wonderland, glistening in the faint glow from lights mounted on the buildings.

"Damn, it's cold for February," I grumble to myself before blowing on my fingers to warm them. I peer down the alleyway but see no trace of Bastian. I'm about to dash inside and snag the wool gloves I left in my room when a slim figure steps from the gloom.

Trepidation coils in my gut as Rowena Moretti saunters toward me. This bitch potentially killed my father, and I'm suddenly cursing my lack of weapons. Yeah. Like I could murder my mate's mother unless it were justifiable self-defense. Based on their interactions, Sebastian loathes her, but she's still his parent, killing her would erect an impenetrable barrier between us never to be scaled.

"Alexandria. I was hoping to have a moment of your time." The beautiful ebony-haired creature with sharp blues eyes requests with a lush smile. The woman looks like she's in her early thirties, not sixth century.

"Actually, I've been searching for you, Rowena," I reply, doing a swift scan down the alley once more. Where is Bas?

"Oh?" The bitch advances closer, causing the hair on my nape to rise.

While I am a proficient fighter, I am no match for the velocity and strength of a vampire, especially one of Rowena's age, but I hold my ground and reach under the neckline of my sweater to yank out the silver chain. The Moretti ring dangles from the center, glinting in the eerie light.

"You wouldn't know anything about this ring and where I found it would you, Rowena?"

A flicker of blue fire ignites in the vampire's gaze as she glances at the gold circle. "If you are questioning me, then I assume my ruse didn't work."

"What ruse might that be?"

"My ongoing endeavor to maneuver my son into killing you, of course," she says with a casual shrug. "If you believed Sebastian butchered your precious father, I held faith you would make an attempt on his life to avenge the weak, pathetic berserker. My boy would have no alternative but to kill you in self-defense." The sapphires, so like Bastian's, burn brighter.

"How could you have possibly known we were fated then? We hadn't met." I need to keep her talking and hope Bas arrives soon.

"I learned you were my son's before you were born, my dear. I paid a hefty price to acquire the information from a witch. Sebastian will *never* have a mate. And while I considered killing you outright myself, he would never forgive me. But if you died by his own hand or the Watchers, I would be there to help him pick up the pieces. Comfort him. Love him. He would finally see that we are meant to be together."

Bile rises in my throat. "Together? As in mother and son, or together as in lovers?"

Her laugh is slick as oil. "Both my dear. Sebastian was the ultimate sexual submissive. I taught him everything he knows." Her smile evaporates. "Until his transition, when my thrall no longer obtained an effect, and physically he became too troublesome to control."

"You sick, twisted bitch." I've only known loving parents, so I'm appalled at her perverted treatment of her child.

She manipulated her son's mind, forcing him to be her submissive. No wonder Sebastian closed off his heart. Is inflicting pain on women his mental revenge against his mother?

"You wouldn't understand, and I have no inclination to justify it to a simpleton like you." One second, she's three feet from me, the next her fingers close around my throat, crushing my larynx before slamming me into the metal door.

I claw at her hand and kick out, aiming for her knee cap. When she buckles slightly, I ram my elbow into her cheek just as the door behind me flies open, sending us both careening into the snow cover ground.

A quick roll, and I'm on my feet once more, fixed to fight to the death. But no longer is it merely for my dad, it's for Sebastian too, for the hell he endured at the hands of this demented monster.

Chapter 37

Sebastian

Joy and anxiety battle for supremacy inside my brain. Over the previous months, remaining away from Alex has been sheer torture, both physically and mentally. I fed only out of necessity, and merely enough to provide me the strength to perform my functions as commander of the Guardians.

Every night I buried myself in work, hit the gym, pounded my body into exhaustion, begged for dawn, and the oblivion of sleep. But even then, she invaded my dreams, twisting them into dark fantasies filled with her luscious body responding to my every stroke and command. Upon waking, my dick was rock hard and throbbing for her flesh.

I worked over several of the more extreme subs at the club, expecting the discipline and control would distract my inner vampire, and I could find a few moments of peace. But I pictured Alex, bound and gagged, red welts rising on her porcelain skin, and it sickened me. I offered them what they sought; pain, but I never touched them sexually.

By day sixty, I conceded defeat. I couldn't survive without her a minute longer. She transformed me and brought my withered heart back to life. I may be the one with all the experience, but she is the one who knows how to love, how to risk it all for what she wants.

I glance at my watch for the hundredth time and pick up speed toward the building. With so many humans milling around, tracing becomes problematic. The inconvenience forces me to walk at a snail's pace, and I am running late.

A fierce cry pierces the night, and my lungs compress. *Alex!* I would recognize her voice anywhere. I break into a run, faster than a mere mortal but not so rapid I invite attention. White plumes of air discharge from my lips as my anxiety escalates. I assumed she would be secure with my family and friends surrounding her at this event, and I left explicit instructions that she was not to go outside until I arrived.

My feet skid around the corner into the alley, and I stop dead in my tracks. Everything inside me ceases to function as my mind struggles to process the scene before me.

Facedown in the snow, red hair spanning out from her head like a fiery beacon, dark blood saturating the ice, is my mate.

I open my senses to her. '*Alex?*' I whisper telepathically. Nothing. No heartbeat, no breaths raising or lowering her torso, and I do not discern her presence.

"Alex?" My anguished shout reverberates through the alley, my gaze glued to my mate's body, hoping and praying to identify some spark of life. A twitch of a limb, a sharp inhale of breath.

Nothing.

Movement snags my awareness, and I recognize Rowena standing over Alex, blood dripping from her fingernails. Rage clouds my vision. I fly at Rowena, not caring who sees, smashing my fist into her throat.

"Why, mother?" I roar as she cowers at my feet, shaking her head, coughing, and wheezing while the damage in her neck repairs.

Beyond rational thought, my soul and mind suffused with the impact of losing my precious Red and the torment at my failure to save her, I yank Rowena up by her hair as Nicole and Logan come barreling through the doorway, shadowed by Liam, Kurtis, and Lu.

Before they can stop me, I plow my fist through my mother's sternum. Sapphire eyes, identical to mine, swell in shock as my fingers close around the beating organ. I refuse to call it a heart. My mother never possessed one.

"Bastian! No!" Logan roars, and I see my brother advancing in my periphery, but it is too late. Without remorse and a feral snarl, I crush it in my fist.

Through a haze of crimson fury, I regard my mother's stunned pupils dilate as her life force evaporates. Her corpse collapses softly onto the snow, her pulverized heart still clenched in my hand.

"Lu," Nicole barks. "Thrall the humans at the entrance. Kurtis, you and Liam stand guard with Lu and don't let anyone in here until we get this mess figured out."

I hear their movements, but a dazed numbness settles over my brain as I stare at the lifeless body of my mate. She's dead. How can this be? I was coming to announce I love her. That I wish to try to make things work between us, assure her we could persuade the Watchers to back off somehow with Icarus or Viessa's help.

Now we will never have the chance. I was too late to spare her from the monster in my past, the creature who defiled my body and blackened my soul against love.

I peer down at the remnants of Rowena's heart oozing between my fingers and the numbness recedes, replaced by despair and anguish the likes of which I have never known before. A dark, bleak future spans out before me, one without the little valkyrie who wheedled her way past my defenses and pierced my heart. A heart now filled with grief, misery, but also condemnation and self-loathing.

What kind of animal possesses the capability to slaughter their own flesh and blood, the female who provided them life? My mother was a vile, devious, manipulative bitch, who controlled my mind for her sick sexual appetite. Maybe she deserved to perish, but not by her own son. Not by me.

I lift my gaze to my brother. Love and sympathy shine bright in the emerald stare, driving the last visage of numbing fog from my brain.

I cannot breathe. Sharp, piercing pain builds and builds, expanding like a gathering storm raging below the surface, demanding an outlet. I throw my head back, peer into the ominous clouds above as large snowflakes land quietly on my face. I do not feel the icy slush only the agony consuming every part of me, and I cannot contain the suffering a second longer.

Flinging my arms out wide, I bellow my torment, rage, and grief to the heavens, fists clenched, bloody gore oozing from my right palm. Tears spill readily from my eyes. My irises smolder with a brilliant light, chasing away the gloom of the alley.

Depleted, I slowly lift my head and glare at the mutilated organ in my fist through a shimmering barrier of tears. Lifting my arm like a pitcher for the Red Sox, I hurl my mother's heart against the side of the building. It strikes with a wet splat, the force bursting the muscle like a squashed tomato. I observe the chunks slide down the brick, dripping without a sound into the snow piled below.

Nicole kneels next to my mate's body, and I cannot be here a second longer. I do not wish to see the vacant stare in those beautiful blue eyes. It would break me. I harness the last ounce of energy, gather my frenzied wits, and scatter my molecules, ignoring my queen's outstretched hand and urgent command to stop.

I am as dead inside as the shell of Alex's body on the ground. I shut down, fortify my mental shields against Nicole and Logan, and draw my pain and anguish around me like a silver blanket.

I failed her. Neglected to protect the most precious element in my life when she needed me the most. All because I could not trace in front of the goddamn humans.

Fuck them. Fuck them all.

Chapter 38

Alexandria

"Where the hell are we?" I demand as Ezekiel lands on a pristine white beach and lowers me to my feet. Gentle waves slap against the shore, advancing and receding in a hypnotic rhythm. "Take me back, E. right now."

My roommate, Ryen, was the one who burst through the exit to the alley. Tears fill my vision—the slideshow of circumstances contributing to her death flashes through my mind.

"Alex? Are you alright?" She paused in the doorway, the light behind her setting her red hair aflame. Her jade eyes flitted between Rowena and me.

"I'm fine, Ry. Just enjoying a little chat. Please go back inside," I urged as calmly as possible, knowing my former shrink could rip my human friend to shreds in the blink of an eye.

Instead of backing up, the idiot advanced further; the door closed behind her with a soft click, sealing her doom.

I sprinted for her, but Rowena was quicker, slit her throat open with a slash of her dagger-like nails.

"No!" I screamed, watching Ryen's terrified expression turn my direction, her fingers clutched at her neck in an attempt to curb the flow of blood.

Right before I reached her, a mighty arm snaked around my waist like a steel band, and I rose backward into the night sky.

Shocked, I observed Ryen fall face-first into the snow, garish red darkened the surrounding whiteness, the crimson curls, so like my own, fanned out in a halo around her head.

"You've violated the laws of your council, Ms. Moretti," Ezekiel warned, continuing to ascend, my spine fused to his chest. "You will suffer the consequences of your actions."

I couldn't understand why he was lifting us away. We needed to annihilate the bitch. As the ground and my target became smaller, I battled against the powerful angel, thirsting to rip Rowena's head clean from her body. "Let me go!" I howled and struggled harder. "We have to kill her."

"I'm sorry, Alex. It is forbidden without permission."

How could he be so fucking calm? He just witnessed the vampire murder a human in cold blood. What more goddamn incentive did he need?

"Then put me down, and I'll do it myself."

"She is extremely powerful. I will not allow harm to come to you."

"You don't get to decide that!" I shouted and renewed my struggles. A streak of lightning flashed by us.

"Please cease, Alex, or you will force me to subdue you."

"You son of a bitch. She murdered my father, Did horrible things to Bastian." Bitter tears coursed down my cheeks as I clawed, kicked, and bit at my kidnapper.

"I am sorry," the angel whispered right before pain burst through the side of my skull, and my world blackened.

As I stand on the picturesque beach, in the middle of fucking nowhere, Ryen's blood oozing into the snow brands my mind forever. Her death was my fault. I should've obeyed Bastian's order and hung inside with my friends. Instead, I disregarded my safety and the security of others for some coveted one on one with my vampire.

Grief clogs my throat, but I force the tears away. There will be time to grieve the loss of my friend later. Right now, I need to figure out a way to persuade Ezekiel to get me out of here.

"Rowena needs to pay for what she did to my father, to the other immortals that night, and for murdering a human." I dig my fingers into his shoulders. "Fly us back, E. Please."

"The vampire is atoning for her transgressions as we speak," the angel replies dispassionately with a shrug. E's muscular chest is bare, the extraordinary black wings spanning out from his back make the dark blue jeans and sneakers comical. His breathtaking beauty and sculpted physique should be draped in a white robe similar to the outfits Icarus wears. "The safest place for you right now is here with me."

"How is she atoning?" I ask, my eyes narrowing in suspicion.

"Mr. Moretti slew his mother."

Oh, my God!

I gape at E, blinking but not actually seeing him. Instead, I visualize my lethal vampire, his mother's blood dripping from his fangs, the sapphires radiating with murderous fury. What possessed Bastian to kill his own flesh? And how the hell do you survive something like that?

Granted, in the eyes of the council, the killing would be warranted, and the bitch more than deserved it, but if I understand anything about my vampire, in his mind, the burden of such an act will damn his soul. I have to get to him. Sebastian will need me whether or not he realizes it. Now, I must persuade the stubborn angel to fly me back to the scene of the crime.

"Where is here, Ezekiel?"

Although the coast is magnificent, the ocean glittering like undulating diamonds in the moonlight, the soaring palm trees swaying gently in the warm, humid breeze, my inner valkyrie is itching to get the fuck gone. I'm confident my friends, along with Bastian, found

Ry's body, and on top of everything else he's dealing with, my mate will go insane trying to locate me.

E ignores my question, tucking the annoying curls floating around my face in the mild wind behind an ear. "There is a dwelling up the path with every amenity you require. The island is extensive enough for you to explore, but we are the sole inhabitants."

"You brought me to a deserted island? Why?"

Son of a bitch. There goes any prospect of freedom. I can't teleport or fly. I don't possess the ability to communicate telepathically, so essentially, unless there's a boat secured to a dock somewhere, or a landline up at this mysterious house, I'm screwed. E is my only way off this gorgeous prison.

"To keep you from the vampire, of course." He shrugs like the statement clarifies everything. Well, it so doesn't, not by a long shot.

"Tell me why it's so damn important to keep Bastian and me apart?"

"I am not permitted to disclose facts before their allotted time. I am sorry."

"Ezekiel? Did the Watchers sanction this little abduction?" His lids lower, and a blush steals over his cheeks. "They don't realize you grabbed me. Do they?"

"No. I acted so because I love you, Alexandria, and I will not permit any harm to your person."

I lurch back a step. "You love me? But... but you're a freaking angel. That has to be against the rules or something."

"We are fallen, free to copulate with whoever we choose as long as it does not interfere with our obligations."

"But it is interfering." My fists perch on my waist. "You defied orders by holding me hostage. And is that your goal here, E? To copulate with me?" If he imagines I'll allow him to touch me intimately, then he truly is cray-cray.

"First off, you are my guest. Secondly, I would never force you into sex, but I will not lie. Everything about you turns me on, and I would cherish the opportunity to explore your luscious body and make love to you. Not for a night, but for all eternity." I try not to recoil when his knuckles brush gently down my cheek. "I would defy God anew to keep you safe and all to myself." His devilish grin diminishes the small spark of optimism I boasted to convince him to return me to Flagstaff.

The reason the Watchers fell is because they opposed God. Like *the* God. Instead of being cast into purgatory, he granted them a second chance by becoming the wardens of the immortal realm. This abduction is just another defiance to E, one he believes rightly overshadows his loyalties and obligations to his brothers and the big man upstairs.

Could the all-powerful being actually want me dead, or is this little witch hunt a product of the fallen's overzealous quest to breach the pearly gates? I choose to maintain it's the latter because if God were out to get me, I'd be lost already.

My thoughts drift to my initial question; Why is it so damn important to keep Sebastian and me apart they're willing to assassinate me to accomplish it? I'm a valkyrie, he's a vampire, but us mating is no longer against council law.

Is it against God's law?

No, that's ludicrous. If that were the argument, the angels would've taken out either Lu or Kurtis, not to mention my mom and Cipher. His bite is bound to develop the second she steps down as queen.

"Please." Ezekiel indicates with a wave of his hand I proceed up the trail toward the house. "You must be starving. Allow me to cook us dinner."

How can he be thinking of food right now? With no fucking way off this island, even if I could kick the angel's ass—the odds being slim to non-existent—I'm stranded with no means to alert any-one where the hell in the world I am.

Anger, fierce and rapid courses through my veins. How dare E dictate my life in this manner? How I live, dangerous or not, is my goddamn choice, not Sebastian's, Ezekiel's, or the fucking Watchers.

A brilliant streak illuminates the beach and E's face, then anoth-er, and another until the midnight sky is cracking with the electrical charge of energy.

E frowns. "Please settle down, Alex."

Oh, is the angel worried someone might detect the unusual dis-play of lightning across the clear sky? Good.

And I believe I warned him once about the consequences of telling a woman to calm down.

Chapter 39

Alexandria

"**Y**ou must eat, love."

I cringe at the endearment and glare at the fish eyeballing me from my plate. After my tantrum on the beach, E threw me over his shoulder and trudged up the path to a beautiful casita nestled among the foliage of this lush tropical landscape.

My 2,000 sq. Ft. prison is all open shutters, cool colors, and mosquito netting around the beds. Huge black barrels on the roof catch rainwater, and with no electricity, a generator runs the essentials. Propane lanterns mounted throughout the house light the way at night.

Any other time, I would've thoroughly enjoyed this little paradise, but a strange anxiety has taken residence in my gut, and not only because of my forced incarceration. An urgency to get to Bastian plagues me night and day. Over the last couple of weeks, my dreams turned sinister, visualizing my mate's death over and over again.

The worst one was watching his body being engulfed in flames as he willfully strolled into the midday sun, my nickname on his lips, tears dampening his cheeks. I cried out to him repeatedly, but he couldn't hear me, and I was forced to watch him burn to ash.

Something is grievously wrong, and if I don't find out what, I'll go psychotic.

"E, please," I plead for the hundredth time in the past two freaking months. "Let me call Nicki. We can inform her Rowena was the one who murdered my father and sought to frame Sebastian, and that I'm fine."

No doubt, my mother, along with Nicole and Logan, and my tenacious mate, are bringing every resource at their disposal into finding me. But, Jesus, how much longer will it take? In the couple months Ezekiel stranded me on this uninhabited island, I've eaten seldom, sustained only by the lightning on continuous display in the hope someone notices it. But the effort is sapping my reserves, and I've dropped a significant amount of weight. Enough that the clothes E bought when we first arrived, hang like sacks on my frame.

"Eat, and I will consider it."

Yup. We pretty much have this same damn conversation every day. Although I'll give the angel credit, he's come up with some innovative approaches to keep me entertained. From poker—which he attempted to turn into strip poker—to scavenger hunts, and even ballroom dance lessons on the beach. It seemed glamorous at first but attempting a graceful spin in the sand was nigh impossible.

Through it all, the Watcher's seduction has advanced by gradual, methodical increments, and it's making me edgy. I understand next to nothing about this being. When his patience runs out, will he resort to violence?

"You recall I can't consume anything while it's staring at me. Eyeballs equal vomitus."

With a frustrated sigh, Ezekiel comes at me with a butcher knife, and I leap back, knocking over my chair. He severs the head of the fish, stabbing it and tossing it out the window for whatever predators live on the island.

"Now eat," he commands with a glower.

Biting my cheek to keep from grinning, I pick up my chair and resume my seat, but simply pick at my dinner. I'm getting to the fallen. If I continue throwing grenades at his defenses, he'll eventually weaken and give in to my demands.

A ridiculous urge to thrust my head backward and cackle like a crazy woman enters my brain. It must be my lack of protein. I reject the impulse and launch another bomb.

"Please, E, I promise I'll eat everything you put in front of me if you allow me to call Nicole."

"I will contact her."

"She's gonna interrogate you about me. Are you going to lie, Angel?" Badgering the witness is a "You're out of order" kind of move, but desperate times and all that. "If you let me speak to her, I agree to do anything you propose." Not really, but a prisoner will blow the biggest smokestack up your ass to get paroled.

He quirks an eyebrow. "Anything?"

Oh boy, does the wicked angel crave a kiss? "Yes. Anything." I lower my voice to a throaty murmur.

Ezekiel runs his tongue over his teeth as he contemplates a response, his eyes darken. "Vow it."

Son of a bitch.

"If you wish me to vow, you need to be more explicit on what you demand."

"I want you to marry me."

Holy fucking God! That I never expected. A kiss. A little make-out session. Yes. But marriage?

"Are you kidding me right now?"

"No." The seriousness in his manner sets my nerves on edge. "I love you, Alex, and in time, you will care for me as well. We could be happy here."

Oh shit. He wants us to live our lives in complete isolation in a happily ever fucking after kind of scenario? Who is this lunatic?

"Um, E… I…" I'm at a loss. My shell-shocked brain isn't behaving. So, when he rises and yanks me to my feet, it doesn't register what's happening until his lips brush mine.

I'm astonished by the skill and hunger in his kiss, held immobile by heavy arms wrapped around my waist, hauling me against the hardness behind his zipper. Holy cripe! Angels get erections. Who knew?

When the black wings come around and enfold us in darkness, the intimacy is too extreme. Who's weakening whose defenses here? My traitorous body responds to the soft insistence of his mouth. The gentle slide of his tongue over my closed lips, begging for entrance, the tender, sweeping caresses along my back, and the pressure of his dick rubbing against my pubic bone.

What the fuck am I doing? This sweet seduction is nice, but it's not the demanding, dynamic, all-absorbing passion Bastian brings out in me. The vampire is who I crave.

I push against the naked chest—I swear the creature doesn't own a shirt—and he maneuvers away several inches. I lick my lips in what I hope is a provocative move. "Phone call first, negotiate marriage later."

"No negotiation, Alex," he pants into my ear, rolling his hips against mine. I swallow down the revulsion. "Vow it or no contact with the outside world."

Anger ignites in my gut. The feathered fucker is blackmailing me into marrying him. "You realize Sebastian is my fated one, right?"

"Yes. But your union will never be. Take what I am offering. We are perfect together." He trails soft kisses down my neck, and I moan low to continue the pretense, but the angel clearly lost his damn mind.

What if I'm powerless to communicate to Nicole where I am, or I need rescuing? What then? An immortal's vow is like a signed contract: binding, unbreakable.

Think, Alex. Think.

"That's a big ask, E. I hardly know you. Not to point it out, but our relationship started with you kidnapping me."

He leans back, the golden head tilts, and I strive not to squirm under his inspection. "Fair enough. Vow to grant me a fighting chance to gain your trust and love. Let me woo you."

"Woo me?" I almost laugh out loud until I realize he's serious. "What precisely are we talking about here?"

"Allow me permission to kiss you, caress you, taste you as an actual boyfriend would, and I yearn for you to do the same. Your affection will grow during our time here if you give it half a chance."

"Wait. Are we talking sex or just make out sessions?" No way I'm having sex with him, even though it was my original goal when we met, until I discovered he was part of a faction that wanted me dead.

"We start with make-out sessions, as you call them, progress into making love, and ultimately marriage. I am skilled in thousands of ways to pleasure a woman, Alex. Once I get my hands and mouth on your exquisite body, you will be thoroughly satisfied and greedy for more. I promise."

Of all the arrogant... "Fine. I vow it."

Chapter 40

Sebastian

Darkness permeates my soul, but I am too much of a coward to stride into the midday sun and end my miserable existence.

The anemic blood of humans denies my beast and my body nourishment. Horrific images of my dead mate in the snow, my mother's beating heart in my hand, and her shocked expression plague my mind. The sapphire eyes, so like my own, damned me to hell.

Night after night, I seek escape in the lowliest dives scattered around the world, steering clear of other immortals who might report my whereabouts to the queen. I felt her persistent nudges in my brain, but the mental barriers remain firm despite my weakened state.

When the agony of starvation cramps my gut, I thrall the pathetic humans to do my bidding. Blood pours freely, their fragile bodies offer empty, sexual release, the pain inflicted doing little to relieve the torment in my heart.

The dawn approaches, and exhaustion rides my back like a jockey with a whip. After the first couple of weeks, I discontinued erasing their memories of me, leaving them with the aftermath of their bruised hearts and bodies, and a pounding hangover.

Why should I give a fuck? These stupid, pathetic creatures are the reason my beautiful Red is gone. If it were not for them, I would have arrived in the alley on time. My mate would still be alive, and my mother's blood would not stain my hands.

After months of self-torture with no relief in sight, I finally concluded nothing can ease this torment. My life is but a deep chasm of darkness and pain without the sparkling blueness of my mate's eyes gazing upon me with love and desire. The fiery, soft curls clutched in my fingers as I pound into her tightness, the sweet vanilla flavor of her skin and blood coating my lips, her moans and cries of ecstasy filling my ears. The beautiful smile will never brighten the world again.

It might as well have been my blackened heart I ripped from my chest because without my mate, my reason to exist on this planet died with her.

Alexandria's death was the fulcrum of my downfall, the eye of the storm that had taken me into madness, the catalyst of my disintegration.

It is past time to end the torment. This dawn, I will meet the sun and join my love in the afterlife.

Chapter 41

Alexandria

"**W**hat do you mean he's gone?" I stare at my best friend's troubled image on the small screen of Ezekiel's phone. Apparently, cell service exists in the middle of freaking nowhere. Thank you, Verizon.

"He assumes you're dead, Alex. He took off before I could verify the body in the snow wasn't yours." She swipes a hand through her hair. "And the fucker is blocking me mentally."

"So, not only did he kill his mother, he believes his mate perished in the alley? Holy shit, Nicki. What will he do?"

'*Where are you, Alex?*' The powerful halfling whispers in my mind across the miles. I present a slight shake of my head.

"I'm not positive, but it isn't good," she continues, as if she's not transmitting a separate conversation in my brain. "I require you here to help locate him before he does something stupid."

'*Blink once for yes and twice for no. Do you understand?*' One blink.

"That is not feasible, Queen Giordano," E butts in, and I scowl at him in irritation. "The Watchers still hunt for Alexandria."

"No shit, Sherlock," Nicki practically growls into the phone.

'*Are you in a city?*' Two blinks. '*A forest?*' Two blinks. '*Wait, I think I hear the ocean.*' I blink once slowly. '*Okay, you're by a beach. He'd need to keep you isolated. Are you on an island?*' I blink in answer when what I truly crave to do is shout it.

My beautiful fanged lover is hurting. We're not fully mated, but the bond between his inner vampire and my valkyrie warrior is strong. The loss would be mentally crippling, even if there were no love or emotion involved. Most bonded males end their lives after losing a mate. They abandon the will to live. Pile on top, the fact he performed a heart-ectopy on his mother, and it's a recipe for disaster.

"I'm guessing your Watcher buddies didn't endorse this little heist of yours," Nicki says, a gray spark kindling in her glare. "Release her, and I'll forget this ever happened." The underlying threat is blatantly obvious. I smile inwardly.

E's eyebrow lifts. "And if I do not?"

"Then I go straight to the dude with the big stick up his ass and tell him all about how you abducted the valkyrie princess to a deserted island to defy God and have your wicked way with her."

I'd laugh out loud if I didn't consider it would piss Ezekiel off. Instead, I extend a quick wink of encouragement.

'Do you see any other islands?' Two blinks. *'Are you producing any lightning?'* One slow, exaggerated blink. *'That's my girl.'*

"You are bluffing, young halfling. You possess no inkling where we are."

"See, that's the problem. Everyone always underestimates me." She turns those steel grays on me. "Hang on, sista. I'm comin for ya."

This time I don't hold my grin in check. "I'll be here."

E immediately ends the call before extracting the sim card and battery. Clever angel. But it won't do him any good. Nicole will zero in on the lightning to pinpoint my position.

He seizes my elbow, whirling me to face him. The anger in his expression makes me giddy, but the apprehension in his gaze tempers it.

"What have you done? You sealed your fate, all for that filthy vampire who beats females."

Whoa. "Shut the fuck up, E!" I shout at him and attempt to wrench my arm free, but his fingers are like a powerful vice keeping me in place. "He doesn't beat women. You don't know what you're talking about."

"Do you desire such rough treatment, Alex? To be strung up and whipped?" The disgust in his tone elevates my rage. How dare he judge Sebastian. Or me. He defied God. Ezekiel will always win the game of 'who's the evilest,' hands down.

"Let go of me, E. You're hurting me."

"But that is what you enjoy, is it not?" A manic gleam enters the hazel eyes, and true fear settles like a stone in my stomach. "Perhaps, I was too patient and gentle, when all along you craved something else altogether."

"Not from you, E. Never from you."

"So, the vow was just a ploy to lower my defenses? Did you carry on a private telepathic conversation with the Halfling? I knew she was powerful, but I held no clue she could communicate such great distances."

"Like she said, people always underestimate her." I can't help the jab. He freaking deserves it.

"Your actions sadden me, Alex. I only had your best interest at heart."

A tiny twinge of guilt tries to invade, but I shove it back. The angel kidnapped me and forced me to play house with him for two months.

"Bullshit. You kidnapped me for your own selfish reason. Did you ever consider asking me what I wanted, Ezekiel?"

"Your decisions will get you killed, and I love you too much to allow that to happen."

When he attempts to throw me over his shoulder once again, I leap and twirl over his bare back, settling behind him. No way in hell,

I'll let him fly me off to God knows where again. Nicki will extricate me soon, and my mate needs me.

I kick out, landing a decent shot on his knee. When he buckles, I hop on his back. No clue if snapping his neck will kill him or not, so I aim for his skull with my elbow, committing all my weight into the blow to knock him out.

Nothing happens. No wait, correction, he sighs, heavily as if I'm a gnat buzzing around his head.

Fuck. Dammit. Shit.

In one abrupt action, the angel's wings unfurl, smacking me in the face and sending me sailing across the room. My poor abused back slams into the wall before I land with a heavy, 'thud' on the tile floor.

Pain ratchets up my spine as I attempt to rise. I make it to all fours when a hand clamps down on my skull, grasping a fist full of curls and yanking me to my feet. Why am I constantly in this predicament?

Gone is the fun-loving angel attempting to woo me. What stands before me is the enraged warrior of God. Fire dances in his eyes, his lips twist in contempt, and the massive wings undulate with each harsh breath.

"You dare to strike a Watcher? After everything I have undertaken to keep you safe, you still choose him over me."

"Every. Damn. Time." I spit out, pleased to see my silver gaze reflected in his irises.

Even though it's a futile endeavor, I punch his rock-hard gut several times before rearing up with an uppercut to his chin. Intense pain reverberates through my fist as bones snap, and I shake my head at my absurdity.

"You cannot win against me, Alex. I wasted enough time. You are mine. If I must tie you up, whip you within an inch of your life, and fuck you senseless to make you see reason, then I so be it."

"Over my dead carcass." I breathe out, cradling my busted hand to my chest.

"And mine."

Relief pounds through me at the sound of my savior's voice behind the livid angel. I feared she would be too late. Guess now I'm the one underestimating her.

"Get your goddamn paws off my best friend."

The Watcher drops me and swings to the crowd gathered. Nicki brought friends, and man are they a sight for sore eyes. Logan, Kurtis, Lu, and Liam are all jammed into the cramped living room.

"I guess you pissed off your brothers, Ezekiel. When I advised them of your actions, they mentioned something about stripping you of your powers." She tsks. "Sounds pretty bad."

The angel has the audacity to chuckle. "You align with the wrong angels, my lady. They are the ones who demand her death."

"Yeah, care to explain why before I kill you?"

My brows draw together as I slowly ease away from E. As pissed as I am with him, I don't want him dead. He did what he did under some misguided notion he was sheltering me. And maybe he was.

"No. They will reveal it soon enough. Circumstances will trigger it." With a shrug, his wings disappear. "Then, there will be no saving Alexandria."

"What will trigger?" I ask, blanching as the bones in my fingers mend.

"A tremendous change to seal your fate." The sorrow in his eyes freaks me out.

"Your riddles are pissing me off, Watcher," Nicki declares, advancing a menacing step in E's direction, but Logan reaches out and clamps a restraining hand on her elbow.

"Easy love. We came here for Alexandria. Leave Ezekiel Sorath to his brothers."

"Just get me outta here, Nic, so we can find Bastian before it's too late."

Never taking her gaze from E, she stretches out her arm, and I step into her warm embrace, never so grateful for such a devoted and powerful friend.

"Alex. Leave the vampire to his own devices. His death ensures your safety."

I gape at the heartless creature before me, prepared to eliminate one soul to preserve another for his own selfish desires. "If you believe I would willingly sacrifice a life for my own, then you don't know me at all, Fallen," I declare before the room darkens, dissolving altogether as Nicki scatters our molecules to the wind.

Chapter 42

Alexandria

As soon as we appear at the vampire castle, my mother and Cipher embrace me, and for once, I bask in my mother's love, pleased to alleviate her stress and anxiety regarding my wellbeing once again.

"I requested all hands-on deck," Nicki reports as she takes her place at the head of the massive table in the grand dining hall.

"Where is the priest?" Liam asks, his dark whiskey eyes scanning the room. No doubt he's hoping Viessa will accompany him.

"We are on our own with this one, kids. Icarus is embroiled in Oracle training with Vi. Whatever the fuck that means."

I stride to the wooden behemoth. It comfortably seats over a hundred immortals and is broad enough to accommodate three chairs at each end. Nicki presides over affairs in the middle, with Logan and Sebastian on either side.

Fear settles like a fiery cannonball in my stomach as I stare at the vacant chair to Nicki's left. A shiver races up my spine despite the warmth of the vast fireplace crackling on the far wall.

Where are you, my love?

Horrible images of my vampire burning alive plague me every second he's missing, and a scream of frustration bubbles below the surface. Why aren't we out there searching for him instead of having a goddamn family meeting?

The rational, 'calm your roll' sector of my brain understands we require a cohesive strategy, but my inner valkyrie doesn't give a rat's ass. He's out there somewhere, hurting, bracing to end his existence because he assumes I'm dead.

Placed between Cipher and my mother, my knee bounces with nervous restlessness, my fingers clench and unclench under the table as I gaze at this force assembled to locate the vampire commander. Each of them risks death by opposing the Watchers. But that's who they are, prepared to do anything for the individuals they care about. I'm proud to be part of such a tight-knit group of immortals.

When Dr. Warn... I mean, Guardian Christoph Nox, materializes with the seven-foot, red-eyed demon king who plundered my memories, I nearly jump out of my skin. The scexy—my rendition of scary/sexy—beast causes my heart to thump in double time. His skilled lips forced my brain into meltdown, oozed my lost history to the surface, and barreled it to the forefront with crystal clarity.

It was an illusion. The instigating event to catapult my past remembrances over the impenetrable barrier the demon erected, but if the kiss was any indication of his prowess, hoo doggie, whoever becomes his fated female is in for a rip-roaring ride. I blush when the wicked brute winks at me with a provocative, knowing grin.

Bastard.

"Thank you all for gathering on such short notice," Nicki begins, seizing the task force's attention. "In addition to our escalating issue with the Watchers, we have another urgent matter. As most of you know, Sebastian is missing, and while we've been working diligently to recover him, we are on borrowed time. I fear if we don't locate him by dawn, it'll be too late. I am open to any and all suggestions."

"As his mate, can you attempt to connect with him mentally, Alex?" Kurtis asks from across the table.

"Although he drank from me, we didn't complete the mating. I tried on numerous occasions during my captivity to reach him. Each time, all I achieved was a splitting headache."

King Ruse and Lucretia exchange an odd look before he nods, and she directs her attention to Nicki. "My queen...."

"Dammit, Lu, I am not your queen anymore. You and Kurtis mated, which makes you the shifter queen, so stop calling me that."

The former Guardian clears her throat. "Nicole does not sit easily with me yet."

"Well, fucking get used to it."

The vampire smiles. "Yes, my lady."

"What were you going to say?" I prompt when she adds nothing further.

"I believe I might be able to pinpoint the commander's location."

"Why didn't you just lead with that?" I throw my hands up in frustration.

"How?" Nicki and Logan inquire at the same time.

"I possess the ability of remote viewing."

Crickets. Every warrior is unmoving as stone. My gaze darts around at the stunned expressions, and I feel like a moron. I'm obviously the only one in this room who does not understand what that means.

"Are you fucking kidding me?" Logan all but growls down the table, and Kurtis tenses. "When did you gain this gift, Lu?"

She swallows. "After my turning."

"It's physically and mentally dangerous and weakens her to the point of collapse," the beefcake shifter chimes in, scowling at Logan.

"When did you use it last?" Nicki asks softly, her stare intense.

"Last year."

"And were there any side effects?"

"Yes," the beautiful warrior admits with a brief sideways glance at her mate. "My spleen nearly ruptured, and I was bedridden for eight hours."

"Jesus," Kurtis mutters.

"And you're prepared to apply this skill again to find Sebastian?"

"Of course." Lu's dedication is commendable.

"What do you need, and how can we help?" I ask, eager to get started. With every second that passes the demand to shriek my desperation and failure, burns my throat.

"Hang on," the werewolf king interjects. "Does Viessa have the same capability?"

Saddened amber eyes peer at Liam. "No. Not that I'm cognizant of, anyway." The hybrid turns her gaze on me. "I need a secure place to lie down and complete quiet to focus."

"Kurtis' tower room is free. Good Enough?" Logan suggests, hope shining in the emerald depths.

"Yes. Please understand, commander, I've only employed this ability twice in my whole life. The first occasion was to uncover my twin's whereabouts when Dimitri kidnapped her. The other was to… view my mate. I have no blood or bond connection to Sebastian, so I do not know if this will work."

"During your years as a Guardian, you never drank from Bastian or he from you?" Logan inquires.

Crap. Don't need that freaking visual in my head.

"No. The warrior allowed no one to consume from him," *Oh, thank God. Pretty confident I'd have lost it if she answered yes.* "And rumor had it; he only fed from his subs." *Son of a bitch, that's worse.*

Putting such thoughts aside, for now, I plead with Lu. "We have to try, though. Please."

When the warrior nods, we all rise in unison. Kurtis and Nicki escort Lucretia to the tower. I move to follow when Logan places a detaining grip on my arm.

"Mayhap you should leave them to it and help facilitate a scouting party in the event she is... unsuccessful."

"Have you ever experienced a crazed valkyrie, commander?" He lifts an eyebrow in response. "It's violent, messy, and loud, so unless you care to see this room destroyed, I suggest you let me pass. Nothing is keeping me out of that chamber."

Logan smirks. "As you wish, princess."

"Alexandria?"

I pivot with a frustrated sigh toward the valkyrie ruler. "Mom. Whatever it is, it can wait."

"Do you love him, or is this urgency to find him simply the bond?"

"Mother, I understand your reservations regarding Sebastian, but he was not responsible for Daddy's death. Rowena murdered him and everyone in that alley. I also recognize my mate's reputation with females precedes him, but let me be quite clear. The vampire possesses my heart, mind, and body. I desire him more than my next breath, and if he perishes, he takes my soul with him."

"If we are successful in locating him, and I hope to the gods we are, if you complete the bond, Alexandria, the Watchers will have your head, and no matter our number, they will triumph." She grips me by the shoulders, her somber eyes frantic. "Are you eager to sacrifice your life and the lives of the people you love to become his mate?"

"I would willingly lay down my life for his, Mother, but I'm not stupid. You and Cipher have loved each other for decades and never sealed the deal. We can do the same."

My mom looks away. "Oh, Alex, some factors are just too tempting to resist. I mated the shifter years ago."

"But..." I draw aside the collar of her blouse. "You don't carry the mark of his bite."

"Circumstances compelled us to hide it. Rest assured, I do bear his mark in a more private spot."

What the fuck? "Did you mate him while married to dad?"

The queen's dark eyes swell with regret, and her arms drop to her sides. "Yes."

"Did he know?" I demand in a harsh whisper as anger brightens my gaze. "Do my siblings know?"

"Gadr knew. It was impossible to keep something so obvious concealed from a husband. I believe your brother suspects. He is quite intuitive for a berserker, but your little sister is too self-absorbed to recognize anything if it doesn't affect her directly."

"You make me sick." How could she betray my father in such a way? He worshiped the ground she walked on and would have faced a battalion of vampires for her.

Her eyes tighten. "Since you have discovered your mate, I assumed you would understand. Accept it."

Is she fucking kidding me? "I'll never understand adultery, mother."

"Gadr knew before we married Cipher was my fated male, and he accepted it. Just as the shifter and I agreed, we could never be together openly. Our species was at war, and it was against council law. A council we helped into fruition."

"I don't have time for this. If your confession is over, I need to get up there and hopefully locate Sebastian before he offs himself." I spin from the sorrow in her expression and dash up the stairs to the fourth floor.

Why the hell did my mother choose this moment to confess her sins? Is she so selfish she can't see her daughter is in turmoil? Never have I required the solace and love of my mom more than tonight, and she takes the opportunity to pour out her heart so she can feel better about herself. She remarked on my sister's self-absorbing ways, well I suppose the electricity doesn't fall too far from the lightning, so to speak.

If... no, *when* we find Bas, and he's safe, my mother and I will cop-a-squat and have a little "come to Jesus" meeting because I foresee more secrets lurking beneath the surface.

Chapter 43

Sebastian

Silver chains sizzle on my flesh, starvation cramps my hollowed-out stomach, muscles, and tendons weaken with each passing minute. Dawn approaches. The tingle of awareness skitters along my nape, and I long for the end to begin.

I am so weakened; I can no longer lift my head. It lolls like a deflated balloon in the breeze against my bare chest, but I need not gaze around to recall the location I chose for my fiery demise.

The Roman Colosseum seemed fitting. Hundreds of warriors lost their lives in the great games to entertain the restless, starving masses. But a tiger or gladiator will not end my life. It will be the blazing heat of the sun upon my flesh.

The silver chains secured to the inner wall ensure I cannot change my mind and slink into the shadows like a weakling. The constant pain and misery entombed in my body from the loss of my mate must cease. And maybe finishing it is the cowardly path, but I cannot live in a world Red does not inhabit. Where the burden of murdering my mother chips away at my sanity.

The demon in my past mutated what passion meant. Sullied it. Defiled it. Rowena was the sole reason I could not love the one thing more precious than life itself. And a part of me is relieved she is dead.

By the time our father married Rowena after the death of Logan's mom, my brother was already out of the house and serving as King Dimitri's Guardian. During most of my childhood, she was loving and caring, to the point, it was suffocating at times, but I felt cherished by both my parents.

It all changed when my father died in battle around my fifteenth year. Rowena changed. The loving caresses made my skin crawl. Her sweet motherly kisses lingered. She used every excuse she could find to keep me at home. Even feigning heartbreak or illness to ensure I stayed at her side.

At first, I was not sure how to act or what to do about it. I passed it off as her grieving my dad and clinging to me for support. But when the caresses strayed below my waist, anger filled me, even as my adolescent body betrayed me by responding.

For years she seduced me, manipulated my young mind into believing she didn't mean to do the things she did; it was the loss and grief of losing her husband controlling her actions. And I was too weak and pathetic to fight back. With my brother embroiled in his duties to the king, my mom was all I had in the world, and I did not want to believe it was any more than the bullshit she was voicing.

Shame and guilt filled my gut the first time she made me ejaculate, and I struck out, slapping her across the face. I cringe remembering the spark of lust in her gaze when she forced me over her lap, stripped me of my pants, and landed blow after blow on my bare backside.

Even as a pre-tran vampire, I smelled her desire to cause me pain, but my body was too weak at the time to fight, so I endured it, vowing to make her pay after my transition when I would be strong enough to exact my revenge.

After the first beating, the bitch influenced my mind to follow her every order, respond to her sexual ministrations, and crave more. And I did. The thrall took hold, and I begged for my mother's touch, obediently followed every command. The lick of pain she inflicted, the sensation of being tied up and at her mercy became more than my need for blood.

The mind control did its job, but in the back of my mind, shock, and disgust at what she was making me do lingered. I wanted to tell Logan, but her influence over me, and my shame, kept my mouth shut.

I slump against the chains, recalling the last few nights right before my transition. She was desperate to hold on to me, instinctively knowing the second I became fully immortal, I would either kill her or leave forever.

For the first time, she'd chained me in her playroom in silver, drove me into a state of such crazed lust I thought I would go mad. The things she did to me and forced me to do to her altered my budding inner vampire. It skewed my perspective of sex and love permanently. I vowed right then and there to never love or trust another female for as long as I lived.

After my transition, which strangely enough she assisted me through, I couldn't bring myself to slay her. As much as I loathed and despised everything she did, the female was still my mom, the woman who raised me, fed me from her own vein as a baby, and bandaged my scrapes and bruises as a child.

In the end, I walked away, and my inability to kill her then caused Alex's death. I am responsible for that monster taking her life. My beautiful redhead with the brightest blue eyes and wide loving smile is gone because of me.

Pain courses through my veins as the dawn approaches. I grip the silver and grit my teeth to prepare for the coming agony. My cowardice all those years ago killed my one true mate, and for that, I deserve to burn in hell for all eternity.

Chapter 44

Alexandria

"If she doesn't locate him in two minutes, I'm ending this." Kurtis declares in a heated whisper towering over his mate, lying prone on the big bed.

Nicki and I perch on the edge of the wing-backed chairs facing the fire, its warmth doing nothing to diminish the tremors in my body. Lu has been in a trancelike state for the past twenty minutes while her spirit mind searches for Sebastian. Finding one vampire among thousands must be like a Where's Waldo painting.

Logan refused to join us, insisting he needed to keep busy with alternate means to uncover his missing brother and strategize with the council on how best to deal with the Watchers if they should breach the castle.

Just another typical day in the land of immortals. Life was much simpler when I thought I was a mere human.

I glance at the clock on the mantle for the zillionth time. Shit, depending on where he is in the world, we either have several hours, dawn is approaching fast, or the sun blazes already, and he's dead.

Unable to sit a moment longer, I hop up and pace the room. Nicki's eyes follow every agitated step. I know she's as anxious as me to bring Bas home, but this newfound, eerie calm she's sporting, is driving me nuts. Nicki is good at masking pesky emotions—her phrase, not mine—but her brother-in-law means the world to her.

By her vigilant expression, she recognizes the loss of my mate will destroy me, and rip Logan to shreds. They've barely come to terms with the miscarriage. They don't need another death piled on top.

NO! Stop thinking like that. He's going to be okay. Lu will locate him, and we'll get to him in time. I have to continue believing that. If I don't remain optimistic, the little valkyrie might go cray-cray.

When the warrior bolts upright on the bed, Kurtis leaps for her, positioning his powerful body behind her to support her lethargic frame.

"Did you find him?" I ask urgently, gripping her fevered hand.

Her head lolls onto Kurtis' shoulder as she attempts to look me in the eye. Her lids droop as if it's a struggle to hold them open.

"Italy," she finally whispers. "Colosseum... hurry."

In the next second, Logan appears in the chamber suited for battle, and I want to howl with relief as he and Nicole embrace me, arranging to teleport. As the room darkens, Kurtis gently turns his mate in his arms and cradles her face at his neck, nourishing his depleted vampire.

A slight sinking sensation tightens my gut, like when you experience a loop de loop on a super-fast roller coaster. I'm not a fan of teleportation, but thank goodness it doesn't make me want to vomit like some species.

As soon as our feet touch solid ground, my frantic gaze scans the tan and golden stone walls of this 2,000-year-old piece of history. But the spectacular beauty of the place is lost on me. Only one thing consumes my mind. Sebastian.

A flash of silver catches my eye. "Holy mother of God," I whisper in stunned disbelief.

This being chained to the wall, his head hung in defeat, is half the male he was two months ago, in weight and musculature. Gone is the vibrant, dominant vampire I've come to love and cherish.

A dark, unkempt beard covers his jaw. The eyes are so sunken I don't even glimpse a flicker of sapphire. Stained, ripped blue jeans hang loose on his hips, showcasing his protruding hip bones and ribs.

Shock cements my feet. Even as Logan strides by me to rescue his brother, and Nicki's arm wraps around my shoulders in comfort, I can't move.

Bastian always declared he didn't have a heart, or it was blackened, hardened by his past, but the shell of the male before me proves him wrong. The strength of his despair over losing me, and the trauma of killing his mother, crippled his will to live. Crushed his spirit. Fractured his magnificent heart.

"Let him see you, Alex. He needs to understand you're alive before we trace out of here," Nicki says, giving me a slight nudge.

It was all I required to snap me out of my frozen state and propel me toward my mate at a full run just as Logan lowers him to the ground, bracing his back against the wall. The sizzling wounds in his palms from removing the silver from his brother already healing.

"Bastian?" I choke out as tears spill down my cheeks, and I stumble to my knees next to him. Deep angry welts on his wrists, ankles, and across his chest ooze blood "Bastian," I whisper again when his head doesn't lift, and his arms hang limply at his sides. "I'm here."

"Alex." My name is but a wheeze escaping his lungs. "I'll be with you soon, my love."

I sweep the long hair off his forehead, grasp his chin, and raise his face to mine. "I'm right here, Sebastian." I lean in and kiss the dry, cracked lips, and my heart weeps. "I'm alive."

The dull sapphires blink several times as they attempt to focus. "Red?"

"Yes." I smile through the tears. "It's me."

"Am I dead?"

"No, my love."

"I saw you. In the snow. So much blood."

"It wasn't me. It was my roommate, Ryen."

I regard the valiant effort his depleted brain is making to comprehend what I'm saying. So I recite it again and again until a faint spark ignites in the sunken blue depths.

"Red," he murmurs. "You are alive."

"Yes, you big dummy. What the hell have you done to yourself?" His rough chuckle has more tears escaping.

"We must depart," Logan says urgently, and strides forward to gather his brother gently in his arms. "Dawn is seconds away."

Sebastian rests his head on Logan's shoulder, too frail to hold it upright. When Logan brushes a kiss on his brother's forehead, I want to burst out in an ugly cry at the beauty of their relationship.

Instead, I grasp Bastian's feeble hand as Nicole wraps her arm around my midriff. The bumpety, bump of the rollercoaster shoots through me until we touch down in what I can only assume is Sebastian's bedroom. Logan sets his brother down on the bed, propping him against the padded headboard.

"Do not ever fucking do that to me again, brother or I will beat you senseless." Unashamed tears glitter in the bright emeralds when he pivots my direction. "He must feed, but be vigilant. As starved as he is, he might consume too much or be aggressive."

"I understand." I simply wish to be alone with him, so I can provide and care for my mate.

Nicki strolls over to the bed, hands on her hips, and glares down at her commander. "You're suspended from duty for two weeks, you feel me? You ever scare me like that again, and I will excommunicate you from vampire society. Or something just as severe."

In other words, she loves him and is delighted he's home.

"Yes, my queen." At his rasp, she stoops, kissing his forehead before her and Logan trace from the room.

For several seconds, we stare, devouring each other with our eyes.

"Bastian...."

"Alex...."

We begin at the same moment, and I grin. "Feed first, talk later, eh?"

When he nods, I see the physical struggle to reach for me, so I race to seize his hand. On the last occasion he drank from me, we were spooning. This time, I prefer to cradle him in my arms to assure myself he's fine.

I mount the bed and straddle his hips. Once again, appalled at the emaciated condition of his body. It will require more than one feeding to restore my male to his former glory, but I'm more than thrilled to oblige. But on the flip side, I must temper my desire. Absolutely no sex while my blood rushes down his throat. No matter how turned on we become, we can't mate until we have a serious discussion about our future.

Easier said than done.

"Stop thinking. I need you," Bastian gasps out, and I lean forward, clasp him around the shoulders, and draw his upper body flush with mine.

"Drink, Bas. Regain your strength." I grip his skull, urging him toward my neck.

"Do not allow me to hurt you."

Even in his starvation, he's concerned about me. "I'm tougher than I look, big guy. Now shut up and sink those sexy fangs into me."

The low, desperate growl is the only warning before he strikes.

Chapter 45

Sebastian

At the first drop of Alex's potent blood, replenishing energy courses through my system, plumping deflated veins, strengthening atrophied muscles and tissue, and easing the cramps in my gut.

In all my years, I have never encountered such power in an immortal's blood. Is it because she is a valkyrie or my one true mate? The female subs I dined from over the centuries nourished and sustained my body and strength, but Alexandria's essence rushes through every part of me as if laced with cocaine.

Muscles and tendons cramp, protesting the rapid revival. For the first time in months, my heart rate accelerates to a normal cadence. A possessive growl vibrates between us at the ring of Alex's moans of pleasure. The delicious scrape of her nails on my scalp and nape as she clutches my head to her neck awakens my cock and my inner vampire.

Red is *mine*, and no force in the universe or beyond will take her from me again.

Strength returns to my extremities in full force. I tighten my arms around her, cherishing the feel of my female in my embrace as her life essence flows down my throat, and the aroma of her desire fills my nostrils.

Unable to hold back any longer, I ease her onto the mattress and settle my groin against the heat of her core. Alex moans deep and claws at my shoulders, undulating her hips along my length. The beast purrs, demanding control, and in my impaired state, I surrender to his call.

I snake a hand between us and unzip her jeans before yanking them down her thighs, using my foot to peel them the rest of the way until they sink to the floor. With a quick jerk, the lace thong rips apart, and for the first time in months, my fingers caress the smooth, silken folds soaked with wetness.

"Bastian." Her breathy moan sets me on fire, and I make quick work of my zipper while keeping my fangs buried deep. "As much as I want this, we can't complete the bond."

The beast growls low and clamps down harder on her neck. Alex is ours. We thought we failed her, and it nearly killed us. Tonight, there is no escape.

In one swift plunge, my cock is encased in utter fucking bliss. I still, savoring the velvet walls convulsing, endeavoring to adjust my girth.

"Oh, God," she exclaims, her thighs tightening around my waist.

My vampire craves this connection with our mate, especially after the last couple of months without her. Even in my frenzied state, I understand her worry about completing the bond. Still, I will only conclude my half of the link to keep her protected. Besides, with a valkyrie's ability to envision an immortal's past by consuming their blood, I will never tolerate the ugliness of my life to desecrate her beautiful mind.

The threat to her life from the Watchers still boils on the back burner. It is imperative I can locate her at all times, be able to sense her emotions, and reach out to her telepathically, even if she cannot answer back. I neglected to protect her once from the bastard Ezekiel, I will not make such a mistake again.

Mentally pushing aside my doubts, I set a vigorous pace. My one obsessive thought; spill my seed while devouring her precious gift to ensure Alex belongs to me.

She grips me tighter, matching me thrust for thrust as her reservations shatter at my aggressiveness.

Our heated breaths, rapid heart rates, and sweat-slicked bodies permeate the air. A yearning so powerful strikes my blackened soul, and a chasm of fire builds to an explosive resolution for us both, shaking me to my very foundation.

Before I withdraw my fangs, the mating bond zings through me like a lightning rod. Alex's desire renews my own, her uncertainty of the unknown breaks my heart, but it is the love emanating from her in waves that strips the breath from my lungs and carries all my old insecurities to the forefront. Deep down, I am not worthy of such a profound devotion. Never will I measure up to her expectations of a mate, and ultimately, I will let her down or disappoint her with my sick desires.

I lick the punctures closed and ease back, ready to roll off and establish some distance between us. Strong legs and arms tighten their grip, and I cannot check myself from peering down into the silver depths.

"Sebastian Moretti, don't you dare shut me out."

"Alex, thank you for your tribute. The power in your blood is astounding and has fully restored my health." Why am I reverting to traditional school etiquette? When what I truly crave is to fuck her senseless again.

"Don't," tears shimmer, and I clench my jaw against the torment at producing even a moment of pain. "Don't treat me like a stranger offering a vein. You mated me, so I assume my emotions are freaking you the fuck out, but please..." She clasps my face between her small palms. "Let go of your fears and simply be mine."

"Red, you do not understand what such a request encompasses. Simple is not an adjective I would use to describe my life." Breaking her hold, I slip out of her glorious tightness, not bothering to re-zip my jeans before leaning against the headboard once more.

Alex sits up, dragging her shirt down over her hips and tucking her legs to the side. Her curls are all over, her skin is devoid of make-up, but she is the most breathtaking creature I have ever encountered.

"Why did you complete your end of the bond if you have no intention of permitting a relationship?"

I shrug, appreciating the wholeness and vitality in my body once more. "If you are in peril, I will sense it and be able to find you in a matter of minutes."

"That's it? That's the reason you bound yourself to me for all eternity?"

I contemplate her with wariness, not certain where this is leading. "You deserve a nice, sensible male who can grant you love, children, and happiness."

"Well, I guess the link didn't work, because you are way off base, dumbass."

She leaps from the bed, tugs on her jeans, and pivots to scowl at me with fists on her hips. I almost grin at the fierce expression, but somehow my addled brain halts. No need to antagonize the little spitfire further.

When those big blue eyes, glistening with indignant tears, drill into me, something in my chest tightens, reliving the devastation I endured at her presumed demise. The rage that gripped my mind toward my mother, and the months of grief and anguish that spiraled me into a black hole of purgatory only death could alleviate.

What the fuck are you doing, fool. You have a second chance with her, and you are completely blowing it.

"I never craved a nice, sensible sort of love, you big idiot. I desired to be ravaged, consumed, and treasured," the lone tear cascading down her flushed cheek crushes me. "That's what you do to me, Sebastian. And if you can't see it after all this time, I'm done. I refuse to beg for your affection."

Panic has me leaping from the bed when she turns toward the door. I catch her around the waist and haul her against my chest. "I do... love you, little Red," I whisper in her ear, and a weight lifts at the proclamation. "But my needs are dark, and I am terrified I will lose you when you discover how demented."

"So, what, you're going to end it without giving me the benefit of the doubt? I realize your history, Bas. It's not like I've never heard of BDSM or the fact you own several clubs and have engaged in the Dom/sub scene exclusively." She twists in my embrace, gripping my biceps. "I also learned what your mother did to you."

Anger ignites fast and swift. "You know nothing," I state harshly and thrust her from me.

"I understand better than you realize. Rowena and I underwent a little chat before she killed my roommate. She murdered my father, and everyone else in the alley. Planted the Moretti ring to frame you. All in the sick hope I would avenge him and seek to kill you."

"When you mentioned the ring, I suspected as much, but how the fuck did she even know you were mine then?"

"Apparently, a witch told her before I was born." Alex's eyes soften. "Your mother was psychotic, Sebastian. Her warped mind hoped you would turn to her in your grief, and the two of you would resume your *relationship*."

"When I thought she killed you, I ripped her heart from her chest." A vision of her stunned expression flashes to the forefront.

"I know." Her reply is soft, and another tear slides down her cheek.

"My feelings for you terrify me." I clench my fists, despising even one small admission of weakness.

"Why?"

"Because... you are so pure and innocent, passionate and loving. I am... the polar opposite."

"You're convinced your appetites, your needs are wrong, dement-ed. But I treasure everything about you, Sebastian. I crave to please you in any way you require." She sweeps a slender hand down my bi-cep. "Do your sexual preferences scare me? Yes. I won't lie. But it's more a fear of the unknown than anything else."

"I could never harm you, Alex. You know that, right?"

"Yes." No hesitation or doubt. Such trust humbles me. "Nor I you."

I close my lids and sigh heavily as dread gnaws at my gut. Am I seriously contemplating pursuing a committed relationship with a valkyrie princess who possesses a heart of gold? But what is the alter-native? A life of misery or death.

"If we do this, we start slow. If at any moment you feel uncom-fortable or uncertain, vow you will tell me."

Her smile brightens my soul. "You bet your ass I promise. But..." She clasps our hands. "I have one stipulation."

Okay, Sebastian. Whatever it is, you can deal with it. After all, you are demanding she enters your world, the least you can do is grant her a boon.

"State your terms."

She swallows, and I sense her anxiety. "Allow me control once in a while?"

Fuck. "Alex, I..." *Fuck.*

"Do you trust me as I trust you?"

"Yes. But it is not you that is the obstacle. It is me. My demons." Just the notion of submitting has sweat beading on my upper lip.

She watches me as I take several deep inhales and work to cram the past in a dark dusty corner for the woman I treasure more than my own life. "What happens if I concede to your stipulation, and I cannot do it?"

"Then we figure out another approach, something you can ac-cept, and we both agree on together."

Okay. Yes. This might work.

Chapter 46

Alexandria

Desire and nervous anticipation simmer below the surface as Bastian grips my hand and leads me through a doorway into the bathroom. It's a beautiful space. Stone floors, granite counters, and a stunning, enormous shower accented with rust and tan stacked stone.

But where is the toilet? It must be behind door number two.

"Shower first, play after."

Oh, man. I crave to experience this with him so damn much, but having only dipped my toes into the kiddie pool in this arena—cause you know, virgin before Bas—my heart-rate jacks, and I'm panting like I just ran a marathon. But at the same time, wetness floods my core at the prospect of surrendering to my male.

I relished the spankings, so I'm hoping whatever else he has planned will turn me on as well. Right? What if I can't tolerate what he so desperately requires? Can the Dom compromise?

"Stop thinking, Red," he says before capturing the bottom of my shirt and hoisting it over my head. "Let go of your fears and simply be mine."

"You know, it's not nice to throw my words back in my face."

He chuckles, and the sound eases the butterflies in my gut. "Trust me, baby. Submit."

I swallow, not loving the word submit. I suppose I could give up some control, but only sexually. If the commander tries to boss me around any other time, his nose will suffer the impact of my knuckles.

"I do trust you, Bas." And to prove my point, I unzip my jeans and slide out of them before tossing them to join my shirt on the floor.

Nude, I remain perfectly still and await his direction. He wants control, he's got it. It's kind of freeing, actually. No need to speculate or fret about anything but following his commands.

His sexy grin tightens my insides. "Remove my pants."

Okay. That tone, all authority and dominance, inflames my passion, and I step forward to obey.

The change in his physique since he fed is astonishing. His muscles are well defined, and while mouthwatering, they have yet to revert to their previous bulk. I glide the jeans down over his hips and note the bones no longer protrude, pass powerful thighs, but it's the enormity of his erection my gaze stays fastened to when the material drops past his calves to the floor. He steps out, and with a flip of his ankle, they land next to mine.

I'm still kneeling, ogling his magnificent cock with mouthwatering anticipation when he stalks away to turn on the shower. That's when I notice the scars marring the perfect ass. Thin white lines slash across each muscled cheek as if sliced with a knife. Or a whip.

Holy shit. Those marks must be from his mother before his transition. That fucking bitch! If I could get my hands on her, I would cut her up into tiny pieces and feed her remains to the vultures.

Sebastian turns to me and stops cold, staring at me kneeling naked on the floor. A hasty glimpse in the mirror reveals my irises are bright silver, my face pinched with fury. I Inhale slowly, imprison it in for a full minute before letting it out, along with my hatred.

"She has no place between us. Ever. Do you understand me?"

The harshness of his tone startles me, and I blink up at him several times. He's right. She is dead, burning in hell for all eternity, I hope. If anyone deserves to rot in the fiery depths of purgatory, it's Rowena Moretti.

When I nod, he holds out his hand. "Come, let us clean this night, and the prior two months down the drain, and concentrate on you and me."

I rise, slip my palm into his, glorying at the strength in his grip, and step beneath the heated spray. Once he enters, he turns another lever, and a wide square showerhead in the ceiling cascades water like warm rain.

"This is fucking fantastic, but can I ask you a question?" He nods, reaching for a bar of soap before handing it to me.

"Wash me. I crave your touch upon me."

Quickly lathering up, I place my soapy palms on his shoulders and begin the wonderfully erotic process of cleansing my mate. The Moretti tattoo swirling and slashing over his pec, shoulder, and bicep is fascinating. The inky blackness of the bold bands snaking around his arm are intricately beautiful.

"What is your question, little one?"

Shit. I was so caught up in finally exploring his body at my leisure, I failed to ask. "Where's the toilet?"

Sebastian bursts out laughing, and I can't help but grin even though he's snickering at me. "What's so funny?" I demand and work to pull off a fierce frown.

"Not the question I was expecting. Do valkyries not understand the physiology of a vampire?"

"No, you arrogant ass. You're not significant enough in our culture to study."

That sobers him. Good.

"When you are the ruler, you might choose to revise that policy. It is a prudent strategy to identify all facts about your allies and enemies."

"Just answer the question," I mutter, realizing he's correct. I allowed my hatred of his race to overshadow my duties.

"Alex, vampires have no use for such a device. The blood we consume converts in our systems to fuel our body's needs. Nothing wasted or eliminated. Hence, no toilet."

"Oh. That's convenient."

"Is it not the same for you? The electrical charge from lightning fuels your strength. You need not ingest food if you choose not to, right?" He asks, lathering shampoo in my hair and massaging my scalp. I groan at the immense pleasure but continue working my soapy hands over his pecs and abdomen, denying us both contact with his erection standing tall and proud.

"Yes, and while many of my kind, mostly elders, do just that, if my entire species lived solely off those bolts, there would be an endless barrage of lightning to attract the scrutiny of humans. I eat infrequently, but I still enjoy food too much to give it up."

"Interesting. Something to keep in mind. My mate requires food and a lavatory."

I stare into the blueness watching me when he draws my head backward to rinse the shampoo. "How will this work, Bastian? Your job is here in Nunavut. My mother is preparing me to be the queen, which means it involves my presence at our home base in Ontario."

"Vampire, remember. Teleportation is kind of my thing," he smirks.

I snort at his attempt at humor. "You're a funny guy, Mr. Moretti."

"Just keep it between you and me, or I might have to spank you."

"Hmmm. I kinda like the spankings."

"Is that so? Then I may have to up my game to keep my female satisfied."

"Yeah. Step up, big boy." I grin and grasp his cock, sliding my soapy hands along his length before cupping his balls.

He groans low, bucking his hips with my tempo. "Be careful what you ask for, Red."

"Fuck careful. I'm a valkyrie, adrenaline is kind of *my* thing." I smirk back.

He chuckles and reverses our positions, capturing the shampoo to wash his own longer locks since it would be impossible for me unless I obtained a step stool. I welcome the opportunity to explore further. Down the muscled thighs completely barren of hair. "Do you shave your groin and legs?"

"No. Vampires do not grow hair below the neck."

Wow. Not only can they teleport, but they also don't have to worry about the pesky task of going to the bathroom. And to never have to wax my legs or sex again would be freaking amazeballs.

But I would miss food and the sun. It saddens me we can never relax on the beach together, or enjoy the thrill of an amusement park, or sightsee during the day. You can do those events at night, but many things are only accessible during daylight.

I shrug and let it go. Now is not the moment to worry about such obstacles when we are both wet and naked. Only one place left to wash, and I'm dying to observe my mate's reaction. If he allows it.

I glide my fingers up the inside of his thighs, circling his taut hamstrings. I yearn to touch him there. I've heard—thank you, Google—it can be an erogenous zone for both men and women.

The cascade of the warm waterfall washes the suds away, and as I ease a finger between the muscular cheeks, his gaze snaps down to mine at the same time I wrap my lips around the head of his cock.

The intense sapphires watch me for several seconds, but instead of protesting, Bastian widens his stance to allow me further access, and a thrill plows straight through me, stiffening my nipples and clenching my core. With one fist gripping the base, and my mouth licking and sucking as deep as I can, my middle finger swirls the tight puckered opening.

Sapphires lock, his dark and stormy, and I see the effort this is costing him in the tightness of his jaw and pinched look around his eyes. He is not relishing this, and I fear his mother is coming between us after all.

I ease away, but Bastian's fingers suddenly grip my skull, compelling me over his length once more.

That's when things shift. No longer am I controlling the situation, my vampire is. His hips undulate as he fucks my mouth. The grip on my tresses causes delicious pinpricks of pain along my scalp, and I respond by gripping the base of his cock tighter and delving the tip of my finger past the tight resistance.

"Yes, fuck me with your mouth and hands," he all but growls, thrusting harder and faster, and I open my throat to keep from gagging, but he tastes so damn good, and I love pleasing him. I will welcome whatever he dishes out, and more, to see the pleasure chase away the darkness.

My finger matches his thrusts, burrowing deep then retreating until it's sliding in and out with ease. I introduce another digit.

"Fuck, yes!" He roars, pitching his head backward as his hot seed shoots down my throat. I moan, gobbling it all and lapping for more.

Chapter 47

Alexandria

Once Sebastian makes sure we are thoroughly clean and dry, he wraps me in a fluffy robe before ordering me to stay put and disappearing into the bedroom. Seconds later he returns with a pair of fresh jeans hugging his hips.

When he ushers me toward door number two, which I now realize doesn't hide a potty, I'm stunned when he opens it and walks into another room. Perplexed, I follow, stopping dead at the entrance.

Great balls of fire.

This thirty by forty-foot area is Sebastian's private playroom. The walls are ebony, the garnet carpet is plush, but that's not what draws my attention. The St. Andrews cross on the far wall holds my gaze. The cherry wood gleams, the leather cushion in the center, and along each post, contrasts with the black shackles attached about a foot down from the end of each point.

All the nervous anxiety from before comes flooding to the forefront as I peel my eyes away and take in all the various apparatuses placed strategically around the room. The belts, floggers, crops, and whips hanging on the wall clench my butt cheeks. A huge, black armoire dominates the far corner, and my imagination runs wild with what secrets lie behind those doors.

In the center of the chamber, two thick chains dangle from tracks in the ceiling running the length of the room, and at the tip of each are leather cuffs with intricate buckles. Right below the chains, secured into the carpet, are two large silver eyelets. What are those for?

I peek at the vampire watching me intently from several feet away and shove the anxiety down deep, remembering he now has the ability to sense my emotions. If I give him even an inkling I'm not on board, he will march us both out of this room and lock it up never to return.

This is what my male needs, and if I wish to be in his life, I either suck it up or walk away because there is no way in hell I can ask him to abandon such an intricate part of himself.

BDSM saved him, aided his tormented mind to heal and overcome the torture his mother forced him to endure, the mental shame and humiliation at his own weakness. This lifestyle gifted him the control he desperately lacked, and if I asked him to walk away from it, he would, but he'd end up resenting me.

I must try it. Hopefully, we can come to some sort of compromise and tone things down a bit, because some of those devices on that wall will never strike my body.

"Alex, stop thinking. I said we would start slow, and I meant it." He saunters over and gently clasps my shoulders. "Please do not be intimidated by everything in this room. All of this," he indicates with a wave of his hand, "is designed for pleasure. Will there be discomfort? Yes. But only as far as you can handle. You are linked to me, all you have to do is open your mind, and I will sense when to give more or ease back. Do you understand?"

I swallow and nod.

"Good. In this room, I control everything. I demand. You obey. But remember, it all comes to a screeching halt the second you use your safe word, and the first couple of times, you are free to ask questions."

"And after that?"

"You do not speak unless given permission. You do not come until I say so. When issued a command, your response is always, yes, sir."

Holy mother of God! I can't.... I'm not a submissive. It goes against everything I am to cower before a male, no matter how much I love him.

"Talk to me, Red. Your emotions are all over the place."

"Stop reading me. It's not fair."

"I never said I would play fair." He tucks a curl behind my ear. "If you say no, we walk out of here and figure out another way."

I may not have drunk his blood, but it doesn't take a biological connection to read the uncertainty in his expression or ridged tension in his frame. Sebastian desperately craves me to submit to his will but is prepared to leave it all behind to keep me by his side. If the dominant Alpha male is willing to compromise for me, shouldn't I do the same?

"No. I wish to try. But I need you to be a little more tolerant with me than your subs. I'm gonna fuck this up here and there. Just the word submission grates my nerves."

"Of course. I am here to guide you every step of the way."

"Okay. What do I have to do?"

He smiles, bending to brush his lips across mine. "First off, try not to look like you are walking to your doom. Just enjoy and trust me."

At the caress of softness, tense muscles relax, and my fears recede, hovering in the background, ready to pop out at a moment's notice. Weirdly enough, my inner warrior, the one I assumed would be shrieking her resistance, appears content to take a wait and see attitude. Fine. If she can, I can too.

"Do you have any objection to being restrained?" He asks as he loosens the belt on my bathrobe.

"I don't think so." I want to trace my fingers around the intricate tattoo on his fucking fabulous pectoral, but I'm assuming touching without permission is a big fat no, no.

"Good." He brushes the soft fleece off my shoulders to pool at my feet. "Now, go stand between the round eyelets in the floor, facing the cross."

Oh shit. He's going to chain me? I thought we were starting out slow.

Despite my reservations, I do as commanded, watching the beautiful vampire as he moves to the huge armoire. I only get a quick glimpse inside before he snatches something and closes the doors. When my gaze lands on the objects in his hands, I finally figure out what the eyelets are for.

Wide leather cuffs with shiny lanyards dangling from the ends of a long silver bar. I'm not so naïve I don't recognize what it is. It's a spreader, and he plans to attach it to my ankles and then to the eyelets in the floor via the lanyards.

Okay, I can handle this. No biggie.

When Sebastian kneels to clamp a cuff around one ankle, a thrill runs through me at the sensation. And as he cinches it down, I nearly groan with pleasure. Who knew an ankle was an erogenous zone.

Strong hands clasp the other one. "Widen your stance, Alex."

I immediately obey, and he secures the other cuff before using the lanyards to lock me down to the eyelet. Sweat breaks out along my forehead. I bite my lip as hunger for the unknown spirals through my core.

Sebastian traces the pads of his fingers along my thighs as he slowly rises. His gentle caress continues up the curve of my hip, and the dip in my waist. I shiver as his knuckles graze the side of my breasts, and my nipples tighten with need.

"Mmmm," the vampire purrs. "You are fucking incredible, and your sweet aroma drives me wild."

I bite my lip to keep from verbalizing that I feel the same. The soft scent of ocean wafts from my mate, ramping my lust higher. He grabs a wrist, lifting it above my head, I follow with my eyes, watching with eagerness as he buckles each one to the leather cuffs.

When done, my legs are spread, locked securely in place, and while my wrists are held tightly by the cuffs, I can move my arms with the flow of the chains.

Sebastian steps back and examines his handiwork. "So fucking beautiful."

I preen on the inside, but my stubbornness refuses to let him see it. Instead, I ogle the bulge in his pants. Man, he's got some incredible endurance. The male has come twice already in the last hour, and it looks like he's raring to go yet again.

My body tightens at the delicious prospect.

"Tonight is about initiation. So, your first time will be soft and gentle." He walks over to the wall of weapons, and I tense, my gaze following his every move.

I'm not sure I could handle a whip. The thought of it has my safe word perched on the tip of my tongue. When he plucks a long, black, leather flogger from the lineup, my trepidation eases somewhat. Okay, I think I can deal with the soft strips against my skin, as long as he goes easy.

"You are overthinking again, Alex," Sebastian murmurs, striding behind me. "Let go. Open your mind and trust me."

Yeah, right? Easier said than done.

Instead of the barrage of hits I was expecting, Bastian's heat penetrates my spine. He brushes my hair to the side and nuzzles my neck, his lips sucking at my vein, while his other hand reaches around and slips between my slick folds.

My head drops on his shoulder with a moan, and I jerk against the chains as intense pleasure spirals through me.

"When I am finished, I will devour this pussy with my mouth and gorge myself on your sweet juices."

Holy shitballs. I almost come apart at his naughty words.

"But first, I still thirst for your blood."

Without warning, his fangs sink deep into my flesh, and I nearly combust. The pad of his finger circles my aching clit, while the other pinches and rolls a nipple. The slight pain, combined with the addictive pull on my vein, is too much. I need to explode, but some part of my brain I didn't realize existed resists the urge until given permission.

All too soon, his warm tongue licks the punctures closed, the scalding heat of his hands slip away, and I want to bemoan the loss of his warmth and expert ministration on my sex. The wicked vampire has me so ramped; I have no idea which way is up.

When the first strike lands on my ass, I cry out, more from surprise than from pain. Don't get me wrong, it stung but not enough to force me to use my safe word. I crave to please him, and if the male gets off on flogging and spanking me, as long as it doesn't become too unbearable, I can endure, enjoy it even, like at the villa.

The slaps on my skin turn into an even cadence. He alternates between my ass and back, and a delicious heat builds. A desperate need clenches my core, my nipples harden into tight, achy points, and my head lolls on my neck.

A strike on the side whips the leather straps around my chest, hitting my breast, and I groan in ecstasy at the pleasure/pain it inflicts. My God, I never understood such intense bliss existed in pain. I finally understand Nicole's need to let go and give up control to the demands and desires of your body. It is liberating.

No. It's fucking orgasmic.

When the tips of the flogger strike my nipple, I jerk on the chains, arching for more. Bastian doesn't disappoint. He moves around me, lashing with precise movements until he is standing before me, and the savage lust in his glowing gaze nearly shoots me over the edge, command or not.

The soft hits to my belly and breasts escalate the raging inferno inside, but I can't even press my thighs together to hold it in. I bite down on my lip and squeeze my core, not wanting this to end.

By the time Bastian throws the whip to the side, my head hangs backward, my tresses brushing the sensitive skin on my back, and my legs are quivering with the effort to keep my orgasm at bay.

Scalding palms land on my thighs, and I jerk, lifting to peer down at the vampire kneeling before me. I squint against the bright blue glow.

"You were fucking perfection, Red." His thumbs spread the folds slick with my desire. "Now come, baby, let me taste everything you have."

The second his mouth makes contact with my swollen, aching bundle of nerves, I skyrocket, shattering into a thousand fragments, his name tumbling from my lips. Bastian doesn't let up, and wave after wave of molten lava blasts through my system and I erupt with the force of a volcano.

The tremors ease as I come down from the most explosive moment in my life, and I hang from the chains, my legs unable to hold my weight.

I hear something land close to me. Cool softness touches the front of my thighs, and I urge my heavy lids to open. It's a rounded, padded bench about hip high. I stare at it, uncertain what it could possibly be for, and the vampire doesn't offer an explanation.

When he moves behind me and wraps a powerful forearm around my abdomen, I lean into his strength, knowing he would never let me fall. With quick movements, he unclips the cuffs from the chains, and my lethargic limbs drop to my sides as if weighted with lead. The only thing keeping me upright is Sebastian's arm.

Slowly, he bends me at the waist until my lower abdomen settles on the cool leather before nudging me forward even further. My chest and arms hang over the other side of the padded apparatus. I'm at a loss on what happens next because my overstimulated brain has checked into la-la land. All I can do is silently watch as he fastens my wrists to the same eyelets as my ankles. My pubic bone rests on the cushion, and my upper torso dangles over the bench.

Bas runs his palm across my sensitive backside, and I moan as tiny sparks fire across my skin. The blood rushes to my brain and the ends of my curls brush the floor. This will either be fucking epic or a complete disaster with me passing out from all the blood draining into my head. It's a tossup at this point.

The second I hear a zipper being lowered, my mind perks up, and a fresh wave of need flows through me. Holy shit. He's going to fuck me while I'm strapped across this bench.

Sure enough, with no preamble, Sebastian seats himself balls deep into my drenched core. I tense at the sudden invasion and attempt to rise. Metal clangs as the lanyards jerk against the silver eyelets. With no escape, I force my muscles to relax to accommodate his girth, the pleasure so intense it's painful, the line between orgasm and agony blending.

Strong hands clutch my hips as he sets an unrelenting pace that has me building toward another orgasm within seconds. A palm snakes up my spine before gripping a fist full of my curls, arching my neck as he pounds into my flesh. Every forward thrust hits the perfect spot, and with no way to leverage myself, I relax against the bench and enjoy the ride.

Every whisper of breath skitters along my nerves, lighting them on fire. The hard-smooth lips on my shoulder and spine, the fingers tangled in my tresses, send tremors through muscles I assumed too languid to move.

"Do you want to come, Alex?" I jerk my head in what I hope is a nod. "Say it." His guttural tone tightens my nipples and clenches the walls around his substantial length.

"Yes, Sir."

He rewards my submission with a gentle kiss on my backside. "Good girl. Now shatter, Red, milk my cock once more."

Chapter 48

Sebastian

"So how do we defend against these tight-ass fuckers?" Nicole demands before lifting a crystal goblet filled to the brim with red wine to her lips.

When I suggested we gather at my villa to hash out our strategy concerning the Watchers, I did not plan on hosting a legion of armies. Nicki and Logan materialized at sunset with Liam and half a dozen of his elite Wardens. The werewolf soldiers set up tents in the east garden.

Not long after, Kurtis and Lu appeared with the former Guardian tracing back and forth until the same number of Sentinels, the shifter version of Guardians, expanded the encampment to the west.

Arra and Cipher showed up with King Darath, who brought his special ops warriors. Even Priestess Tanagra, the land nymph ruler, arrived with her infamous Storm Walkers, and I cannot help but notice the excitement in the demon king's expression every time his eerie red gaze settles on the beautiful Kleora. Rumor has it she has led him a merry chase over the last few months.

I peer over at my mate, lounging in an armchair by the fire, and my cock tingles. I admit, when I escorted her into my playroom, it was with the sole purpose of giving her more than she bargained. A sick, twisted part of me wanted her to be appalled enough at the sight of the area to run away in disgust. It would deliver me from the guilt of introducing such an innocent into my dark, unbalanced world.

But my mate took everything I dished out and seemed to rejoice in it. Her body sang for me, came alive under my ministrations. She was so exhausted by the end, once I removed the restraints, I carried her to bed, snuggled in next to her before positioning her already snoring body over my chest. Only then did I let the sleep drag me into oblivion.

Her mind, on the other hand, is the mystery eating away at me, nibble by little nibble. When I woke at dusk, the sheets were stone cold. The damp towel on the bathroom floor proved she showered before deserting me.

After my own shower, I caught up with my mate in the kitchen, flanked by Nicole and Logan. We have not received an opportunity to talk about what transpired.

"Earth to Sebastian," Nicole prods, and I cast my gaze to my queen.

"As far as I am aware, and my brother can chime in, only another angel or God possesses the ability to slay a Watcher."

"Or an Oracle," Logan adds.

"Speaking of, has anyone heard from the little blue weirdo," Liam asks. "We sure could use him right about now."

"No," Nicki all but growls. "I assume he's still entangled with training your mate."

A collective gasp from various immortals, either loitering by the bar or relaxing on my furniture, permeates the space.

"Your fated female is an Oracle?" Kleora's stunned expression says it all. "I did not think such a situation was possible."

"She was," the werewolf king mutters between clenched teeth. "By now, I'm sure Icarus has eliminated our bond."

"You won't know that Liam until you see her," Alex pipes in. "Try to stay positive."

See. Right there is the essence of who Alexandria is; optimistic, upbeat, loving, and fucking pure. How can I proceed to poison her with my sinister desires? This morning's scene was just the tip of the iceberg.

I never enjoyed vanilla sex until I met my sarcastic little spitfire. My yearning for her is tremendous. I would fuck her any which way she wanted, and if she requested no kink, I would certainly seek to keep that side of myself at bay. For her.

But I know my needs. The only avenue to tame the carnal beast and manage the demons of my past is with absolute control through BDSM play. Most of the subs I enlisted over the years were extreme sex slaves. They expected an excessive degree of suffering to get off. The more violent and severe, the more appealing. It quieted the depravity of my childhood, removing my mother's voice from my head. My inner vampire recoils at the mere notion of levying such a high degree of pain on our mate, even if she permitted it.

Alex hushes the monster with a mere touch, a sideways glance silvered with heat, or her soft, sexy moans in my ear. When I recall what transpired in the shower, it is all the proof I require. Never would I have tolerated such intimacy with a sub. Initially, I balked, and old ghosts threatened to intrude, but one glimpse into my mate's gaze darkened with hunger, and I could refuse her nothing.

"Do we have any means of contacting the Oracle to enlist his aid?" Jagorach inquires of Nicki.

"Believe me, demon, I tried. I got nada."

"Then we are on our own, and since we cannot kill or injure them, our best course of action is arbitration." I cite and saunter over to my mate, needing to be closer. She stiffens when I halt at the back of her chair. Son of a bitch. She is lamenting the playroom.

"Great idea, Sebastian, but what do we have to negotiate?" My brother asks with a frown.

"First, we must identify the reason behind their demand to keep Alex and me apart in order for us to figure out an alternative."

Nicki's gaze jerks to Arra. I analyze the valkyrie ruler, noting her downcast eyes and fidgeting fingers. Even Cipher turns a concerned glance on his mate.

"Anything you care to contribute, Queen Arra?" My question elicits the scrutiny of everyone in the room and directs it toward the agitated blond.

"I wish I could help, but I have no idea why the Watchers are prepared to execute my daughter to keep her from you, commander, but the prudent course of action is not to mate her or better still, stay away from her altogether."

I observe Nicole wince in my periphery. I may not have the hybrid's empathic abilities, but I can tell Arra is withholding something, and by the glower on Cipher's face and Nicki's watchful countenance, they sense it as well.

"Too late, my lady. I completed my end of the link." I grin viciously and her eyes swell. The queen and I have never seen eye to eye.

"Goddamnit, Sebastian!" Alex erupts, rising from the chair to spin and glare at me. "Was that fucking necessary?"

No, probably not, but it felt fantastic. "I apologize, Alexandria, but it would have come out sooner or later."

"Sorry, not sorry, written all over your face."

"Too true," Nicki chimes in with a smirk.

"Not helping, my love," Logan chides his mate.

A shift in the atmosphere is the only thing to alert our group before Ezekiel Sorath appears in the center of the living room, wings unfurling, chest bare, and the saber of death affixed to his waist.

Jagorach grabs Kleora around the midriff, teleporting her across the room a nanosecond before a deadly wing would have smacked her in the face.

"You conspire against the Watchers," he accuses, his gaze aimed at Alex. "The fallout will be the annihilation of all you hold dear."

I step forward, partly blocking my mate, my vampire quivering with the need to hack the angel's head from his body. "Inform me why they are so intransigent regarding our mating, Ezekiel. I sense you care for Alex, help us keep her safe."

"Nothing you do can alter the conclusion of this night, commander."

Ezekiel's words create movement. The occupants in this villa gathered tonight for one reason; to defend Alexandria. They assemble around us in a protective circle. Nicole and Logan front and center.

"See, I don't like those odds," The vampire queen sneers, her gunmetal irises sparking. "Maybe it's time to call in my marker with the Oracle."

"The Watchers have surrounded the perimeter. Your troops are impotent against our vast strength, young halfling. Resistance is futile."

Nicki chortles. "As much as I dig Star Trek, I'm more team Kirk, than team Picard."

Who the hell are Kirk and Picard? And what the hell is Star Trek?

Alex snorts. My brother glances at me with a bewildered shrug. Okay good. It is not just me.

"Hold on a minute."

The small voice snags everyone's regard as my mate tries to shove her way forward. When the three of us refuse to budge, she leaps up on the mantle, squatting there like a magnificent hawk ready to strike.

"Nobody is dying because of me. I freely present myself up to the Watchers."

"Like fuck you are!" I bellow at the same time Nicki rages. "Not fucking happening!"

The angel does not move, watching my mate intently. It is all I can do to keep my vampire at bay. He charges against my ribcage, bellowing with violence in my brain.

No way will I let them take her.

I peer down at the silver sword at Ezekiel's waist, the weapon designed to obliterate an immortal with one stroke. Could it also kill a fallen?

"If I give myself up, do the Watchers vow to leave and never trouble my friends again?"

"Shut up, Alex," I snap, the blue gleam from my eyes spotlighting the fierce valkyrie.

When those sapphires lower to mine, fear tightens my jaw. I see acceptance and a savage resolve to protect us all from harm. As I glance around the room at the group of immortals, I call friends and family; I understand her rationale, but I will not survive if she is taken from me again.

"I have another solution." I shift to the Watcher. "If the intention is to keep Alex and I from mating, for whatever fucking reason you refuse to divulge, take me. The result is the same."

A chorus of no's in varied and colorful descriptions echo around the room. Alexandria leaps from the mantle to land next to me, grabbing onto my arm.

"No. I will not allow you to sacrifice yourself for me."

"Yet you were willing to do the same," I counter softly, brushing a curl behind her ear.

"The Watchers agree with your proposal, Guardian," Ezekiel announces with a gleam in his eyes.

When the angel draws his sword, I see my death on the mystical surface, but I push Alex away to draw my own sword strapped to my back. No way I'm going down without a fight. I am a Moretti. We do not yield.

The second our steel clashes, a powerful force throws me clean across the room. My body slams into the wall, paintings plummet to the floor around me. I shake my head to impede the encroaching darkness and glance around to see what the hell happened.

Nicole is helping Logan to his feet. It appears Jagorach shielded Kleora with his body if the massive concave in my wall is any indication. Lu stands unharmed behind Kurtis' large frame. In fact, the only beings unaffected by the explosion were Liam, Nicki, Kurtis, and Cipher. Instead, they appear suspended in shock, their wide-eyed gazes glued to something on the other side of the couch blown across the room with me.

Quickly, I send healing energy throughout my body before clutching the edge of the sofa, determined to learn what the hell just erupted in my living room.

In the center of all the destruction, facing off with the Watcher, is a lethal 400-pound lioness. The impressive, sleek muscles along the flanks quiver, bracing to pounce. Low menacing growls permeate the place. When the massive head with the piercing amber eyes of a predator turns my direction, instant recognition plows through my brain like a silver bullet.

Alex!

Chapter 49

Sebastian

I stare in disbelief at the stunning, formidable lion in the midst of my living room. My mate.

It makes sense now why Alex continued to eat food instead of absorbing all her energy from lightning. It justifies her peculiar connection to animals Christoph reported during her time at the veterinary hospital, and the immense potency of her blood.

Most notably, it explains the Watchers need to intervene in our mating. A vampire/valkyrie/shifter offspring would tip the balance of power and nature—their sole reason to exist.

Lu's shifter side has never made an appearance. Maybe it never will since the fallen did not interfere in Kurtis and Lu mating. Based on her lineage, a child of theirs would merely be a Hybrid: half-Vampire, half-shifter.

With quiet, cautious strides, I edge closer to Alex, needing to touch her, feel the strength beneath the rough tawny coat. The long tail twitches at my approach.

"Careful, Sebastian," Logan warns. "If this is her first shift, she might attack out of fear."

"Arra?"

I halt at the menacing tone from Kurtis' father, glancing at the large shifter. I perceive shock and outrage in the blue eyes laser-focused on my mate. It suddenly dawns on me; Gadr was not Alex's father, Cipher is. This means, even though there is no seeable evidence of their mating, they were bonded, and Alexandria was the result.

"Cipher, I..." Arra begins, stuttering to a stop when he twists and grips her biceps.

"How could you not inform me she was mine? For a century, you have lied to me."

Tears fill the small queen's eyes, pleading with her mate for understanding. "Please. I did it for her protection."

"You did not consider entrusting me with such knowledge?" Abruptly he surrenders his hold as if he cannot bear to touch her. "I am your goddamn mate, woman. You stripped me of the opportunity to be her father, to be a part of her life."

"That is precisely why I resolved not to tell you." Arra reaches for the former shifter king, but he jerks back. "You would have demanded parental rights, which in turn would have exposed, not merely our mating, putting us both at risk, but her lineage to the immortal world."

"After all this time and everything we have been through together, your faith in me is despicable. Not once did you count on me enough to understand the risks or allow me the opportunity to protect my own child?"

A lone tear slips down the valkyrie queen's cheek. "I put my baby first, my love. I am sorry."

"Wait," Liam interrupts. "Shouldn't Cipher have sensed their connection?"

"I... Icarus placed a protective spell on her at my behest. No one detected she was a Hybrid. Not even her father."

"Did Gadr know?" Cipher's tone, along with the flicker of yellow in his blue irises, indicates she would be wise to answer in the negative.

"No. He had no idea she wasn't his."

A savage roar penetrates the standoff between the valkyrie queen and former shifter king, capturing everyone's attention once more. My beautiful lioness snarls, announcing her displeasure at her mother before angling back to the actual threat in the room.

"Your shift sealed your doom, Alex," Ezekiel says, stepping forward. "The Watchers no longer agree to Sebastian's alternative. They demand your life to avert the probability of future matings outside your own species. I apologize. I did everything in my capacity to protect you."

I lunge for the angel, hell-bent on shielding my mate from his sword when I am abruptly frozen mid-leap.

"Wait just a goddamn minute," Nicki says in a rough growl, her power freezing everyone but Ezekiel and Jagorach, who contemplates the Watcher with eerie disdain, blocking the land nymph with his broad frame.

"Why don't you take on someone more equal in strength, you lowlife piece of shit." She moves swiftly through the frozen chaos to go toe to toe with the fallen angel.

"Nicole." I shift my eyes to my brother, and my heart stutters at the fear in the emerald depths. "Please, baby. Do not engage."

The pleading tone appears to give my queen pause. We all understand the power she has. She might maintain her own in a duel, but the second that sword touches her, it is all over, no coming back this time.

"No immortal is equal to an angel," Ezekiel says with jaw clenched. To demonstrate his point, he grabs Nicole by the neck, lifting her off the ground above his head. Logan roars, battling against Nicki's telekinetic hold.

All I can do is watch in dismay as he flings my queen across the room like she is a rag doll. Her body slams into the wall with such force she plows right through it into the other chamber.

King Darath steps forward with a sneer. "You dare harm the prophesied halfling, the bringer of peace? I expect my father might have a little something to say about that, Fallen."

His father? Jesus. The rumors were mistaken. Jagorach Darath is not a descendent of Lucifer. He *is* Lucifer. The original fallen angel.

"She is impeding the directive. We must restore balance." For the first time, I witness apprehension in the angel's face as his eyes scan the room beyond for Nicole.

"You are a miserable excuse for an angel. What the fuck would you know about following orders? You rebelled against him the same as I did. Instead of standing by your decision, you and your pathetic followers crawled on your bellies like cowards, wallowing in self-pity until you established the Watchers in the pathetic hope you could somehow earn your way into paradise." Darath's laugh tightens my nerves. "News flash, dumbass, all you had to do was plead for forgiveness. The old softy would have welcomed you with open arms."

"We discovered a better path to serve our Lord and care for his children." Ezekiel lifts his chin defiantly but doubt swirls in the hazel depths. Not as confident as he declares.

'On the count of three, I will release you all. Charge the bastard. Get that damn sword away from him.' Nicole's livid voice bounces in my brain, and when I notice everyone else acknowledging with a slight nod, I am astonished. She communicated telepathically to everybody at the same time.

'One.'

"Yes, but is your group sanctioned by God, Ezekiel?" Darath asks, keeping the fallen distracted.

'Two.'

"We would not exist if it was not."

"Ah. Have you ever heard of the ludicrous concept of free will? He's a huge proponent of it."

'Three!'

The constrictor of her shield dissipates. Despite the fact it will be my last action, I tense to tackle the angel when Gadriel, Manakel, and Kalaziel materialize next to Ezekiel in a display of tremendous force.

Everyone is astute enough to break off their advance. Mayhap we could have subdued the one, but we are no match for four.

"Enough," the tall blond Kalaziel barks. "Your warriors outside are dead. This wretched resistance is over." The black regard sinks to Alex. Quiet snarls puff her rib cage, she drops low. Large claws extend, drilling into the floor, bracing to leap. "Come willingly, or we will take you by force. The death of everyone here will be on your head."

Fuck. Fuck. Fuck.

Large yellow cat eyes find mine. Fear constricts my heart. Defeat stares back.

Sudden energy traverses the room, not as potent as when she transformed into the lion, but adequate to cause me to brace against the onslaught.

Even with the impending catastrophe, I am fascinated to watch my mate alter her body. I have witnessed many shifts over my centuries, and it is not like in human movies. Every joint and bone do not crack or break. They do not shed their outer skin to mutate. It is barely a pop of sound, a spark of energy, and poof, standing before me is Alex in all her naked splendor.

I shrug out of my jacket, draping it across her shoulders, and supple leather pools around her feet. The lithe beauty of her body is for my eyes alone. Sorrow brightens the peacock depths staring up at me. It squeezes my heart, causes my vampire to rage at the terrifying prospect of failing our mate. Again.

"Oh, my God! I'm a shifter, Sebastian."

The pleasure and excitement in her tone fracture my soul. Never will she enjoy another shift, the freedom of running through the woods in beast form, or the thrill of a hunt. These bastards will snuff out her precious life. Her smile. Her joy. Forever.

"I love you, Sebastian Moretti." She reaches up to caress my cheek, and I lean into her touch. "I regret nothing. Last night was the most profound moment of my existence. I embraced every second."

"Red." My throat clogs with emotion. We just discovered each other. I cannot bear the anguish of her death once more. "You brought light into my darkness. I never realized what love was until you." I clasp her precious face between my palms.

"Come forward, valkyrie. Your time is at hand."

Chapter 50

Alexandria

This can't be the end? I've just discovered my inner beast, and she is glorious. Her primal impulses are strong; defend, protect, love. She is fierce, respects strength in others, purrs with pleasure in the presence of her Alpha male but would rip your head off without thought or regret if you dare threaten what's hers.

Last night or I should state the wee hours of the morning, was intense, erotic, and fucking incredible. I crave more. I've merely scratched the surface with Sebastian, and I seek to experience all he has to offer.

My broken Guardian needs to understand true love for the first time in his long existence. His bitch of a mother stole that from him. I want to be the one to open his heart, expose his soul, and cherish it for the rest of our lives.

Instead, I'm being condemned to perish because of some erroneous belief my death brings harmony to the immortal world. The Watchers fear the potential in an offspring between Bas and me. A Tribrid. The first one in history.

I glance over at my mother. Anger fuses my spine. The anguish in her shimmering gaze, the way she wrings her hands together in misery, fails to trigger an iota of sympathy. She fucking knew this would happen. She could've warned me, helped to prepare me somehow.

I understand Cipher's resentment. It saddens me we never obtained a chance to get to know one another as father and daughter.

Not that I didn't love my father—Gadr, I did. Even though he was an intense dude, he was a fine male who adored me like his own, but I can't help feeling I missed out on a real relationship with the shifter.

"There has to be an alternative, Ezekiel." The regret in the being I once considered a friend is etched in the deep grooves around his mouth and eyes. Maybe I can persuade him to side against the others. "Don't let them kill me. Please."

A loud thud snags my attention. Nicole steps through the gaping hole in the wall, bricks falling in her wake. She traces to me, shoving me behind her.

"I just got her back. No fucking way I'm letting you take her from me." A sharp clang of metal rings through the air as the vampire queen, my best friend, draws a sword from under her coat before palming a smaller dagger strapped to her thigh.

The Watchers answer, brandishing their death swords in unison.

"Nicole!" Logan bellows, fear for his mate bringing his vampire raging to the forefront.

The Moretti brothers are a formidable sight. Their muscles bulge and strain, attacking the force field trapping their bodies. Enormous fangs, fit to rip flesh, protrude past their bottom lip as they snarl and growl like caged animals. The brilliance of their irises blanket the room in a kaleidoscope of blue and green with Lucretia's amber and Nicki's gunmetal gray thrown in the mix.

I always adored the way vampires' eyes brighten with intense emotion—a reminder of the beast prowling below the surface.

"Nicki, stop." I clutch handfuls of Bastian's enormous jacket, hoisting it off the floor as I leap around the individual with the ability to save my friends. So, not a great moment to trip and tumble face-first at the Watcher's feet. My grip tightens, struggling to hold the front closed. The last thing I wish to do is expose my girly bits to everyone in the room. "No one is going to die for me."

"Get out of my fucking way, Alex."

My friend's manner is harsh, but I notice the battle to maintain the tears at bay. This woman loves intensely, whether she recognizes it or not. She would freely lay down her life for anybody here. Not too long ago, she did precisely that. Plunged a silver dagger through her heart to kill her father and spare us all.

Now it's my turn.

"Oblige me to handle this, my lady." At the sound of the polished melody of the High Priest Oracle, hope fills my breast, and I pivot with a wide smile.

"Icarus!" I want to weep or wrap the blue tattooed priest in a big bear hug, but that would require letting go of Bastian's jacket. Hell will freeze over before I allow the Oracle to see me naked.

"Your timing is impeccable as always, Icarus," Nicki grins.

The priest smiles congenially, and that's when I notice Lucretia standing next to him. No wait, wasn't she behind Kurtis? I peek over my shoulder, and sure enough, Lu stands beside her mate, sword drawn at the ready, but frozen like the others.

The powerful being, a mirror image to the former Guardian, adorned in a white flowy gown, must be Viessa, the Oracle in training.

"Viessa?" Liam's low tentative inquiry snags the vampire's regard. Their gazes lock. The female examines him for several seconds without a lick of emotion.

Oh, no. Icarus removed the mate bond. My heart breaks for the werewolf as the hope drains from his eyes.

"Sweetness," Liam whispers before lowering his head.

The vampire Oracle turns from the wolf to challenge the line of Watchers shoulder to shoulder with her mentor. Well, not shoulder to shoulder per se, since the priest is my height and Vi is like close to six foot.

"We mean no disrespect, but this does not involve you, Oracles." Manakel, the dark-skinned, quiet one, states with a slight bow.

Isn't this delightful? The angels fear Icarus and Viessa. Hope flares in my breast. I might survive this night yet.

Viessa's amber gaze drills into the Watchers as she strides forward. "You wish to destroy this female because you dread an offspring with the vampire?"

"Yes, Oracle. It would unsettle the balance."

"Because it would be a Tribrid?"

"Yes," Kalaziel answers, observing the Oracle with what appears to be trepidation.

"My dear fallen, am I not the ultimate Tribrid? Shifter, vampire, and Oracle. By all accounts, you should seek my death."

The Watchers appear alarmed by her declaration. "Nay, my lady," Kalaziel responds. "You are a mediator of God. Sacred. No harm would ever befall you by our hand."

Viessa's smile is beautiful and cruel. Enormous fangs descend. "It appears you encounter an impasse, Fallen. You will have to go through me to get to Alexandria. I have foreseen her death, but not the here and now."

Wow. The magnitude of this situation suddenly sinks into my brain. I glance at Sebastian. The sapphire glow shifts to mine briefly before returning to scowl at the Watchers. I guess the old saying is true; It's not what you know, but who you know that makes all the difference.

The angels blink with uncertainty. If they couldn't communicate telepathically, I visualize them huddling up like a football team to draft their next move. Simultaneously, the four close their lids while the rest of us wait in tense anticipation. After several seconds and a collective nod, their focus is on Vi once more.

Goodness. Were they listening to God? Goosebumps break out on my skin at the notion the big man upstairs is observing and actively engaging in our lives, out of billions across the globe.

"We have been instructed to provide you an alternative."

I glare at Nicki, and her eyebrow lifts in question. When I gesture with my head toward our friends, signaling she might want to release them, she nods and waves her hand.

While the majority shift to a more comfortable position in place, Logan traces to his mate, just as she puts her sword away. A huge palm grips the nape of her neck, using it as a fulcrum to swing her to his chest.

"Why do you insist on freezing my heart with terror, baby?"

Nicki shoots me an eye roll, but the slight lift of her lips says she enjoys his protective tendencies. In response, she leans up and brushes her lush mouth across his before twisting in his embrace to focus on the angels.

Bastian's broad frame partially blocks me from the Watchers. He clasps my free hand in a death grip, proof of his anxiety at nearly losing me again. I squeeze back.

"We are all ears, Fallen," Icarus replies, his head cocked to the side in curiosity.

"The Hybrid and vampire must vow never to conceive a child."

"Or what?" I ask with a frown.

"We will return and eliminate any offspring."

The judgment, given with a callous shrug, ignites my seething anger. I peek up at my mate to gauge his reaction to such vile bullshit—a muscle pulses in his jaw.

"Agreed," Bas says with a rough grunt.

Outraged, I jerk my hand from his, turn my back on the angels, and face off with the vampire. "Now wait a goddamn minute. I have a voice in this decision, Mr. Moretti."

Pure determination peers down at me, and I swallow. "Would you willingly sacrifice your life to bear a child?"

Well. When he presents it like that. "They are ordering me to surrender being a mother."

"No, Red." He grips my biceps—the hold painful. "They are demanding you give up conceiving a child with *me*. If you truly yearn to be a parent, you and I can never complete our bond. You will need to locate a shifter or berserker to mate, and if that is your decision—as much as it breaks my heart—I would rather abide by your wishes, walk away, and know you are happy, than crush your spirit or see the bitterness grow between us for my own selfish reasons."

What the fuck kind of choice is that?

Yes, I've always fantasized about being a mother, having X number of kids to love and cherish, a daughter to train and raise to take over the reign of queen one day, as I will from my mother. But if those choices mean I must throw away the one thing my heart and soul cries out for to obtain it, all of a sudden, motherhood dims in comparison.

Glancing at Nicki, I'm reminded of the devastation she suffered at the loss of her unborn child, and I recognize I never wish to understand such extreme emotional pain.

I stare at the heavy sorrow burning in the cerulean depths. This vampire is prepared to sacrifice his happiness to ensure mine. Little does the idiot realize; he's my happy place—an existence without my brooding, dark, and sexy as fuck vamp is no life at all.

Never turning from his gaze, I respond to the angels. "I comply with your demands, Watchers." Bastian's eyes grow in wonder. "I choose you, Sebastian. Always."

The vampire wraps those big, powerful arms around my midriff, hoisting me off the floor, before devouring my lips in too brief a kiss. "Your words sealed your fate, Red. I will never let you go."

I smile. "I'm counting on it."

"I detest being the bearer of bad news," the demon king interjects, strolling forward, Kleora's small hand engulfed in his. The discrepancy in their heights is comical. The top of her head barely reaches the well-defined pecs. But isn't that the pot calling the kettle thing? Or however that phrase goes. "Modern contraceptives have no effect on bonded mates. And since abstinence is impossible with a mated couple, how will they keep from conceiving?"

"Can't an immortal tie their tubes or get a hysterectomy like humans?" Nicki asks.

"Nay, young queen," Manakel answers. "An immortal's regenerative process prevents such a procedure from success. Whether the reproductive organs are tied or removed, they repair or grow back."

"I believe I can eliminate the risk of pregnancy." Icarus' quiet declaration has all eyes focused on him.

"The same goddamn way you disposed of the mate bond, priest?" Liam questions with a bitter growl, but the intensely serene Oracle ignores him.

"If you declare it, and vow it, Oracle, the Watchers will depart and torment you no more on this matter."

Yeah, meaning if we screw up on anything else, they'll be back?

"I vow it," Icarus promises. The angels bow before disappearing.

Chapter 51

Alexandria

The second the powerful beings dissipate, an enormous weight lifts from the place, energizing everyone into action, slapping each other on the back or hugging their relief at still being alive after an encounter with fallen angels.

Logan hugs his brother, and I take the opportunity to peer at Liam's dark brooding gaze studying Viessa from across the room. If he possessed the ability to trace, no doubt, the wolf would be long gone rather than endure the indifference from his mate.

"My lady."

I spin toward the tattooed priest. My heart hiccups at the tempestuous sea swirling in the blue irises. Oh, shit. He meant right now.

"Can you give us a minute, Icarus?" Bastian asks, securing me to his side with a protective arm over my shoulders.

"Of course, my lord."

"Nicole, would you please trace to Newport and retrieve some clothes for Alex?"

"I'll do it." Lu steps forward. "I'm sure Alexandria would appreciate her best friend by her side."

"Thank you, Lucretia," I respond with a grateful smile before she and Kurtis disappear.

Sebastian steers us to a corner for a little privacy, although that's an illusion in an area crowded with immortals, but it's the thought that counts.

"Are you okay?"

I nod. "Yes. Are you?" I never considered inquiring if he was alright with never being a father.

He seems taken aback by my query. "Never contemplated being a mate, let alone a parent. My position as the commander to the queen's Guardians, as well as my personal lifestyle, never allowed for such a possibility." Rough knuckles graze my cheek. "So, in answer to your question, as long as I have you, I'm perfect."

Lu and Kurtis appear with a pair of jeans, and a blue sweater draped over the shifter king's arm, with black boots dangling from his fingertips. Sebastian takes the offerings and the Guardian leans in, whispering she placed underwear and socks inside a boot.

I smirk at her discretion. "Thank you."

One minute I'm grinning at the tall warrior, the next Bastian and I are standing in the center of his chamber, and he's sliding his jacket from my shoulders.

"No eyes will gaze upon your exquisite body but your mate's." He plucks the undergarments from the footwear with a grin.

Geez, freaking vampire hearing. I move to seize the lacey material, but he holds them out of reach.

"Allow me to dress my female."

"What? The Dom is lowering himself to service a woman?" I tease, but the smile dies a swift death at the fierce expression.

"A Dom must see to his sub's needs. Especially after a vigorous session. But you are more than a submissive to me, my fierce little lion. You are my mate, which means I will do everything in my power to make certain I fulfill your every need and desire." He swoops in and claims my lips, and suddenly I am cognizant of the fact I'm standing stark naked in his bedroom—the same room where he claimed my virginity along with my heart.

Lust pools hot and lively in my core and I grip his shirt, countering with all the pent-up fear, anxiety, and heartbreak we've both survived in our short relationship. A liaison that began for the sole purpose of regaining my lost memories and a misguided plan for revenge but became so much more—more than I ever considered possible.

Too quickly, the vampire breaks away, kneels before me, presenting the pretty red thong. I've never experienced a man dress me before, and based on the heat swirling in my mate's gaze, he's as turned on as I am.

I grasp the mighty shoulders and step into the underwear. Before shifting the lace upward, Sebastian leans forward, deposits a tender kiss on my sensitive mound. My stomach tightens in response to the gentle pressure of his lips.

"God, I cannot wait to devote hours to tasting and exploring your sweetness." His rough tone ramps up the fire spreading through my veins, and I want to ignore our family and friends waiting downstairs, and Icarus' plan to sterilize my innards.

I'd be lying if I claimed the prospect of never carrying or giving birth to a smaller rendition of Sebastian didn't cut deep, but the alternative would destroy me.

With the barely-there piece of cotton in place, Bas helps me into blue jeans, socks, and boots before rising and sliding my arms through the matching bra, gliding the soft cashmere over my head.

When I finish gyrating the ladies into a more comfortable position in the lacey cups, the vampire lifts my hair clear of the sweater with a smirk.

Cheeky bastard.

Strong fingers brush my curly mane to the side, and he places his lips gently over my jugular. "Are you ready for this?"

I exhale and tilt my head to give him further access. "Yes. I want to get this bullshit over, complete our bond, and start our life together."

Soft nuzzling grazes the erogenous zone at the tip of my ear, causing shivers to dance along my spine. "Our life?" Bastian straightens. "How do you envision that exactly?"

I ponder. How *will* it work? I have obligations to the throne, my people, which will demand a considerable amount of my time. But the commander does as well. He may not be a king, but the enormous task of commanding the infamous Guardians and protecting his queen consumes his life.

"I'm not sure," I answer, sincerely. "But as you mentioned before, with your teleporting ability, we'll be able to carve out more time for each other than if restricted to conventional travel." I step closer and wrap my arms around his waist, craning my neck to peer into his focused gaze. "Also, we'll communicate telepathically, and since you're an IT guru, we can perform vexting instead of plain old sexting."

"Vexting?" he frowns at my made-up word, and I snicker.

"Video sex, my love. You command me from afar and watch to make certain I obey."

"Hmmm, I will get right on developing a secure network for us," he says with eager anticipation brightening his gaze. "I can't wait to observe you put on those adorable unicorn pajamas and order you to pleasure yourself, utilizing the softness against your beautiful sex."

"You say the nicest things," I laugh even as his words harden my nipples. "I love you, Sebastian, and I'll cherish every single second we have together."

"As will I," he grins. "Let us get this over with. I crave you in my playroom."

"Yes, Sir," I beam as the room darkens, and we head to our future.

THE SECOND WE MATERIALIZE back in the living room; the milling immortals gather to construct a semi-circle behind us. Viessa and Icarus take front and center.

My heart is fixed to pound out of my chest as sudden doubts plague my mind. Is this going to hurt? Will my psyche miss my reproductive organs, drive me to feel less than, like a significant part of being a female is missing? I'm sure occasions will occur down the road when sorrow weighs heavy on my mind, and I'll lament this decision. Like on the occasions I observe a mother with her child, a tinge of melancholy will prick at my soul.

Sebastian lifts my chin. "I sense your qualms, Alex. I will ask you one last time. Are you certain?"

His gentle stroke, the unrelenting need to make sure I'm happy, even at the expenditure of his own, thrusts all the worries away. I grasp the nape of his neck, drawing his forehead down to mine. "I wish to spend the rest of my life with you, vampire. I've never been surer of anything."

"Good answer," he smiles, but it doesn't expunge the worry in his gaze.

"As long as we have each other, nothing else matters."

Next to me, I see my mother step forward, tears glistening in her dark eyes. I pivot to confront her.

"Alex, please forgive me. I did what I assumed was best for your safety."

Without thinking it through, I haul off and slap my mom, my queen, across the face. Her head jerks to the side, and my newfound inner lioness preens in satisfaction at the red handprint on her cheek.

Cipher's daunting presence moves in behind the queen, no doubt his beast objecting to anyone hurting its mate, no matter how furious he is with her himself.

My mom straightens with sovereign grace to peer at me with conviction. "Hate me all you want, both of you, but I do not regret my decision." Cipher grips her shoulder, tugging her backward to our line of friends. I let go of my bitterness to refocus on the two Oracles.

"Viessa and I will require laying our hands on your abdomen, my lady." He glares at the immortals circling us. "Utter silence is required for absolute concentration."

"Is it going to hurt?" I ask.

"Yes, my lady, but you must remain standing. Your mate can support you." He nods to Sebastian, who moves behind me, folding an arm around my midriff just below my breasts.

Nicole and Logan step forward, clasping my right hand and shoulder, while Kurtis, Lu, and Liam hold on to the other side. The rest surge in around us. Holy crap. I feel like we are about to perform an exorcism, and I'm the bat shit, projectile vomiting, head swiveling crazy girl with the demon inside.

When Vi and Icarus lay their palms on my stomach, I jerk in surprise. Sebastian presses me into his chest. "Relax against me, Red. I have you."

A jerky nod and the Oracles begin a weird chanting in a dialect I've never heard before. The priest's irises swell and undulate in bright swirls of blue, the tattoos along his torso and arms above the white toga pulse in cadence with his eyes.

Viessa's gaze shines a magnificent golden amber, but instead of swirling like the priest's, hers blaze brighter with each passing second until my belly is awash in the translucent hue.

Immense power suddenly fills my abdomen. At first, it's simply a penetrating warmth, similar to a heating pad on your stomach. This isn't awful. A little hot but tolerable. Maybe it won't be as bad as they...

Fire. Pain. Agony.

The dangerous combination spears through my gut. I jerk against my captors, pressing against Sebastian to evade the violent blaze, but their grip tightens. The oracle's chant becomes louder. The light from Viessa sockets is blinding.

Another streak of fire, this one so sharp, I arch and cry out against the suffering. Tears escape, not merely at the horrendous pain infusing my belly, but at the loss—a sacrifice I willingly make to have a life with the beautiful vampire behind me.

'Easy, love. Breathe.' Sebastian's deep voice in my mind relaxes the tense muscles along my spine. *'I love you, Alex, and I plan on spending the next millennia, showing you how much.'*

Pain. Fire. Agony.

Sweat plasters my thick curls to my neck, trickles between my breasts. It's too extreme. I... I can't stand anymore. My torso is going to burst into flames or split in two.

A scalding poker stabs through my abdomen. I clutch my friends, arch my back, and let loose a tormented scream to the rafters. No way I will survive this, it's more than my fragile body can handle.

"Stop," I wail, slumping against the powerful frame behind me. "I can't take it anymore. Please stop."

But the fiery bolts of pain remain, one after the other until my brain shuts down to escape the torture. My head slumps forward, and blackness encroaches.

'Red. Concentrate on my voice. Stay with me.' I blink several times to expel the darkness, striving to obey my mate. *'I'll never forget the excitement on your face when you saw my Bronco. Remember that night?'* He chuckles, and I grit my teeth to remain conscious. *'I realized you were more turned on by my vehicle than me.'*

Somehow, I manage to shake my head in answer. As much as I loved his ride, nothing compared to my passion for this warrior.

'Alex,' his voice cracks, and it rips my attention away from the torment in my gut. *'Thank you for loving me enough to sacrifice the possibility of a family. And even though the sheer prospect of being a father terrified me more than facing a legion of Centaurs, I would have done it for you. I would undertake anything for you, my love, and I finally*

understand you would for me as well. I don't deserve your love or this sacrifice, but I praise the gods every second of every night you are mine.'

Too weakened to respond and remembering the Oracles orders for complete silence—although I suppose my screaming doesn't count—I nod my understanding. Sebastian leans down and kisses the side of my neck. His lips are like ice against my feverish skin and I moan at the contact, desiring the soothing coolness on my burning stomach.

After what seems like ages of incessant heat and misery, with Bastian whispering words of love and encouragement in my mind, the white-hot fire weakens to a dull burn, eventually dissipating altogether.

I want to bawl with relief as the Oracles step back. My knees buckle, but Sebastian catches me up into his arms. Exhausted, I curl up against my mate's solid chest and let the darkness drag me into oblivion.

Chapter 52

Sebastian

My heart is teeming with so many emotions I have no inkling how to process them all.

My female carried out the ultimate sacrifice. For me. No sick, perverted ulterior motive. No underhanded manipulation. Just pure, selfless love. For me.

I stride over to the big chair by the fire and relax into it with my precious bundle held securely against my chest, mindful to keep her head against my shoulder.

"Will she be all right, Icarus?" Arra questions the priest, never taking her worried gaze from her daughter in my lap.

"Yes, my lady. She will recover with no side effects in a few minutes."

My lids lower in relief. With the intense level of pain she just suffered, I feared she would agonize for several days. She moans but does not waken. Gently I smooth her damp hair from her forehead and press my lips to her warm skin.

"I'm pissed it came to this," Nicole says to Icarus and Viessa. "But I am grateful to you both. As distasteful as this procedure was, it saved her life."

The Oracle bows low. "I am ever at your service, Queen Giordano."

"Yeah, but the whole keeping vital information from me has to stop."

Icarus peers at Nicole with a diabolical grin, and I blink several times at the display. "Only so much one can reveal, my lady. "

"Well, well, well. You do have a sense of humor," Nicki grins.

He sets his index finger over his smiling lips before twisting to Lu's sister. "Come, Viessa, we must return."

"May I have a moment to speak with my twin? I'll join you shortly."

The priest hesitates, darting a glance at Liam across the room. A crystal highball, with at least three fingers of my finest whiskey, dangles from his fingertips as he leans against the sidebar. His bleak, resentful gaze bores into the priest. I cannot say as I blame him for his rage. Icarus took the one thing an immortal lives and dies for: it's mate.

"Of course," he finally responds. "I will await you shortly."

The second the priest vanishes from the room, instead of traipsing over to her sister, Viessa spins on her heel to face the werewolf king. Surprise has him straightening before setting the tumbler on the bar.

For several moments they stare at each other, neither acting nor even breathing, I think. A stillness settles over the area as we all wait to discover what will transpire.

"Sweetness?" Liam breaks the standoff, and it triggers Viessa into action.

In a blink, the vampire is across the den. Her arms wrap around the wolf's collar before ravaging his lips in an impassioned kiss. With a deep groan, Liam's brawny arm enfolds her slim waist, forcing her tight, while his other hand sinks in the long, dark tresses cascading down her spine, angling her head for greater access.

I cannot help being stirred by their intense passion, and I squeeze my mate closer in response. I glance sideways at Lucretia, comforted to notice her smiling at the couple, her fingers intertwined with Kurtis'.

When Viessa eases back, I am rather disappointed the show is over, until her fangs extend. She jerks Liam's head to the side by his hair, striking his jugular with lethal precision.

Liam grunts at the assault, but his lids lower, and a growl of satisfaction rumbles through the room, provoking us all to fidget with our own desire. The big wolf palms her skull to hold her at his throat. My fangs descend with a hunger for my mate, and my erection presses against her hip.

I peer down and am startled when two sapphires watch me beneath dark lashes. A relieved smile lifts my lips when her slender arms fold around my neck.

"What's going on?" she whispers, no doubt sensing the sexual energy around us.

Instead of responding, I position her between my thighs, her luscious ass pressing against my firmness, her back to my chest. I hear her breath hitch when she notices Viessa staking her claim on Liam, and her heart rate accelerates.

The erotic potency undulating in waves from the wolf and Oracle affects every couple here. My brother, his chest pressed against his mate's back, nuzzles Nicole's neck. In answer, she slides a hand between them, and if the soft emerald glow in his eyes is any indication, she is no doubt fondling my brother's raging erection.

Kurtis clutches Lu to his chest as she licks and nibbles at his vein, undulating her hips into his.

The demon king ogles the petite land nymph, devouring her frame with those crimson orbs like she is a feast laid out before him, and he is starving. Kleora does her best to ignore him, but the rapid beat of her pulse indicates she is not as unaffected as she would like him to believe.

Cipher bends low, tosses Queen Arra over his shoulder before stalking from the room. Based on the harsh breathing from the shifter, and the blue eyes flickering yellow, I see an angry fucking in their immediate future.

Unable to help myself, I lick and nuzzle Alex's neck, inhaling her sweet vanilla scent into my lungs. Her hips grind against my aching length, and I crave nothing more than to delve my fingers into her jeans and observe her come apart.

I am about to do just that, uncaring if we have an audience, when Viessa edges away from Liam, licking the last residual of his blood from her lips, but the werewolf refuses to let her move from his embrace.

"I thought Icarus removed the bond?"

"He tried," she smirks, caressing his cheek. "He would have been successful if I hadn't struck a compromise."

Liam's irises, the exact color of the whiskey in his glass, tighten, but his hands continue to travel over her body like he cannot believe she is in his arms. "What kind of compromise?"

Viessa's eyes soften with sadness. "I pledged to complete my training, no matter how long it takes, and to stay away from you unless required until it's done. In exchange, the bond remains."

"How long are we talking?" Liam asks, unease etched on his expression.

"It could be years, Liam," she confesses, and my heart goes out to the king. Alex and I were separated for two months, and it nearly killed me. Not to mention the two-month agony when I assumed she was dead.

"Years. As in a couple or a decade?" He persists.

"I can't answer that, Liam. My mind is still a jumble. Sometimes I have a hard time distinguishing the past from the future or present."

"You seem better. More focused."

"I always am in your presence, but Icarus says I've improved. Although, I have a long road ahead before I am of any value to the immortals. Tonight, my presence was to help bolster the priest's power, nothing more."

The king's somber eyes search our group, not actually seeing us, I suspect, but contemplating his next step with his mate. When his gaze returns to the beautiful Oracle, determination shines bright.

"It doesn't matter. I don't give a rat's ass how long it takes. When you're done, I will be waiting."

"No."

"What do you mean, no? You violated your vow when you kissed me, drank from me. Now you're informing me not to wait for you?"

"Liam. I needed your strength. I'll require your potent blood every couple of months. Since I've sampled you, I can locate you anywhere when the craving becomes too extreme, and I have need of you."

"When you have need of me?" Bitterness edges into Liam's tone. "Is that all I am to you, a bag of blood?"

She laughs. "You are much more, wolf." Viessa steps closer before placing both palms on his cheeks. "Form a vow, Liam, in front of all your friends."

He contemplates her warily even as his gaze drops to her lips, and his fingers clutch her waist. "What vow?"

"Pledge to me, you will continue to flourish in your life, as you always have while I'm in training. Be happy as if I never existed. Fuck as many females as you desire until my return. But, when I conclude with all this tedious study, and my mind is completely right, make no mistake, you'll be mine and mine alone."

Wow. I have never heard of a bonded vampire okay with their mate having sex with others. It is not how we are designed. It goes against every instinct we possess. She either has ultimate command over her inner vampire, or her brain is in such chaos she ignores the beast.

"You wish me to fuck other women?" Liam is clearly flummoxed and angry by her remarks.

"What I want isn't relevant right now. It's cruel of me to demand you to abstain." The tenderness in her gaze hardens, and her chin lifts. "Vow it, Liam."

The authority in her tone causes my eyebrow to lift in surprise. Put this Oracle in latex or leather, and she could be a dominatrix in any one of my clubs.

"And if I don't?" The Alpha's concentration narrows, his beast objecting to the command.

"I'll find another source of nourishment," she states simply.

"The fuck you will," the king growls. The dark eyes flash blue as his wolf fights for control.

Viessa grins. "Then, vow it, my king."

For having a muddled brain, she certainly has a handle on manipulating the werewolf.

Liam regards his mate. "When you return to feed, sweetness, how much time will we have together?"

Smart wolf. He's calculating if he will have sufficient time to fuck her. If so, I would wager this villa, Liam will abstain and remain true to his fated one.

"An hour, no more."

Jesus. Sixty minutes every couple of months? That would be the sixth level of hell.

"Then I vow to be utterly faithful to my female, but hear me now, woman. Our time together will be more than feeding. And when your training is complete, your flesh will bear the mark of my bite. Right here—" Liam glides a finger across the muscles between her neck and shoulder— "for all to witness and know you belong to me." His smug grin has the males in the room chuckling softly in understanding.

Viessa licks her lips. "So be it. Your vow seals the contract. No matter what arises in that hour, you must abide by your promise."

Liam scowls. Alex glances up at me in bewilderment, and I share the sentiment. The Oracle has something up her sleeve, and whatever it is, the werewolf king just conceded to honor it.

Viessa leans in close, brushing her lips to his before whispering. "See you in two months, my king. Be ready for me." With a hasty wave to her twin, she disappears.

The werewolf rakes his fingers through his black locks, plainly uneasy with the unknown component in his arrangement.

"Well, now that you got everyone juiced up, Liam, and the immediate crisis is over. For now," Nicki says. "I think we need to take care of the dead outside." Sadness darkens her gaze. "My Guardians will burn with the sun, but we should bury the others."

The weight of their deaths crushes my sternum. So many. Too much blood tarnishes my hands.

"Sebastian?"

I stare down at the beauty in my lap. "Yes, Red?"

She swivels to straddle my hips, whispering in my ear. "I need to make you mine now."

In a blink, I am on my feet; my shifter/valkyrie clutched in my arms. "Okay, you freeloaders. Take care of the dead, then get the fuck out of my home. My mate and I desire privacy."

"Oh, my God!" She mutters. "Subtle, Bastian. Real subtle."

Chapter 53

Alexandria

"No playroom tonight?"

As soon as we said our goodbyes to family and friends, Bastian traced us to his bedroom. After my brush with purgatory, sweat caked my skin, and I demanded a cool shower before he touched me. He chuckled and left me to it, declaring some business demanded his attention and to take my time.

In the large enclosure, I washed the perspiration from my hair and body, ran Bastian's razor carefully over my girly bits and armpits, wrapped a fluffy towel around me, and exited the tiled behemoth to flip on the hot water valve in the gigantic jacuzzi tub.

While the whirlpool fills, I investigate the cabinets for any bathing salts or bubble bath. In the last one, of course, clear in the back, I spy a jar of vanilla beads, along with my favorite vanilla-scented shampoo, conditioner, body wash, and lotion.

Holy shite. Did he purchase all my shower supplies? How the hell did he know which brands? Out of curiosity, I open the drawer above, and sure enough, a fresh toothbrush still in the package, as well as the same toothpaste and razors I use lie nice and precise on the bottom.

Either he went through my bathroom at the apartment, or he memorized my toiletry bag from my last stay here. The first option is kinda creepy. The second is an "aww" moment and incredibly thoughtful.

Not certain I care to learn which answer is correct.

With a shrug, I brush my teeth, grab the bath salts, scattering the pellets into the steamy water, shut the taps off, open the new razor, before relaxing down into the fragrant hotness.

Oh yeah. I needed this.

I can't believe I'm a freaking shifter, or Cipher is my father. I guessed something was off with my peculiar animal whisperer abilities, and now I understand why. I stretch my limbs in the scented water, glorying in the newfound predator lurking below the surface.

It's not hard to imagine myself racing through the endless, uninhabited woodlands around the vampire stronghold with Sebastian running along beside me, or hunting with Kurtis and Liam. I could shift with Cipher, get to know him better, have him teach me the ins and outs of being a shifter. I smile. The possibilities are boundless.

Underneath the awe and wonder at my future, lies a heavy sorrow. I will never have the opportunity to advise a child how to fight, hunt, shift, or if it were a vampire, watch Bastian school him/her to consume blood. My child. I freely surrendered the primary factor—besides the whole he has a penis, I have a va-jay-jay thing—that sets females apart from males—our ability to carry a life inside us and give birth. And it's not like there are a plethora of orphaned immortals out there demanding a home. The delivery rate in our world is paltry, and we covet children immensely.

But I would make the same choice again. I can survive without a kid in my life, but I can't live without my vampire.

After about ten minutes of letting the warmth ease the tense muscles along my spine, and emptying my mind, I pick up the shaver, hike a limb out of the water and slide the blades repeatedly over my shin and calf.

I finish with one and am about to start on the other when Sebastian strolls through the door completely naked.

I freeze, leg suspended several inches above the fragrant steam and eyeball the glorious pecs, eight pack abs, and the colossal erection jutting tall and proud from his hairless groin.

Damn. Am I drooling?

"Mind if I join you?"

Slowly, I lower my foot. "Not at all."

Observing the huge male ease into the steaming water across from me is an appetizing sight and my mouth waters to get my lips around that beautiful cock.

He plucks the forgotten razor in my fingers, captures my calf, and plants my toes on his chest right over the Moretti tattoo. His long, powerful thighs slide along my hips. Without a word, he begins to efficiently and methodically shave my leg. Good grief, it's the most erotic thing I've ever encountered.

Sebastian may be a true Dom, but underneath all the discipline and commands lies a gracious, loving heart. Yeah, it's bruised and battered, but it craves to cherish and be cherished in order to heal.

Who knew having a male shave me would be such a turn on and relaxing at the same time? I lay my head against the rim and lower my lids with a soft sigh, savoring the slow sensual glide of the blades and Bastian's touch.

When he lowers my foot into the water, my eyes crack open to meet the heated glow in my mate's irises. But I likewise take note of the clenched jaw and nervous swallow.

Is my fierce vampire anxious about me drinking his blood?

"Alex, when you complete the bond, you will learn things I..." he falters, his chest rising and falling rapidly.

I grasp the porcelain edge, rise out of the water to move over him, and straddle his hips. His gaze devours my breasts and stomach. "Bastian, it doesn't..."

"No," he interrupts, gripping my waist. "Let me finish." I nod. He obviously needs to bring this out in the open. "The abuse started when I was a juvenile. The initial moment she touched me inappropriately, I slapped her across the face, but as a pre-tran, I was no match for her strength. She controlled my mind, twisted it against me, and compelled me to crave her. I lusted after the pain and humiliation she inflicted, the games she played with me and others."

Sebastian swallows, refusing to meet my eyes. My heart aches for him. "When you observe those situations, it might appear like I was enjoying what was transpiring, but deep down, below the thrall, I wished to wrap my hands around her throat and snuff the life from her. Do you understand?"

"Bastian." I clasp his cheeks, urging him to look at me. "I understand. I love you, no matter what. Your mother was a vulgar, monstrous creature, and her death by your hand was justified and long overdue."

He studies me for several minutes as if seeking verification of my words.

I squeal in surprise when he stands abruptly, lifting me with him. Water cascades from our bodies to saturate the mat as he steps from the enormous tub, snags a fluffy bath towel off the rack, before lowering my feet to the rug, and proceeds to dry my skin. The soft fabric brushes my aching nipples, producing a needy moan and I clutch the bulky shoulders.

When his cotton-covered hand slips between my legs, I gasp at the contact on my throbbing bundle and widen my stance.

"Fuck, I love how you respond," the vampire says before dipping his head and drawing a hardened nipple between his lips.

I thread my fingers through his hair, holding him to my breast as he teases the peak with tongue and teeth. Electricity shoots straight to my clit, and my hips grind against the cloth pressed between my legs.

"Bastian," I grumble when the towel disappears until his expert fingertips replace the fabric—doing that glorious swirly thing. But too soon he's stepping back, and I whimper in protest.

His broad palm engulfs mine. "Come, Red. I prepared something specifically for our mating."

Naked, I follow the muscular perfection of my mate's ass into the bedroom, and gasp in stunned disbelief at the metamorphosis to the chamber.

Candles flicker on every surface, casting shadows along the walls, soft classical music circulates from a speaker by the bed, and the heat from a roaring fire warms my flesh. But it's not the romantic ambiance stopping me in my tracks. It's the St Andrews cross smack dab in the center of the room.

Chapter 54

Alexandria

Sweet anticipation clenches my core, and I gnaw on my lip, imagining all the wicked things my mate is about to do to me on that thing. I mosey over and run my fingers the length of the ornate wood, up over the leather shackles positioned at each point. Instead of standing vertical, it's suspended horizontally on its frame.

"I lost count how many occasions my mother strapped me to a similar device." His words stun me, and I whirl to stare at him in dismay.

"Then why…"

"To replace those memories with new ones. With you." He steps next to me, gazing at the apparatus for several moments before turning those haunted sapphires on me. "I want you to bind me to the cross. Torment me in any fashion you desire, then drink my blood while you impale yourself on my cock to complete our bond."

"Sebastian, I…"

"I need this, Red." The desperation is apparent as day. I thrust aside my reservations and nod. "Besides," he smiles, and my tension eases some. "This will be the only occasion I allow you control over me, so enjoy it while it lasts."

"Oh, I don't know," I respond with a devilish grin, tracking my nail down his chest. "You might love it enough; you beg for it again."

He chuckles before moving between the branches of the cross and arranging his wrists and ankles in the straps.

Nervous anticipation grips my tummy, even as I buckle him in, and I'm reassured to discover the manacles have no silver. If Bastian wants out, breaking free of the restraints will not be a problem.

By the swift rise and fall of his rib cage, and the clenched jaw, I'd surmise he's contemplating escape right now. I take a moment to examine my options. My mate needs this. To him, this loss of control to me will purge his mind of the past. How can I make this remarkable and gratifying enough it overshadows the vileness of his past?

A bright bulb explodes in my brain, and I grin, peering around the room. That's when I notice the heavy armoire from his playroom at the castle. The vampire traced the whole damn thing here, all while I was in the shower. I never heard a peep.

With a bemused shake of my head, I meander over and open the cabinet doors, scanning the shelves. I sense Bastian's gaze boring into my backside, but I ignore him and snatch several items.

I pivot and shove them behind me so the piercing azul irises can't observe my choices and move to his head cushioned on a leather pad. Unable to deny myself those tempting lips, I bend, dropping the pieces under him before he can see them and ravage him— licking, sucking, and nibbling.

Bastian growls low, angles slightly to capture control of the kiss. His warm tongue duels with mine, and it would be so easy to surrender to the skillful mouth, but first things first.

I inch away, severing contact, and grab the black silk off the floor. The height of the contraption places Bastian's face about mid-thigh. I could straddle those talented lips with ease. Convenient.

"I'm going to blindfold you, Sebastian."

"No," he barks. "I need to see you, Red."

"I want you to utilize your senses. Listen to my voice, inhale my scent, and relish every touch. Push everything else away, and focus entirely on me."

The reluctant nod strengthens my resolve to make certain he enjoys each second of this. I drape the black material over his eyes, and he lifts his head slightly so I can tie the straps, mindful to keep his hair out of the knot.

The objective tonight is to exterminate the bitch from his mind if it's the last thing I do.

I arrange the remaining devices in a row on the bench at the end of the bed and snatch my first pleasure tool.

With slow, sensual movements, I twirl the slim feather duster up over his toes, the top of his masculine foot, and along his shin. He jerks in response at the initial contact but soon relaxes at the delicate approach.

"You've only known anguish on this cross. That ends. Tonight, you will experience great pleasure, enjoy the gentle strokes, relish the slight sting of pain, and realize every command and touch is offered with love. Do you understand, Sebastian?"

"Yes," he murmurs.

I rotate the plumes over his tightening sac several times. His spine arches, but I bypass the immense girth laying rigid along his abdomen to skim his chest, neck, and down one arm before proceeding to the other side. I can't help lingering and tormenting his balls once more. The powerful muscles bunch and flex, but no longer in trepidation—they pursue the willowy touch. I smile.

"Are you enjoying this, Sebastian?"

"Yes," he grunts.

"Do you require something more?"

"Yes."

I seize the next piece on the bench. Each one increases in intensity, hopefully ramping up my male's lust to a fevered pitch.

The smooth, supple skin of the riding crop can either elicit a slight sting or a fierce burn, depending on who's wielding it.

I start at the bottom of his foot once more, letting him get the sense of it before gently striking each sole. He jerks in response, the powerful thighs tense, but the sight of his dick twitching, his balls drawing tighter, is all the green light I require to proceed.

Quick little slaps along the inside of his legs, provoke my mate to jerk against the shackles. Not to elude the blows, but to seek the slap of leather on his skin.

I position myself between his spread legs, and run the crop over his taut abdomen, scraping the edge across his puckered nipples, before striking each one. Sebastian jerks, his fists clench, his breathing harsh.

I can't believe how turned on I am at having this powerful vampire at my mercy, pleasuring him this way. No wonder Bas gets off on being in control. It's downright addictive.

"How does that feel, Bastian?"

"Fucking amazing." His guttural response wets my opening.

"Say my name," I order, needing to make sure he's in the here and now.

"Red. My precious, lioness."

"Good. Very good." As a reward, I kneel, run my tongue along his tightened sac, swirling around each ball.

"Alex," His deep moan is a beautiful sound.

"Mmm, you taste like a spicy ocean breeze, my love." I take my time licking and nibbling up his shaft, lapping at the bead of yummy goodness pooling at the tip, and his hips thrust upward for more.

When I ease back, Sebastian growls low in protest, and I grin as I turn to fetch the last item on the bench. I hesitate, investigating the weight of the flogger in my grip, recalling the delicious burn of it against my flesh.

"The aroma of your desire surrounds me, Red."

In reply, I give a gentle slap across his pulsing dick and Bas arches. "Fuck!" he shouts. "More."

With the command, I set in, working to maintain a steady rhythm while gradually increasing the severity of my strikes. Pre-cum drips from the bulbous head. Bastian writhes and moans in bliss as I stroll around the cross, making certain to cover every square inch of his exposed skin. Red welts appear before disappearing. My clit pulses in time with the whack of leather.

Unable to stand it any longer, I toss the whip to the side and stride to Bastian's head. "Make me explode," I order before pivoting ninety degrees to straddle his face, my butt cheeks resting on his collarbone. His growl changes, from needy and lustful, to possessive predator right before he devours me like a crazed animal. Within seconds, I implode. Convulses shake my frame, and I grip the vampire's forearms to remain standing as wave after wave of glorious heat spreads through my body.

Once the tremors ease, my remarkable male continues to devour my sex with his, oh so talented, mouth, but I step away and remove the blindfold.

A tremendous blue brilliance fills the room. The vampire arches his neck in order to pin me with his beautiful otherworldly gaze.

"Come back here. I need more of that sweet pussy."

In two strides, I'm to him, but instead of letting him have his way, I climb over his face, plant my shins on his shoulders, and stretch across his torso with one hand planted on the wood by his hip.

"Fuck me, that's a delicious sight," he groans

I grip his erection, and set in, sucking and licking my mate with vigor. The commander growls low, jerking his hips, straining to get to my sex just out of reach on his chest.

"Come for me, Bastian," I command before setting in once more, lusting after his salty spice. His muscles strain. Powerful arms break loose from the restraints to grasp my hips and yank me to his greedy lips.

The bite of his fang on my sensitive bundle ignites a fire in my core and I grind against his face, moaning as his hot seed shoots down my throat, and I voraciously swallow every last drop.

With a strength that constantly astounds, Bastian reverses my position, my palms land on his chest to steady myself, and with legs dangling off either side of his hips, my toes barely touch the floor. But there's no need. The glorious vampire controls me, lifting my lower body before impaling me on his still rigid cock, his grip on my waist brutal.

"Oh, God! Bas." I cry out as my inside's spasm around his hardness, working to accommodate his size and never let him go. Sebastian sets a vigorous, unrelenting pace, regulating the momentum, using the restraints at his ankles as leverage.

The blue fire in his gaze promises ecstasy, but when he twists his head to the side, baring his neck, my focus zeros in on the rapid pulse of his vein.

The beautiful lioness surges to the forefront. Upper and lower canines extend. My one thought is to claim my mate. Make him ours. My attack is pure instinct, zeroing in on the meaty flesh at the base of his collar while making sure to puncture his jugular at the same time—Sebastian tenses at the savagery of my strike.

The second his potent essence gushes over my taste buds, my eyes roll back, and I drink my first glorious gulp of my mate. His flavor is sublime, like the man himself; clean, fresh, and spicy. I grip fistfuls of his dark tresses, hold him immobile, and clamp down harder while he pounds into my core with wild abandon.

Image after image of Sebastian's life flashes behind my closed lids. His father and Logan's love. Even his mother's affection and devotion as a small child.

The incident he revealed earlier plays out when she touched him, his slap, and the harsh consequences. My heart aches for the helpless teenager. I perceive the unwanted lust and contempt for his mother, the two sides warring with each other.

Scene after scene of every depravity the evil bitch forced him to endure captures my brain, and I can't cease the tears spilling from my eyes to pool on the floor beneath us.

Bastian senses my distress, locks those massive arms around my waist, breaks free of the ankle cuffs, and strides over to the bed. He eases me down on the mattress, settling his weight on my pelvis, all the while careful to keep my canines connected at his neck.

I clamp my thighs on his hips, grip his shoulders, and hold on for dear life as the vampire renews his thrusts.

The images with his mother shatter, replaced by visions of him as an adult. His lethal precision on the battlefield. The joy and pride he received at fighting side by side with his brother. The rejoicing after a significant victory, indulging in mass amounts of blood and women, Logan right there with him. The sorrow over fallen comrades.

When the pictures alter, to showcase his BDSM lifestyle and the extreme measures various subs required—the lust and euphoria he experienced having ultimate control—instead of repulsing me, my desire soars brighter, magnifying my need. Not that I would ever require or desire something so harsh, but I finally understand his demand for supreme control, and all of it is a part of who my love is. I rejoice in sharing the memories of his life. Good and bad.

"Come with me again, Red. Complete the bond."

At his command, I swallow another gulp of his potent essence, only this time, instead of images flashing, my insides convulse. My muffled cry against his neck shoots Bastian over the edge once more. The second his warm seed enters my body, and his blood fills my gut, a lightning bolt of energy zings through my mind, shattering every doubt and uncertainty into oblivion.

The vampire Guardian, one-half of the legendary Moretti brothers, is now mine. Forever.

Carefully, I unlock my jaw, sliding all four canines from his thick muscle. When they recede, I gaze at the grave, violent punctures. My lioness purrs with satisfaction, knowing even when they heal, every immortal will still see the bite and sense my claim. I raise my lids, and brilliant sapphires meet mine.

"Sebastian Roman Moretti, you are mine. From this moment forward, we are one. One mind. One heart. One soul. Forever."

The irises pulse and his emotions, desires, and needs become my own. "I am yours, as you are mine. From this moment forward, we are one. One mind. One heart. One soul. Forever." Tears leak from my eyes as Bastian's vow cements our commitment.

"I love you with all my heart, Red, and proudly wear your mark. I will never let you go."

"No matter what the future holds, Mr. Moretti, we meet it together."

His sexy smile brightens my world. "Yes, ma'am."

The End

ABOUT THE AUTHOR

A.R. VAGNETTI IS AN American writer who grew up in the scalding Tucson desert. Her debut novel, Forgotten Storm, is the first book in her Storm Series and won the Top 20 Best Indie Books of 2019. Book 2, Forbidden Storm won the Readers Favorite Five Star Award in 2020.

She does her best writing while camping, traveling, and on the beautiful shores of Lake Huron where she is now blessed to spend her summers away from the Arizona heat.

A.R. loves to transport readers into a fantastical world of paranormal romance where bold Alpha males will sacrifice anything for the strong, deeply scared, kickass females they love.

FRACTURED STORM

Book four in the Storm Series
Available Spring, 2021

Tormented all her life by visions of past, present, and future, Viessa Bramen discovers a refuge in the presence of the sexy werewolf king. Control over his body means the incessant voices bombarding her every waking moment vanish, freeing her mind. But her new job as Oracle to the immortal world forbids a mating. Will Vi defy the gods to claim her one true mate, or will the Alpha male's resistance to submitting force her mind back into chaos?

Burdened under the duties as king, Liam Scott always found release in women, booze, and music, until he came face to face with his fated female. The potent Tri-Brid's control issues and his beast's powerful objections could destroy their newfound love and fracture her delicate mind?

For updates on new releases, join the Stormster Club!
https://www.arvagnetti.com

About the Publisher